Instrumental Jazz Arranging
A COMPREHENSIVE AND PRACTICAL GUIDE

By MIKE TOMARO and JOHN WILSON

To access music templates and audio visit:
www.halleonard.com/mylibrary

Enter Code
"2037-3718-2186-4055"

ISBN 978-1-4234-5274-4

7777 W. BLUEMOUND RD. P.O. BOX 13819 MILWAUKEE, WI 53213

In Australia Contact:
Hal Leonard Australia Pty. Ltd.
4 Lentara Court
Cheltenham, Victoria, 3192 Australia
Email: ausadmin@halleonard.com.au

Visit Hal Leonard Online at
www.halleonard.com

ABOUT THE AUTHORS

Mike Tomaro has been the Director of Jazz Studies at Duquesne University in Pittsburgh, PA since 1997. He holds a B.S. degree in Music Education and an M.A. degree in Saxophone Performance. Mike is a Yamaha Performing Artist and endorses Vandoren reeds, mouthpieces, and ligatures. A former member of the Army Blues jazz ensemble, Mike served as its Enlisted Musical Director and performed for Presidents Reagan, Bush, and Clinton as well as heads of state from around the world. He also composed and/or arranged much of the Army Blues repertoire and was featured as a soloist on several of the group's albums and CDs.

Mike has four nationally released recordings, including *Forgotten Dreams* (Seabreeze Jazz), *Dancing Eyes* (Seabreeze Jazz), and *Home Again* (Positive Music). His latest CD, *Nightowl Suite* (Seabreeze Jazz), features his compositions and arrangements as performed by the Three Rivers Jazz Orchestra. Additionally, Mike has also been featured on many other CDs, most notably on Nancy Wilson's two latest GRAMMY® award-winning CDs, *RSVP* and *Turned to Blue*, and the New York Voices' *A Day Like This*.

Mike's music has been performed by the likes of jazz greats Randy Brecker, Mike Stern, Ernie Watts, Bobby Shew, Claudio Roditi, New York Voices, Al Vizzutti, and many more, encompassing elementary to professional ability levels. As a performer, Mike has worked with such diverse artists and groups as Rosemary Clooney, Ray Charles, Michael Feinstein, Linda Ronstadt, Johnny Mathis, Terence Blanchard, Louis Bellson, Terry Gibbs, Dizzy Gillespie Tribute Big Band, New York Voices, Woody Herman Orchestra, and the Smithsonian Masterworks Jazz Orchestra.

Mike is a member of the International Association for Jazz Education and was a long-standing associate of its prestigious resource team in the area of arranging and composition. He was also inducted into the Pittsburgh Jazz Hall of Fame in 2005. For more information on his activities, visit Mike's website at *www.miketomaro.com*.

Dr. John Wilson's career as a jazz trumpeter and arranger has encompassed all facets of the profession, including big bands, small combos, recording, radio, television, and movies. Some of the bands that he played in and wrote for included Benny Goodman, Claude Thornhill, Eliot Lawrence, Pete Rugolo, Neil Hefti, Les Elgart, and the Sauter-Finegan Orchestra. He has recorded with Gerry Mulligan, Bob Brookmeyer, Phil Woods, and Jimmy Raney, and has also worked with Frank Sinatra, Tony Bennett, Peggy Lee, Billy Eckstein, Louis Armstrong, Lena Horne, and Martin and Lewis, as well as legendary entertainers George Burns, Jack Benny, Sophie Tucker, and Jimmy Durante.

In 1975, John instituted the first Jazz Studies Degree Program in Pennsylvania at Duquesne University, where he continued as Director of Jazz Studies until retiring in 1997, when he was succeeded by Mike Tomaro. During his tenure at Duquesne, his arranging career continued to flourish. His credits include Gerry Niewood, Tony Williams, John Schofield, Stanley Turrentine, Louis Bellson, Elaine Elias, and the Dizzy Gillespie Alumni All-Star Band.

In 1999 he was commissioned by the Pittsburgh Ballet Theater to arrange a musical tribute to Billy Strayhorn called "Indigo in Motion." He has been a major contributor to Nancy Wilson's last three albums, two of which won GRAMMY® Awards. John was inducted into the Pittsburgh Jazz Hall of Fame in 2003. He is currently teaching classes at the University of Pittsburgh and Carnegie Mellon University.

CONTENTS

PREFACE

One might ask, "Why write another arranging book when there are so many good ones already available?" There has to be a better reason than mere repetition of material presented many times before. The conviction that there is a need for such a book grew out of our classroom experiences at Duquesne University. We have a combined fifty years of experience in teaching jazz arranging and during that time have yet to find a book that addresses all of the basic needs for beginning jazz arrangers. Most books focus on orchestration, rather than arranging. They serve as excellent reference material for more advanced students, but do not deal with the basic elements in enough detail.

This book has evolved from efforts dating back to the 1970s to develop a systematic presentation of the essential techniques and materials of jazz arranging. It is a result of the constant refinement and reorganization of countless handouts and examples. It is also a reflection of several well-defined points of view in regards to the teaching of jazz arranging.

For instance, we have tried to maintain a balance on both the horizontal and vertical aspects of music writing. Counterpoint is no longer a required subject in many college curriculums today. As a result, students are not adept at linear writing. We have attempted to remedy this deficiency through the early emphasis on two-part writing which establishes the importance of independent lines and proper voice leading.

Most college students are also deficient in the knowledge of jazz harmony. Traditional theory curriculums do not go far enough in bridging the gap between the common practices of the eighteenth and nineteenth centuries and contemporary harmony. We have tried to address this problem as effectively as possible within the scope of the book by including exhaustive chord compendia, suggestions for harmonizing non-harmonic tones, methods of tonicization, modulation, etc. We feel the easiest way to assimilate the concept of added-note harmony is through four-part writing. Three-part writing then becomes a process of subtraction, while five-, six-, and seven-part writing becomes a process of addition.

Beginning arranging students frequently have no background in composition and are wary about undertaking the various parts of an arrangement which involve this process. Our approach offers encouragement to even the most reluctant composers by providing solutions which require a minimum of original material. Hopefully, once the student has gained some experience and confidence in his creative ability, this will cease to be a problem.

We wish to express our sincere thanks to the many people who have played a part in some way in the creation of this book: Jo Dallas, for successfully amalgamating our diverse writing styles; the hundreds of students, whose assignments, both good and bad, have unwittingly assisted us in the honing of our teaching methods; Eric Lauver, Charlie Doherty, Jim Emminger for their contributions; and Dan Maske, our editor, who helped tie up all the loose ends in the book.

A special thanks also to the musicians, our good friends, who recorded the examples found on the accompanying audio tracks.

Finally, special thanks to our families: Mike's wife Nancy, and his children Natalie and Andrea; and John's wife Barbara, for their incredible patience throughout the past five years.

HOW TO USE THIS BOOK

This book is divided into four sections, excluding the appendices. The first deals with the basic techniques of arranging. It is important that these are assimilated without reference to specific orchestration. The second section is devoted to a discussion of the instruments found in jazz ensembles. Concepts for specifically sized ensembles are presented in the third section, while the fourth breaks the typical jazz arrangement into its component parts. The appendices contain pertinent supplemental material as well as the complete scores for the two full-length arrangements discussed in this book.

It is assumed that the reader possesses some knowledge of jazz harmony, including chord to scale relationships and nomenclature. A basic understanding of improvisation can be helpful, but not necessary.

This book can be used by the individual or as a classroom textbook. The following are suggestions for use in each situation.

For Individual Instruction

Those with no experience are urged to follow the sequence of learning presented in the class schedule found in appendix 9. Written assignments should be completed as directed. These *must* be created using music notation software to permit a successful aural evaluation. If possible, seek the opinions of an experienced arranger.

Those with some background in arranging are also encouraged to read through the entire book, as each chapter will provide fresh insight. Areas of weakness could be improved by completing the suggested assignments from the pertinent chapters.

For Use as a Classroom Textbook

This book can serve as a text for a one- or two-semester course in jazz arranging. In a one-semester course, it is recommended that the emphasis be on basic techniques and the small ensemble. The second semester would concentrate on larger ensembles.

Appendix 9 contains detailed descriptions of the suggested assignments as well as week-by-week class schedules. These schedules are based on a fourteen-week semester with the class meeting twice a week. There are three types of assignments: reading, writing, and revisions. Reading assignments are given on the first day of each week and are discussed on the second. Writing assignments are given on the second day of each week and are due the first day of the following week. After these are submitted and discussed in class, the instructor can make the necessary remarks on the comment sheets found in Appendix 10. These are designed to eliminate some of the tedium involved with the correction process by assigning numbers to the most common mistakes. The instructor can place one or more of these into the provided grid at the appropriate measure. Space is also provided for additional comments. The sheets are then given to the students.

Merely correcting the assignments is not enough, as students do not learn from doing something poorly. If an assignment is unsatisfactory, it should be revised. These revisions are due one week later. Those that are still deemed unsatisfactory would necessitate a private consultation with the instructor so that the student does not fall behind.

If the length of any assignment proves to be too long, it could be shortened. This is preferable to the omission of a chapter as the maintenance of the class schedule is of paramount importance.

Each semester culminates with the creation of a full-length arrangement. The live performance of the arrangements is essential. The feedback from the performers on the playability and readability of the parts can be invaluable. The students can also hear the instruments in various registers and dynamic levels and begin to catalog this information. These subtleties cannot be duplicated on a computer.

Listening is also a strong component of learning. The suggested listening examples and lists located throughout this book were selected because they represent the best of small and large ensemble writing. But these are only a small cross section of the cumulative efforts of the great arrangers throughout jazz history. These should constantly be supplemented with other examples to continue the growth process as an arranger.

ABOUT THE AUDIO AND TEMPLATES

The audio that accompanies this text contains live performances of selected examples. Those that were selected for performance were chosen because they helped to further illustrate the topic being discussed.

Also included are templates for each assignment formatted for Finale® 2011 and Sibelius® 7. This enables the student to submit each assignment as a file, creating a paperless setting for the class. Depending on the class size, as many assignments as possible should be heard and discussed during class, in the manner of a master class. The computer's sound output should be connected to a stereo system. If a laser projector is available, scores could be projected onto a screen or wall so that all the students could see each other's work and participate in the discussion. If this is not possible, students could either gather around the computer monitor or simply listen to each assignment.

Credits

Recorded at Heid Studios, Aspinwall, PA

Saxes: Jim Guerra (Alto & Baritone), Eric DeFade (Tenor), Rick Matt (Tenor), Jim Germann (Baritone)

Trumpets: Steve Hawk (Lead – Large Ensemble), Galen McKinney, Justin Surdyn, Ralph Guzzi, James Moore (Solo on "Charming William" & Lead – Small Ensemble)

Trombones: Bob Matchett (Lead – Large Ensemble), Clayton DeWalt (Solo on "Bar Flies"), Gary Piecka, Chris Carson (Bass)

Guitar: Eric Susoeff

Piano: Ron Bickel

Bass: Paul Thompson (Large Ensemble), Brian Stahurski (Small Ensemble & Solo on "Bar Flies")

Drums: David Glover (Large Ensemble), Lenny Rogers (Small Ensemble)

Engineers: George Heid, Jim Barr

PART 1
Basic Techniques

Chapters 1 through 9 contain the following topics:

- Melodic Paraphrase
- Countermelody
- Harmonization from Two to Five Parts
- Close and Open Voicings
- Accompaniment Devices

These topics are presented without regard for specific instrumentation so that each subject can be explored without the constraints of orchestration.

CHAPTER 1
Melodic Paraphrase

Melodic paraphrase, according to the *New Grove Dictionary of Jazz* (pp. 556–557, St. Martin's Press, New York, 1995), is "the ornamentation of the melody ...The paraphrasing of the melody may be no more complex than the introduction of a few ornamental flourishes into an otherwise faithful repetition of the original tune. But at its most inventive it may involve a highly imaginative reworking of the melody, which remains recognizable only by its outline or the preservation of certain distinctive turns of phrase or figure. The underlying harmonic structure...remains essentially unchanged, though that too may be subjected to local alteration and embellishment." In much simpler terms, it is the transformation of a non-jazz-oriented melody into a jazz-oriented one.

Identification of Jazz and Non-Jazz Oriented Melodies

Jazz-oriented and non-jazz oriented melodies differ in their use of syncopation and ornamentation. Most songs from the American popular songbook fit into the category of non-jazz-oriented melodies. The majority of these were composed in the second quarter of the twentieth century by such luminaries as Jerome Kern, George Gershwin, Cole Porter, Hoagy Carmichael, Richard Rodgers, Harold Arlen, and countless others. This is not to say that American popular songs are limited to this time period. The genre has continued into modern day through the songs of composers such as Johnny Mandel, Leonard Bernstein, Henry Mancini, Michel LeGrand, and others. These songs were originally composed to be sung in Broadway shows, musical revues, and motion pictures; they were not intended as vehicles for jazz musicians. The pervading characteristic of these tunes is their lack of syncopation and ornamentation.

The Old English tune "Billy Boy," will be used as the primary example for this chapter. Below is the original version of this song in 4/4 with chord changes similar to the ones heard on Miles Davis's 1958 *Milestones* recording (Original LP issue: Columbia CL1193; 2001 CD release: CK 85203).

EXAMPLE 1-1.

This melody is comprised solely of whole, half, and quarter notes, and contains no syncopation or ornamentation. Many American popular songs are similar to this model. Even in those where eighth notes predominate ("Everything Happens to Me," "My One and Only Love," etc.), there is little or no syncopation.

If one of these is compared to any tune written by a jazz composer, the difference is immediately noticeable. The following shows the first eight measures of "Bar Flies," a tune composed for this book that is based on an American popular song.

EXAMPLE 1-2.

While "Billy Boy" contains no syncopation or eighth notes, "Bar Flies" is highly syncopated, with eighth notes comprising the majority of the tune.

The objective, then, of melodic paraphrase is to turn a melody with no syncopation or ornamentation into one that contains these characteristics. This process is essential to jazz arranging! No matter what song is to be arranged, the first step is the creation of a melodic paraphrase. As mentioned above, these alterations can be subtle or dramatic. Some melodies require great amounts of alteration, while others need only a few subtle enhancements. Even when arranging a bop tune, which tends to be full of syncopation and ornamentation, an attempt should be made to personalize the arrangement by applying some form of paraphrase. However, an overabundance of this can destroy the tune.

Melodic paraphrase is primarily a linear function as it deals with the melodic line. A common misconception is that it is solely linear. In order to create an effective paraphrase, the vertical aspects of the music (harmony) must always be considered when creating a melodic line. In fact, both functions should always be taken into account when performing any arranging task.

Devices for Melodic Paraphrase

Melodic paraphrase should ultimately be an innate process. Ideas, for the most part, should flow freely to create a natural-sounding reinterpretation of a melody. However, first attempts must be methodically created. There are eight devices used to conceive melodic paraphrase.

1. Rhythmic Alteration
2. Fragmentation
3. Connecting Tones
4. Neighbor Tones
5. Fills
6. Articulations
7. Dynamics
8. Ornaments & Inflections

The first two devices deal with the rhythmic aspects of a line. Devices 3–5 are melodic in nature, and 6–8 are nuance-oriented.

Rhythmic Alteration

Rhythmic alteration is the most important device available for paraphrase. It involves the creation of syncopation through the use of **anticipation** and **delay**. Following is a rhythmic alteration of "Billy Boy." (Note: articulations have intentionally been omitted so that they may be discussed later as a separate entity.)

EXAMPLE 1-3.

Notice in the previous example that:

- Rhythmic anticipations and/or delays occur in every measure.

- There are more anticipations than delays (nineteen vs. eight).

- All the alterations involve moves of a half beat with the exception of the B♭ in measure twelve (a full-beat move). Rhythmic alterations longer than a half beat tend to produce a more dramatic effect and should be used sparingly.

- The most common anticipations occur across the bar line (of the nineteen, eleven fall into this category).

- Not every note has been altered; several remain in their original rhythmic positions. Some downbeat references are essential to an effective melodic paraphrase.

The next two examples show ineffective applications of rhythmic alteration. The first demonstrates an insufficient amount of modification, and the second is an extreme example in which every note has been moved.

EXAMPLE 1-4.

Neither of these is acceptable. The first is lackluster and has an insufficient swing feel. The second is confusing because it lacks downbeat references.

There is no one way to rhythmically alter any phrase. The example below presents four entirely different, yet acceptable versions of the first phrase of "Billy Boy."

EXAMPLE 1-5.

Subsequent occurrences of the same section of a song should be altered for variety. For example, when working with typical song forms (AABA, ABAC, etc.), each of the recurring A sections should be paraphrased in a different manner. The literal repetition of a paraphrase in a song, especially an AABA form, can be monotonous.

Musical sensibility must be exercised in the paraphrasing process to determine its effectiveness. The best way to ascertain this is to sing or play it. This is a subjective matter, and it is only with practice that an arranger can be certain that a correct amount of alteration has occurred.

When paraphrasing an American popular song (or any piece that originally contained lyrics) for instrumentalists, there is no need to be concerned with an exact rendering of every syllable on any one pitch. The following is the original version of "Billy Boy" with the note repetitions circled.

EXAMPLE 1-6.

The recurrence of a single pitch can be tedious, even when rhythmically altered. Next is a paraphrase that effectively eliminates all note repetitions except for mm. 9–10. Here, the five E♭'s have been truncated to two.

EXAMPLE 1-7.

This is not to say that note repetitions are undesirable. The next example shows a paraphrase that retains all note repetitions and even adds a few. All retentions and additions have been indicated.

EXAMPLE 1-8.

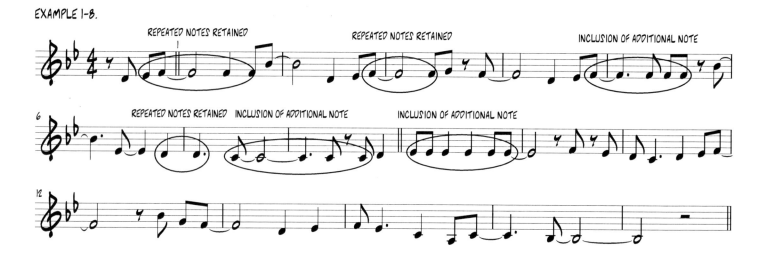

Melodic paraphrase provides the basis for all the other devices and should be applied first.

Fragmentation

Fragmentation refers to the shortening of note values for the purpose of creating space in a melody. For the novice, it is best to begin with a rhythmic alteration.

EXAMPLE 1-9.

Fragmentation can then be accomplished by merely converting some or all of the held pitches to shorter note lengths, with rests occupying the remainder of the space. Compare the fragmentation of example 1-10 with the paraphrase from example 1-9.

EXAMPLE 1-10.

TRACK 2

Connecting Tones

Connecting tones can be used to fill the gaps between melody notes, no matter how large or small the interval. They can be diatonic, chromatic, or a combination of both.

EXAMPLE 1-11.

A working knowledge of chord-scale relationships is essential to the effective use of this device. As with fragmentation, first attempts at using connecting tones should begin with a rhythmic alteration.

EXAMPLE 1-12.

Next, locate the intervallic gaps. The above example reveals intervals as small as a whole step and as large as a minor sixth (m. 2). Finally, fill selected gaps with connecting tones.

EXAMPLE 1-13.

The following are two important points regarding connecting tones.

- All gaps should not be filled; a few carefully chosen applications of this device are most effective.

- The original melody becomes less clearly defined as more connecting tones are added.

Neighbor Tones

Neighbor tones are non-harmonic tones that are inserted between two repeated pitches. There are two types, upper and lower, that occur either a half or whole step above or below the given pitch.

EXAMPLE 1-14.

Neighbor tones can be used separately or together. When upper and lower neighbors are combined (one after the other), it is called a **changing tone**.

EXAMPLE 1-15.

As with the other devices, the best way to illustrate the proper use of neighbor and changing tones is to begin with a rhythmic alteration.

EXAMPLE 1-16.

Next, locate repeated pitches and insert neighbor or changing tones between the repeated target notes.

EXAMPLE 1-17.

U.N. = UPPER NEIGHBOR, L.N. = LOWER NEIGHBOR, C.T. = CHANGING TONE

TRACK 4

There are three methods for applying this device.

- The length of the first of the two repeated notes is shortened so that neighbor or changing tones can be positioned directly before the second of the two repeated notes (mm. 1, 5, 9, and 14). The inverse of this is also possible (shortening the second note in length), but is not used in this example.

- The neighbor tone is used in place of a rest (m. 6).

- The neighbor or changing tone is inserted by first creating two repeated notes from one held note (mm. 7, 11, and 13).

This brief introduction to neighbor and changing tones is by no means complete. Both will be discussed in further detail in chapter 5.

Fills

Fills are fragments of newly composed music that are inserted into periods of inactivity. These can be comprised of chord arpeggiations or combinations of harmonic and non-harmonic tones. Unlike many of the earlier devices that were created through the use of methodical procedures, the successful application of this device relies on the compositional creativity of the arranger. Continuity must be maintained when inserting fills; the flow of the music should not be interrupted.

After a rhythmic alteration has been created, longer note or rest values should be located.

EXAMPLE 1-18.

These spaces can then be filled with lines that logically connect the note at the beginning of the space to the next movement. The original melody notes are indicated in this example with arrows.

EXAMPLE 1-19.

TRACK 5

Moderate use of this technique can add further interest to a melodic line without obliterating it. Extreme use, written sensibly as in the example above, can create a new melody that contains only the skeleton of the original.

Articulations

Articulations are required in any piece of music to ensure its correct interpretation by defining note length and amount of emphasis. There are five commonly used articulations in jazz and commercial music: **legato**, **staccato**, **accent**, **accent w/legato**, and **"cap" accent**.

EXAMPLE 1-26.

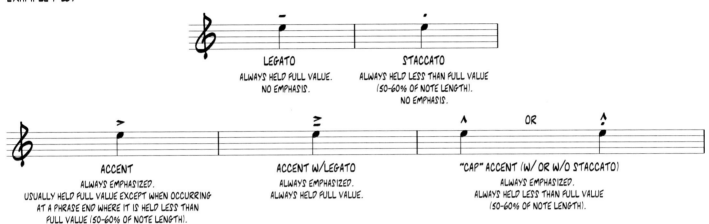

The ability level of the group should govern the amount of articulations inserted in the music. Experienced players can immediately assess all the nuances of the music and play them correctly. Younger players require more assistance; articulations can guide them toward the proper interpretation of melodic contours and rhythms.

EXAMPLE 1-21.

The notation of **natural line accents** (notes in a melody that seem to demand an accent, naturally) becomes crucial when writing harmonizations of a line. These may not be apparent in all the voices, especially if contrary motion is present in the harmonization. If there is any doubt as to whether a line will be interpreted correctly, it is best to include all necessary accents.

EXAMPLE 1-22.

The definition of note lengths is critical for all players. In eighth-note oriented music, quarter-note lengths may be unclear. In sixteenth-note oriented music, this lack of clarity extends to the eighth note as well. The examples below illustrate the ambiguity that occurs when note lengths are not defined.

EXAMPLE 1-23.

Whether appearing one at a time in syncopated figures or in succession, the length and emphasis of these notes must be defined with articulations.

Articulations can also add interest to any musical passage. The paraphrase below contains an insufficient amount of rhythmic alteration.

EXAMPLE 1-24.

The judicious use of articulations can transform an otherwise unusable paraphrase into a viable musical statement.

EXAMPLE 1-25.

TRACK 6

Dynamics

Dynamics define overall volume (*p*, *mf*, *f*, etc.), gradual changes in volume (crescendos and decrescendos), and attack nuances (*fp*, *sfz*, etc.). The following is a paraphrase that contains a moderate amount of rhythmic alteration.

EXAMPLE 1-26.

In the next example, dynamics have been added. An overabundance of dynamic symbols have been inserted for purposes of demonstration only.

EXAMPLE 1-27.

TRACK 7

Ornaments and Inflections

Ornaments and inflections include effects such as the **ghost** or **swallowed note**, **shake**, **turn**, **smear** or **gliss**, **short fall**, **long fall**, **rip** (or upward gliss.), **drop**, **doit**, **grace note**, **scoop**, and closed and open horn indications (these define plunger mute positions for brass or alternate fingerings for saxes and trumpets).

EXAMPLE 1-28.

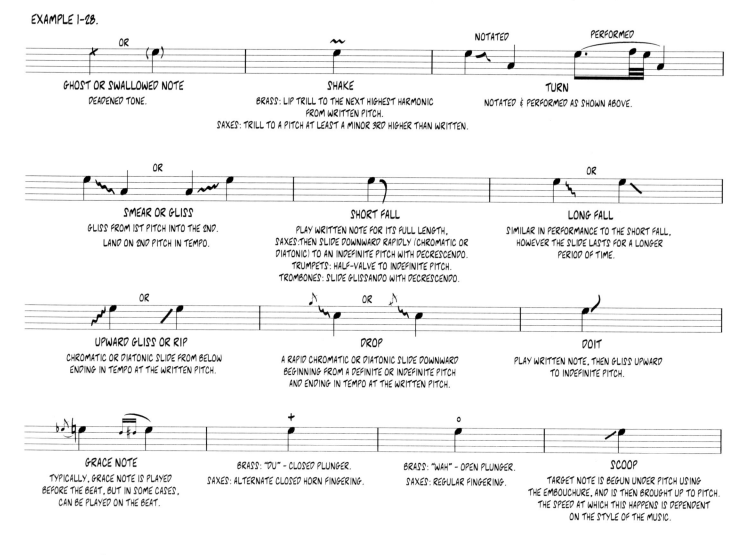

GHOST OR SWALLOWED NOTE
DEADENED TONE.

SHAKE
BRASS: LIP TRILL TO THE NEXT HIGHEST HARMONIC FROM WRITTEN PITCH.
SAXES: TRILL TO A PITCH AT LEAST A MINOR 3RD HIGHER THAN WRITTEN.

TURN
NOTATED & PERFORMED AS SHOWN ABOVE.

SMEAR OR GLISS
GLISS FROM 1ST PITCH INTO THE 2ND.
LAND ON 2ND PITCH IN TEMPO.

SHORT FALL
PLAY WRITTEN NOTE FOR ITS FULL LENGTH.
SAXES: THEN SLIDE DOWNWARD RAPIDLY (CHROMATIC OR DIATONIC) TO AN INDEFINITE PITCH WITH DECRESCENDO.
TRUMPETS: HALF-VALVE TO INDEFINITE PITCH.
TROMBONES: SLIDE GLISSANDO WITH DECRESCENDO.

LONG FALL
SIMILAR IN PERFORMANCE TO THE SHORT FALL.
HOWEVER THE SLIDE LASTS FOR A LONGER PERIOD OF TIME.

UPWARD GLISS OR RIP
CHROMATIC OR DIATONIC SLIDE FROM BELOW ENDING IN TEMPO AT THE WRITTEN PITCH.

DROP
A RAPID CHROMATIC OR DIATONIC SLIDE DOWNWARD BEGINNING FROM A DEFINITE OR INDEFINITE PITCH AND ENDING IN TEMPO AT THE WRITTEN PITCH.

DOIT
PLAY WRITTEN NOTE, THEN GLISS UPWARD TO INDEFINITE PITCH.

GRACE NOTE
TYPICALLY, GRACE NOTE IS PLAYED BEFORE THE BEAT, BUT IN SOME CASES, CAN BE PLAYED ON THE BEAT.

BRASS: "DU" - CLOSED PLUNGER.
SAXES: ALTERNATE CLOSED HORN FINGERING.

BRASS: "WAH" - OPEN PLUNGER.
SAXES: REGULAR FINGERING.

SCOOP
TARGET NOTE IS BEGUN UNDER PITCH USING THE EMBOUCHURE, AND IS THEN BROUGHT UP TO PITCH. THE SPEED AT WHICH THIS HAPPENS IS DEPENDENT ON THE STYLE OF THE MUSIC.

The next example shows the proper use of all of the effects listed above. Once again, an excessive amount of these effects has been added for the sake of demonstration.

TRACK 8

EXAMPLE 1-29.

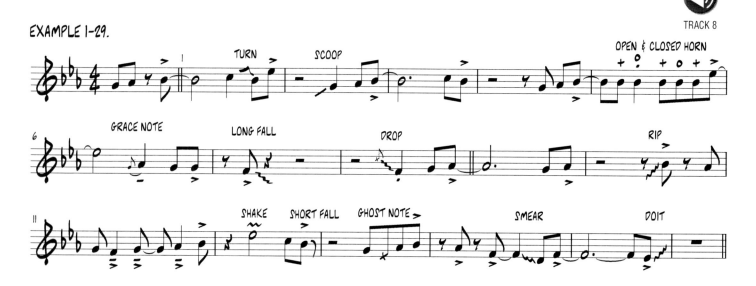

Discretion must be used when adding these effects. An excess of ornaments and inflections will clutter a melodic line and sometimes make it difficult or impossible to play.

Time Signature Alteration

Another idea for creating a fresh interpretation of a melody is the alteration of its time signature. This conversion can involve simple (2/4, 3/4, 4/4) or **compound** (5/4, 6/4, 7/4, etc.) meters. It requires the **augmentation** (multiplying/lengthening) or **diminution** (dividing/shortening) of note values and **harmonic rhythm** (the rate or rhythm at which chords change). The first step in this process is to choose the new time signature. The most probable alteration for any 4/4 tune such as "Billy Boy" is to change the meter to 3/4. The next decision involves the "measure to measure" ratio between the two time signatures. The two possible ratios for a 4/4 to 3/4 conversion are 1:1 or 1:2; a 1:1 ratio indicates that one measure of 4/4 will equal one measure of 3/4, while a 1:2 ratio denotes that one measure of 4/4 will equal two measures of 3/4.

The 1:1 alteration involves the diminution of the 4/4 note values and harmonic rhythm to fit four beats of music into three. Below is a 4/4 to 3/4 alteration of the original version of "Billy Boy" found at the beginning of this chapter (Ex. 1-1) using a 1:1 ratio.

EXAMPLE 1-30.

Because of the long note values and moderate speed of the harmonic rhythm, the change from 4/4 to 3/4 at this ratio is a fairly simple one. However, it cannot be considered complete until some melodic paraphrase has been applied.

EXAMPLE 1-31.

TRACK 9

There are three important points concerning the 1:1 ratio alteration from 4/4 to 3/4.

- The diminution of note values does not provide much space for the insertion of new melodic material such as connecting tones, neighbor tones, or fills.

- Due to the compression of the harmonic rhythm, there is limited space for further reharmonization.

- This alteration is most effective when applied to tunes containing a majority of longer note values. The compression of an occasional eighth-note line is a bit cumbersome, but possible at slower tempos; the diminution of several successive measures of these can be tedious and unmusical.

The 1:2 ratio alteration from 4/4 to 3/4 involves the augmentation of the 4/4 note values and harmonic rhythm to extend four beats of music into six. The characteristics of this conversion are as follows.

- This stretching of the music allows both melody and harmony to breathe, and provides more freedom to reinterpret both of these musical aspects.

- This conversion can be applied to any tune, no matter how many eighth notes are present.

The following is a 1:2 ratio version of "Billy Boy" that contains new melodic and harmonic material.

TRACK 10

EXAMPLE 1-32.

The two possible ratio options when altering a time signature from 3/4 to 4/4 are 1:1 or 2:1. A model for this alteration is the public domain tune "Home on the Range."

EXAMPLE 1-33.

Contrary to the 4/4 to 3/4 conversion above, the 1:1 ratio alteration, when applied from 3/4 to 4/4, produces the more spacious rendering of the melody. Its effect is comparable to the one produced by the 1:2 alteration going from 4/4 to 3/4. The example below utilizes this conversion in conjunction with melodic paraphrase.

TRACK 11
Part 1

EXAMPLE 1-34.

The application of the 2:1 ratio when moving from 3/4 to 4/4 produces a more compressed version of the melody with the same effects as the change from 4/4 to 3/4 using a 1:1 ratio.

TRACK 11
Part 2

EXAMPLE 1-35.

The conversion of tunes from simple to compound meter also involves 2:1 and 1:1 ratios, albeit in a slightly different manner. The 2:1 ratio alteration involves the subtraction of one beat from every other measure of the standard meter and the compression of the note values to fit into one measure of the complex meter. In order to preserve the inherent rhythmic qualities of the simple meters contained within the compound ones (5/4 = 3/4 + 2/4, 7/4 = 4/4 + 3/4, etc.), the first of the two simple meter measures usually remains rhythmically intact with the compression occurring in the second measure. The next two examples illustrate conversions from 3/4 to 5/4 and 4/4 to 7/4 using this ratio.

EXAMPLE 1-36.

The 1:1 ratio works only when creating a 4/4 to 5/4 conversion (3/4 to 4/4 has already been shown and 3/4 to 5/4 involves the use of a 2:1 ratio). Here, the 4/4 note values are stretched

to five beats. In actuality, this conversion involves two processes. As mentioned above, the qualities of the simple meters contained within the compound one should be retained. Consequently, the most efficient way to create a 4/4 to 5/4 alteration using a 1:1 ratio is to first create a 4/4 to 3/4 alteration using a 1:2 ratio.

EXAMPLE 1-37.

Next, alter this 3/4 version to 5/4 using a 2:1 ratio and the method outlined earlier.

EXAMPLE 1-38.

TRACK 13

The rhythms of all the odd-numbered measures have been retained while the even numbered measures contain rhythmically compressed versions of the original 3/4 alteration.

This two-step process may seem a bit lengthy, but its use will ensure the rhythmic retention of the 3/4–2/4 division of this compound meter. As experience with simple meter subdivisions of compound meters is acquired, this two-step process can be eliminated in favor of a single alteration.

Conversions to the larger compound meters (9/4, 11/4, etc.) cannot be expressed easily using ratios. Effective alterations to these meters are dependent upon the creativity of the arranger.

Melody Reconstruction

The alteration of jazz standards and American popular song has proliferated throughout jazz history. Their modifications range in complexity from simple melodic paraphrase, reharmonization, and time signature alteration, to elaborate reworkings incorporating all of these elements. An inventive writer can take any tune, no matter how trite, and transform it into a brand new piece of music that barely resembles its model. The next example shows one possible alteration of "Billy Boy" that incorporates time signature shifts, drastic reharmonization (covered in chapter 2), and radical rhythmic alteration.

EXAMPLE 1–39.

TRACK 14

Summary

Melodic paraphrase cannot be accomplished effectively through the use of any one device (with the possible exception of rhythmic alteration). It should be a combinatory process involving the intelligent integration of all of them. Below is a fully-realized version of "Billy Boy" that utilizes all the devices discussed in this chapter. They are indicated in the example by numbers as follows:

1) Rhythmic Alteration
2) Fragmentation
3) Connecting Tones
4) Neighbor Tones

5) Fills
6) Articulations
7) Dynamics
8) Ornaments & Inflections

TRACK 15

EXAMPLE 1-40.

In terms of frequency of use, rhythmic alteration is the predominant device; it is found in every measure except the last. Articulation is next most used with sixteen appearances; however, this number is misleading due to the marking of some of the natural accents of the line. If articulations were inserted solely for the definition of note length, they would only have appeared in five measures. Fragmentation is third, with appearances in eight measures. Dynamics occur in six measures, ornamentation and inflections in five, connecting tones in four, fills in three, and neighbor tones in two.

The order of priority culled from this example, though random, is indicative of typical frequency of usage. Rhythmic alteration and fragmentation are the principal devices, with the other six used in varying lesser degrees.

The paraphrase should ultimately be conceived as a single entity containing many different elements. The experienced arranger does not decide to add only neighbor tones or fills in any particular section of music. It is the subtle mixture of all these devices that creates an effective paraphrase that can provide the foundation for an arrangement.

CHAPTER 2
Two-Part Harmonization

Once the paraphrase of a melody is complete, the next step in the arranging process is to harmonize it. The simplest, yet most instructive way to begin is with a two-part harmonization. When creating a harmony part, both vertical and horizontal (linear) implications should be considered. These decisions require much care because the resulting vertical sonorities will define tonality and chord quality and provide momentum.

It has been a long established practice in two-part harmonization to use an effective mixture of consonances and dissonances. While these terms are subjective and debatable, intervals are traditionally classified as follows.

EXAMPLE 2-1.

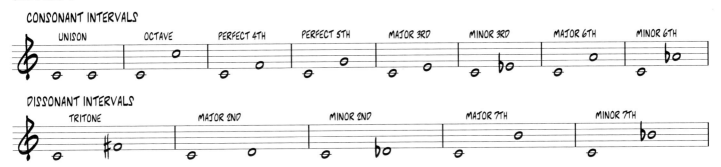

The concept of consonance and dissonance not only differs from one individual to another, but from one style of jazz to another. The history of this music has shown an increasing tolerance to dissonance in each succeeding style. But this does not alter the fact that there is a finite number of intervals available, and that a hierarchy of dissonance among them exists. Therefore, regardless of style, a disciplined control in the use of consonance and dissonance is essential.

Definition of Basic, Guide, and Color Tones

Before proceeding, it is necessary to clarify the terminology used in this book to identify specific chord tones.

- Roots and perfect fifths are **basic tones**. Because they are the first two overtones of any given note, they epitomize firmness and stability.

- Thirds and sevenths (both minor and major) are **guide tones** (diminished fifths function as guide tones in half-diminished chords as do perfect fourths in dominant suspended chords). These notes are essential in defining basic chord quality.

- Ninths, elevenths, and thirteenths (both natural and altered) are **color tones**. These notes add complexity and density to a chord.

The following is a list of the common chord types and their basic, guide, and color tones.

EXAMPLE 2–2.

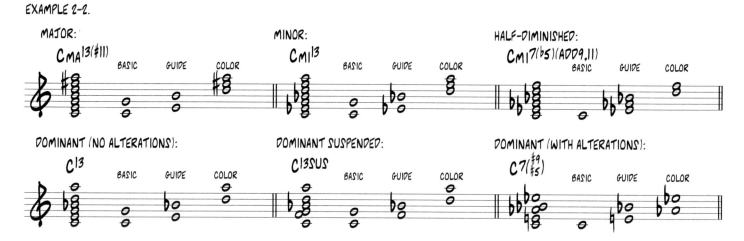

When creating a two-part harmonization, it is imperative to consider chord quality. The use of guide tones is essential in establishing this. A vertical sonority with two guide tones is the most definitive. One with a single guide tone is less definitive, but usable in most contexts. Those with no guide tones can be vague and ambiguous. In a sonority containing only a root and fifth, for example, the quality of the chord cannot be determined. The lack of a seventh further inhibits identification of chord quality. If the melody note is a root or fifth (both basic tones), the obvious choice for a harmony note is a third or seventh (guide tones). If the third or seventh is in the melody, the root and fifth work well in the harmony. This simple "guide tone versus basic tone" procedure results in a consonant third or sixth interval between parts, and is a good first step in harmonization.

EXAMPLE 2–3.

The most frequent use of two guide tones occurs between the third and seventh of a dominant seventh chord. It is important to resolve these correctly whenever possible. The seventh of the dominant should resolve to the third of the next chord, and the third should resolve to the seventh (or root). This rule of voice leading can be expanded to include any cycle progression, that is, one in which the root movement is down a perfect fifth. The most common cycle progression in jazz is the ii7-V7-I7. Here, the guide tones alone, if correctly resolved, can establish tonality. The addition of the chord roots achieves a sense of completeness.

EXAMPLE 2–4.

Jazz harmony is highly chromatic and tends to shift frequently to other tonal centers. This movement is called **tonicization**. Unlike a modulation, which is of longer duration and requires cadential confirmation, tonicization usually encompasses a measure or two at most.

Guide-tone movement plays a central role in implementing tonicization. A detailed analysis of this process can be found in chapter 5.

EXAMPLE 2-5.

In the beginning, two-part harmonizations should be constructed by using as many guide tones as possible. This will provide valuable insight into the way these tones function in creating vertical sonorities and chord movement.

A typical two-part harmonization should also contain a large proportion of consonant intervals. Dissonant intervals will provide contrast and momentum. The guide tones will aid in defining chord movement and tonality.

EXAMPLE 2-6.

Four Types of Movement

As the harmonization evolves, the linear aspects will become apparent and the combination of the two parts will result in four types of movement: parallel, similar, oblique, and contrary.

- **Parallel**: the two voices move at the same interval (e.g., thirds) in a diatonic fashion; the quality of the interval (major or minor) may be continually adjusted to fit the chord-scale of the moment.
- **Similar**: the two voices move in the same direction; intervals can be mixed.
- **Oblique**: one voice moves while the other is stationary.
- **Contrary**: as one voice moves upward, the other moves downward.

EXAMPLE 2-7.

Harmonizations are typically placed below the melody so as to retain the proper focus on it. Since the harmony part is subordinate or accompanimental in nature, independent movement is not of primary importance. A typical two-part harmonization will contain a great deal of parallel or similar movement, with oblique and contrary motion providing relief.

EXAMPLE 2-8.

The construction of a two-part harmonization should not only sound good, but also impart a sense of the underlying harmony. This is especially important at the beginning of phrases and in instances where movement to other tonalities occurs. But once the tonality is firmly established, there is more freedom in the choice of harmonies.

Another factor to be considered is that harmonizations do not typically exist in isolation, but are integrated with the rhythm section. While this harmonic framework should not be seen as an opportunity to be less discerning in the choices of harmony notes, it does open up many new possibilities. This is especially true when harmonizing chromatically altered tones and color tones. By choosing the chord tone immediately above or below, ninths, elevenths, and thirteenths can be harmonized with the melody, producing consonant thirds or sixths.

EXAMPLE 2-9.

Most of these two-note combinations contain no guide tones, so a passage using these types of sonorities might not impart the true sense of the underlying harmonies. But integration with the rhythm section will provide the proper guide-tone references that will help bring the harmonies into focus.

Throughout this chapter, the first eight measures of "Bar Flies," an original tune that was introduced in chapter 1, will serve as a model for two-part harmonization.

EXAMPLE 2-10.

By simply applying the "guide tone versus basic tone" procedure outlined above, a simple but quick harmonization may be achieved using only parallel thirds or sixths.

TRACK 16

While these harmonizations may sound pleasing to the ear, they have some serious short-comings.

- There is no interplay between consonance and dissonance. The resultant sound is bland and one-dimensional.

- The harmony is completely subjugated and has no identity of its own. Although this may sometimes be desirable, it is not always the case.

- The underlying harmony does not always impart the true sense of the tonality. This is most obvious in mm. 5–6.

By using a combination of thirds and sixths, a more useful and interesting harmonization may result as shown in the next example. Notice how the wide leaps in the melody in mm.1 and 2, as well as the octave span in mm. 3 and 4 are counteracted by switching from one interval to the other in the harmony. The use of contrary motion in mm. 5–8 provides variety and makes the harmony part more interesting.

TRACK 17
Part 1

By way of contrast, the next example shows an ineffective combination of thirds and sixths that produces the opposite effect. It creates a succession of even wider intervals in the harmony part that is disconcerting and actually diverts attention from the melody.

TRACK 17
Part 2

EXAMPLE 2-13.

These examples illustrate that there is much more to writing a good harmony part than merely finding two notes that sound good together. For an experienced arranger, extensive experimentation has refined the decision-making process to the point where it is almost intuitive. However, for the novice, this procedure must be explained in detail. The following section presents a step-by-step method for creating an effective two-part harmonization.

Steps to Creating an Effective Two-Part Harmonization

1 – Examination of the Melody

When planning a harmonization, the first step should involve an examination of the melody to determine the following.

1. **Important target notes**: It is sometimes helpful to find the best harmonization for a target note and then work backward. This combination of working forward and backward helps to maintain a sense of where the line is going, and will improve the linear aspects of the harmonization. Target notes may be identified as:

   - First note of a phrase, or phrase segment
   - High or low notes in a phrase
   - Notes of long duration
   - Final note of a phrase, phrase segment, or cadential progression

In the next example, the target notes of "Bar Flies" are circled, and a letter is placed below each one to indicate the reason for its selection.

EXAMPLE 2-14.

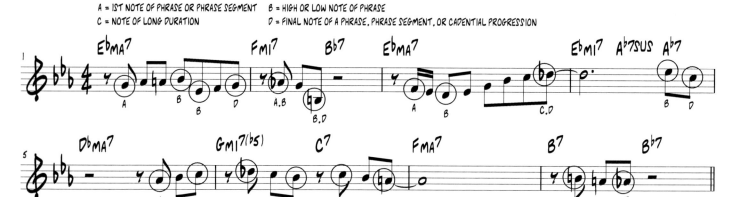

2. **The presence or absence of guide tones, especially with regard to the target notes**: When guide tones are present in the melody, this may preclude their use in the harmony, whereas the absence of guide tones in the melody necessitates their use in the harmony. The following section of "Bar Flies" contains an unusually high percentage of guide tones (twelve of the thirty-one notes are guide tones). This important observation plays a key role in determining the number of acceptable harmonizations.

EXAMPLE 2-15.

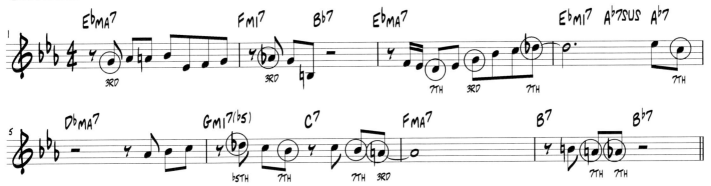

3. **Presence or absence of non-harmonic tones**: If the melody to be harmonized has been paraphrased, several passing tones, neighbor tones, and rhythmic anticipations and delays may have been added. These non-harmonic tones are important elements in providing movement in a musical phrase. They were briefly defined in chapter 1 and will be explained in further detail in chapter 5.

The decision as to whether a note should be considered a non-harmonic or color tone can sometimes be a complicated one. Those notes pitched at an interval of a second, fourth, or sixth above the chord root may be treated as non-harmonic tones or harmonized as color tones (ninths, elevenths, or thirteenths). When thought of as color tones, there is a risk of harmonic stagnation, so it is wise to consider the possibility of treating these notes as non-harmonic tones.

EXAMPLE 2-16.

4. **Temporary changes of tonal center**: One way to identify these is to look for ii7–V7–I, V7–I, or ii7–V7 progressions. A new key center means a new scale, and will affect the choice of harmonies. "Bar Flies" begins in the key of E♭ major, moves to D♭ major in mm. 4–5, to F major in mm. 6–7, then returns to E♭ in m. 8. These key changes are shown in the following example and are accompanied by the appropriate theoretical symbols that explain how these tonicizations were achieved.

EXAMPLE 2-17.

The rhythmic anticipations in this piece are not really non-harmonic tones because the chords that harmonize them have been anticipated as well. In the following example, the chord symbols have been moved forward a half beat and placed above the notes that they harmonize to demonstrate this point. Of course, these anticipated chords would not appear this way in the rhythm parts; they would fall on the next downbeat.

EXAMPLE 2-18.

II – Harmonization of Phrase Segments

After this four-step analysis is completed, preparation for the actual harmonization should begin by breaking the melody into smaller sections; first into phrases, and then into phrase segments. A phase segment is an arbitrary division that may consist of anything from a few notes to a measure or two. Phrase segments are separated from each other by rests, notes of longer duration, large leaps, or target notes.

The following example shows the first eight measures of "Bar Flies" broken down into both phrases and phrase segments. It consists of three phrases; the first and second are comprised of three segments, while the third contains four. Each phrase segment begins and ends with a target note.

EXAMPLE 2-19.

The next step is to harmonize each of these phrase segments by working both forward and backward to connect the target notes. The "guide tone versus basic tone" method is predominantly used to harmonize most of the target notes. When another method is used—that is, "basic tone versus basic tone," or "basic tone versus color tone"—the target note should be approached and/or left by contrary motion.

Each segment is presented below with several options for harmonization. This is not to say that every option must be considered for every phrase segment. In actual practice, a few possibilities are sufficient. This exhaustive listing is provided only to show that there are numerous ways to harmonize any given segment.

The first phrase segment consists of two target notes (see example 2-14) connected by two non-harmonic tones. The target notes are the third and fifth of the tonic triad. The harmonizations of these two notes are especially important as they establish the tonality. The choice of notes to accompany the non-harmonic tones should move logically from the first target note to the second. All other non-harmonic tones should be dealt with in the same manner. The following shows some acceptable harmonizations of phrase segment one.

EXAMPLE 2-20.

Since the tonic E♭ chord was clearly defined in segment one, the harmonization of the first note of segment two is not so critical. More important is the movement to the last note (G), which is a color tone (the ninth of the F chord labeled on beat 1). This can be harmonized by the chord tone immediately above or below it. The chord tone above is the eleventh (B♭), the chord tone below is the seventh (E♭). When it was harmonized by the fifth (C), the resulting interval of a perfect fifth was approached by contrary motion (basic rule of counterpoint).

EXAMPLE 2-21.

Because F minor was already defined in the last note of segment two, the harmonization of the first note of segment three becomes less crucial. More important is the harmonization of the last note (B♮). Since this is a color tone (flat ninth), it may be harmonized with the chord tone immediately above or below. The chord tone above would be the third (D); the chord tone below could be either the seventh (A♭) or the thirteenth (G).

EXAMPLE 2-22.

The first four notes of segment four constitute a sort of changing tone (consisting of upper neighbor, chord tone, lower neighbor, chord tone) around the tonic E♭. Since the tonic has been well established by now, it is not essential to harmonize both E♭s with consonant intervals, but rather focus on the final note (G). Here, the "guide tone versus basic tone" method is in effect.

EXAMPLE 2-23.

The first note of segment five constitutes the seventh appearance of a member of the tonic chord, and its harmonization is again not critical. The most important note is the last one, which is the beginning of a tonicization of the key of D♭. When the last note is harmonized with a consonant third or sixth, it is approached by parallel motion. When harmonized as a perfect fifth (D♭–G♭) it is approached by contrary motion.

EXAMPLE 2-24.

Every note of segment six is important because of the tonicization process that is in effect. Here, guide tones play a central role. Because achieving contrary motion into the last note is difficult, it is best harmonized with either a consonant third (A♭) or sixth (E♭). Notice that three of the segment phrase examples end with a perfect fifth that is not approached by contrary motion. When contrary motion is difficult, similar motion is acceptable, but parallel motion should be avoided at all costs.

EXAMPLE 2-25.

Segment seven is the most challenging to harmonize. The last note (C) is the most important because it is the beginning of another tonicization; this time to the key of F. This note is the eleventh of the G half-diminished chord, but harmonizing it with the chord tone above or below it does not work; both D♭ and B♭ are only a major second away, making for an undesirable dissonance, and neither A♭ (flat ninth) nor E♭ (thirteenth) will convey the tonality of the G half-diminished chord. Chromatically altering them to A♮ or E♮ creates a jarring effect coming from the key of D♭. This leaves F and a unison or octave C as the only workable harmony notes.

EXAMPLE 2-26.

Fortunately, the first note in segment eight (D♭) is in the same chord and is much easier to harmonize. Any of the other three notes of the chord are acceptable. The focus should be on the last note, being the dominant of the new key of F. Since guide-tone action is essential in tonicizations, the most effective harmonization would be with the other guide tone (E). However, other choices are possible.

EXAMPLE 2-27.

The guide-tone resolution (B♭–A) in segment nine defines the key of F very clearly. This opens up many different possibilities for harmonization.

EXAMPLE 2-28.

The last segment constitutes a return to the original key of E♭. Since the last two melody notes are guide tones, several harmonizations are possible. The most definitive one would use both guide tones on the last note.

EXAMPLE 2-29.

III – Combination of Phrase-Segment Harmonizations

After all the segments have been harmonized, each group of segments can be reunited to form a phrase. In each of the following three examples, a matrix has been created in a "Chinese menu" fashion with most of the possible segment harmonizations. By merely drawing lines between each segment, endless possibilities, both good and bad, will emerge for each phrase. Many of these can immediately be eliminated due to improper voice leading or awkward movement between segments. The remaining combinations should then be closely scrutinized to find the most effective ones.

EXAMPLE 2-30.

EXAMPLE 2-31.

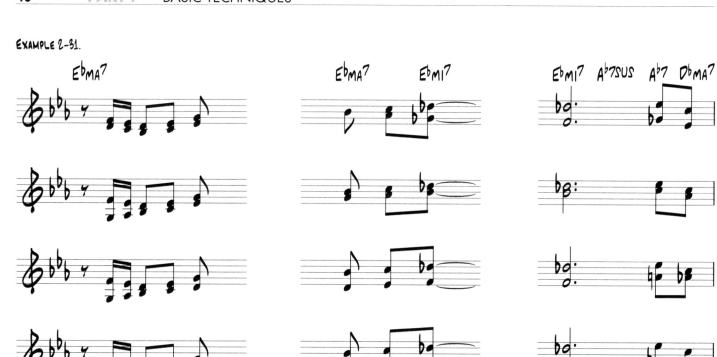

EXAMPLE 2-32.

As mentioned earlier when discussing segment harmonizations, it is not necessary to locate every possible segment combination. This detailed presentation is only meant to once again amplify the point that there are literally hundreds of ways to harmonize any given phrase.

For purposes of illustration only, three harmonizations are presented that exclusively exploit one type of motion throughout the entire eight measures of "Bar Flies." Example 2-33 uses only oblique motion; 2-34, contrary motion; and 2-35, contrary motion combined with the use of unisons or octaves.

TRACK 18

EXAMPLE 2-33.

TRACK 19

EXAMPLE 2-34.

TRACK 20

EXAMPLE 2-35.

Examples of parallel and similar motion have already been shown in examples 2-11 and 2-12.

In actual practice, an effective two-part harmonization usually contains a combination of all types of motion. Here are three examples culled from the segment matrices presented earlier in this chapter.

TRACK 21
Part 1

EXAMPLE 2-36.

TRACK 21
Part 2

EXAMPLE 2-37.

EXAMPLE 2-38.

Before concluding this chapter, it is worthwhile to mention a technique referred to as **planing**. This involves "harmonizing" a melody at the interval of the perfect fourth or perfect fifth, either above or below. Actually, this is not really a harmonization, but rather a thickening of the melody. It is reminiscent of organists' use of mutation stops, which add overtones to enrich a melodic line. This technique is best used in modal or pedal situations or in tunes with extremely slow harmonic rhythm.

EXAMPLE 2-39.

CHAPTER 3
Countermelody

The transition from writing a harmony part to creating a countermelody represents a rather large step. Not only does it require a basic knowledge of counterpoint (the combination of two or more independent lines), it also involves some original composition. The jazz format also imposes some restrictions that may hinder this creative process.

- It must operate within a preset harmonic progression.
- The contour of the countermelody is conditioned to some extent by the nature of the given melody.
- Practical considerations, such as instrumentation, may restrict the range of the countermelody.

During the process of combining two independent melodies in a coherent, meaningful manner, two opposing factors are constantly at work: *contrast* and *unity*. While contrast is inherent in any contrapuntal design, unity is also necessary when combining the two melodies to produce a cohesive whole. The implementation of this correlative process will be more easily understood if the two components are discussed separately.

Methods of Providing Contrast

There are four distinct ways to achieve independence between two melodic lines.

- Relative motion
- Rhythmic activity
- Register
- Timbre

Relative Motion

This term refers to the contrasting contours (or melodic curves) of the two melodies. The possible shapes of melodic curves are too numerous to catalogue. But the four basic contours may be shown graphically.

EXAMPLE 3-1.

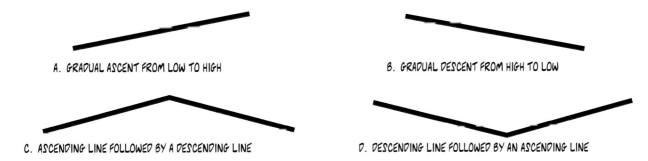

A. GRADUAL ASCENT FROM LOW TO HIGH

B. GRADUAL DESCENT FROM HIGH TO LOW

C. ASCENDING LINE FOLLOWED BY A DESCENDING LINE

D. DESCENDING LINE FOLLOWED BY AN ASCENDING LINE

The shapes of types C and D are not always symmetrical; the peak of a line may occur early or late as well as in the middle.

EXAMPLE 3-2.

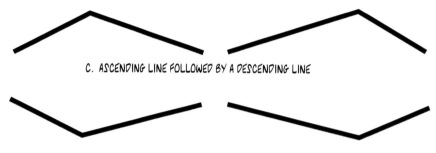

These diagrams are obviously simplified; all melodies possess secondary curves within the broad overall design, but secondary curves do not alter the basic contour of the line. Example 3-3 illustrates how these four basic designs may be expressed melodically.

EXAMPLE 3-3.

The combination of the countermelody with the melody will result in any of the four types of relative movement described in chapter 2. They are: parallel, similar, oblique, and contrary.

EXAMPLE 3-4.

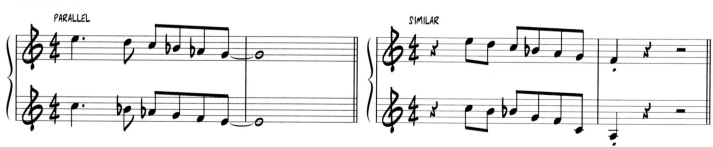

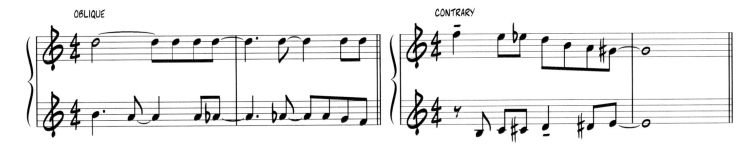

To achieve the desired independence, it is imperative that the contours of the two lines are dissimilar. Therefore, contrary motion is the primary choice, and next is oblique. If similar and parallel motion are used excessively, the feeling of independence between the lines is lost, and the countermelody will sound more like a line created simply to fill out the harmony instead of a distinctive melody.

The natural resolution of tendency tones may occasionally take the countermelody in an undesirable direction. This is particularly the case in **cycle progressions** (chords that progress via fourths or fifths), where the natural movement is downward.

TRACK 22
Part 1

EXAMPLE 3-5.

There are several ways to interrupt or reverse this movement.

- Leap or arpeggiate to the octave above.

TRACK 22
Part 2

EXAMPLE 3-6.

- Leap, arpeggiate, or move stepwise to the other guide tone above and start a new line.

TRACK 23
Part 1

EXAMPLE 3-7.

- Create an ascending line through the use of chromatic alterations.

TRACK 23
Part 2

EXAMPLE 3-8.

Descending lines were chosen for the purposes of illustration, but the same principles apply for ascending lines, only in reverse.

- Leap or arpeggiate to the octave below.
- Leap, arpeggiate, or move stepwise to the guide tone below and start a new line.
- Create a descending line through the use of chromatic alterations.

Rhythmic Activity

If providing contrast between the two lines was merely a matter of contour, the possibilities would soon be exhausted. To achieve true distinction, the rhythmic independence of the lines is essential. True contrast occurs when each line consistently employs its own rhythmic patterns.

TRACK 24
Part 1

EXAMPLE 3-9.

A well-established formula is to have one part moving in animated rhythms, while the other employs longer note values. This interplay not only maintains the rhythmic flow, but causes attention to be shifted from one part to the other.

TRACK 24
Part 2

EXAMPLE 3-10.

Another effective device is to use the same melody in both parts, but start the two lines at different times. This creates the effect of one line imitating the other, in a delayed fashion (imitative counterpoint). Here, the judicious use of rests and ties can be helpful as long as the continuity of the countermelody is not impeded.

EXAMPLE 3-11.

TRACK 24
Part 3

The melody and countermelody together must not contain too many different rhythmic patterns if unity and cohesion are to be retained. The following example demonstrates how the overabundance of rhythmic patterns may result in clutter and confusion.

EXAMPLE 3-12.

TRACK 25
Part 1

The following excerpt also has a wide variety of rhythmic patterns, but it contains enough unifying devices to create a balanced effect.

TRACK 25
Part 2

EXAMPLE 3-13.

Register

The normal position of the countermelody is below the melody, but it may occasionally be written above. The next example shows the same countermelody written both above and below a given melody.

EXAMPLE 3-14.

The register of the countermelody may be predetermined to some extent by the range and **tessitura** of the instrument assigned to play it. (Tessitura is the general or overall range of a melody, i.e., most of the melody may consist of high notes with just a few very low notes. One would refer to this as having a high tessitura, even though the range may be fairly wide.) But it need not be a concern at this point. The main objective is to maintain a separateness of the two lines. Wider spacing results in greater contrast. One of the most common errors, especially when writing for two like instruments (or two closely pitched instruments), is to write the lines too close together.

EXAMPLE 3-15.

Here the two lines are not only too close; they actually run into each other. It is important not to let the clef being used restrict the range of a melody (only the range of the instrument playing the line). The clef may be changed at any time to accommodate the range of the countermelody. One should just be mindful of keeping enough distance between the two melodies, and then change the clef if need be.

EXAMPLE 3-16.

It is possible that the two lines might cross occasionally. This should occur naturally as a result of the energy created by the countermelody. The parts should not remain crossed for long, or they might lose their identity.

EXAMPLE 3-17.

Timbre

Tone color or **timbre** can play a significant role in creating contrast between two lines. Two instruments with different ranges and timbres will provide greater contrast than two like or two closely pitched instruments. Here the contrasts would be both registral and timbral. But the focus should be entirely on the musical aspects at this time.

Unifying Devices In Contrapuntal Writing

If two melodies are to be combined successfully, they must have enough in common melodically, rhythmically, and stylistically to form a convincing whole. These common elements can most often be identified as **motives**. A motive is defined as a short figure with its own characteristic rhythmic pattern and melodic contour. The following melody contains several identifiable motives.

EXAMPLE 3-18.

In their endeavor to achieve contrast, beginning arrangers often fail to isolate these motives and utilize them as a unifying device. The three most common ways to manipulate and develop motives are as follows.

- Repetition
- Variation
- Sequence

Repetition is a fundamental means of achieving unity in music; it is rooted in the concept of *motivic development*. One way repetition may be employed is through an exact duplication of a motive in another voice. It is acceptable for the same rhythmic patterns to be shared by both parts. When these patterns are shared, but not sounded at the same time in the different voices, this is referred to as imitation.

EXAMPLE 3-19.

Variation retains some features of the original motive, while other areas are altered.

EXAMPLE 3-20.

In a sequence, the motive recurs immediately on another pitch. There are three types of sequences:

- **Diatonic**: no chromatic alterations involved; tonality is preserved.

EXAMPLE 3-21.

- **Real**: intervals of the original are preserved exactly (literal transposition).

EXAMPLE 3-22.

- **Chromatic**: combination of the first two.

EXAMPLE 3-23.

It is also possible to subject only the rhythmic design of the figure to variation.

EXAMPLE 3-24.

These devices are excellent for creating interest and variety while maintaining unity. Repetition alone can become monotonous; monotony can be overcome by variety.

There are other means of motivic variation that are inherent in contrapuntal writing. But they are a bit more involved, so they will only be mentioned briefly here.

- **Augmentation**: multiplying the note values
- **Diminution**: dividing the note values
- **Inversion**: arranging the intervals in contrary motion (upside down)
- **Retrograde**: beginning with the last note and proceeding to the first (backward)

Augmentation and diminution are useful compositional techniques and are worth pursuing. Inversion and retrograde are considered more intellectual pursuits. Most people have difficulty recognizing a melody when it is played backwards or upside down. Many of these devices may seem too academic for the task of writing a countermelody. But, later on, when attempting to write a developmental section, they will prove very helpful.

These concepts of contrast and unity will be applied to the writing of a countermelody to "Bar Flies," which was introduced in chapter 2.

Form

Because an entire piece of music is being used for the first time, it is necessary to examine its **form**, or organizational structure. When confronted with a new composition, whether for arranging or performing, the first task should be a formal analysis. A complete version of "Bar Flies" is presented below to aid in this process.

EXAMPLE 3-25.

"Bar Flies" is a thirty-six measure **ternary** (three-part) form. By assigning letters to each of the phrases, it can be expressed as ABA. If the repeat of the first phrase is acknowledged, it becomes:

Formal element: A A B A' (Extension)
No. of measures: 8 8 8 12 (8+4)

Because the first two A sections are identical, they are notated with a repeat with first and second endings. In the final version, this repeat will be written out to accommodate different treatments of the two sections. Due to the slight modification in measure one of the final A section, plus the four-measure extension, it is designated as A'.

Writing a Countermelody: Three-step process

In the previous chapter, preparations for writing a successful harmony part entailed a detailed, four-step analysis. Each melodic fragment was examined for the purpose of finding the most suitable vertical sonorities for each note. The preparation for writing a countermelody requires a different focus. The note-to-note analysis will be replaced with a broader, three-step process with the emphasis on the following.

- **Melodic curves**: Both overall and secondary curves will be identified so that contrasting ones can be employed in the countermelody.

- **Rhythmic content**: This includes characteristic rhythmic patterns as well as areas of rhythmic activity and inactivity. Identification of these areas is key to the establishment of independent rhythmic patterns in the countermelody and the proper distribution of rhythmic activity between the two lines. Selective use of imitation and variation of motives from the original melody helps maintain unity and continuity.

- **Target notes**: Harmonizing these notes is still essential for establishing the harmonic progression and identifying shifts in tonality (tonicizations). But in the actual working-out process, the other forces at work will cause the harmonization of many target notes to be weakened and, in some cases, abandoned altogether.

The following lists the recommended three-step procedure for preparing to write a countermelody.

1. Scan the melody to determine its overall curve, as well as secondary curves. The chief concern at this point should be with the broad outline—not the secondary curves.

   Mm. 1 and 2 of the A section have a kind of "wavy" curve centering on the note G before a sudden descent to B in m. 2. There is a steady ascent to the high E♭ in mm. 3 and 4. This E♭ is the climax of the A phrase. Mm. 5–8 form a gentle arch.

EXAMPLE 3-26.

Mm. 1–4 of the B section are centered on high E♭. Mm. 5–7 form a gradual descent from E♭ to G, followed by a sudden plunge to low E in m. 8.

EXAMPLE 3-27.

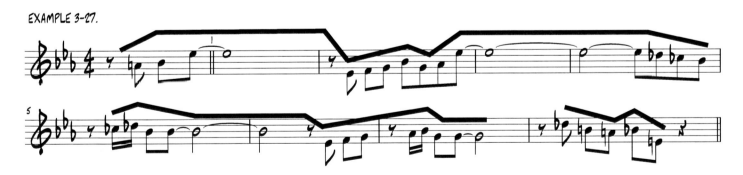

Because of the energy expended in m. 8 of B, the first four notes of the final A have been deleted to provide some breathing space. The first two measures now create a simple arch form. The four-measure extension of the final A is an inverted arch form, starting on high G♭, descending to G and rising to a high A at the end.

EXAMPLE 3-28A.

EXAMPLE 3-28B.

By utilizing the four types of motion, with emphasis on contrary motion, some feasible outlines begin to emerge. Other factors, such as register and spacing will enter into this early planning. The results will be sketchy, but some possible contours will gradually appear.

2. Examine the rhythmic structure of the melody to find the points of activity and inactivity, and the types of rhythmic figures used.

   The A section of "Bar Flies" contains a steady eighth-note rhythm interspersed with points of rest. The long notes in mm. 4 and 7 and the rests in mm. 2, 5, and 8 make up the areas of inactivity.

EXAMPLE 3-29.

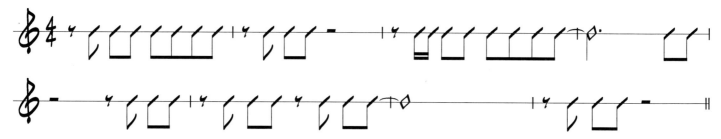

The B section is an excellent example of alternating long and short note values.

EXAMPLE 3-30.

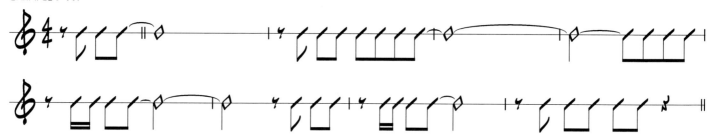

Not counting all half-beats, there is a sustained note of four beats in m. 1, six beats in mm. 3 and 4, four beats in mm. 5 and 6, and two beats in m. 7. These are connected by steady eighth-note patterns. Eighth-note rests are inserted to provide offbeat entrances for all the eighth-note figures. By creating movement in the countermelody at these points of rest, a distribution of rhythmic activity between the two lines can be easily achieved. This interplay of activity will result in a constant shift of emphasis between the lines, and assure their individuality.

EXAMPLE 3-31.

The most recognizable rhythmic figure is the three eighth-note pattern which appears five times in the A section and four times in the B section. Sometimes it is separated by rests; other times it is tied to a longer note value.

The other distinguishable figure is the seven eighth-note figure in m. 1 (as shown below in example 1). It appears three more times in altered form (examples 2–4) . In m. 3, the first eighth-note is broken into two sixteenths, and the contour is altered; in m. 2 of the B section, it is tied to a whole note; in m. 8 of the B section, the rhythm is retained but the contour is altered, ending one beat short of the complete figure.

EXAMPLE 3-32.

3. Identify the target notes and determine the presence or absence of guide tones. The same procedure that was devised for writing a harmony part will be used here. The "basic tone versus guide tone" relationship and proper resolution of guide tones are still important in establishing and maintaining chord movement and tonality. However, there is a shift in emphasis from the vertical to the linear. The need for independence between the two lines dictates that the focus should be concentrated on important junctures such as cadences, phrase endings, and shifts in the tonal center and not on the vertical sonorities for every target note. The momentum of the countermelody may obliterate the consonance normally found at some target notes, and the harmonies might not be readily apparent at these points. But this broader approach is necessary if the lines are to maintain their independence. It will not be clear which vertical sonorities will be retained until the final version of the counter-melody is completed. So, it is still important to identify all of the target notes at the beginning. Below is a complete version of "Bar Flies" with the target notes circled.

EXAMPLE 3-33.

The following examples show how the three steps outlined above can be utilized in working out the countermelody. The first version deals almost exclusively with implementing contrary motion.

TRACK 26

EXAMPLE 3-34.

The next version concentrates on establishing independent rhythmic patterns.

EXAMPLE 3-35.

The third version incorporates elements from the first two. The result is a better balance between contrast and unity.

TRACK 28

EXAMPLE 3-36.

For many writers, contrapuntal skills do not come easily. They may lag behind other skills, such as melodic paraphrasing and vertical harmonizations, for some time. But it would be disastrous to abandon them. Counterpoint is an essential component of an arranger's technique. It is the best way to provide variety in an arrangement that contains mostly vertical sonorities.

Also remember that many melodies—or parts of melodies—do not lend themselves readily to this kind of process. Melodies with incessant eighth-note movement, vaguely defined contours, or irregular harmonic rhythms often resist contrapuntal treatment.

Most good two-part arrangements do not consist of just one style or texture. They are generally a combination of unison, octaves, quartal (in fourths), or quintal (in fifths) planing, melody with harmony, and melody with countermelody.

CHAPTER 4
Four-Note Close-Position Voicings

The first three chapters were mainly concerned with the linear (or horizontal) methods of combining notes. This chapter will focus on the construction of vertical sonorities. In both small and large ensemble writing, the stacking of several notes under (and sometimes over) a melodic line has been fundamental to jazz arranging since its inception, and continues to be the most widely used method of melody harmonization.

The first step toward the creation of any voicing involves an analysis of the melody and chord progression. Many lead sheets contain only the most basic chord spellings. It is the arranger's job to extend a lead sheet's harmonies to their most logical density by adding color tones or altered tones, to change the quality of a chord, or to use substitutions. Melody notes are a determining factor in this decision-making process.

EXAMPLE 4-1.

When selecting tunes for arranging, be sure to use a reliable source. The newer compilations have been carefully edited and are generally reliable. They also contain some reharmonizations of older standards that reflect current jazz practices. Older fake books and original sheet music contain many incorrect chord notations. The piano arrangements on original sheet music were faithfully harmonized with the composers' harmonies, but quite often the guitar chord symbols reflected only what appeared in the right hand. The correct bass notes were usually present in the music's bass clef staff, but not in the chord symbol. Early fake books merely copied these chord symbols without taking the entire chord into consideration. This practice resulted in a distortion of the true harmonies.

Even though a workable four-part harmonization might be fashioned from these symbols, the rhythm-section parts would be incorrect, and the information essential to creating alternate harmonizations would be lacking. The following are some examples of these types of chord misspellings.

- Mi6 chords are frequently half-diminished chords and part of a II–V–I progression.

EXAMPLE 4-2.

- Dim7 chords may actually be V7♭9 chords.

EXAMPLE 4-3.

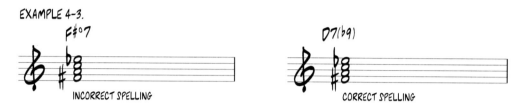

- Mi7 chords may be ma9 chords.

EXAMPLE 4-4.

- Major chords with added sixths may be mi7 chords.

EXAMPLE 4-5.

The logical starting point for constructing vertical sonorities is four-note voicings in close position. It might seem that three-note voicings would be the next obvious step after two-part writing, but the process of combining basic, guide, and color tones into vertical sonorities in a controlled manner is more easily accomplished by using four-note voicings. The addition of the fourth note greatly expands the number of options in the selection of chord tones and facilitates the creation and control of dissonance. After this process has been assimilated and a vocabulary of four-note voicings has been acquired, three- and five-note voicings may then be created more effectively through the process of subtraction or addition.

The term **four-note voicing** refers to a top voice (melody) with three notes placed underneath. **Close position** indicates that all four notes are contained within an octave. This is also known as **block voicing**.

EXAMPLE 4-6.

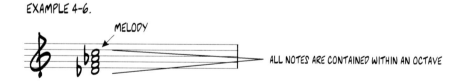

All close-position voicings, regardless of the number of notes, possess several distinctive characteristics.

- They are the densest of all voicing possibilities as the component intervals are primarily seconds and thirds. The compass of close-position voicings is no larger than a major seventh and can be as small as a perfect fourth.

- Because of this density, these voicings produce a homogeneous sound. The resulting timbre is an amalgam of all the instruments involved.

- The individual lines resulting from this type of harmonization are not easily discernible.

Voicing Construction

The following is a general procedure for creating four-note, close-position voicings. The first consideration is the inclusion of all guide tones, which are essential in defining chord quality. The remaining notes will be basic tones, color tones, or a combination of both. The most important factor in this decision-making process is that of *tension level*. This term refers to the amount of dissonance contained in a vertical sonority and will be discussed in detail later in this chapter.

First, determine the function of the melody note (top note of voicing) in the chord (basic, guide, or color tone).

- If it is a basic tone, add all applicable guide tones beneath, keeping the distance between the top and bottom notes within an octave. In most situations, one note will remain to be added. Choose either a basic or color tone and place it within an octave below the melody note.

EXAMPLE 4-7.

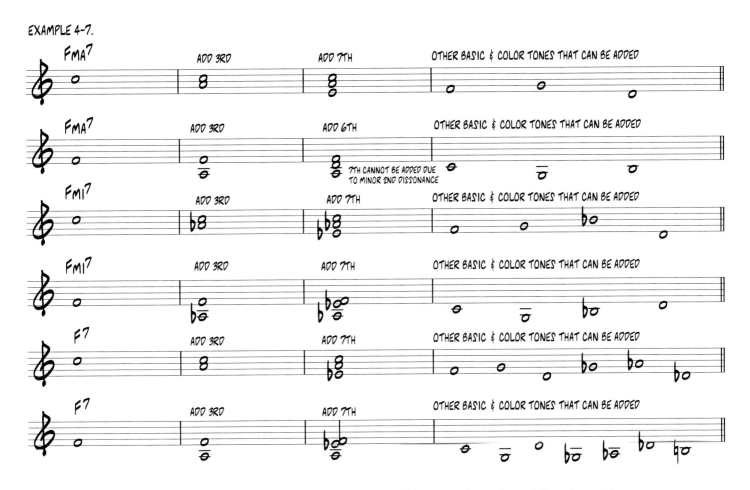

There is one situation where the voicing will be complete after adding the guide tones. This occurs when harmonizing a half-diminished chord where the root is the melody note.

EXAMPLE 4-8.

- If the melody note is a guide tone, add all other applicable guide tones beneath, keeping the distance between the top and bottom notes within an octave. One or two notes will remain to be added. Choose basic or color tones and place them within an octave below the melody note.

EXAMPLE 4-9.

- If the melody note is a color tone, add all applicable guide tones beneath, keeping the distance between the top and bottom notes within an octave. In most situations, one note will remain to be added. Choose either a basic or color tone and place it within an octave below the melody note.

EXAMPLE 4-10.

On the whole, voicings cannot function alone. The chord's root must be heard in combination with any voicing to create a "complete" sound. Without it, a chord's quality can easily be misinterpreted.

EXAMPLE 4-11.

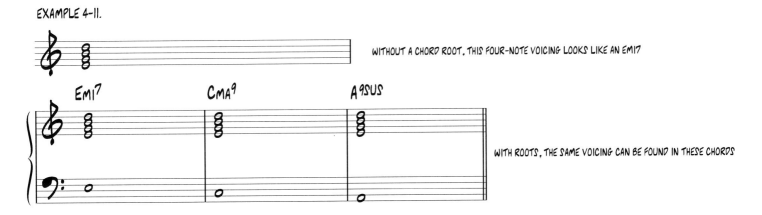

In chapter 6, the notes of these voicings will be manipulated to create new sonorities. Consequently, it is important to identify each note of a voicing. They are referred to in the following manner; the top note (melody) is the first voice, the one directly below the top voice is the second, the one below that is the third, etc. The numbering continues similarly to the bottom of the voicing.

EXAMPLE 4-12.

These voices, when given to different instruments, are almost always distributed according to pitch order and voice number (for exceptions to this, see the section on cross-voicing later in this chapter). For example, when distributing a four-voice harmonization to trumpet, trombone, alto sax, and tenor sax, the first step is to determine the pitch order of the instruments (highest to lowest). The pitch order of this particular group is trumpet, alto sax, tenor sax, and trombone. Therefore, the trumpet will always receive the first voice, alto the second, tenor the third, and trombone the fourth, throughout the entire harmonization.

EXAMPLE 4-13.

Traditionally Unacceptable Dissonances

A four-note chord can be written in four different positions, with each of the notes appearing in the top voice.

EXAMPLE 4-14.

Many chords, when written in root position (with the root on the bottom), span the interval of a major seventh.

EXAMPLE 4-15.

When these chords are written in any of the other three positions, the major seventh is inverted and becomes a minor second.

EXAMPLE 4-16.

This dissonant interval is acceptable anywhere except between the top two voices. The placement of a minor second directly below the top (melody) note creates an unacceptable effect and should be avoided. An interval of at least a major second should be maintained between the top two voices.

EXAMPLE 4-17.

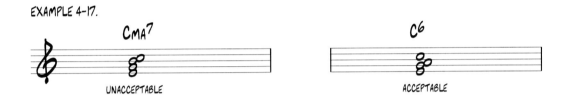

This is not to say that voicings containing a minor second between the top two voices are never used. Many arrangers use this vertical arrangement for special effects, but it is not advisable in melody harmonization. (A complete listing of all the minor-second clashes that should typically be avoided in multiple-note voicings, along with possible solutions, can be found in appendix 2.)

There is an additional rule regarding unacceptable dissonances that must be mentioned.

- When the natural fifth or ninth is present anywhere in a voicing (not just in the top voice), do not use either of its altered versions in the same voicing. In other words, natural and altered ninths cannot be mixed within the same voicing. This also applies to natural and altered fifths. However, altered ninths can be mixed with natural fifths and vice versa.

EXAMPLE 4-18.

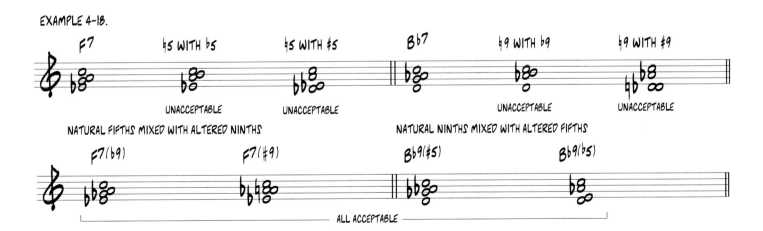

An often-used exception to this rule pertains to the use of both natural and lowered fifths in major and dominant chords when the natural fifth is not the top note of the voicing. Examples of this can usually be found in denser voicings containing larger numbers of notes where the natural fifth is placed below the lowered fifth, thereby approximating the pitch order of the natural overtone series. Use in four-note voicings is rarer, though feasible.

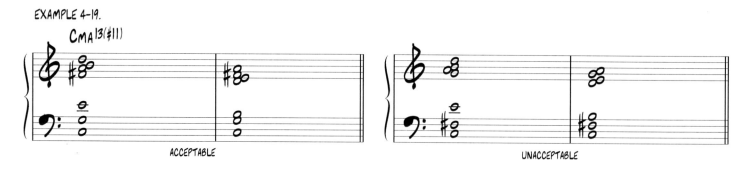

EXAMPLE 4-19.

CMA¹³⁽♯¹¹⁾

ACCEPTABLE   UNACCEPTABLE

A compendium of all available four-note voicings in close position containing all applicable guide tones is included in appendix 4. An inspection of this will illustrate the many possibilities for harmonizing each chord tone of any given chord type.

Tension and Density Levels

Two other important concepts to grasp before attempting to create any voicing are that of **tension** and **density**. When discussing chord voicings, tension level refers to the amount of dissonance contained in a vertical sonority. Dissonance is increased as major and minor seconds and tritones are introduced. A major second creates a mild dissonance, while a minor second creates a sharper one. The tritone creates either a mild or sharp dissonance, depending on the musical context. Density level refers to the thickness of a voicing. For example, a chord that contains only the ninth is less dense than one containing the ninth, eleventh, and thirteenth or alterations of these notes. Tension and density levels should be taken into account at all times when creating vertical sonorities of any size.

Appropriate levels of tension and density are dependent on many circumstances: the type of music being arranged, the ability level of the performing group, and the performing situation. For example, an arrangement of a pop tune would contain lower chord tension and density levels than one of a jazz tune due to the nature of pop harmony. An arrangement of a tune written for a beginning jazz ensemble might contain lower levels of tension and density than one written for a more experienced group due to the difficulty associated with the tuning of these chords. Levels of tension and density can even change within an arrangement. A sax soli in a big band arrangement may contain a slightly lower level than a full ensemble section simply due to the larger number of horns.

The assessment of these levels is a highly subjective matter. Generally speaking, the more seconds found in a voicing, the sharper its tension. However, there are flaws in this statement. This is why chord density is also taken into account. Ultimately, the best way to judge a chord's tension and density levels is to listen to it. Below is a table that illustrates the general progression of movement from mild to sharp tension and density.

Tension Levels	Mild	⟶	Moderate	⟶	Sharp
Voicings contain:	7ths ⟶ 9ths & 11ths	⟶	13ths & a few altered 5ths, 9ths, 11ths, & 13ths	⟶	Many altered 5ths, 9ths, 11ths, & 13ths

As a rule, consistent tension and density levels should be maintained throughout a harmonization.

EXAMPLE 4-20.

TRACK 29
Part 1

However, gradual movement across the spectrum is also typical and acceptable.

EXAMPLE 4-21.

TRACK 29
Part 2

Abrupt moves from sharp to mild tension and density, especially at points of rhythmic inactivity, should be avoided. These are often ineffective due to the lack of color present in the sustained chord, as shown in the next example.

EXAMPLE 4-22.

TRACK 30
Part 1

Sudden movement from sharp to moderate tension and density is typical in cadential progressions. For example, a heavily altered dominant chord can resolve to a tonic chord of moderate dissonance; this is the tension and release characteristic of all tonal music.

EXAMPLE 4-23.

TRACK 30
Part 2

Leaps from mild to sharp tension and density can be useful to add impact to a phrase.

EXAMPLE 4-24.

TRACK 31

(For a listing of a more specific sequence of tension and density levels for each chord type, consult appendix 3.)

Basic-Tone Substitutions

Even after a thorough examination of tension levels, inexperienced arrangers tend to create voicings that lack color. These invariably contain too many basic tones. The chord root, though it can provide stability, is frequently redundant when used in a voicing because it is assumed that the bass will already be playing this note.

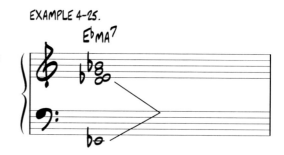

EXAMPLE 4-25.

This also applies to chord inversions, where a note other than the root is in the bass. In the example below, the root of both the Cma7 and Cma7/E chords is C. However, the redundant pitch in the first chord is C, while in the second it is E (both of these notes are already being played by the bass).

EXAMPLE 4-26.

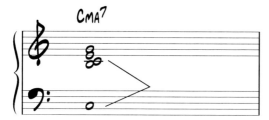
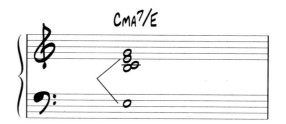

When the natural fifth is a basic tone, it can also be omitted in a voicing because of its occurrence in the overtone series. This overtone is very strong, and even if it is not present in a voicing, it can be felt. Therefore, it can be omitted in favor of a color tone.

EXAMPLE 4-27.

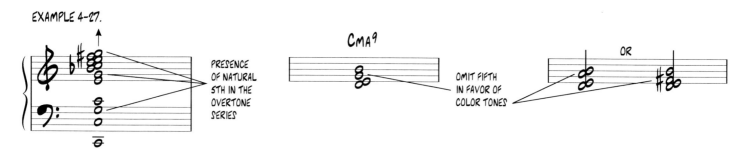

For the most part, basic tones are the least necessary notes in a voicing and should be used only when a more colorful voicing exceeds the desired tension level. The following table of note substitutions for both basic tones is offered as a solution to this problem.

Basic-Tone Substitutions

If the voicing contains:	For major chords, substitute one of these notes:	For minor chords, substitute one of these notes:	For dominant chords, substitute one of these notes:	For half-diminished chords, substitute one of these notes:
root	9th	9th	natural 9th, ♭9th, ♯9th	natural 9th
5th	♯11th, 13th, (6th)	11th, 13th, (6th)	♭5th, ♯5th, natural 13th	11th

EXAMPLE 4-28.

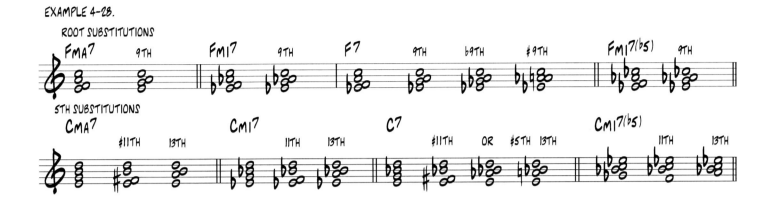

When replacing basic tones with color tones, the note that has been replaced is usually not included in the new voicing. This is a general rule of thumb; however, exceptions are not uncommon, especially when a basic tone is the melody note.

EXAMPLE 4-29.

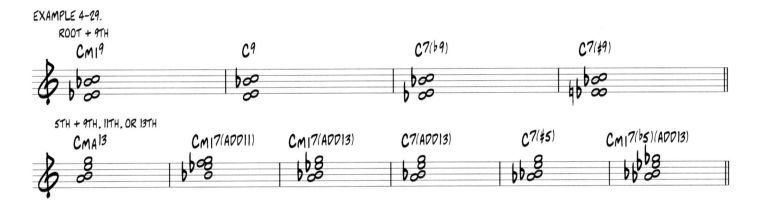

Guide-Tone Substitutions

The method for constructing voicings with all guide tones is a dependable one as every voicing will clearly define a chord's quality at all times. However, there are instances where a guide tone might be omitted from a voicing in favor of a color tone. For example, when the melody note is a basic tone, only one color tone can be added due to the inclusion of all guide tones in a voicing; the probable solution is to omit a guide tone and replace it with a second color tone.

EXAMPLE 4-30.

Another circumstance involving a possible guide-tone substitution occurs when several melody notes appear within one chord. A harmonization that contains all necessary guide tones in every voicing may be lackluster. After the basic sonority has been established within the initial notes of the line by using all necessary guide tones, the remaining notes can be harmonized more freely.

EXAMPLE 4-31.

TRACK 32

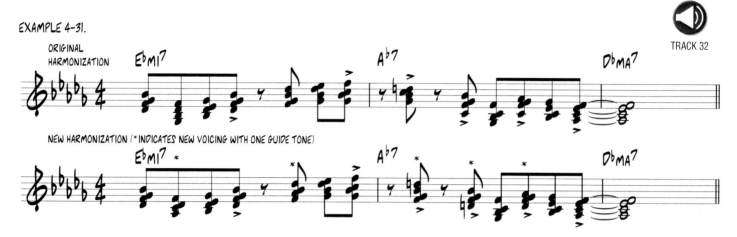

The two examples above illustrate that guide tones, though necessary for chord definition, do not always have to be present; many interesting voicings can be created using only one of the guide tones. There are even some usable voicings that contain no guide tones (see example 4-34).

The following is a list of note substitutions for guide tones. As with the basic-tone substitutions, the rule of thumb is to not include the note that has been replaced in the new voicing.

Guide-Tone Substitutions

If the voicing contains:	For major chords, substitute one of these notes:	For minor chords, substitute one of these notes:	For dominant chords, substitute one of these notes:	For half-diminished chords, substitute one of these notes:
3rd	9th, ♯11th	9th, 11th	natural 9th, ♭9th, ♯9th	natural 9th, 11th
7th	13th	13th	natural 13th, ♯5th	natural 9th

EXAMPLE 4-32.

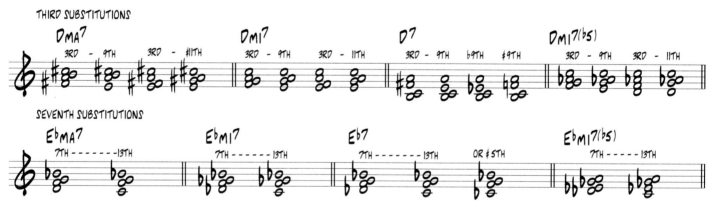

When using both the basic- and guide-tone tables, apply no more than one or two note substitutions at a time. These voicings rarely exist in isolation. Even if some are incomplete (i.e., lacking all necessary guide tones), a pianist or guitarist's comping will provide any missing notes. This is true even when a bassist is playing a walking line where the chord root might only be heard for one beat in any particular measure. Once the chord root has been heard in conjunction with a voicing, the ear retains that quality until a new one is introduced.

EXAMPLE 4-33.

Below are some possible four-note close-position voicings containing only one or no guide tones (with one exception in the C half-diminished 7 chord). These should provide guidance in the creation of voicings and not be used to construct an entire harmonization.

EXAMPLE 4-34.

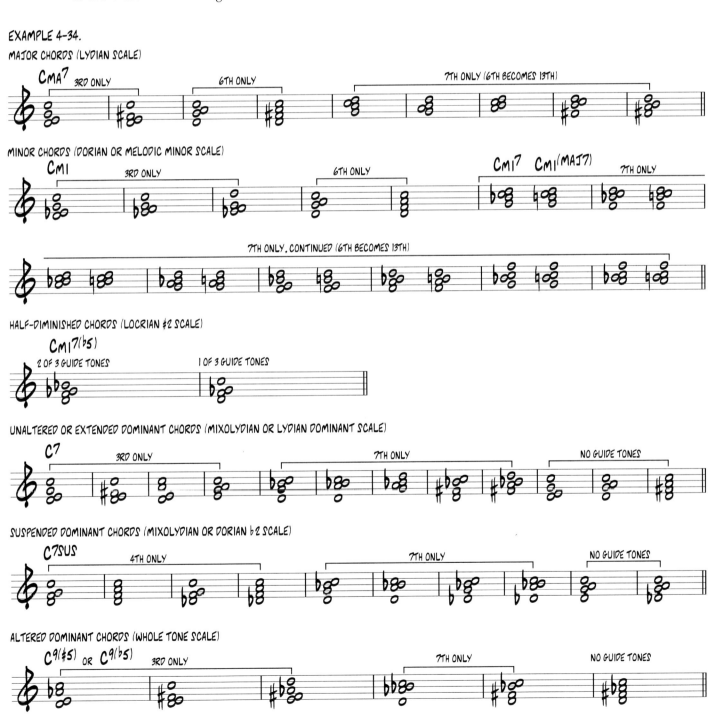

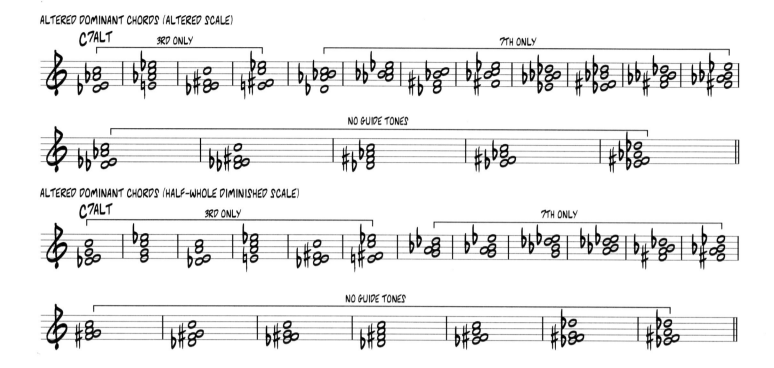

ALTERED DOMINANT CHORDS (ALTERED SCALE)

ALTERED DOMINANT CHORDS (HALF-WHOLE DIMINISHED SCALE)

Range Considerations for Close-Position Four-Note Voicings

Since no discussion of arranging for specific instruments has yet transpired, there is little concern at present for writing a close position voicing that is too high. However, these higher voicings, when written for certain wind groups (mixed instruments are the most typical case), may place some of the lower instruments at the top or out of their range, making them difficult or impossible to play. Solutions to these problems will be discussed in chapter 6.

Low voicings in close position are another matter. It is possible, even when arranging for a non-specific instrumentation, to write voicings that are too low. These sound muddy and lack clarity.

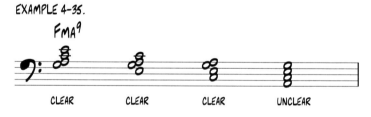

EXAMPLE 4-35.

FMA9

CLEAR   CLEAR   CLEAR   UNCLEAR

Generally speaking, chords with milder dissonances can be written lower than chords with sharper ones. This is especially true when the dissonances or color tones appear nearer the bottom of the voicing.

EXAMPLE 4-36.

Eb6	EbMA7	EbMA9	EbMA7(ADD13)	EbMA9(#11)
CLEAR: MILD DISSONANCE AT BOTTOM OF VOICING	CLEAR: SHARP DISSONANCE IN MIDDLE OF VOICING	CLEAR: MILD DISSONANCE AT TOP OF VOICING	UNCLEAR: TWO MILD DISSONANCES AT BOTTOM OF VOICING	CLEAR: SHARP DISSONANCE IN BOTTOM OF VOICING

If the top voice drops below middle C, there is a possibility that a close position four-note voicing may sound muddy. This statement is also applicable when the bottom voice reaches one octave below middle C. Listen very carefully to these voicings with the chord root to determine clarity. If the chord is unclear, use the following solutions, in listed order, until clarity is obtained.

1. Lower the chord's tension level.

EXAMPLE 4-37.

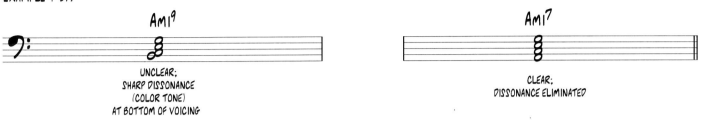

2. Substitute a three- or two-note voicing with doubled pitches.

EXAMPLE 4-38.

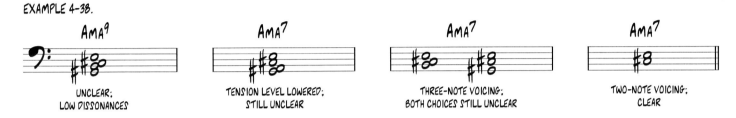

The most typical method for distributing a three-note voicing among four instruments is to double the top note to strengthen the melody.

EXAMPLE 4-39.

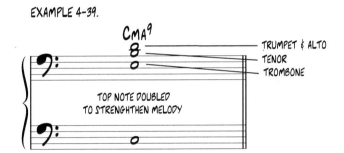

Doubling two pitches among the four instruments typically splits a two-note voicing. However, if this method creates awkward individual lines or the lower note is out of range of the third voice, a two-note voicing can be divided by placing three instruments on the top voice and one on the bottom. Never divide a two-note voicing in the opposite manner with one instrument playing the top voice and three on the bottom.

EXAMPLE 4-40.

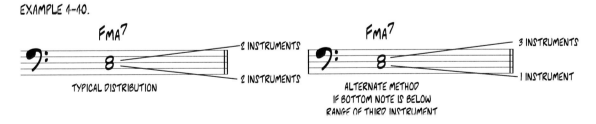

3. Abandon the chord altogether and place the entire group of horns in unison.

EXAMPLE 4-41.

For those chords that border on muddiness, the following criteria may be followed to determine their usability.

- What is the dynamic level at the moment this chord is heard? If the volume is loud and it puts most, if not all the instruments, near the bottom of their ranges, it cannot be played as loudly and will not be compatible with the dynamic level of this section. If the volume is softer, there will be fewer problems.

- Where is the chord situated in the phrase? If it begins a phrase, it may not have enough impact. If the chord is contained in a quickly moving passage where it will be heard only for an instant, it is probably usable.

Harmonization of Pickup notes

Pickup notes precede the first full measure of a tune. In a typical lead sheet, no harmonies are placed above these notes. However, there is implied chord movement that must be considered if these notes are to be harmonized. Pickups typically assume a dominant relationship to the first chord in the first full measure of a song. Many songs begin on the tonic chord. In these cases, the pickups would be harmonized using a V chord (or a similar tonicization) in the tonic key. (For more on tonicization, see chapter 5.)

EXAMPLE 4-42.

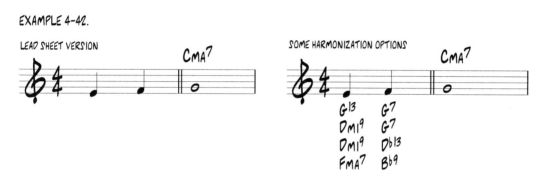

However, there are numerous tunes that begin on a chord other than the tonic. Here the pickups must be harmonized using the V chord relative to the first chord of the song. Two examples of this are "Just Friends" and "Speak Low." "Just Friends" begins on the IV chord, so its pickup note would be harmonized using the V of the IV chord. "Speak Low" begins on the II chord; its pickup note would be harmonized using the V of II.

EXAMPLE 4-43.

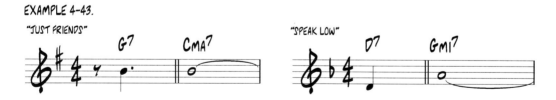

As the number of pickup notes increases, so do the options for harmonization. For two pickups, a II chord relative to the V might be used. For three, a VI chord relative to the II and V can be used. By working backward from the last pickup note to the first, an elaborate harmonization can be created using nothing but tonicization. Because of the quick harmonic rhythm, these work best at medium to slow tempos. The following example contains two possible harmonizations: the top one consists of a series of cycled II–Vs, while the bottom one uses tritone substitutions to create a more melodic bass line.

EXAMPLE 4-44.

Sometimes, due to a tune's tempo or harmonic design, this elaborate type of harmonization may be inappropriate. If so, a simple II-V relative to a tune's first chord can be used to harmonize an entire measure of pickups. Simply divide the number of notes equally between the two chords. For example, if there are four pickup notes, assign the first two to the II chord and the last two to the V.

EXAMPLE 4-45.

Harmonization of Measure-Length and Unequal Note Values with Changing Chords Underneath

The harmonization of two equal note values with different chords above each is a typical situation that is easily handled by harmonizing each with its corresponding chord. However, there tends to be some confusion concerning the harmonization of measure-length and unequal note values with changing chords underneath. When the melody plays a longer note, but the chords are indicated to change, the other voices may have to change during this note, or be altered rhythmically to accommodate this. The most typical instances of longer-note melodies with changing harmony underneath found in 4/4 and 3/4 are shown in the following example.

EXAMPLE 4-46.

The solution for measures 1 and 4 is a simple one. The top voice (melody) sustains the written note full value while all the other voices change halfway through the measure to accommodate the second chord. The changing chord can be anticipated or delayed with no major consequences.

EXAMPLE 4-47.

There are three solutions for measures 2, 3, 5, and 6. The chords change halfway through the measure as in the first two examples. However, due to the rhythm of the melody, these changes occur before (dotted half-quarter in 4/4 and half-quarter in 3/4) or after (quarter-dotted half in 4/4 and quarter-half in 3/4) the melody note has been attacked. The three solutions to these problems are dependent upon time signature and tempo.

The first is to alter the rhythm of the second chord so it changes at exactly the same time as the melody. All voices, as well as the bass, move together. In 4/4, this is the least desirable solution at any tempo, as it tends to upset the natural harmonic rhythm of a progression.

EXAMPLE 4-48.

However, in 3/4, this is a possible option because of the uneven number of beats in the measure. Here, the second chord only needs to be moved a half beat to accommodate the rhythm of the melody. This move is less jarring to the harmonic rhythm and works at any tempo.

EXAMPLE 4-49.

The second solution is to alter the rhythm of both the melody and harmony in order to lessen the awkwardness created in the first solution. Here, all the voices move together while the bass retains the original harmonic rhythm. The result is much more desirable and works well in both time signatures and at all tempos. (Note: the solution is the same for measures 5 and 6 of our original example 4-46.)

EXAMPLE 4-50.

The third solution is to retain the original rhythm of both the melody and harmony. This creates a chorale-like effect where the bottom three voices move in opposition to the melody. The bass retains the original harmonic rhythm with the bottom voices. This works best in 4/4 at slower tempos.

EXAMPLE 4-51.

At moderate to fast tempos, altering both the harmonic and melodic rhythm can decrease downbeat movement.

EXAMPLE 4-52.

This option is not usable in 3/4, due to the smaller number of beats in the measure. If the chord changes halfway through the measure and the melody is unchanged, the half-beat difference between the attacks will sound like a mistake.

EXAMPLE 4-53.

Any time two or more notes are harmonized in succession, it is possible that one or more of the lower voices may retain the same pitch from chord to chord. When harmonizing a line that is syncopated or contains eighth or sixteenth-note strings, or when emphasis is necessary, the voices that retain the same pitches will typically re-attack the note.

EXAMPLE 4-54.

——INDICATES RE-ATTACKED PITCHES

However, when writing *pads* (these are sustained multiple-note-voicings that provide harmonic underpinning—discussed in chapter 9) containing longer note values (whether at fast or slow tempos), it is often desirable to create smoother transitions between chords. This is accomplished by adding ties between notes of the same pitch, even across bar lines. This creates a flowing, chorale effect.

EXAMPLE 4-55.

Then, if the ties within a measure create awkward-looking rhythms, change these to their equal note values, without the tie, which will split the lines into multiple voices.

EXAMPLE 4-56.

Creation of Internal Movement Between Chord Voicings

There are occasions when *homophonic* harmonizations (ones where all the voices move in exactly the same rhythm) can be uninteresting. This can happen anytime a melody note is sustained and, though the harmonies may change, there is no forward motion in the music. Examples of this can be found in AABA song forms where the phrase ends in measure 7 and the note is held through measure 8. One way to add motion to these otherwise static chords is to create internal movement between voices. First, choose a voice other than the melody to alter. Then, using that voice's existing movement between chords, compose a melodic line that targets those notes. Example 4-57 demonstrates this in the second voice.

TRACK 34
Part 1

EXAMPLE 4-57.

The above example shows internal movement in one voice. It can also be passed from one voice to another as in the following, between the second and third voices.

TRACK 34
Part 2

EXAMPLE 4-58.

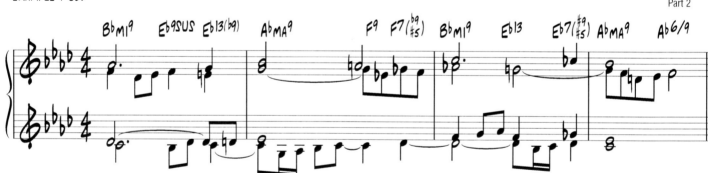

In addition, internal movement can be created in more than one voice at a time.

TRACK 34
Part 3

EXAMPLE 4-59.

Cross-Voicing

After harmonizing a passage, it is possible that repeated notes may occur in any of the lower voices. These tend to become more pronounced, especially when repeated several times. At slower tempos, this may not be an important concern because the passage will not be awkward to play. However, these lines become more cumbersome as the tempo increases. Attempts should be made to re-harmonize the passage to eliminate as many of these as possible. If repeated notes still exist, *cross-voicing* can be used. In this technique, the voices literally cross for one or two notes and then resume their normal positions. Below is the original version of three measures of a harmonized eighth-note line. Notice the inordinate number of repeated notes in the lower voices.

EXAMPLE 4-60.

By crossing the voices, the individual lines become less stagnant while the harmonization remains intact.

EXAMPLE 4-61.

In this example, it wasn't possible to eliminate every repeated note without creating unusually large leaps in some of the parts. However, all the lines are much easier to play now that the voices have been crossed.

Anticipation of Harmony

As discussed in all the earlier chapters, if the melody anticipates the harmony, so do all the lower voices.

EXAMPLE 4-62.

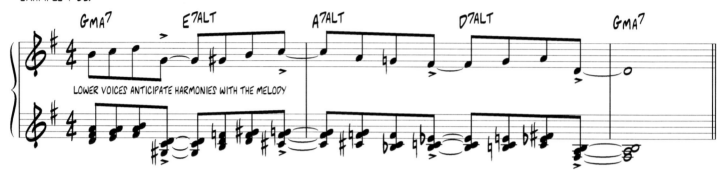

Any phrase—no matter how short—that ends a half beat before a chord change should be considered an anticipation of that change even though it rhythmically appears under the previous chord.

EXAMPLE 4-63.

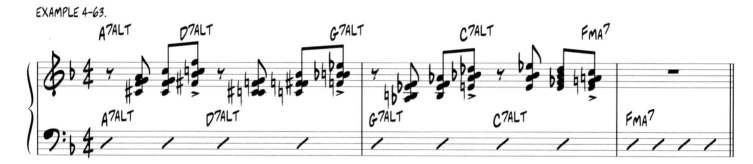

The Final Product

As mentioned in chapter 3, both variety and unity are essential to effective countermelody writing. These are equally as vital in vertical harmonizations. Other variable elements such as density, tension, color, texture, and dissonance can be controlled throughout the harmonization process. Some of these may remain constant whereas others may be varied. Below is a four-note close position harmonization and note-by-note harmonic analysis of an original tune titled "Windswept." This melody is comprised mainly of guide, color, and altered tones; there are only a few basic tones. Consequently, its harmonization easily maintains a moderate to sharp level of tension. The measure-by-measure commentary that follows the tune will serve to elucidate the manner in which these elements have been controlled.

TRACK 35

EXAMPLE 4-64.

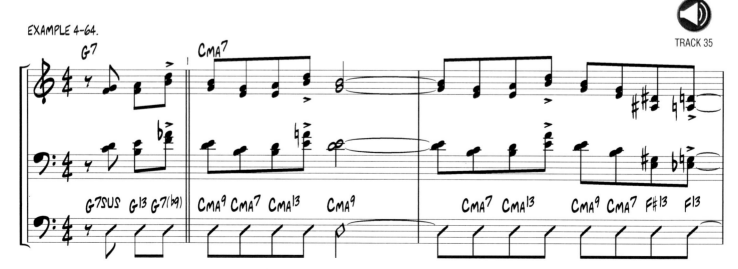

Pickup notes: These use a simple dominant to tonic relationship. Harmonic interest is achieved through the use of all three characteristic dominant chords: suspended, resolved chord with color tones, and resolved chord with altered tones.

Measures 1 and 2: Identical melody notes (B-G-A-D) within and between each measure are harmonized exactly the same for cohesion.

Measure 2: As the melodic line descends (upbeat of two through upbeat of three), the harmonic density decreases.

Measure 2: Non-harmonic tone on the fourth beat (D♯) is harmonized using chromatic planning, a minor second above the upbeat of four (see chapter 5 for more on this).

Measure 3: The two Ds in the melody (downbeat of one and upbeat of two) are harmonized differently to attain variety.

Measure 5: Melody is identical to the first measure; consequently, the harmonization is identical to achieve unity.

Measure 6: These harmonizations were chosen to eliminate possible repeated notes in the lower voices.

Measure 7: As the melodic line descends (upbeat of two to the end of the measure), the harmonic density decreases.

Measure 8: The altered chord at the beginning of this measure appears unaltered on the upbeat of three, and then is re-altered on the downbeat of four for harmonic interest.

Measure 9: Internal movement in the bottom voice adds melodic interest to the sustained chord.

Measure 10: Cross-voicing occurs between the bottom two voices to eliminate repeated notes.

Measure 11: The suspension of the D♭9 on beat two is chosen as a passing chord so that two voices move instead of only one.

Measure 12: The density in this descending line increases from the first note to the third, as it is considered an important target note.

Measure 13: Melody is identical to the ninth measure; accordingly, the harmonization is identical to achieve unity. The internal movement is even duplicated, though harmonized this time between the bottom two voices for added interest.

Measure 14: The melody and harmonization are identical to measure ten except for the different chord at the end of the measure. Cross-voicing is also retained.

Measure 16: More cross-voicing has been employed to eliminate repeated notes; this time between the second and third voices.

Measure 17: Internal movement in the second voice adds melodic interest to the sustained chord.

Measure 19: The two A's in the melody are harmonized differently; the first contains a lower level of tension than the second. Also, internal movement is added in the second voice.

Measure 21: Internal movement in the second voice adds melodic interest to the sustained chord.

Measure 22: There is a considerable amount of cross-voicing in this measure to avoid repeated notes. This first occurs between the bottom two voices, then between all three lower voices.

Measures 25–26: Identical melody notes (C, low F, and high F) within and between each measure are harmonized exactly the same for cohesion.

Measures 27–28: Identical melody notes (C and B♭) within and between each measure are harmonized exactly the same for cohesion.

Measures 29–30: Melody is identical to mm. 25-26; harmonization is identical to achieve unity.

Measure 31: First half of this measure is melodically identical to m. 27; harmonization is identical.

Measure 32: Three different alterations of G7 were chosen for harmonic interest.

Choosing Tunes

At this stage of development, tune choice for practicing the creation of four-note voicings is very important. Choose tunes that contain no or few nonharmonic tones. In this chapter, those notes that are considered nonharmonic tones are the natural fourth of a major chord and any notes that are not contained in the chord scale.

EXAMPLE 4-65.

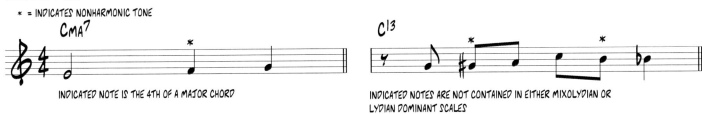

INDICATED NOTE IS THE 4TH OF A MAJOR CHORD

INDICATED NOTES ARE NOT CONTAINED IN EITHER MIXOLYDIAN OR LYDIAN DOMINANT SCALES

In other words, every note of a melody should be able to be harmonized using the chord indicated above it.

EXAMPLE 4-66.

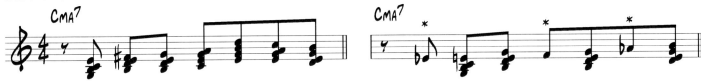

ALL MELODY NOTES CAN BE HARMONIZED USING SOME FORM OF C MAJ; NO NONHARMONIC TONES

ASTERISK INDICATES NOTES THAT CANNOT BE HARMONIZED USING CMAJ; THESE ARE NONHARMONIC TONES

When identifying nonharmonic tones, always consider all the possible scale choices for any chord. The less specific a chord is, the larger the number of scale choices. In conjunction with this, always take into account the chord's function in the progression.

EXAMPLE 4-67.

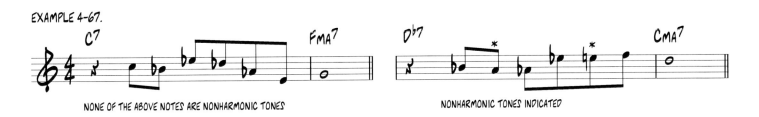

NONE OF THE ABOVE NOTES ARE NONHARMONIC TONES

NONHARMONIC TONES INDICATED

In the first example above, the C Altered scale is the appropriate choice for the C7 chord due to the V–I chord progression. All the notes that fall under this chord are contained in that scale. In the second example, the D♭ Lydian Dominant scale is the correct option for the D♭7 chord because of the ♭II–I progression. There are two nonharmonic tones in this example that are not contained in that scale.

There are other nonharmonic tones beside those mentioned above that will be discussed in detail in chapter 5.

The following list contains titles of tunes whose first eight measures are comprised solely of chord tones or contain no more than one or two nonharmonic tones as described above. Do not harmonize these notes; skip them until a thorough examination of chapter 5 has occurred.

A Child Is Born	I Could Write a Book
Afternoon in Paris	I Remember You
Airegin	I'm Beginning to See the Light
Alice in Wonderland	In a Mellow Tone
All the Things You Are	Indiana
Alone Together	It Don't Mean a Thing
All of Me	Just Friends
All of You	The Lady Is a Tramp
Always	Laura
Anything Goes	Lazybird
Autumn in New York	Lil' Darlin'
Autumn Leaves	Moment's Notice
Baubles, Bangles and Beads	Mood Indigo
Beautiful Love	Moonlight in Vermont
Black Orpheus	Naima
Bluesette	On Green Dolphin Street
Chelsea Bridge	Our Love Is Here to Stay
Cherokee	Peace
Come Rain or Come Shine	September Song
Countdown	Solitude
Daybreak	Some Day My Prince Will Come
Days of Wine and Roses	Sophisticated Lady
A Foggy Day	Stardust
Get Out of Town	Summer in Central Park
Giant Steps	Tangerine
Girl Talk	Three Little Words
Gregory Is Here	The Touch of Your Lips
I Could Have Danced All Night	Without a Song
I Mean You	You Took Advantage of Me

CHAPTER 5
Harmonization of Nonharmonic Tones and Tonicization

Most notes in a melody correspond to the underlying harmonies. But there are notes that are not members of the chord against which they are sounded. These melodic dissonances, or *nonharmonic tones*, are essential for good melodic design and maintaining a balance between consonance and dissonance. Because this dissonance is an integral part of the musical structure, it would seem advisable not to disturb this balance. In many musical settings this is true. But *block-chord* harmonization presents a unique situation. Here, all of the instruments have the same rhythmic content and general direction as the melody. To allow for nonharmonic tones in the melody, the other voices would have to sustain or repeat the accompanying harmony. This interrupts the rhythmic flow and cohesion inherent in block voicing. The harmonization of these nonharmonic tones does not really upset the balance of consonance and dissonance because the chords chosen are, in themselves, dissonant to the surrounding chords, and the balance is maintained.

Types of Nonharmonic Tones

The challenge for the arranger is to identify the nonharmonic tones and find a suitable harmonization for them without disturbing the underlying tonality. The majority of non-harmonic tones are found in scalar passages or other stepwise movement. This movement may be diatonic, chromatic, or a combination of both, and this type of melodic configuration falls into two categories: *passing tones* and *neighbor tones*.

Passing Tone

The passing tone connects two different chord tones through stepwise movement, in one direction. These two tones may be members of the same chord or different chords. Passing tones are usually unaccented, falling on weak beats or upbeats. (Though upbeats in jazz are often accented, this term comes from traditional harmony, where upbeats are the weaker, unaccented parts of the beat.)

EXAMPLE 5-1.

Accented passing tones are not uncommon, however. They have more impact than unaccented tones because their placement on the beat delays the appearance or resolution of the chord tone.

EXAMPLE 5-2.

Through the insertion of chromatic half steps, two or more passing tones may occur between chord tones.

EXAMPLE 5-3.

Neighbor Tone

Neighbor tones lie immediately above or below the chord tone. The melody line either rises or falls to the neighbor tone and then returns to the chord tone. Neighbor tones are used less frequently than passing tones because excessive use results in a static melodic situation.

EXAMPLE 5-4.

Chromatic alterations are often applied when a neighbor is a full step away from the chord tone, especially when a *lower neighbor* is involved. In major scales, the lower diatonic neighbors of scale tones two, three, five, six, and seven can be raised; in minor scales, the lower diatonic neighbors of two, four, five, and seven can be raised.

EXAMPLE 5-5.

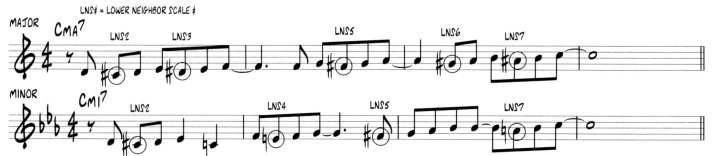

Upper neighbors may also be altered to a half step. In major keys, the upper diatonic neighbors of scale tones one, two, four, five, and six can be lowered; in minor, the upper diatonic neighbors of one, three, four, six, and seven can be lowered.

EXAMPLE 5-6.

A more decorative use of the neighbor tone is called a *changing tone*, or *double neighbor*. This occurs when the melody skips from one neighbor to the other before returning to the chord tone.

EXAMPLE 5-7.

Neighbor tones are usually unaccented. But when they are accented, the result can be quite dramatic. Because of their effectiveness, they are often found in sequential passages.

EXAMPLE 5-8.

Suspension and Appoggiatura

There are two other types of nonharmonic tones: the *suspension* and the *appoggiatura*. Unlike the passing tone and neighbor tone, they are always accented. They have been important compositional tools in classical music for centuries. But in the context of jazz harmony, they usually sound too sentimental. While their melodic configurations appear frequently in jazz, their harmonic treatment in block voicing is often altered. Instead of treating the dissonances as nonharmonic tones, they are harmonized as part of a vertical sonority.

A *suspension* occurs when one part is rhythmically delayed, creating a temporary dissonance before resolving. There are three events in a suspension: Preparation (P), Suspension (S), and Resolution (R).

EXAMPLE 5-9.

This type of treatment causes a slowing down in harmonic movement and is not suitable in many jazz settings. In block voicing, the suspended note is harmonized and becomes a chord tone.

EXAMPLE 5-10.

This kind of harmonization of a suspended fourth in a dominant seventh chord is really the origin of the ii7–V7–I7 progression in jazz. If the root of the dominant chord is placed under the ii7 chord as well, a temporary feeling of suspension is created. This type of unresolved third gave rise to the term "sus."

EXAMPLE 5-11.

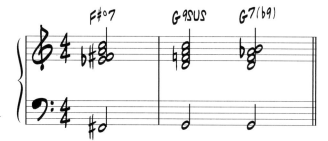

An *appoggiatura* is the only nonharmonic tone that is approached by leap (more than the interval of a second) and resolved by stepwise motion, usually in the opposite direction. It is always accented.

EXAMPLE 5-12.

In block voicing, an appoggiatura is harmonized and becomes part of the chord. There are three ways of harmonizing an appoggiatura.

1) Half-step planing.

EXAMPLE 5-13.

2) Harmonize as a color tone.

EXAMPLE 5-14.

3) Create an appoggiatura chord. That is, precede all of the notes of the chord of resolution with notes a half or whole step above or below, so they all resolve somewhat like leading tones.

EXAMPLE 5-15.

As with the suspension, if the root of the chord of resolution is placed under the appoggiatura chord it can create a striking dissonance.

EXAMPLE 5-16.

Anticipation

The *anticipation* was discussed in chapter 1. In classical music it is a nonharmonic tone. In block voicing, when there is a rhythmic anticipation, the chord is also anticipated, so it is no longer harmonized as a nonharmonic tone.

Identification

Since nonharmonic tones constitute a significant part of most melodies, their identification is a very important step toward melody harmonization. Suspensions and appoggiaturas are easy to identify because of the unique approach to them and their strong rhythmic placement. Neighbor tones are also easily recognized because of their distinctive configuration. Passing tones are more elusive. In many scalar passages it is not always obvious which are chord tones and which are passing tones due to the extended harmonies that are the norm in jazz. When a seventh chord is enlarged to include the ninth, eleventh, and thirteenth, all seven notes of the scale are represented. Therefore, any note of the chord scale could be harmonized with the tonic chord. Though theoretically correct, this can create a melodic line that is stagnant due to the continual inverting of the tonic chord.

EXAMPLE 5-17.

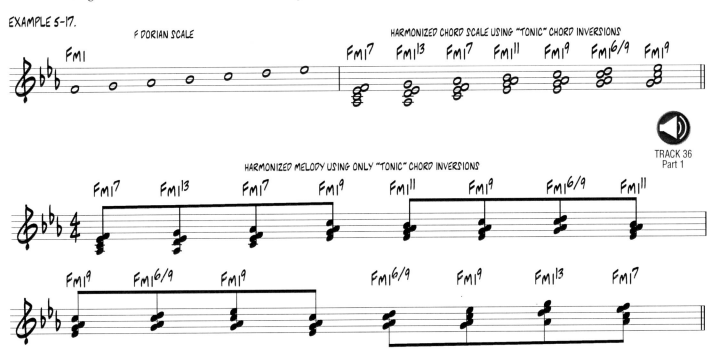

TRACK 36
Part 1

A more practical approach might be to consider notes one, three, five, and seven of the chord scale of the moment, as chord tones, and notes two, four, and six as nonharmonic tones requiring reharmonization. However, allowances must be made for the fact that notes two, four, and six could also be upper partials of the tonic chord.

EXAMPLE 5-18.

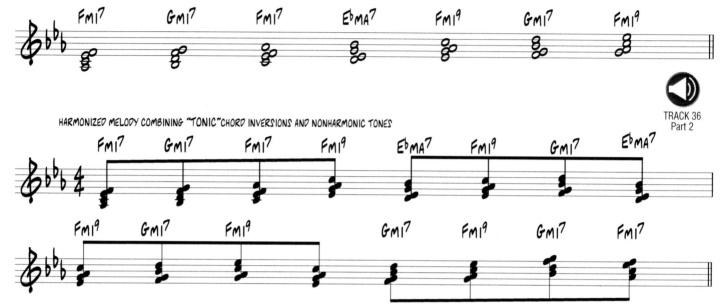

1, 3, 5, & 7 HARMONIZED AS "TONIC" CHORDS; 2, 4, & 6 HARMONIZED AS NONHARMONIC TONES

HARMONIZED MELODY COMBINING "TONIC" CHORD INVERSIONS AND NONHARMONIC TONES

TRACK 36
Part 2

The key to making the right choices when deciding whether tones are chordal or non-harmonic lies in a careful examination of the melody. The following factors should be taken into account.

- **Melodic Placement**: Is the tone a target note or merely providing movement? Target notes must be harmonized with the written chord while those providing movement can be considered nonharmonic tones.

EXAMPLE 5-19.

- **Rhythmic Placement**: Is it on a strong or weak portion of a beat? Those notes falling on strong beats are usually harmonized with the written chord while those on weak beats (or weak portions of the beat) can be considered nonharmonic tones.

EXAMPLE 5-20.

- **Emphasis**: Is it accented, repeated, or of long duration? All these notes must be harmonized with the written chord.

EXAMPLE 5-21.

- **Melodic Contour**: Is it a high or low note in the phrase? High notes are usually harmonized with the written chord, while low notes can be considered non-harmonic tones.

EXAMPLE 5-22.

Methods of Harmonization

Once the nonharmonic tones have been identified, the next step is to select an appropriate method of harmonization for each tone. The most frequently used methods are diatonic parallelism, chromatic parallelism, and tonicization

Diatonic Parallelism

Diatonic parallelism involves the harmonization of a nonharmonic tone using a diatonic seventh chord derived from the scale used over that chord. Parallelism implies that if the melody moves up or down by step, so does the chord.

EXAMPLE 5-23.

In Example 5-23, the F connects the third and fifth of the Cma7 chord. Since the melody is moving up stepwise, so should the chord. Therefore, the F is harmonized using Dmi7, the diatonic seventh chord built on the second degree of the C major scale. The process could be continued to include the next chord as well. Because the melody continues upward by step, the G could be harmonized with Emi7, the diatonic seventh chord built on the third degree of the C major scale. When combined with the C root, this chord is actually a Cma9.

The following examples illustrate all possible solutions for scale members two, four, and six using diatonic parallelism. "Scale 2" melodically connects the root and third of the chord.

EXAMPLE 5-24.

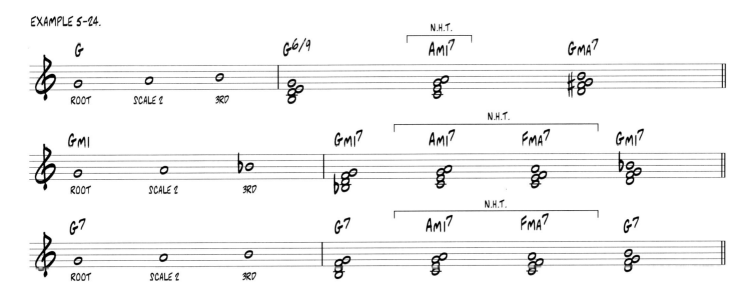

"Scale 4" melodically connects the third and fifth of the chord. It is the most consistently active of the three and in need of reharmonization.

EXAMPLE 5-25.

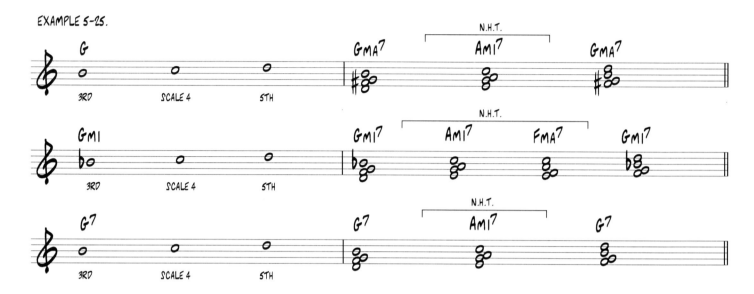

"Scale 6" melodically connects the fifth and seventh of the chord.

EXAMPLE 5-26.

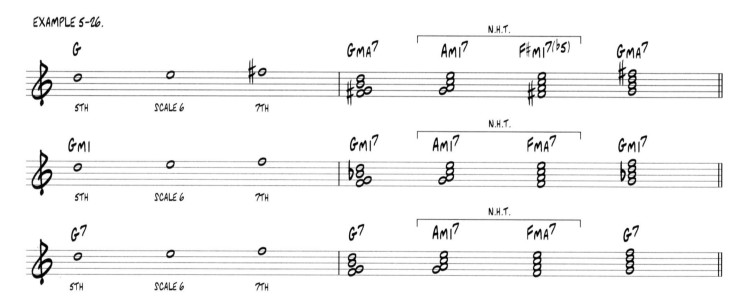

The advantage of diatonic parallelism is that its use results in cohesiveness and a strong sense of tonal center.

TRACK 37
Part 1

EXAMPLE 5-27.

The disadvantage is that its overuse may sound bland and lacking in interest.

TRACK 37
Part 2

EXAMPLE 5-28.

Some tunes that employ this device are Oliver Nelson's "Stolen Moments," Freddie Hubbard's "Little Sunflower," and Benny Goodman's "Soft Winds," as well as the shout chorus to his arrangement of "Oh, Lady Be Good."

Chromatic Parallelism

Chromatic parallelism, or *planing*, is the process of retaining a chord's quality and voicing exactly from note to note.

EXAMPLE 5-29.

As shown in the example for diatonic parallelism, an F once again occurs in a line between an E and G over a Cma7 chord. Here, the E and G are both harmonized as Cma7 chords. The F could be harmonized as a D♭ma7 chord (a chromatic parallelism a half step above the Cma9 harmonization of the E), or as a B♭ma7 (a chromatic parallelism a whole step below the Cma7 harmonization of the G).

Though the word "chromatic" may imply half steps, this type of parallelism can occur at any interval since "chromatic" also simply means non-diatonic. The next example shows movement other than half steps.

EXAMPLE 5-30.

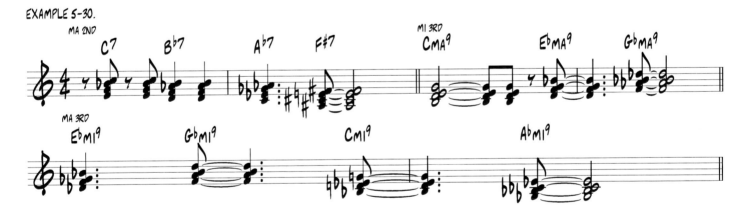

Examples of this style of parallelism can be found in Gil Evans' setting of Miles Davis' "Porgy and Bess" and Horace Silver's "Nutville" and "Silver's Serenade."

There are also advantages and disadvantages to using chromatic parallelism. The advantages are that it is extremely easy to accomplish, is quite colorful, and provides movement in all voices.

TRACK 38
Part 1

EXAMPLE 5-31.

The disadvantage is that it contains little or no functional harmonic movement. One or two chromatic moves in succession can add color to any line, but its overuse can become harmonically confusing.

EXAMPLE 5-32.

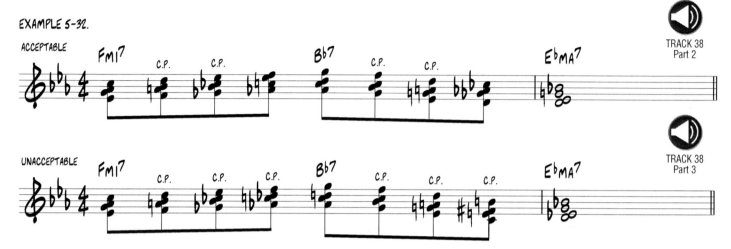

TRACK 38
Part 2

TRACK 38
Part 3

There are situations where extended use of chromatic parallelism can be very effective. These occur in areas of extremely slow or static harmonic movement and over an extended bass pedal.

EXAMPLE 5-33.

TRACK 39

Tonicization

Tonicization is the process by which a chord other than the original tonic temporarily assumes a tonic function. The difference between tonicization and modulation is one of emphasis and duration. A modulation is more prolonged and requires cadential confirmation, while a tonicization is brief and transitory in nature.

TONICIZATION IN THEORY

Two-Chord Tonicizations

Many tonicizations involve only two chords. These momentary excursions into other key areas do not impart the sense of having truly arrived at a new key center. They pass so quickly that the tonicized tones are never really heard as tonics, but retain their function in the original key. In fact, the overall effect is an enrichment of the original tonality.

Theoretically, twenty-two tonicizations from any given tonal center are possible. The most frequent targets are the diatonic chords of the original key. In major keys they are ii, iii, IV, V, and vi. In minor keys they are III, iv, v, VI, and VII. (The vii in major and ii in minor are diminished triads and cannot be tonicized because these have no dominant.) Those triads further removed from the original tonality require more preparation and are not usually involved in two-chord tonicizations.

There are five ways to tonicize using two chords. They are listed below, followed by an explanation for each.

1) V7–I (or i)
2) vii dim7– I (or i)
3) ♭II7–I (or i)
4) ♭VII7–I (or i)
5) VII7–I

V7–I (or i)

Since tonal harmony revolves around the interaction of tonic and dominant, it is not surprising that this is the most commonly used method of tonicization. It merely involves preceding the chord to be tonicized with its relative V7. Chromatic alterations are always necessary to create these chords, which are called *secondary* (or applied) *dominants*.

The following example shows the diatonic triads of the key of C major, preceded by their relative V7 chords.

EXAMPLE 5-34.

Note that except for the F♯ in the B7 chord, all of the alterations involve guide tones. Four of the five leading tones (scale seven in the tonicized key) are created through chromatic alteration. However, the ear readily accepts this leading-tone movement, and the results are smooth and decisive.

The next example lists the diatonic triads in C minor with their relative V7 chords.

EXAMPLE 5-35.

Since the III chord in C minor (E♭) is the tonic chord of the relative major, and both keys share the same scale degrees, the V7 of III requires no alterations. This makes movement between these two keys very natural.

vii dim7–I (or i)

This diminished-seventh chord is found diatonically as the leading-tone (or vii dim7) chord in the harmonic-minor mode, but it is frequently used in the major mode as a borrowed chord. Note the similarity between this chord and the V7♭9.

EXAMPLE 5-36.

The root and fifth of the diminished seventh are the original tritone of the dominant seventh and resolve the same way. So this chord is just as effective at tonicizing as the V7. In addition, the third and seventh also constitute a tritone. This kind of "double leading-tone" action results in very smooth voice leading in all parts and makes it very effective in two-chord tonicizations. The following example shows the diatonic triads of C major and minor, preceded by their vii dim7 chords.

EXAMPLE 5-37.

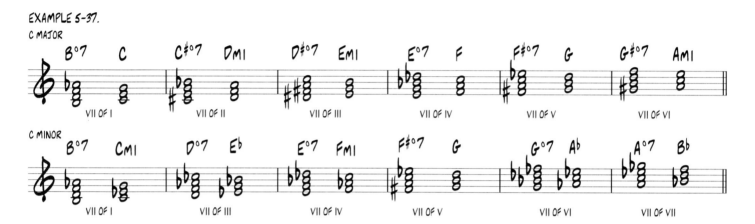

♭II7–I (or i)

This device is known as a *tritone substitution*. The rationale is that since any two dominant seventh chords a tritone apart share the same guide tones, they can substitute for each other. As shown in the example below, the guide tones of G7 are B and F, while the guide tones of D♭7 are F and C♭ (an enharmonic spelling of B).

EXAMPLE 5-38.

As stated, however, this explanation is a bit simplistic. To adhere strictly to this rule would lead to problems of voice leading and chord spelling. For one thing, in the tritone substitution, the guide tones are reversed. In the above example, B is the third of G7, but the enharmonic C♭ is the seventh of D♭7; F is the seventh of G7, but it is the third of D♭7. So if the inherent tendencies of the guide tones, as outlined in earlier chapters, are adhered to, the guide tones of the tritone substitution would not resolve correctly. The correct resolution of the seventh of a dominant chord is to the third of the next chord, while the third is free to move (usually stepwise) to a note in the next chord. Therefore, as shown below, when a tritone substitution is used, the spelling and resolution of the original tritone is retained.

EXAMPLE 5-39.

Here the tritone of the D♭7 chord does not adhere to its normal resolution, which would be to a G♭ chord, but instead follows the tendencies of the G7 chord, the original dominant.

Chord spelling presents another problem. Since the tritone substitution for a V7 is spelled as a ♭II7 (Neapolitan) chord, not a #I chord, the correct spelling of this chord in most flat keys would involve the use of double flats. In the key of A♭ for example, the tritone substitution would be a B♭♭7. And because it is common practice to avoid these awkward spellings, this chord would be enharmonically spelled as A7. But the spelling of the tritone of the original dominant (E♭7) would be retained.

EXAMPLE 5-40.

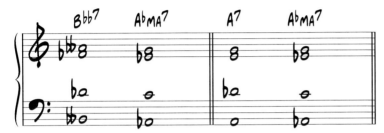

While this may seem a bit confusing at first, two simple rules emerge that will take care of most situations.

- Let the voice leading determine the chord spelling.
- Use enharmonic spellings to avoid double sharps and flats.

It is the responsibility of the arranger to write individual parts that are logical and easy to read; always check chord spellings.

The ninth and thirteenth are effective added tones to the ♭II7. The raised eleventh is the most typically altered tone added to the ♭II7.

EXAMPLE 5-41.

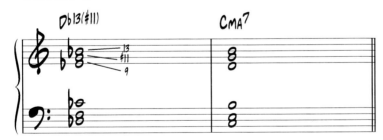

Other alterations are possible, but they should be used at a minimum. The addition of too many alterations will result in the appearance of the original V7 chord and obliterate any sense of chromaticism.

EXAMPLE 5-42.

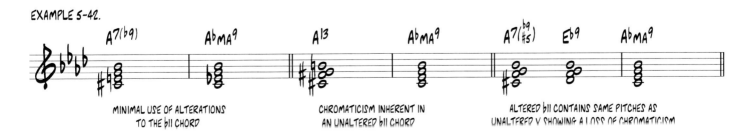

MINIMAL USE OF ALTERATIONS TO THE ♭II CHORD   CHROMATICISM INHERENT IN AN UNALTERED ♭II CHORD   ALTERED ♭II CONTAINS SAME PITCHES AS UNALTERED V SHOWING A LOSS OF CHROMATICISM

The tritone substitution has been in use for a long time, but is still effective. A couple of its advantages are as follows.

- In cycle progressions, it provides an alternative to the leaps of fourths and fifths in the bass. These leaps can become monotonous, and are often awkward to play.

EXAMPLE 5-43.

- The upper extensions of the tritone substitution provide interesting contrasts of color.

EXAMPLE 5-44.

♭VII7–I (or i)

The ♭VII chord is an outgrowth or augmentation of the minor iv chord, and the ♭VII–I progression strongly resembles the plagal (IV–I) cadence. The effect is a quieter, more passive resolution in contrast to the assertive tension-release effect of the other tonicizations. This is because there is neither the leading-tone action nor the conventional tritone resolution found in the other progressions. Because the ♭VII is a dominant-quality chord, there is a tritone between the third and the seventh of the chord. But its resolution is not as active. Here the seventh resolves down by half step, while the third resolves up by whole step.

EXAMPLE 5-45.

Even the addition of color tones (ninth, raised eleventh, thirteenth) does not significantly increase the assertiveness of the progression. They are identical to the notes of the tonic triad and contribute to the relaxed effect of the progression.

EXAMPLE 5-46.

To fully exploit the subdued characteristics of this progression, the ♭VII chord should not be altered. The lowered fifth is enharmonic with the raised eleventh that was mentioned earlier as an acceptable addition to the chord. But the use of any of the other three alterations would only lessen the desired effect.

EXAMPLE 5-47.

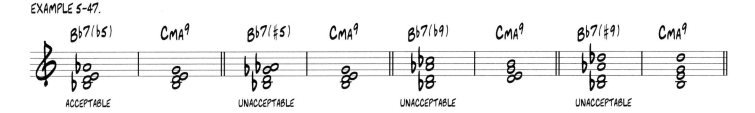

The lowered ninth creates a leading tone, as well as a tritone with the fifth of the chord. The raised fifth creates an augmented sixth with the seventh of the chord. This interval is a very assertive one and inappropriate here. The raised ninth, since it is the raised root of the key, would negate the smooth resolution, and is also unacceptable.

VII7–I

This is used only when tonicizing major chords. It is ineffective in minor tonicizations because the thirds of both chords are the same. Since the root of the chord is the leading tone, it is similar to the first three types. Its guide tones also have definite resolution tendencies.

EXAMPLE 5-48.

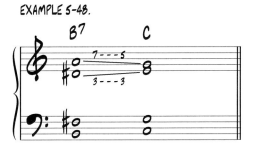

Alterations of this chord can be effective. It is interesting to note that many of the altered tones belong to the original V7 chord.

EXAMPLE 5-49.

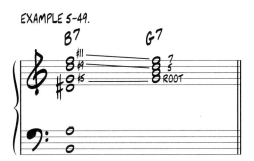

Three-Chord Tonicizations

Two-chord tonicizations can be expanded to three by placing another chord in front of the other two. The added chord usually has a *supertonic* (ii) relationship to the middle chord. The four three-chord tonicizations are as follows.

1) V–I becomes II–V–I.

2) ♭II–I becomes either II–♭II–I or ♭VI–♭II–I (the II is the supertonic of the V chord from which the tritone substitution was derived, while the ♭VI is the supertonic of the ♭II).

3) ♭VII–I becomes IV–♭VII–I.

4) VII–I becomes #IV–VII–I.

Note that the vii dim7–I is not listed above. It remains a two-chord tonicization.

The list above intentionally excludes chord qualities as these choices are quite extensive. The following are the most frequently used combinations.

II–V–I

- Minor–dominant (unaltered or altered)–major or minor
  (In C: Dmi7–G7–Cma or mi)
- Dominant (unaltered or altered)–dominant (unaltered or altered)–major or minor
  (In C: D7–G7–Cma or mi)
- Minor–minor–major or minor
  (In C: Dmi7–Gmi7–Cma or mi)
- Major–major–major
  (In C: Dma–Gma–Cma)
- Half diminished–dominant (always altered)–major or minor
  (In C: D half dim–G7–Cma or mi)

II–♭II–I

- Minor–dominant (altered as little as possible; ♯11 is most typical)–major or minor
  (In C: Dmi7–D♭7–Cma or mi)
- Dominant (unaltered or altered)–dominant (altered as little as possible; ♯11 is most typical)–major or minor
  (In C: D7–D♭7–Cma or mi)

♭VI–♭II–I

- Minor–dominant (altered as little as possible; ♯11 is most typical)–major or minor
  (In C: A♭mi7–D♭7–Cma or mi)
- Dominant (unaltered)–dominant (altered as little as possible; ♯11 is most typical)–major or minor
  (In C: A♭7–D♭7–Cma or mi)
- Major–major–major
  (In C: A♭ma7–D♭ma7–Cma)

IV–♭VII–I

- Minor–dominant (unaltered)–major
  (In C: Fmi7–B♭7–Cma or mi)
- Dominant (unaltered)–dominant (unaltered)–major
  (In C: F7–B♭7–Cma or mi)
- Major–major–major
  (In C: Fma–B♭ma–Cma)

♯IV–VII–I

- Minor–dominant (unaltered or altered; altered is preferable)–major
  (In C: F♯mi7–B7–Cma)
- Half diminished–dominant (always altered)–major
  (In C: F♯ half dim–B7–Cma)

TONICIZATION IN PRACTICE

The first attempts at mastering this technique should entail applying all of the above methods to the existing tonic chord of a piece. The choice of which method(s) to use will depend on the melody notes that precede the target chord. Altering the existing melodic fragment, or writing an original fragment that accommodates the selected tonicization can expand the number of choices.

EXAMPLE 5-50.

The second phase involves the tonicization of the other diatonic chords of the key. The vii dim7 chord in major and the ii chord in minor cannot be tonicized because they are diminished triads and have no dominant. All other diatonic chords can be subjected to some form of tonicization. The major chords are receptive to all of the methods, with a few exceptions. The first three methods work with minor chords. The #iv dim7–VII7 does not work for the reasons stated earlier. The iv7–♭VII7 creates undesirable modal effects. The following example shows the diatonic chords of C Major and the chords that best tonicize them.

EXAMPLE 5-51.

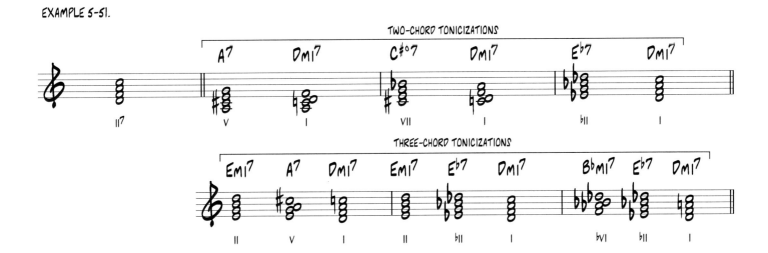

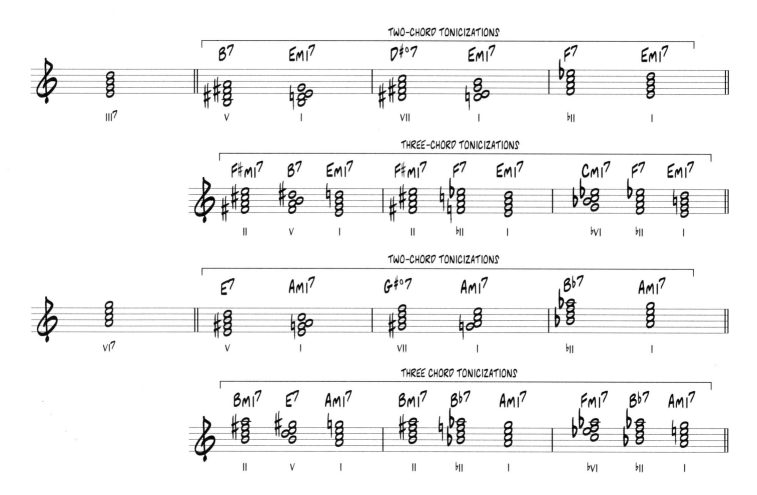

The ii–V–I tonicization can be expanded by using different forms of the ii chord–minor, half diminished or dominant. When tonicizing minor chords, the half-diminished chord is often the preferred choice. The justification for this is found by envisioning the harmonic minor scale for each of these chords. Notice that the flatted fifth in the ii chord is usually retained and becomes the flatted ninth in the dominant chord.

EXAMPLE 5-52.

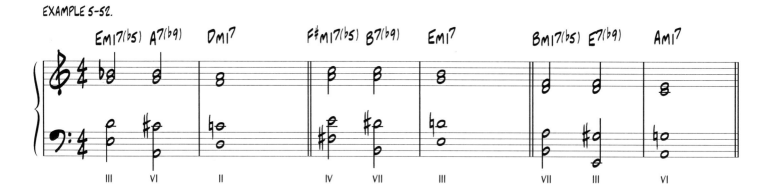

The half-diminished chord works for tonicizing the major chords as well. Borrowing chords from the parallel minor and using them in the major key is a well-established practice in tonal music. The chromaticism resulting from these lowered scale tones creates a pleasant darkening effect.

EXAMPLE 5-53.

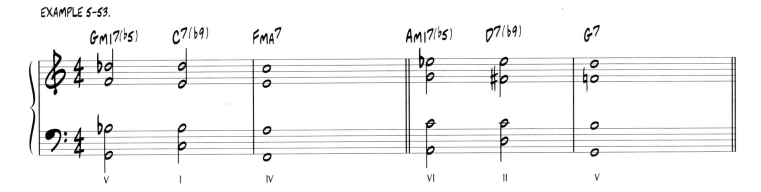

Since these tonicized chords still retain their function in the original key, the whole process becomes merely a momentary shift; it might involve as little as a beat or two. Avoid excessive chromaticism in these brief digressions. The prevailing sense of tonality and modality should not be disturbed.

Another tactic that may involve only a few beats or a measure is the reinterpretation of a melody note as another note of a chord. For example, if the existing chord harmonizes the note as a root, reharmonize it so that it becomes a third, fifth, or seventh (even ninths, elevenths, and thirteenths are possible). This might involve only a single chord or may be preceded by one or two tonicizing chords for greater emphasis. This would temporarily create a feeling of movement to another key. But the logical orientation of the melody itself would counteract this feeling and the overall tonality would be preserved.

EXAMPLE 5-54.

A variation of this procedure would be the reharmonization of a chromatic note of a melody in the same fashion. This can be a bit tricky, since the chromatic note may suggest another key. The reharmonization will take it farther away from the original key and the return may be difficult to manage in a short amount of time. But some striking effects are possible using this process and it is worth exploring.

EXAMPLE 5-55.

The final phase in this process is to create longer tonicizations from two to four measures in length. These expanded tonicizations create a much stronger sense of departure from the original key. But these deviations are an integral part of contemporary jazz and are valuable in maintaining interest. Below are some examples from the standard literature that contain three-chord tonicizations.

I Remember You: mm. 4–5

Gone with the Wind: mm. 5–6

All the Things You Are: mm.6–8; 14–16

Silver's Serenade: mm. 11–13

It's You or No One: mm. 9–11; 12–13

Satin Doll: Bridge (two examples)

Confirmation: Bridge (two examples)

Joy Spring: Bridge (four examples)

Tune Up: mm. 1–12 (three examples)

Solar: mm. 3–11 (three examples)

Summary

The process of harmonizing non-harmonic tones and the use of tonicization is undoubtedly the most involved part of the arranging process discussed so far. It may be summarized as follows.

1. Scan the melody for misnamed chords. This was explained in detail in chapter 4.

2. Make sure all diminished-seventh chords are spelled correctly. They are invariably leading-tone seventh chords and the correct spelling will lead to better voice leading later.

3. Examine the melody to identify nonharmonic tones.

4. Select the best method of harmonization (either form of parallelism or tonicization).

5. Look for existing tonicizations and possible ways of expanding them. These tonicized notes may be:

   • Notes of longer value

   • Last note of a phrase

   • Top note in a line

   • First note of a phrase that is harmonic

6. Find places where additional tonicizations may be used: notes of long duration, cadences, turnarounds, etc.

7. Look for other areas that may suggest reharmonization.

The importance of mastering the procedures discussed in this chapter, especially tonicization, cannot be stressed strongly enough. Tonicization is one of the hallmarks of a great arranger. This technique, more than any others in this book, establishes one's identity. A few well-placed tonicizations can create unforgettable moments in an arrangement.

Below is an updated four-note block voicing of "Windswept" that contains examples of both diatonic and chromatic parallelism, as well as two- and three-chord tonicizations.

EXAMPLE 5-56.

D.P. = DIATONIC PARALLELISM   C.P. = CHROMATIC PARALLELISM

2 C.T. = TWO-CHORD TONICIZATION   3 C.T. = THREE-CHORD TONICIZATION

TRACK 40

CHAPTER 6
Four-Note Open-Position Voicings

A thorough knowledge and understanding of four-note block voicings will provide an excellent foundation for mastering the various types of open voicings. In fact, all open voicings should be derived directly from block voicings, at least in the beginning.

Concept

Any block voicing may be converted to an open one by lowering one or more of the notes under the top voice by one octave. As mentioned in chapter 4, voices are identified by their position in the voicing (the top voice is number one, the note immediately under the top voice is number two, followed by three and four). The process of lowering the pitch of these notes one octave is called *dropping*.

EXAMPLE 6-1.

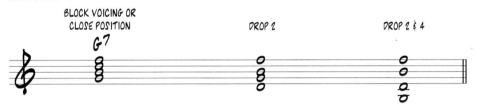

After a block voicing has been converted to an open one, only the top voice retains its original number. In the drop-two illustration above, the second voice was lowered an octave and now becomes the fourth. The original third voice is now the second, and the fourth becomes the third. Remember that the order of instruments remains the same so that when a voicing is changed, all except the lead instrument will be playing different notes. The following illustration will clarify this.

EXAMPLE 6-2.

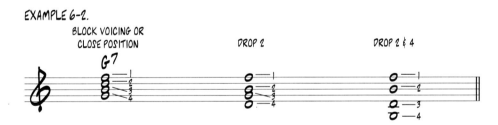

An exhaustive list of four-note block voicings is included in appendix 4 to show the range of possibilities in that format. Including a similar compilation for each type of open voicing would not only be overwhelming, but might actually hinder the creative process. Success can be achieved only through the trial and error process. Once a voicing has been selected and used, its characteristics can be assessed and stored in the memory. This cataloging of sounds is slow and time-consuming because it can only be done one voicing at a time. Nevertheless, it is the only way to develop a musical vocabulary that is unique and personal.

Reasons for Use

The main reason for utilizing open voicings is to achieve a variety of colors and textures and improve voice leading. While block voicing is a very effective and versatile tool, its sound can be tiring if used for too long.

Other factors which may dictate a change of voicing are as follows.

- **Tempo**: As a general rule, block voicing works better in faster tempos (or shorter note values), while open voicings are more effective at slower tempos (or longer note values).

- **Timbre**: Block voicing creates a compact, integrated sound. The larger intervals inherent in open voicings tend to highlight the timbral qualities of each instrument and the individual lines become more discernable.

- **Range**: When choosing a key for a given melody or original thematic material, range, tessitura, and transposition of the lead voice must always be taken into account. But these criteria should be applied to the other voices as well. When scoring for like instruments (i.e., four trumpets or four trombones) there should be no range problems in the other voices. But in mixed instrument scoring, those below the lead are usually pitched in a lower key. In block voicing this means that their transposed pitches will place them relatively higher in their effective ranges. So when the lead voice approaches the upper limits of its range, the other instruments may be at the extreme limits of their upper range, or perhaps out of range. This will create serious problems of balance, blend, and intonation, or even make the passage unplayable.

EXAMPLE 6-3.

Shifting to an open voicing will eliminate these problems.

EXAMPLE 6-4.

In the next example, the bracketed chords have been opened even further. This not only provides additional relief for the two bottom voices, but also introduces some contrary motion between the two outer voices.

EXAMPLE 6-5.

Factors such as sudden leaps and the overall contour of the melody may contribute to potential range problems.

Sudden leaps in the melodic line
Range again comes into play because a large upward leap in the top voice is apt to place the other voices in an uncomfortable range.

EXAMPLE 6-6.

Changing to an open voicing will reduce the size of the leaps in the other voices, resulting in a smoother, more controlled effect. This also creates more contrary motion between the outer voices.

EXAMPLE 6-7.

Contour of the melodic line

Instead of a large leap, the melody may gradually move upward through arpeggiation or scale lines until the same range problems occur.

EXAMPLE 6-8.

The solution is to find the most appropriate place to make the change of voicing.

EXAMPLE 6-9.

- **Emphasis or dramatic effect**: Voicings can play a significant role in controlling dissonance and consonance. Even though these are relative terms, they have real meaning within a context, and one is ineffective without the other. Dissonance is more striking in close voicings; less so in open ones. Voicings that have wide intervals at the bottom tend to be stable and well-balanced; those comprised of smaller intervals are less stable.

- **Stability and motion**: Chord spacing is an important factor in determining the expressive quality of the music and contributes to the effects of movement and arrival. Block voicings are comprised primarily of seconds and thirds. In open voicings, wider intervals such as the fourth, fifth, sixth, and seventh are commonplace. Even compound intervals (those wider than an octave) may occur. When a wide interval is placed at the bottom of a chord, it can bear a resemblance to the distribution of overtones in the harmonic series.

EXAMPLE 6-10.

Notice the wider intervals of the perfect fifth and perfect fourth at the bottom. Also present are the major sixth (between the second and fourth overtones) and the compound interval of the major tenth (between the first and fourth overtones). Chords that are constructed on this model epitomize balance and stability and convey the most explicit harmonic meaning.

EXAMPLE 6-11.

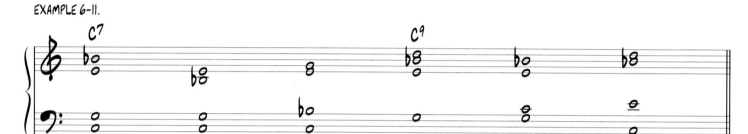

This pertains as well to chords that contain minor thirds, diminished fifths, and major sevenths. Even though these chord types do not occur naturally in the overtone system, following this model will impart the same firmness and clarity.

EXAMPLE 6-12.

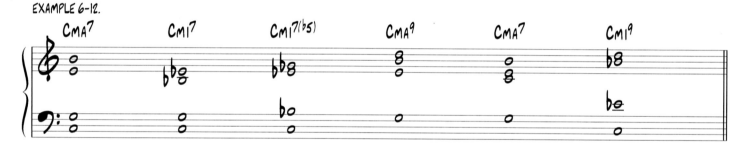

These intervals can also occur between other notes of the chord, but they may not belong to the primary overtone series of that chord. The following shows a few of the many possibilities.

EXAMPLE 6-13.

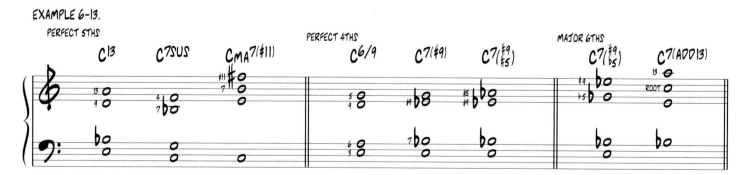

Problems with low-register intervals

A problem may arise when these intervals occur singly or in combination at the bottom of a chord in the low register. Here they can assert themselves as primary overtones and distort the true meaning of the chord. In the following example the chord is intended to be a Gmi9. But in this register, the intervallic construction of the first chord suggests a B♭ma7. The subsequent versions define the chord more clearly.

EXAMPLE 6-14.

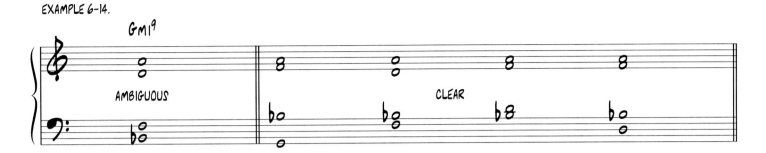

Here is another problem of ambiguity involving an Fma9 chord.

EXAMPLE 6-15.

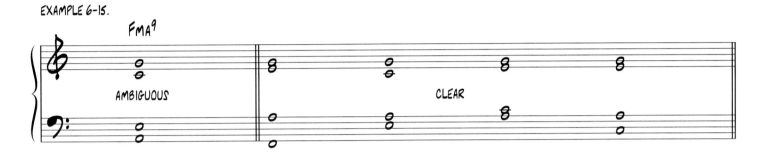

The problem, then, is not one of spacing, but of register. The solution is to use the overtone series model when voicing low-register chords in order to impart the true meaning of the chord. There will be more discussion on this as the various types of open voicings are examined. However, at this point, there should be no great concern for these possible ambiguities. A chord's quality is determined more by its usage than its spacing. Its interaction with the surrounding chords plus the sounding of the true bass note will dispel uncertainty in most instances. The remainder of the chapter will be devoted to the examination of the various types of open voicings, beginning with those that are most useful.

Types

Drop-Two Voicings

This is the most frequently used open voicing because of its versatility. It is effective in both high and low ranges, which makes it possible to use in extended passages.

To convert a block voicing to a *drop-two*, the second note (the one immediately under the lead voice) is lowered one octave. This simple octave displacement results in a rather distinctive change in the sound of the chord. The brilliant, homogeneous sound of the compact version is replaced with one that is richer and mellower. The overall range of the chord now exceeds an octave, thus lowering the center of sound. The intervals between the two top and two bottom voices is also increased. This wider spacing results in a more transparent texture, and the timbral characteristics of each instrument become more discernable. Only the interval between the original third and fourth voices remains intact, and these now become voices two and three in the new configuration. The fact that each of the lower three voices will be played by an instrument of lower pitch contributes to the increased richness of the voicing. (The only exception to this would be if two like instruments are used.)

The possibility of misinterpreting drop-two chords is not great. The main concern is when the interval of the perfect fourth appears between the second and fourth voices in block voicing. In a drop-two version, this interval is inverted and a perfect fifth appears on the bottom of the chord. As explained previously, this resemblance to the overtone series model could cause an ambiguous situation if the chord is placed in a low register. However, if the bottom note of the drop-two is the root, it can be used to good advantage, especially in cadential situations. The next example shows how the same vertical sonority can be ambiguous in one setting, but provides harmonic stability in another.

EXAMPLE 6-16.

Here are the first eight measures of "Windswept" from chapter 5 (p. III), converted from block voicing to drop-two. Notice how easily the conversion is made.

TRACK 43
Part 1

EXAMPLE 6-17.

The increased range of all open-position voicings has a tendency to place the bottom voice close to the bass register at times. This voice should be examined throughout to check for this situation. The lowest notes of the bottom voice of the previous example can be found in mm. 2 and 3.

The last two chords in m. 2 contain unclear voicings. This is due to the low placement of the guide tones in the F♯13 (beat 4) and F13 ("and" of beat 4) chords. The two chords in the second beat of m. 3 are also unclear. These contain the raised eleventh of the F♯13 (C) and F13 (B) in the bottom voice. (For these chords, see example 5-56 in chapter 5, p. III for the detailed harmonic analysis.) These voicings are even more unclear due to the low placement of this color tone. In order to retain this drop-two voicing throughout, the entire harmonization would have to be transposed upward to alleviate this undesirable situation, even though the rest of it is satisfactory. In actual practice, this is not typically possible unless either the key of the entire arrangement or the chorus where this harmonization appears is raised. The correct solution for this problem involves closing those voicings that are unclear. Consequently, the four voicings mentioned above would revert to close position as shown in the next example.

EXAMPLE 6-18.

Drop-Two and Four Voicings

Drop-two and four voicings are also very useful. The majority of block voicings work well in this format. They are more manageable in middle and upper registers, although they can be very effective in the lower register, with some restrictions. This versatility enables drop-two and four voicings to be used in extended passages.

This voicing is created by lowering the second and fourth voices of a block voicing one octave. Now the intervals between all voices are increased and the chord extends to almost two octaves. When a combination of mixed instruments uses this voicing, the timbral characteristics of each instrument, as well as their individual lines, become even more pronounced than in drop-two.

The increased span of this voicing places some restrictions on the placement of the top voice. The range of the lead instrument defines the upper limit. But if the melody descends below B♭ below middle C, the bottom voice enters the bass register and can create problems. Voicings with color or altered tones in the bottom voice become unusable. Those with basic or guide tones in the bottom voice are generally workable, but their effectiveness should be determined in each specific situation. As with drop-two voicings, those configurations that follow the overtone series model can be ambiguous in the low register. The following example contains a sampling of versatile drop-two and four voicings.

EXAMPLE 6-19.

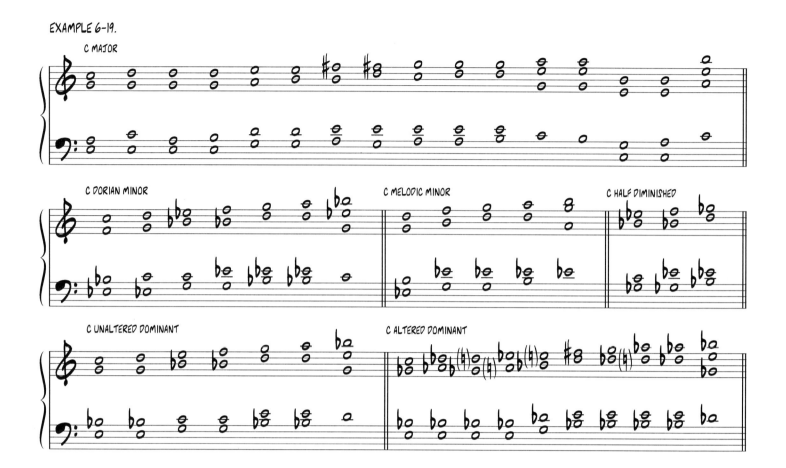

Here are some drop-two and four voicings that sound good in the low register, but whose meaning could be unclear. In the following example, the intended interpretation is shown above the chord while the possible misinterpretation is shown below.

EXAMPLE 6-20.

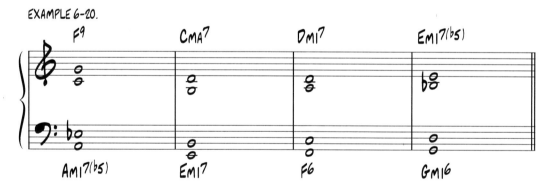

The following example shows the "Windswept" excerpt expanded to a drop-two and four format.

EXAMPLE 6-21.

The increased range of these voicings has created some serious problems in the bottom voices. In its original key, there are only a handful of voicings in the entire eight measures that are clear. Closing the unclear voicings would involve changing a majority of them. Consequently, the only way to successfully employ this voicing here is to transpose the key of the entire arrangement, or this chorus, upward. In the next example the key is raised a major sixth so all the drop-two and four voicings are acceptable. In doing so the lead voice has been placed in its upper range, but the passage is still playable.

TRACK 44

EXAMPLE 6-22.

Other Drop Voicings

Drop-two and drop-two and four voicings are the only drop voicings that are used with any consistency. This is because these formulas tend to spread the voices in an even manner. However, there are times when other types of drop voicings can be employed as a remedy to undesirable drop-two or drop-two and four voicings. These additional drop voices include the following.

- Drop-three
- Drop-four
- Drop-two and three
- Drop-three and four

These voicings are typically used to improve voice leading or to place more stable notes at the bottom of a voicing. Some examples are shown below, which show how a standard drop-two or drop-two and four voicing may be unclear.

EXAMPLE 6-23.

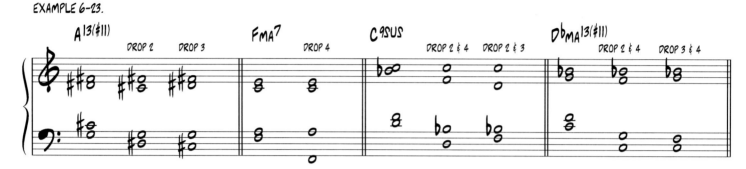

In the A13 chord, a drop-two voicing places its raised eleventh on the bottom. In this range, it is ambiguous, sounding like E♭7(♯9)/A. A drop-three voicing will place the third of this chord on the bottom resulting in a clearer sound. In the Fma7 chord, a drop-four voicing places the root further into the bass register. This is rare, but could be used in a cadential progression. In the C9sus chord, the drop-two and four voicing places its ninth on the bottom. This color tone could make this chord unclear. A drop-two and three voicing places the fourth of this chord (a guide tone) on the bottom, making it more stable. In the D♭ma7 chord, a drop-two and four places its seventh on the bottom. This note is acceptable albeit on the low side. However, the third voice contains the raised eleventh, which may be unclear in this register. A drop-three and four voicing places both guide tones on the bottom and presents a more stable situation.

Spread Voicings

To qualify as a spread voicing, the chord should contain at least two intervals of a sixth or greater. This makes it possible to extend the overall range of a four-note chord to more than two octaves. To convert a block voicing to spread voicing, follow the procedure listed below.

1. Retain the original interval between the outer voices.
2. Invert the interval between the two middle voices.
3. Lower this interval one octave, placing it on the bottom of the chord.

The four positions of an Am7 in block voicing are used to demonstrate this procedure. The numbers above each voicing correspond to the numbered steps above.

EXAMPLE 6-24.

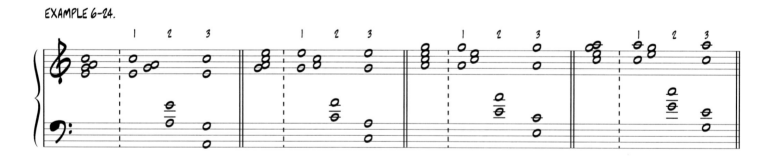

Because these voicings have a spread of more than two octaves, the bottom note may extend into the bass register. The effectiveness of the chord in this situation is determined by which note is in the bottom voice. As in the case of the other open voicings, basic tones work best, guide tones are less effective, and color and altered tones are least effective. The next example shows the same voicing twice; first in a low position and then one octave higher. Only the first two voicings are acceptable in the lower position. The higher voicing is acceptable in all cases, but each one places the top voice in the upper register.

EXAMPLE 6-25.

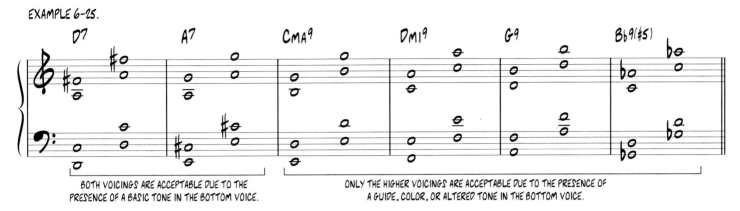

BOTH VOICINGS ARE ACCEPTABLE DUE TO THE
PRESENCE OF A BASIC TONE IN THE BOTTOM VOICE.

ONLY THE HIGHER VOICINGS ARE ACCEPTABLE DUE TO THE PRESENCE OF
A GUIDE, COLOR, OR ALTERED TONE IN THE BOTTOM VOICE.

The top note should not go below third space C. The upper range of the lead instrument
would determine the highest note possible, so unless the lead instrument was a high-pitched
one (i.e., a flute), the overall melodic range would be limited to about an octave. But these
limitations need not be a deterrent to the use of this voicing. It can be combined effectively
with other types of voicings that will not only increase the melodic range, but also may
improve voice leading and create opportunities for contrary motion.

EXAMPLE 6-26.

Below is a selected list of spread voicings that includes all the chord types in different registers and inversions.

EXAMPLE 6-27.

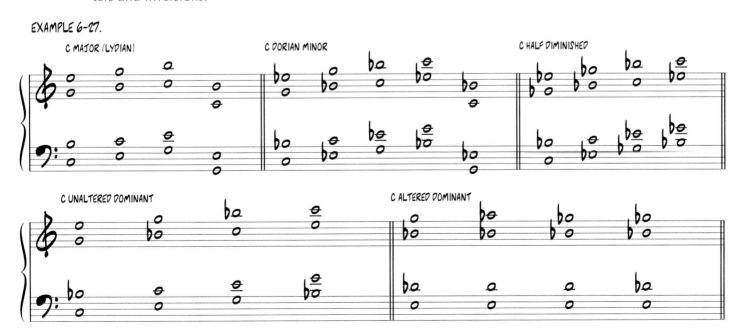

Efficient handling of this voicing requires a great deal of skill. Its extensive use is not recommended until the other voicings have been mastered. Here is an extended passage using
spread voicings.

EXAMPLE 6-28.

TRACK 45

Chorale Voicings

As the name implies, this is a type of spread voicing reminiscent of four-part choral writing with emphasis on proper voice leading. The most effective uses of this voicing are as follows.

- Ballads or pieces with slow harmonic rhythm
- Cadential progressions
- Passages requiring a feeling of strong root movement
- Pads or backgrounds for solos

Unlike the other methods of creating open voicings by starting with a block voicing and transposing notes downward by octaves, these are constructed from the bottom up. The structure of a chorale voicing is as follows.

- The root of the chord is in the bottom voice. The only exception to this rule would be if inversions occur as part of the bass line.

EXAMPLE 6-29.

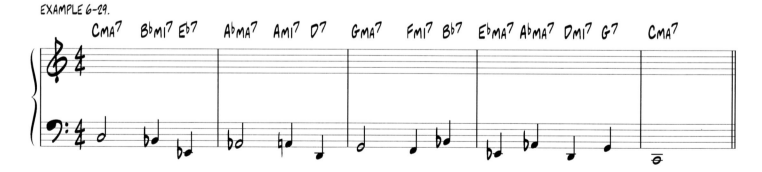

To achieve the proper sonority, the bottom instrument should be a low-pitched one, like a baritone saxophone or a bass trombone.

- The first note above the root should be a guide tone.

EXAMPLE 6-30.

If the seventh of the chord is selected, the interval between the two bottom voices will be a seventh. If the third of the chord is selected, the interval between the two bottom voices will be a third. It is possible to expand this third to a tenth by dropping the bass note an octave. This interval may seem excessively large, but in fact it is a very sonorous one when employed between the two bottom voices because it emulates the overtone model. This kind of spacing is not as effective between other voices and should not be used elsewhere except for special effects.

EXAMPLE 6-31.

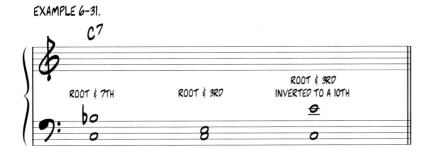

- The remaining guide tone should be placed immediately above. This three-note combination provides a very cohesive unit, but for it to function properly at least one guide tone (and preferably both) should resolve correctly. In cycle progressions, this means either moving stepwise or remaining stationary as a common tone.

EXAMPLE 6-32.

- Once the root, third, and seventh have been added, only one voice remains to add any color to the chord. This top voice would consist mostly of fifths, color tones, and altered tones. Obviously, the only way these restrictions can be adhered to is by composing an original line, rather than dealing with an existing melody.

TRACK 46
Part 1

EXAMPLE 6-33.

In actual practice, this chorale voicing could function as a "pad" (see chapter 9) and would probably look more like the following.

TRACK 46
Part 2

EXAMPLE 6-34.

Harmonizing a given melody in this fashion would be difficult due to the need to include the root and guide tones in the bottom three voices. This leaves one remaining voice to add either stability (basic tones) or color (color or altered tones). The placement of an existing melody atop this configuration may result in uninteresting sonorities due to the possibility of note duplications. The addition of a fifth voice (see chapter 8) would eliminate this problem and make colorful melody harmonizations easier to achieve.

Beware of becoming too enamored with this sound; its overuse can create a heavy, plodding effect. As mentioned earlier, it is most effective in cadential progressions, tonicizations, and passages where strong root movement needs to be emphasized. One such situation involves a horn soli with no rhythm-section accompaniment. Here, the bottom voice must define the root movement. An example of this is shown below. The diminished chords in mm. 1 and 2 and the tritone substitutions in mm. 5, 7, and 8 were chosen to soften the angularity of the cycle progression.

TRACK 47

EXAMPLE 6-35.

A further extension of this softening involves the use of chord inversions. Notice in the next example that there are only five root-position chords. The other nine are inversions.

TRACK 48

EXAMPLE 6-36.

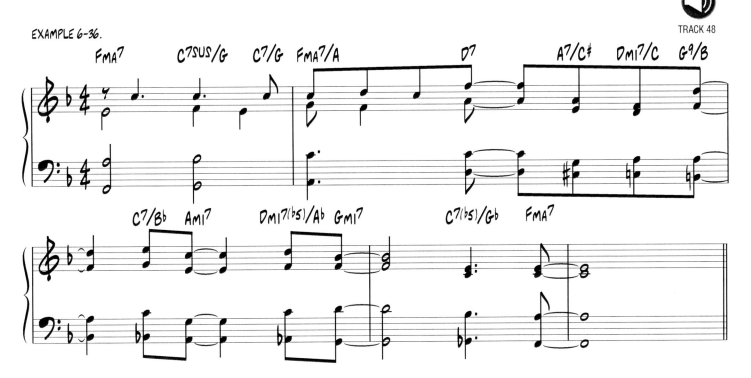

Sections of a harmonized line of any kind rarely contain just one type of voicing. Instead, combinations of close- and open-position voicings are used. The final example of this chapter presents a full chorus of "Windswept" taken from chapter 5, containing parallelisms and tonicizations. The original key of the melody has been retained and the voicing types have been changed to accommodate it. Changes of voicing are indicated throughout.

EXAMPLE 6-37.

THE NUMBERS BELOW EACH STAFF REFER TO THE TYPE OF DROP VOICING. BLOCK AND SPREAD REFER TO THOSE SPECIFIC VOICING TYPES.

TRACK 49

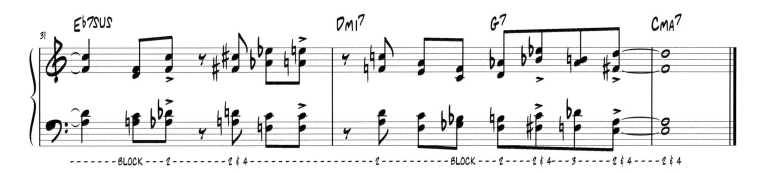

There are several points of interest in this example.

- Drop-two is the most-used voicing throughout the harmonization.

- The more open-voicing types are used only when the melody ascends and all eventually return to drop-two (mm. 6–7, 22, 26, 30, 32).

- For the most part, close-position voicings are used as a necessity, when the melodic line descends to the point where drop-two voicings are unusable (mm. 9–16, 20–22). This type of voicing is also used to provide tension between two open voicings (mm. 25, 25, 29, 31).

- The smoother the melody contour is, the less often the voicing position changes (mm. 17–24, 25–29).

- The more angular the melody contour is, the more often the voicing position changes (mm. 6–7, 22, 25–27, 29–32).

The various open-position voicings described in this chapter are a means, not an end. The decision of which position to use should never be made arbitrarily. With the exception of drop-two, no one position can successfully harmonize extended passages, let alone an entire chorus.

CHAPTER 7
Three-Note Voicings:
Close and Open Positions

Now that techniques for creating four-note voicings in both close and open positions have been assimilated, the next procedure is the creation of three-note voicings. Contrary to the obvious mathematics, three-note voicings are actually more challenging to create than four-note voicings. Due to the decreased number of notes in the voicing, maintaining a balance between guide tones and color tones is more difficult and sometimes impossible.

Methods of Creation

There are three methods of creating three-note voicings.

1) Subtraction of one note from a four-note voicing

2) Extraction of a tertian structure from a chord

3) New construction from a melody note

Each can yield similar or significantly different results. As mentioned in chapter 4, the starting point for all voicing construction is close position.

Subtraction of One Note from a Four-Note Voicing

Deciding which note to eliminate

This method involves the elimination of one note from a four-note voicing. It is a simple, but effective way to create this type of voicing due to the stability of the four-note voicing. The difficult task here is deciding which note to eliminate. The following is a detailed description of this method.

• Construct a four-note voicing in close position using the guidelines in chapter 4.
• Eliminate one of the three notes below the melody note.

1. Basic tones should be omitted first, as they do not define a chord's quality. If the voicing contains both basic tones, eliminate the root first as it is probably already being played by the bass.

EXAMPLE 7-1.

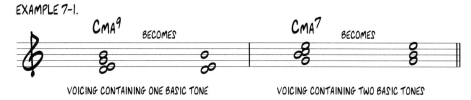

VOICING CONTAINING ONE BASIC TONE   VOICING CONTAINING TWO BASIC TONES

2. If there are no basic tones, omit a guide tone. The ear tends to naturally hear major thirds over minor thirds due to their stronger position in the overtone series. When working with major or dominant voicings, the third can be omitted without greatly affecting the chord's basic sonority.

EXAMPLE 7-2.

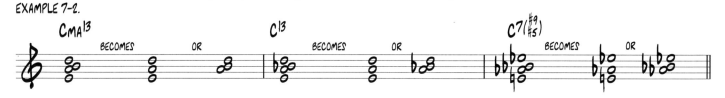

However, when working with minor chords, the third should usually be present to clearly define the quality. This is especially important when creating the initial voicing of a minor chord.

EXAMPLE 7-3.

In the previous example, the first three-note voicing clearly defines the tonality by the presence of the minor-third guide tone. The second, if used as an initial voicing, could easily be misinterpreted by the ear as a dominant suspended chord because of the missing third. However, it could be used effectively elsewhere in the measure.

- Listen to the remaining three pitches with the chord root to determine whether the harmony is still discernable. If not, execute one or both of the following procedures:

  1. Exchange one guide tone for another.

EXAMPLE 7-4.

  2. Omit any color or basic tones (except for those in the melody) and use only guide tones.

EXAMPLE 7-5.

While it is important to listen to all voicings for effectiveness, it is imperative to listen to three-note voicings due to the possible omission of a guide tone in favor of a color tone and vice versa. The following questions should be addressed:

- Does the voicing properly define the harmony when heard with a chord root?

- Does the voicing contain enough color?

The answers to these are dependent on two factors.

1) **Length of the time a voicing will be heard**: Longer note values should gravitate toward a clear definition of the harmony while shorter ones are less crucial. The first and last chords in the following example clearly define the C-minor tonality as they are the longest notes in the passage.

EXAMPLE 7-6.

2) **Place in the measure relative to the first sounding of the chord**: As soon as the chord quality has been established, the remainder of the notes under that same chord can be harmonized more freely. Of the thirteen voicings in the example below, only five contain both guide tones of the Cmi7 chord. The rest contain only one or no guide tones.

EXAMPLE 7-7.

TRACK 50

Extraction of a Tertian Structure from a Chord

"Tertian structure" refers to a group of three notes constructed by the superimposition of two thirds of any quality. The term is used to describe not only the root position, but both inversions as well. In traditional harmony, the most basic tertian configuration is a triad consisting of the root, third, and fifth of a chord. However, these structures exist throughout a chord, from the root to the thirteenth. The following method involves the extraction of one of these structures from a given chord.

Here is a list of all available tertian structures constructed from a C root.

- C Major (Lydian scale): C, Emi, G, Bmi, D, F# dim, Ami
- C minor (Dorian scale): Cmi, E♭, Gmi, B♭, Dmi, F, A dim
- C minor-major 7 (Melodic Minor scale): Cmi, E♭ aug, G, B dim, Dmi, F, A dim
- C half diminished (Locrian #2 scale): C dim, E♭mi, G♭, B♭, D dim, Fmi, A♭
- C dominant unaltered (Lydian Dominant scale): C, E dim, Gmi, B♭ aug, D, F# dim, Ami
- C dominant suspended (Mixolydian scale): C, Emi, Gmi, B♭, Dm, F, Ami
- C dominant altered (Altered scale): C dim, C#mi, E♭mi, G♭, A♭, A♭ aug, B♭ dim
- C13 with altered 9ths and/or #11th (Half-whole Diminished scale): C, Cm, C dim, C# dim, E♭, E♭mi, E♭ dim, E dim, F#, F#mi, F# dim, G dim, A, Ami, A dim, B♭ dim
- C fully diminished (Whole-half Diminished scale): C dim, D, Dm, D dim, E♭ dim, F, Fmi, F dim, F# dim, A♭, A♭mi, A♭ dim, A dim, B, Bmi, B dim

EXAMPLE 7-8.

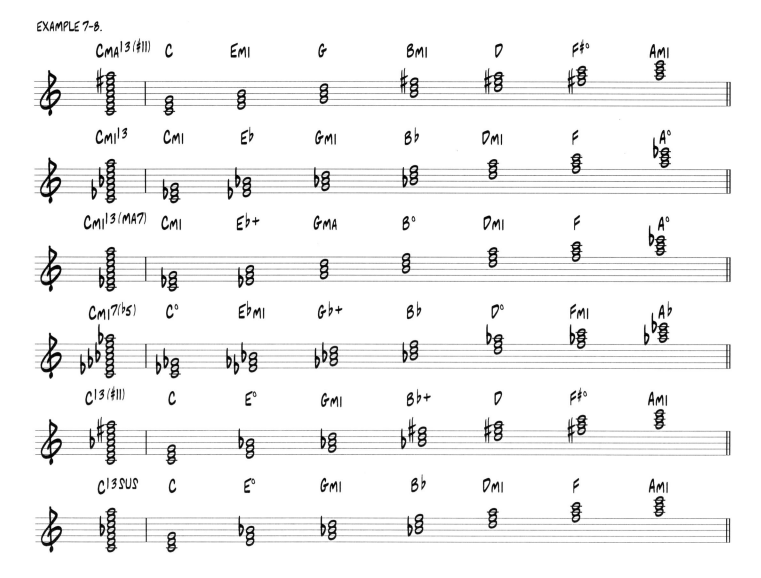

When root position and inversions are considered, there are three possible tertian structures available for any melody note—it may function as the root of a first-inversion triad, the third of a second-inversion triad, or the fifth of a root-position triad.

EXAMPLE 7-9.

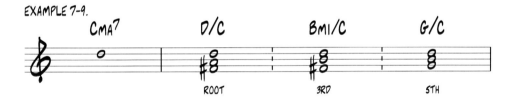

In the above example, the "D" melody note in the Cma7 chord can be voiced as a D major triad (the root of a first-inversion triad), a B minor triad (the third of a second-inversion triad), or a G major triad (the fifth of a root-position triad).

The choice of the most effective tertian structure involves the following factors.

- The combination of color, basic, and guide tones

- Smooth line movement to and from the voicing

Tertian structures are strong and can be used effectively within a harmonization when coupled with other voicing types. They are indicated with asterisks in the next example.

EXAMPLE 7-10.

TRACK 51
Part 1

However, in most situations, they should not be used exclusively, as they do not contain any whole- or half-step tensions.

EXAMPLE 7-11.

TRACK 51
Part 2

New Construction from a Melody Note

The two previous methods utilize existing structures from which to cull three-note voicings. This next one deals with the actual note-by-note construction of this type of voicing.

Determine the melody note's function in the chord (basic, guide, or color tone), then proceed while minding the basic tenets of close position voicing: maintaining the distance between the outer voices within an octave and at least a major second between the top two voices.

- • If the melody note is a basic tone, there are three options.
    - 1. Add two guide tones. This combination will yield stability due to the presence of the guide tones, but a lack of color due to the absence of any notes above a seventh.

EXAMPLE 7-12.

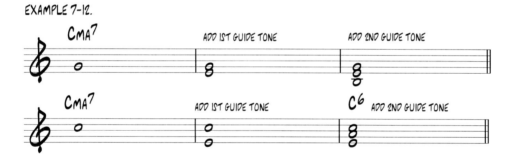

- 2. Add one guide tone and one color tone. This is less stable due to the presence of only one guide tone, but it contains more color.

EXAMPLE 7-13.

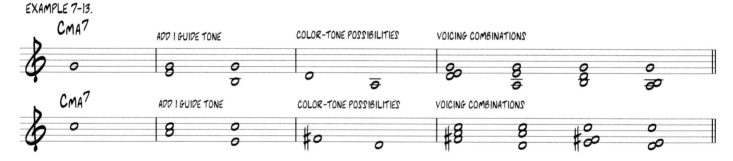

- 3. Add two color tones. This is the least stable, but the most colorful.

EXAMPLE 7-14.

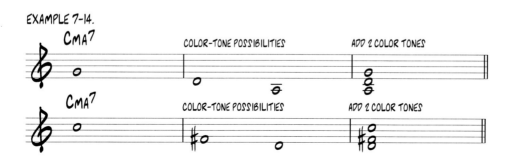

- If the melody note is a guide tone, there are two options.
  1. Add another guide tone and one color tone. This will create a stable voicing that contains some color.

EXAMPLE 7-15.

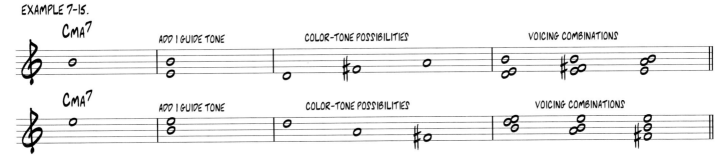

  2. Add two color tones. This is a less stable, but more colorful voicing.

EXAMPLE 7-16.

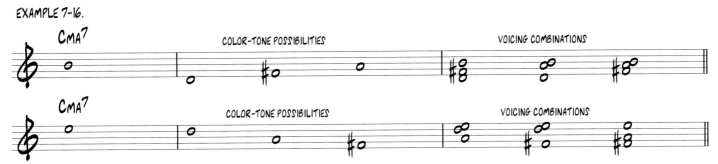

- If it is a color tone, there are three options:
  1. Add two guide tones. This will create a stable voicing that contains some color. Though this voicing is very effective, there may be more interesting possibilities.

EXAMPLE 7-17.

  2. Add one guide tone and one color tone. This is less stable, but more colorful. In the example below, the substitution of an altered fifth for the seventh creates a more colorful voicing.

EXAMPLE 7-18.

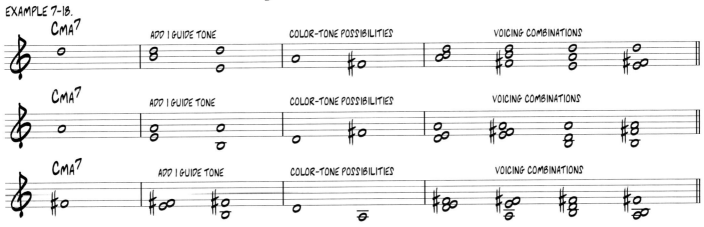

  3. Add two more color tones. This is the least stable, but the most colorful.

EXAMPLE 7-19.

In all the above situations, the most effective note choices are dependent on the factors mentioned earlier in this chapter. One last comment concerning the third method: basic tones were not included as note possibilities because of the redundancy of the root and the tacit presence of the fifth. In actuality, these notes could be used in any of the above situations to improve individual voice movement. One such example is shown below.

EXAMPLE 7-20.

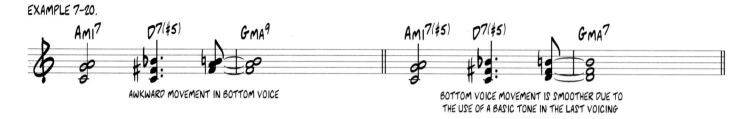

A compendium of close-position three-note voicings has been provided in appendix 5 that contains all the possible note combinations for every melody note within the chord scale. They were formulated using all three of the above methods of construction.

Open-Position Voicings

Open-position voicings, as discussed at length in chapter 6, are used to achieve variety of color and texture. The decision to use them involves tempo, timbre, and range. In three-note voicings, the only consistently practical open position is drop-two. It is created by simply dropping the middle note an octave.

EXAMPLE 7-21.

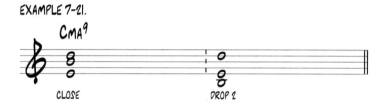

In the case of triadic structures, this transposition creates a more sonorous voicing because of the larger expanse from top to bottom.

EXAMPLE 7-22.

When a three-note close-position voicing that contains the interval of a second between the top or bottom two notes is opened in this manner, the dissonance is softened in both situations due to its inversion.

EXAMPLE 7-23.

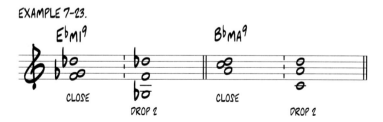

Though the drop-two voicing is the only consistently usable open one for three-note configurations, there are two other possibilities: drop-three and drop-two and three. However, a cursory examination of both will yield an understanding of their very limited usage. A drop-three voicing would place the bottom note too far below the top two, while drop-two and three would place the bottom two notes too far below the melody.

EXAMPLE 7-24.

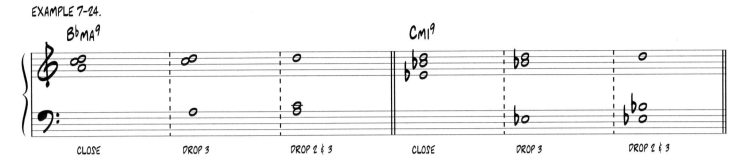

When dealing with the harmonization of a musical passage using standard three-horn instrumentation, these voicings are rarely usable.

The Development of Simple Four-note Voicings from Existing Three-note Voicings

There are two simple methods for creating four-note voicings that incorporate three-note voicings. The first involves the doubling of the melody note of a three-note voicing an octave lower, and the second involves the addition of a chord root to the bottom of a voicing.

Doubling the melody note an octave lower adds body to the chord and accentuates it.

EXAMPLE 7-25.

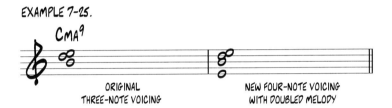

Though it adds density to a voicing, this fourth voice adds no further color. Entire choruses can be harmonized in this fashion.

EXAMPLE 7-26.

TRACK 52

The addition of the chord root below the bottom note of a three-note voicing provides stability in a progression.

EXAMPLE 7-27.

Its use is limited to pieces with slow harmonic rhythm, pads, and cadential progressions. It should not be used in extended passages due to the continual leaping of the bottom voice from root to root.

EXAMPLE 7-28.

Three-Note Voicings in Practice

The final example in this chapter contains another full-chorus harmonization of "Windswept," using three-note close- and open-position voicings. Unlike the previous chapter, this harmonization is not based entirely on the one presented in chapter 5 containing parallelisms and tonicizations. Due to the reduced number of voices, it is necessary to create a new harmonization to realize the full potential of the different types of three-note voicings. Open- and close-position voicings have been indicated as well as both diatonic and chromatic parallelisms (D.P. and C.P.) and the use of tertian structures (T.S.).

EXAMPLE 7-29.

TRACK 53

Upon examination of this example, several points should become apparent.

- Block voicings were used to harmonize the majority of the notes of this song. Drop-two voicings were applied only when necessary (mm. 6–7, 18–19, 24–26, 28–30).

- Anytime the voicing types changed, an attempt was made to create smooth lines within each harmony part during the transition (mm. 6–7, 18–19, 24–26, 28–30).

- A modicum of parallelism was used, consisting of diatonic movement in scalar passages (mm. 6, 10, 14, 22, 28), and chromatic movement in chromatic passages (mm. 7–8, 31).

- As each chord changed throughout the harmonization, the tonality was immediately established with at least one voicing containing all necessary guide tones. After this, the harmonization was freer.

- Tertian structures were used in isolation. The only occurrence of two used in succession can be found in mm. 7–8.

- Tonicizations are essentially nonexistent in this harmonization. This is due to the inherent difficulty of defining complete chord structures with only three notes. This is not to say that tonicizations are impossible when writing three-note voicings. One tonicization occurs in m. 20. It was easily accomplished because the melody notes of the B7 and E7 chords are color tones. This allowed for the placement of both guide tones beneath the melody, creating a clear definition of the chord movement, while maintaining a sense of color.

Summary

Though more challenging to create, three-note voicings are quite remarkable because of the fullness that can be achieved with one less voice. Three-horn groups have been popular since the origin of jazz with Dixieland and swing. They continued into the hard bop era with groups led by Art Blakey, Horace Silver, Cannonball Adderley, and many others. The groundbreaking album *Kind of Blue* also used this format. Today, groups led by Kenny Wheeler, Dave Holland, and others uphold this tradition. The three-horn group is still a viable format due to the surprising richness of harmony that can be attained and the further arranging possibilities not available with two horns, while retaining the intimacy of the small group.

CHAPTER 8
Five-Note Voicings: Close and Open Positions

In the previous chapter on three-note voicings, the focus was on eliminating notes from a chord while retaining its quality and controlling dissonance. Now, with the addition of a fifth voice, the process becomes an additive one. Also, the choices of vertical sonorities increase dramatically. The root may now be reintroduced as a chord member, and it is also possible to include as many as three color tones. The levels of tension and dissonance can be heightened significantly.

Methods of Creation

There are three methods of creating *five-note voicings* from existing four-note chords.

1) Doubling the top note of a four-note voicing an octave lower

2) Addition of a chord root below the bottom note of a four-note voicing

3) Addition of a fifth note to a four-note voicing (other than the melody note an octave below) that will create a sonority consisting of five different notes

As in previous chapters, these voicings will be built in close position.

Doubling of the Top Note an Octave Lower

This is the simplest method: add a note to a four-note close position voicing that is one octave below its top note.

EXAMPLE 8-1. DOUBLING THE MELODY NOTE OF A FOUR-NOTE VOICING AN OCTAVE BELOW

This doubling adds body to the chord and accentuates the melody. It works well at any tempo, but is especially effective when harmonizing a fast moving line.

TRACK 54

EXAMPLE 8-2.

One disadvantage is that though it adds density to a voicing, it adds no further color. The obvious instrument choice for this fifth voice would be a low-pitched one. This type of voicing has been proven to be a very serviceable method of scoring for five saxophones.

In this doubled melody situation, the lead alto and the baritone saxophone play exactly the same written part, which then sounds in octaves.

EXAMPLE 8-3.

The use of this type of voicing is not limited to saxophone writing; it works with mixed instruments equally as well. In situations where the main focus is on the melody, it is still the most functional method of scoring.

Addition of a Chord Root

This method adds a chord root below the bottom note of a close-position four-note voicing. The interval between the added root and the fourth voice can vary significantly, depending upon which chord tone is in the fourth voice.

EXAMPLE 8-4.

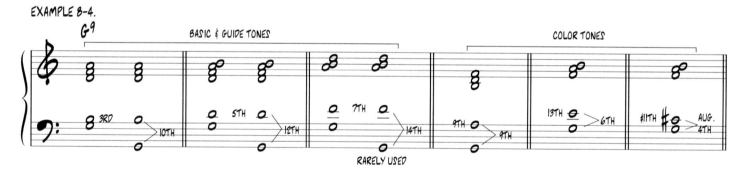

As shown in the previous example, if the third of a chord is in the fourth voice, the interval between the two bottom voices will be either a third or a tenth. If the fourth voice is the fifth of a chord, the interval will be either a fifth or a twelfth. If it is a seventh, the interval will be a seventh, but the compound interval of the seventh would rarely be used in this type of voicing. The appearance of color tones in the fourth voice is possible, but should be handled carefully. A progression with successive color tones in the fourth voice could be difficult to control.

The addition of a root provides stability and firmness in a progression. It is most effective in ballads or pieces with slow harmonic rhythm.

TRACK 55

EXAMPLE 8-5.

It is also effective when used in pads and cadential progressions. However, this voicing should not be overused. Long passages harmonized in this manner tend to sound heavy and plodding due to the constant skipping of the bottom voice from root to root in the low register.

Addition of a Fifth Different Note

The final method adds a note other than the melody to a close-position four-note voicing that will create a sonority consisting of five different notes. This note may be placed anywhere within the voicing.

Considering the seven notes (root through thirteenth) that are available for harmonization, the maximum number of five-note voicings of any given note is fifteen. However, some are less acceptable than others for a variety of reasons, depending on the musical situation. Here is an example that shows all of the possible choices of harmonizing a major-seventh chord with the third as the melody note.

EXAMPLE 8-6.

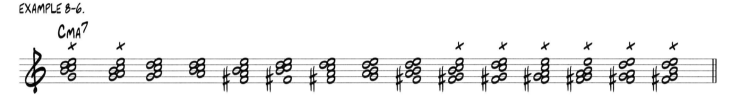

The voicings that may be less acceptable are marked with an X. Their undesirability is due to one or both of the following reasons:

- The inclusion of both basic tones results in a harshness or lack of color.
- The inclusion of both the fifth and the augmented eleventh could produce an undesirable dissonance.

The next example shows all of the possible harmonizations of an unaltered dominant-seventh chord with the thirteenth as the melody note.

EXAMPLE 8-7.

Here, the chords marked with an X could be objectionable because:

- Either the third or seventh are not present, which weakens the sense of chord quality.
- The inclusion of both the fifth and the thirteenth could be undesirable.

A compendium of five-note voicings can be found in appendix 6. It does not contain every possible combination of notes (some have been eliminated for the reasons stated above), but the list is nonetheless comprehensive. These chords have been written in close position with all five notes within the octave, rather than the traditional root-position configuration of stacked thirds. The purpose of this type of organization, as was the case with four-note voicings, is to show all of the possible melodic harmonizations for each chord. When analyzing these chords, it is important to identify each chord tone, especially the color tones. Because of the close spacing, ninths may look like seconds, elevenths like fourths, and thirteenths like sixths. In many instances they appear below the root. These factors may make identification difficult at first. But a thorough study of this compendium is essential to comprehend the range of possibilities that exist in five-note voicings. Each of the chords contains at least one color tone; many have two or three. The amount of dissonance and tension in each chord is determined by the number of color and altered tones present.

When one color tone is included as in the next example, the chord would also contain both basic tones and both guide tones. (Also in this example, as well as the next five, the voicings are presented in root position for easier chord-tone identification.)

EXAMPLE 8-8.

When two color tones are present, the chord should most likely contain one basic tone and both guide tones.

EXAMPLE 8-9.

There are a few instances where the makeup of a chord might consist of two basic tones, one guide tone, and two color tones. These occur in situations where the absence of the third might not interfere with chord recognition. Specifically, these are major, half-diminished, and extended dominant chords.

EXAMPLE 8-10.

When three color tones are present, the chord should contain two guide tones and no basic tones.

EXAMPLE 8-11.

An exception to this formula exists when a basic tone is in the melody. The content of the chord should then be one basic tone, one guide tone, and three color tones; or one basic tone, two guide tones, and two color tones.

EXAMPLE 8-12.

A combination of both basic tones, no guide tones, and three color tones would be rare. The effect would be stark and colorless, sounding rather like a polychord.

EXAMPLE 8-13.

The number of choices available for harmonizing each melody note may seem staggering at first. But it is important to have several options available for each chord quality in order to control dissonance, voice leading, and tension levels.

An intervallic analysis of the chords in the compendium reveals another significant fact: they all contain at least two seconds. Chords that are dominated by adjacent seconds are called *cluster chords*.

EXAMPLE 8-14.

These clusters create a very dense texture, as shown in the next example.

EXAMPLE 8-15.

Although these are functional in block voicings, clusters, like any extreme device, have a striking effect but can easily become tiresome. They are more resonant in open positions. The wider spacing permits more flexible voice leading, and the dissonances become more focused. (See the section on drop-two and four below.)

The three methods of converting four-note voicings to five can be applied to all of the open voicings with equal success.

Drop Voicings

Drop-Two Voicings

When creating a drop-two voicing with a doubled melody, begin with a block voicing and drop the second voice one octave. The resultant effect is quite different from block voicing. The doubled melody is less assertive since it is inside the chord and somewhat covered by the larger tone of the instrument playing the dropped voice.

EXAMPLE 8-16.

TRACK 56

Adding a root below a drop-two voicing can result in a much richer texture than the block-chord version. The chord tones are more evenly spaced and spread over a wider range.

EXAMPLE 8-17.

TRACK 57

The wider spacing enables this texture to work very well when writing pads (discussed in detail in chapter 9).

The drop-two version of a five-note voicing is effective because it alleviates some of the harshness of the clusters. Although a cluster may still be present in the inner voices, it is softened by the larger intervals above and below it.

EXAMPLE 8-18.

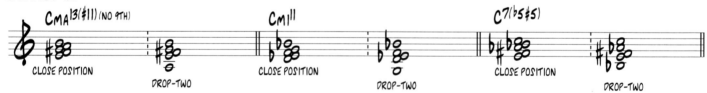

Here is Example 8-15, converted to drop-two voicings.

EXAMPLE 8-19.

Drop-Two and Four Voicings

When creating a drop-two and four voicing with a doubled melody, begin with a block voicing and drop the second and fourth voices one octave. Since the doubled melody is now in the middle voice, it is even less prominent than in the drop-two version.

EXAMPLE 8-20.

TRACK 58

Adding a root below a drop-two and four is another matter. This addition extends the range even further downward and narrows the workable range of the top voice. But within these narrow confines it can be a very strong and assertive voicing, useful in intros, interludes, endings, and short dramatic passages.

EXAMPLE 8-21.

TRACK 59

Five-note drop-two and four voicings open up a whole new area of chord construction called *quartal harmony*. It has been widely used by twentieth-century composers, but still retains its freshness. A chord may be termed "quartal" if it contains two or more perfect fourths between two adjacent voices. These are obtained by inverting the perfect fifth intervals that are present between every other chord tone.

EXAMPLE 8-22.

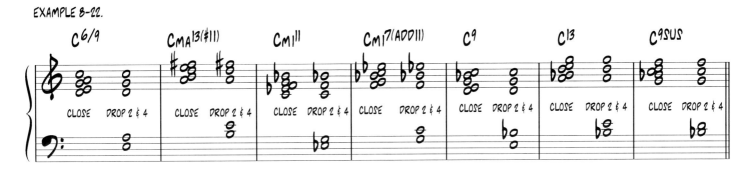

Perfect fourths are rather neutral in quality, so the character of the chord is often determined by the other intervals present. This is especially true of dominant chords. It might seem that these would offer fewer possibilities for quartal construction due to the necessity to retain the tritone between the guide tones. But altering the color tones and doubly altering the fifths and ninths greatly expands the choices here. This is illustrated in the following example; all of these chords possess two perfect fourths and are arranged in order of increasing dissonance.

EXAMPLE 8-23.

Half-diminished chords are limited in the number of choices because of the tritone interval.

EXAMPLE 8-24.

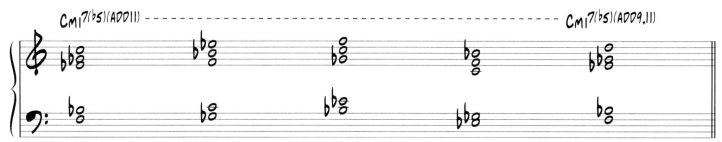

A five-note voicing constructed entirely of perfect fourths has a strong pentatonic flavor. The notes of the chord make up a major or minor pentatonic scale.

EXAMPLE 8-25.

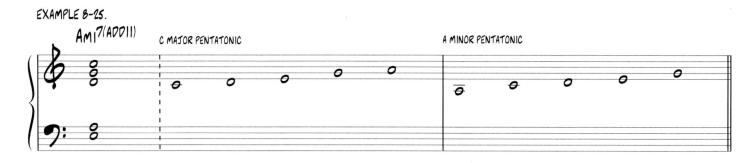

The following chord/voicing is a possible choice for harmonizing a pentatonic motive.

EXAMPLE 8-26.

This parallelism cannot be sustained for very long but is a useful device for a few chords.

Avoid becoming too rigid when employing quartal harmonies. They mix well with other types of open voicings. Always let variety, voice leading, and tension levels determine voicing choices.

Here is Example 8-15, converted to drop-two and four voicings.

EXAMPLE 8-27.

Other Drop Voicings

The addition of the fifth voice offers several more dropped-voicing opportunities compared to four-note voicings.

One-Note Drops:	**Two-Note Drops:**
drop-three	drop-two and three
drop-four	drop-two and five
drop-five	drop-three and four
	drop-three and five
	drop-four and five

As was the case with four-note voicings, these are not suitable for harmonizing extended passages, but can frequently provide acceptable alternatives for unworkable drop-twos and drop-two and fours. Specifically, these alternate configurations can:

- Eliminate undesirable minor-ninth intervals between inner voices.

- Alleviate harsh clusters in the middle voices.

- Isolate the guide tones in the bottom voices for better clarity.

- Place guide tones in the bottom voices to provide more stability.

The following example illustrates how relatively ineffective drop-two and drop-two and four voicings can be improved upon by using one of the alternative drop voicings.

EXAMPLE 8-28.

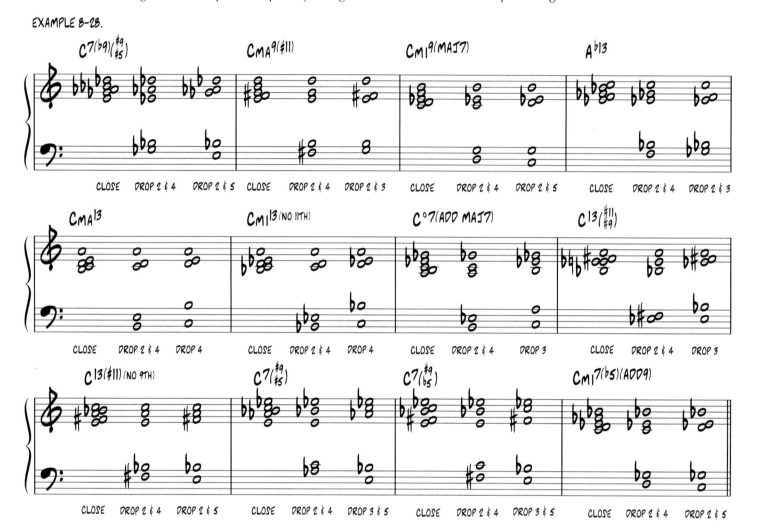

Additional Voicings
Chorale voicing

The method for constructing five-note chorale voicings is essentially the same as that for four-note voicings. Here, briefly, is the procedure outlined in chapter 6.

- Place the root in the bottom voice.
- The first note above the root should be a guide tone.
- Place the remaining guides tone immediately above the first one.
- The next voice, which is placed above the guide tones, will be either a fifth or a color tone.
- The completeness of this four-note sonority now allows total freedom in the construction of the top voice. It may add a fifth note to the chord or double an existing one. The melody can be composed without concern for any specific harmonic implications.

If the top voice is a given melody, the procedure may be adjusted somewhat. The range, melodic contour, and harmonic content of the given melody must be taken into consideration during this process so that there is proper spacing between the two top parts, and that the five voices form a cohesive whole.

Sometimes existing drop-two or drop-two and four voicings can be converted to chorale voicings by placing a root on the bottom of each chord. The conversion of the next example to chorale voicing was possible because the guide tones were already on the bottom of the four-note voicing.

EXAMPLE 8-29.

Short, rhythmic passages like the one above can be effective in delineating certain harmonic progressions. They are useful in introductions, interludes, shout choruses, and setting up solo breaks. However, the caution against the overuse of this voicing cited in chapter 6 still applies here.

Spread Voicing

Here is a procedure for constructing spread voicings from close-position voicings that works for the majority of melody harmonizations.

1. Extract the guide tones and place them at the bottom of the chord. To achieve the proper register and desired spacing, it is sometimes necessary to reverse their position.

EXAMPLE 8-30.

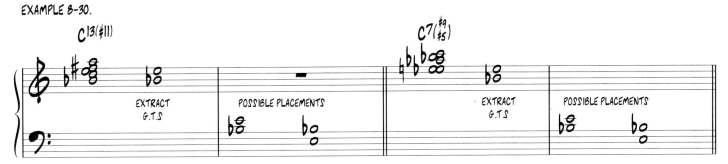

2. Create a drop-two voicing with the remaining three tones.

EXAMPLE 8-31.

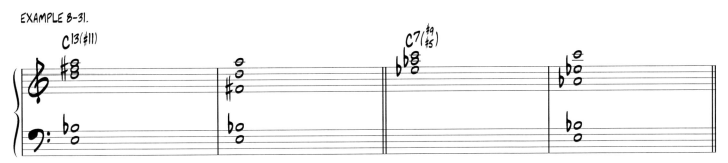

While this formula works when basic or color tones are in the melody, it obviously will not work when a guide tone is the top voice. Here are some solutions for this situation.

1. Extract the remaining guide tone and place it on the bottom of the chord. If basic tones are present in the voicing, extract one of these as well and move it to the bottom of the voicing. The exact placement of these two notes should be determined by the voicings preceding and following the target voicing. Then, as explained above, create a drop-two voicing with the remaining three tones.

EXAMPLE 8-32.

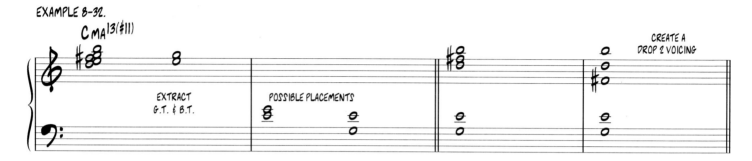

2. Extract the remaining guide tone and place it on the bottom of the chord. If only color or altered tones remain, arrange these three notes to provide an even spacing between the two guide tones (melody and bottom note).

EXAMPLE 8-33.

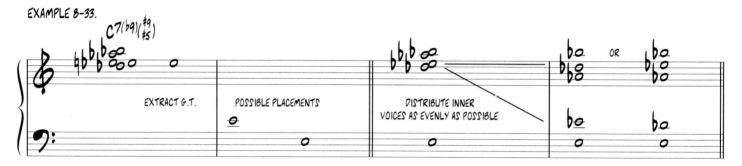

3. Double the melody note in an inner voice. This will temporarily reduce the sonority to four notes. But if enough color is present in the chord, the change will not be too noticeable.

EXAMPLE 8-34.

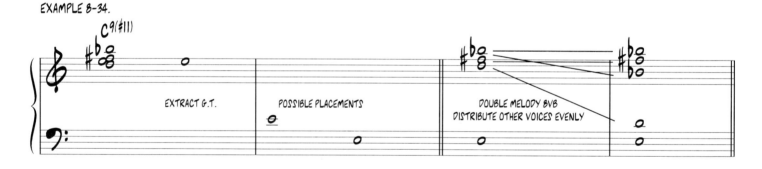

The choice of method depends on which one provides the suitable vertical sonority and the smoothest voice leading. Since this problem will only involve a few chords in any given passage, the best approach is to harmonize the other chords first. Then, by working forward and backward, find the most appropriate voicing for the remaining chords.

Here is Example 8-15, converted to spread voicings.

EXAMPLE 8-35.

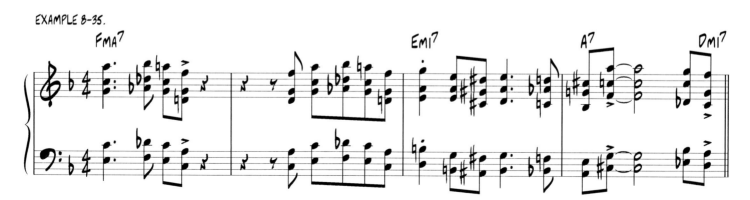

Here is a full chorus harmonization of "Windswept" containing five-note voicings in varying combinations of close and open positions. The parallelisms and tonicizations presented in chapter 5 have been retained and expanded to five notes.

EXAMPLE 8-36.

TRACK 61

CHAPTER 9
Accompaniment Devices:
Pads, Punches, Melodic Fills, and Riffs

In classical music, the combination of melody and accompaniment is considered a homophonic texture; that is, one element. However, in jazz and commercial music, these devices are so striking that they are considered separate elements. To this point, the only other independent element discussed has been the countermelody. Accompaniment devices, like countermelodies, involve newly composed material. They differ from each other for the following reasons: a countermelody divides the listener's attention between it and the melody and assumes an almost equal importance with the melody, whereas a background device is intended to enhance the melody without diverting attention from it. All of these devices are derived from piano and guitar comping techniques. They can be found in any section of an arrangement and will be alluded to in subsequent chapters. Here, they will be discussed in terms of their use when accompanying an existing melody as this situation presents the most critical need for specific guidelines.

There are four different types of accompaniment (or background) devices.

- Pads
- Punches
- Melodic Fills
- Riffs

The effectiveness of each device is wholly dependent upon the arranger's creativity.

Pads

Pads are sustained multiple-note voicings that provide harmonic underpinning. They should create a backdrop for the melody and support it without overpowering it. The most effective way to construct a pad is with the composition of a secondary melodic line that consists mostly of sustained notes. The example below shows the A section of "Bar Flies" along with this new secondary line.

EXAMPLE 9-1.

This line can then be harmonized, transforming it into a pad.

TRACK 62

EXAMPLE 9-2.

Unlike a countermelody, which can be quite active and usually contains a number of guide tones that help to define the harmony, a melody composed as the top line of a pad should be much less active and contain many color and altered tones, and relatively few guide tones. A comparison of the line in Example 9-1 and the countermelodies in examples 3-34 through 3-36 in chapter 3 will illustrate these differences.

The pad line should complement the melody both rhythmically and harmonically. If the melody anticipates the harmony, the pad should either correspond directly with it or avoid a rhythmic clash by anticipating or delaying its entrance until at least a full beat before or after the anticipation.

The following example points out both of these situations in the "Bar Flies" pad. The arrows indicate those notes that correspond harmonically and rhythmically to the melody. The solid lines indicate the anticipation or delay of the pad to avoid a rhythmic clash.

EXAMPLE 9-3.

The existence of basic and guide tones in a melody tends to inhibit the use of richer harmonies in block harmonizations. When composing the top line for a pad, these are no longer problematic. Here the arranger has the freedom to compose new lines that can accommodate more interesting harmonizations.

EXAMPLE 9-4.

Any line composed as the top line of a pad should be able to stand alone as an interesting melody. A common mistake is that of choosing a starting pitch and then merely finding the closest movement between chords or retaining like pitches. This often results in a line with little melodic interest as in the top voice of the bass-clef part in the next example.

EXAMPLE 9-5.

The following are some solutions for this problem.

- Avoid retaining pitches between chords for more than one or two measures. There is a tendency to become enamored with the chord movement below a single pitch. Though in theory there is nothing wrong with this, in actual practice, this creates a top line that is static and dull. A few retained pitches are acceptable, but avoid extended harmonizations in this manner. The next example shows the retention of a single pitch through seven chords and two possible remedies.

EXAMPLE 9-6.

- The introduction of rhythmic elements can add energy to an otherwise lifeless pad. Though chord movement usually occurs in four-, two-, and one-beat increments, this does not mean that a pad must move at exactly the same rate. The result would be a pad built entirely of whole, half, and quarter notes. The addition of anticipations, rhythmic suspensions, and syncopation can offer some much-needed rejuvenation.

EXAMPLE 9-7.

- Chord arpeggiation and the insertion of diatonic passing chords can create a sense of movement where none exists. A pad does not have to be comprised of only one note per chord change. If this were the case, tunes with slow harmonic rhythm would yield an excruciatingly stagnant pad. The careful and occasional use of these can increase forward momentum.

EXAMPLE 9-8.

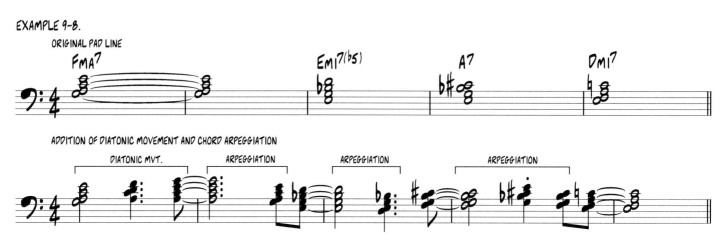

A pad can exist above, below, or around the melody. Its position is dependent on both the pitch of the melody instrument and of those playing the pad. For instance, if the melody instrument is a higher-pitched one such as trumpet, and the pad is to be played by lower-pitched instruments such as saxophones or trombones, it would be positioned below the melody. Close-position voicings are usually employed in this pad placement, though drop-two voicings are also possible.

EXAMPLE 9-9.

TRACK 63
Part 1

If the melody is played by a lower-pitched instrument such as trombone, and the pad is to be played by higher-pitched instruments such as muted trumpets or fluegelhorns, the pad would be placed above the melody. Close-position voicings are typically used in this pad positioning.

EXAMPLE 9-10.

TRACK 63
Part 2

If the pad instruments are saxophones, it would be positioned around the melody. That is, some notes of the pad would be above the melody while some would be below. Unlike the previous situations, this one necessitates the use of open-position voicings.

EXAMPLE 9-11.

TRACK 63
Part 3

In actual practice, pads do not have to remain in any one position, but can change positions as long as this is accomplished musically.

Punches

Punches are short, mainly rhythmic ideas that punctuate a melody. They can be as short as one note or as many as five or six. The basic premise is that a punch contains syncopations, anticipations, and/or rhythmic delays.

EXAMPLE 9-12.

Punches can be placed on both downbeats and upbeats.

EXAMPLE 9-13.

Some are purely rhythmic. Single note punches, as well as those whose top line is static, fall into this category.

EXAMPLE 9-14.

Most punches incorporate a combination of both rhythmic and melodic elements.

EXAMPLE 9-15.

Even when both elements are present in a punch, it is the rhythmic aspects of this device that define it. Of the two examples below, the first would be considered a punch due to its highly rhythmic nature, while the second would be considered a melodic fill because of the lack of syncopation and the preponderance of eighth notes (melodic fills are discussed later on).

EXAMPLE 9-16.

Punches can be written in unisons or octaves, harmonized, or combinations of both.

TRACK 64

EXAMPLE 9-17.

Punches typically appear in four places.

- **At the natural accent points of a melody**: Here, they usually consist of only one or two notes and are almost always purely rhythmic. This type adds further emphasis to the top or bottom notes of a line, phrase endings, and all other naturally accented notes.

TRACK 65

EXAMPLE 9-18.

- **Before a phrase**: Here, they can be purely rhythmic or contain melodic elements. This type sets up a phrase by adding emphasis directly ahead of it.

TRACK 66
Part 1

EXAMPLE 9-19.

- **After a phrase**: The same rhythmic and melodic qualities apply as above. This type provides an afterthought to a phrase.

TRACK 66
Part 2

EXAMPLE 9-20.

Regardless of whether the phrase ends with a short or sustained note, a punch can be placed as soon as a phrase becomes inactive.

- **At periods of inactivity in a melody**: The same rhythmic and melodic qualities apply as above. This type fills in the gaps between segments.

TRACK 66
Part 3

EXAMPLE 9-21.

Due to the uneven quality of swing eighth notes, the proximity of the punch to the last note of a phrase is dependent on the endpoint of the phrase. If it ends on a downbeat, the punch can begin on the upbeat of the same beat as the phrase ending.

TRACK 67
Part 1

EXAMPLE 9-22.

If the phrase ends on an upbeat, thereby anticipating the next downbeat, the punch should usually not begin until the next upbeat, a full beat after the phrase ending.

TRACK 67
Part 2

EXAMPLE 9-23.

If the punch begins on the downbeat directly after the phrase ending, it tends to obliterate the anticipation of the phrase and causes the punch to sound like a continuation of the melody. This is not to say that it can never be placed here. However, this is the exception rather than the rule.

TRACK 68
Part 1

EXAMPLE 9-24.

If the phrase begins on an upbeat, a punch used before the start of the phrase can end as late as the downbeat of the same beat as the phrase beginning.

TRACK 68
Part 2

EXAMPLE 9-25.

If the phrase begins on a downbeat, the punch should end no later than the prior downbeat, a full beat before the phrase beginning.

EXAMPLE 9-26.

If the punch ends on the upbeat immediately before the downbeat phrase beginning, this creates a rhythmically confusing situation where the strong anticipation of the chord progression created by the punch is immediately followed by an equally strong downbeat reference of the new phrase. Again, this is not a totally unacceptable situation. Some exceptions are shown in the following example.

EXAMPLE 9-27.

There is also a possibility that the first and/or last notes of phrases and punches will share the same downbeat or upbeat in a measure.

EXAMPLE 9-28.

When dealing with straight eighth-note grooves, punch placements are less problematic. However, the guidelines mentioned above can be applied to this genre with equally acceptable results.

An often mistaken supposition is that punches should completely fill the space between a melody's phrases. Often, one well-placed note is more effective than several. Notice the situation in the next example where there are four beats between phrases. Beginning with a single note, each of the subsequent punch figures adds another note to the prior example.

EXAMPLE 9–29.

All of these are acceptable. However, depending on the situation, a well-placed single-note punch might deliver more impact than several.

The amount of space between a punch and a phrase beginning or ending is also dependent on the tempo of the music. At slower tempos, less space is necessary because of the longer time between beats. This is not to say that punches cannot be written within small spaces at faster tempos. In fact, these can be used to create a more intense effect.

TRACK 71

EXAMPLE 9–30.

There are three means by which punches can be employed: horns only, rhythm section only, or in combination. The most passive punches are those involving only the horns. The rhythm section retains the time feel while the horns accentuate the melodic line. The drums have the option of keeping time or setting up and kicking some or all the punches.

EXAMPLE 9-31.

TRACK 72
Part 1

A more active approach involves only the rhythm section playing punches. This interrupts the groove. Those horns not assigned to the melody may be resting or playing a countermelody or pads.

EXAMPLE 9-32.

TRACK 72
Part 2

The situation with the most impact utilizes both horns and rhythm section. Again, the time feel is interrupted by the rhythm section, while the horns add even more emphasis by playing a vertical harmonization of the punch chords with the rhythm section.

EXAMPLE 9-33.

TRACK 72
Part 3

Melodic Fills

Melodic fills and punches are relatively similar. The main difference is that punches are more rhythmic. This is not to say that melodic fills do not possess rhythmic qualities. Lines composed for this purpose should contain the rhythmic elements associated with jazz: syncopation, anticipation, and rhythmic suspension.

EXAMPLE 9-34.

Melodic fills can be played in unison (or octaves), harmonized, or a combination.

EXAMPLE 9-35.

TRACK 73
Part 1

Another significant quality of a melodic fill is that, unlike a pad or punch, it tends to temporarily divert attention from the melody due to its melodic content and generally longer length.

EXAMPLE 9-36.

TRACK 73
Part 2

Melodic fills should be placed in exactly the same manner as punches. Refer to the guidelines discussed in that section of this chapter.

Pads, melodic fills, and punches can be combined to create an exciting accompaniment that both supports and accentuates the melody.

EXAMPLE 9-37.

TRACK 73
Part 3

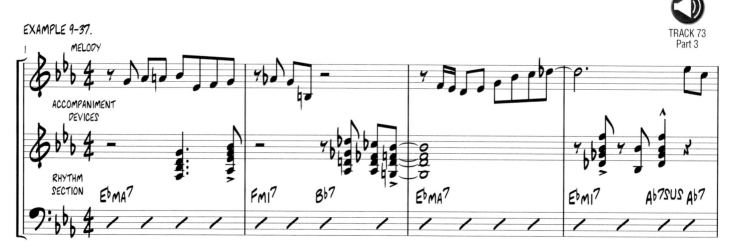

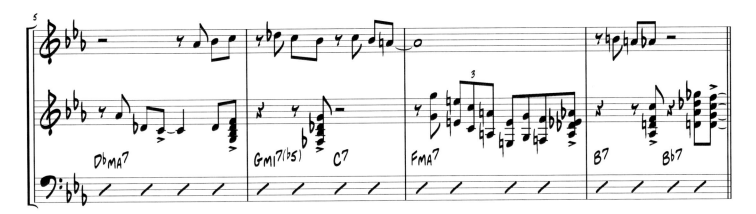

Riffs

The main characteristic of *riffs* is repetition. Their rhythmic and melodic content can vary greatly. They can be as short as one or two beats or last as long as one or two measures, and can be played in unison, harmonized, or a combination of both. But unlike any of the other accompaniment devices, riffs are the only ones whose definition hinges on repetition. The phrases in the following example show some typical riff rhythms.

EXAMPLE 9-38.

Any of these would be considered punches if played only once. But, when repeated several times, they become riffs. In Example 9-39, the rhythmic figure in measure 2 of the first example is a punch. In the second example, the same figure is a riff due to its repetition.

EXAMPLE 9-39.

Riffs work best over progressions with a slow to moderate rate of harmonic rhythm. The traditional blues progression is the most typical song form in which to employ them.

EXAMPLE 9-40.

TRACK 74
Part 1

When a riff occurs over a progression, its melodic line must usually be adjusted slightly to accommodate the harmonic shifts, typically by no more than a whole step up or down. If it is harmonized, the vertical sonorities must also be changed.

EXAMPLE 9-41.

TRACK 74
Part 2

A moderate amount of melodic alteration and reharmonization is to be expected over most progressions. The more melodically complex a riff is, the more likely the need will be to alter it. Consequently, a simpler riff will present fewer needs for adjustment. For this reason, simpler riffs are generally more effective than those that are more complex. In the next example, the rapidly moving harmonies of the bop blues progression combined with the complexity of the riff negate its effectiveness because of the constant compensation for the natural downward motion of the cycle progressions.

TRACK 75
Part 1

EXAMPLE 9-42.

Unlike punches and melodic fills, the collision of rhythms and harmonies between a melody and riff is of no concern due to the riff's repetitive nature. In the next example, diagonal arrows located between the two staves indicate rhythmic collisions and vertical lines designate harmonic collisions.

TRACK 75
Part 2

EXAMPLE 9-43.

Riffs can also be combined. The most famous example of this can be found in the shout chorus of Buck Clayton's "One O'Clock Jump." This section contains three separate riffs played by each of the horn sections that interlock, constituting one of the most exciting moments in jazz history.

PART II

Instruments and Notation

Chapters 10 through 12 contain the following topics:

- Wind Instruments
- Large Ensemble Horn Sections
- Rhythm Section

These chapters present the ranges and characteristics of the instruments commonly found in the jazz ensemble, both individually and in sections, as well as an in-depth discussion of the proper methods of notation for the rhythm section.

CHAPTER 10
Wind Instruments

The previous chapters have dealt only with arranging techniques, without reference to specific instrumentation. The next three chapters will be devoted to acquiring the knowledge and skills necessary to utilize these techniques in various settings. Specifically, this knowledge encompasses the ranges, transpositions, characteristics, and limitations of the various instruments. Only the ones currently used in jazz are discussed. Rather than treat the others superficially, they have been eliminated. If the need to write for one of these should arise, the essential information is readily available in the many excellent texts on orchestration.

The ranges of the instruments are given in the following manner.

- **Possible Range**: This represents the entire range of the instrument. The parenthetical notes indicate that they are available on specially equipped instruments. The arrows refer to extended ranges that are dependent on the ability of the performer.

- **Practical Range**: This may eliminate a few notes on the high or low end of the possible range because they are difficult to control in all situations. This range will not accurately describe the limitations of every performer, but making unrealistic demands in these areas may result in problems with intonation, balance, and flexibility.

This practical range is not absolute. In order to compensate for even the youngest player, it may be necessary to eliminate further high and low notes from the listed practical ranges. The range limitations of any instrument can only be accurately determined when the abilities of the players being written for are known. Otherwise, it is best not to exceed the practical ranges, except for a very good reason.

Transposition

Transposition, even in the age of music notation software, is a necessary skill. Most of the instruments used in jazz ensembles are not in concert pitch and require transposed parts. Remember that all transposing instruments (except piccolo) are pitched *below* concert key, so the transposed parts will always appear higher than concert pitch.

The most common method of transposition is by interval. Compare the key of the instrument to C; the resulting interval will be the interval of transposition. If, for example, the instrument is pitched in B♭, the interval between B♭ and C is a major second. Therefore, the transposed part will be written a major second higher than the desired concert pitch.

EXAMPLE 10-1.

Consequently, B♭ instruments transpose up a major second; E♭ instruments, up a major sixth; F instruments, up a perfect fifth; and G instruments, up a perfect fourth. Some larger instruments, such as the tenor and baritone saxophones and bass clarinet, require an additional octave transposition as well.

EXAMPLE 10-2.

Another method of approach is that when a transposing instrument plays a written C, it will sound the note in which the instrument is pitched. When an E♭ instrument plays a written C, the actual sound is E♭, a major sixth lower. Accordingly, every transposed note on that instrument will sound a major sixth lower than written.

EXAMPLE 10-3.

This method is the reverse of the previous one, starting with a transposed note and realizing the concert pitch.

Understanding both concepts will help in dealing with the dual aspects of transposition, moving from concert pitch to transposed part, and vice versa.

Assimilating the ranges and transpositions of the instruments is a fairly straightforward process; it is largely a matter of memorization. In truth, transposition does not actually require memorization, except to remember what key the instruments are in. Once this principle is grasped, it becomes almost second nature.

Characteristics and Limitations of Wind Instruments

Learning the characteristics and limitations of the wind instruments is a more involved and ongoing process. Timbral characteristics cannot accurately be described by such subjective words as "dark," "brittle," or "shrill." Every arranger needs to create a set of terms that will convey the sound of the instruments in their various registers and commit these tonal images to memory.

The idiosyncrasies of the instruments are also learned through experience. Every arranger has at some time or other been subjected to the disappointment (and perhaps embarrassment) of hearing the performance of a passage for which there had been great expectations, only to find out that it was unplayable, inaudible, or just downright ugly. The first reaction in these situations is to blame the performers, but one may soon realize that a more intimate knowledge of the instruments is the only real solution.

With these goals in mind, each of the instruments used in the jazz ensemble will be examined in detail.

WOODWINDS

Saxophones

The *soprano, alto, tenor,* and *baritone* are the only saxophones currently found in the jazz ensemble (*sopranino* and *bass* are rarely used). They are very agile instruments, capable of playing complex lines. They also possess a wide dynamic range and can balance with the brass at all levels. The lowest perfect fifth of their range is full and rich at louder volumes. The soprano is especially reedy in this register. Below mezzo-forte, it becomes mellower and subdued. The next octave and a half (G up to C) is the most easily controlled. The tone ranges from smooth and delicate at softer volumes to vibrant and intense at louder volumes. The high register (from D up to F♯) is somewhat thinner, but very brilliant and assertive. The baritone thins out less than the other saxophones in this register. Endurance is rarely a factor; saxophonists are capable of playing for a long period of time without rest. The full range of the instrument is available to the arranger, although both the high and low registers have some limitations. Both contain awkward fingerings, and fast passages in these registers are difficult to execute. The high register also has some intonation problems, except in the hands of more capable performers. The low register is difficult to play softly without using a *subtone* (an alternate embouchure which produces a breathy, "half tone"). Delicate attacks in this register are also problematic.

Contrary to many older texts that assign F as the top note of the saxophone range, the F♯ key is now standard on most new instruments, making this pitch easier to play. Also, due to the now-common practice of extending the range of the instrument well into the third and fourth octaves through the use of nonstandard fingerings, this F♯ is readily attainable even by those whose instruments do not possess this key.

The following are three more important points about the extended upper range of the saxophone.

- The use of this F♯ in a written passage to be played by two or more saxophonists should only be employed when writing for more experienced players.

- Any pitches beyond this F♯ should be written only for a single instrument due to the possibility of severe intonation problems.

- The attainment of *altissimo* (higher range, above the treble staff) notes is incremental in difficulty to saxophone size; the larger the instrument, the more easily these notes can be reached. In other words, it is much more difficult for soprano sax to play in the extended range than it is for baritone.

The **soprano saxophone** is pitched in B♭ and transposes up a major second.

EXAMPLE 10-4.

The **alto saxophone** is pitched in E♭ and transposes up a major sixth.

EXAMPLE 10-5.

As mentioned above, transposition for tenor and baritone is a little more involved. Here, an additional octave upward is required.

The **tenor saxophone** is pitched in B♭ and transposes up a major ninth (the original major second required for all B♭ instruments plus an octave).

EXAMPLE 10-6.

The **baritone saxophone** is pitched in E♭ and transposes up a major thirteenth (the original major sixth required for all E♭ instruments plus an octave).

EXAMPLE 10-7.

Most new baritones are equipped with a low-A key, but there are many still in use that are not. When writing a low A, there is a possibility that the baritone player may need to take this note up an octave.

The transposition for the saxophones is the most difficult of all the instruments. Because they all read treble clef and have the same written range, this presents an awkward situation for the beginning arranger. The concert pitches played by the soprano and alto fall mainly in the treble clef range. The baritone pitches are primarily in the bass clef range. The tenor presents a unique challenge as its pitches traverse both the treble and bass clefs. When working with a concert sketch (score), the tenor notes can be problematic, because they are constantly moving from one clef to another. One way is to use dotted lines to keep track of a part as it moves from one clef to another in a concert sketch.

EXAMPLE 10-8.

When using music notation software, it may be helpful to see the score in both concert and transposed forms to be sure that all saxophones are in the proper registers.

An unusual phenomenon occurs when transposing for the baritone. When a concert pitch in the bass clef is transposed for the baritone into the treble clef, it falls on the same line or space.

EXAMPLE 10-9.

This is not offered as a foolproof method of transposing for the instrument. As the above example illustrates, because of the two different keys involved in the transposition, the accidentals frequently do not match. But for the beginner, it is a useful tool to make sure the transposed part is in the correct octave.

Saxophones do not all have the same peculiarities; each has different strengths and weaknesses. For instance, the lower the pitch of the saxophone, the less dramatic the change in tone quality will be from one register to another. The higher the pitch, the more dramatic the change will be.

If one had to choose a particular saxophone as the middle voice in three-voice writing (trumpet, saxophone, trombone), the overall choice would be the tenor, for two reasons.

- It has a fuller, meatier sound in all registers compared to the other saxophones.

- It traverses the ranges of the two outside instruments better than the alto or baritone. (The soprano sax would be a poor choice for this kind of writing because it has roughly the same range as the trumpet.)

The next group of woodwind instruments discussed form the woodwind choir of the symphony orchestra. In that setting they are played by virtuoso performers. The jazz ensemble presents a different situation. Here the primary woodwind instrument is the saxophone; the others are secondary. These woodwinds are referred to as "doubles" and the saxophonist who plays them is referred to as a "doubler." The arranger should expect to encounter a wide range of abilities on these secondary instruments.

Flutes

The **soprano flute** (typically referred to simply as **flute**) is a non-transposing instrument and possesses the following written range.

EXAMPLE 10-10.

Most American flutes have a low-B foot, but it should not be considered standard. Due to the weakness of tone in the low register and the intonation problems inherent in the very high register, the suggested practical range for a doubler would be:

EXAMPLE 10-11.

The first octave of the flute (C to C) has a warm, dark sound, but very little projection. It can easily be covered and does not balance well with other instruments. Using two or even three flutes in this register will result in a fuller, rounder sound, but will not significantly increase the projection. If the sensuous quality of this register is to be presented properly, it should have a sparse accompaniment and sufficient amplification. This also applies to the other members of the flute family. The second octave is clear and bright, with more projection.

Here, two or three flutes in unison can significantly increase the carrying power of a line. The high register is brilliant and penetrating, but intonation and control problems are likely above high G.

The flute is an extremely agile instrument. Fast scales and large leaps are commonplace. It can provide an interesting color when doubling the melody an octave higher in both small and large ensembles. In this role, it should be written in the upper register (second octave E to third octave G). The flute requires a large amount of air, so frequent opportunities to breathe should be provided.

The **piccolo** is pitched an octave higher than written and is the only wind instrument used in the jazz ensemble that transposes downward.

EXAMPLE 10-12.

The piccolo has no foot joint and cannot play pitches below D. The recommended range for a doubler would be the same as the practical range for the flute. The first octave of the piccolo (D to D) has a soft, haunting quality. It has very little projection in this octave, but perhaps a bit more than the flute. The second octave is very assertive, becoming increasingly shrill and piercing in the high register. The piccolo also requires a lot of air. Extended passages should be avoided, as they can be very tiring for both the player and the listener.

The **alto flute** is pitched in G and transposes up a perfect fourth.

EXAMPLE 10-13.

Its possible range is the same as for the C flute, but the practical range is much smaller. This is not due so much to the limitations of the players, but to the instrument itself. The low register is full, rich, and dark. It has slightly more carrying power than the (soprano) flute in this register, but is still easily covered and should be used only with sparse backgrounds. In the middle and upper registers, the sound is rather ordinary, without much brilliance. The suggested practical range for the alto flute is as follows.

EXAMPLE 10-14.

Anything written above this should be given to the flute or piccolo. Even more air is required for the alto flute, so frequent spaces for breathing must be provided.

The **bass flute** is rarely seen in the jazz ensemble, mainly due to its unavailability and cost. It is used in studio orchestras and recordings, where its unique sound can be effectively exploited. It is pitched in C, but transposes up an octave.

EXAMPLE 10-15.

The bass flute is similar to the alto flute, with all its assets and liabilities magnified. Amplification is essential. Again, breathing is the biggest problem, along with the sheer weight of the instrument. The alto and bass flutes are not a regular part of the doubling arsenal, but are by no means rare.

Clarinets

The clarinets typically heard in the jazz ensemble are the B♭ soprano and bass. The E♭ soprano, alto, and contrabass clarinets are rarely used.

The **soprano clarinet** (typically referred to simply as **clarinet**) is pitched in B♭ and transposes up a major second.

EXAMPLE 10-16.

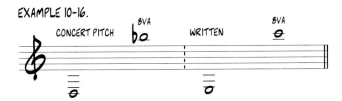

The clarinet has three distinct registers. The lowest register, from E to F♯, is called the *chalumeau* register and is very dark and woody in quality. The next four notes, G to B♭, are referred to as the *throat tones* and are rather pale and thin sounding. Experienced players learn to compensate for this so that the difference in tone is almost unnoticeable. Beginning with B, the next octave is called the *clarion* (or clarino) register. Here, the tone becomes clear and bright. The highest register—any note above high C—is referred to as the *altissimo* register and tends to be shrill, especially when played at loud volumes.

EXAMPLE 10-17.

The clarinet has the largest range of any woodwind and is the most versatile. It does not possess the idiosyncrasies of the other woodwinds in either the high or low registers, and can play the entire dynamic spectrum, from pianissimo to fortissimo, in all registers. It is also very agile and can play long phrases with ease. Because of its variety of tone colors and the fact that it blends well with other instruments, it is indispensable as a woodwind double. The combination of one or several clarinets with muted brass is a time-tested one. It can double in unison, octaves, thirds, or sixths with other instruments or combination of instruments. The clarinet can add warmth in the low register and brilliance in the upper register.

There was a time when almost all saxophonists started on the clarinet, and every member of the saxophone section was expected to double on it. This is no longer true. Fewer and fewer saxophonists are skilled performers on the clarinet.

When writing for clarinetists with limited experience, the following cautions should be observed.

- Avoid the throat tones in sustained passages. They will sound thin and may be out of tune.

- A phenomenon called the *break* occurs between the notes B♭ and B♮ in the instrument's second octave. While the B♭ is played with no holes covered, the B natural requires all holes to be covered. This is a difficult maneuver for less-advanced players, but with experience the problem disappears.

- The very high register above C can be difficult to control and play in tune. This area is best left to the flute.

The recommended practical written range for performers (and/or doublers) at this level is as follows.

EXAMPLE 10-18.

The **bass clarinet** is also pitched in B♭ and, like the tenor saxophone, transposes up a major ninth (the major second required for all B♭ instruments plus an octave).

EXAMPLE 10-19.

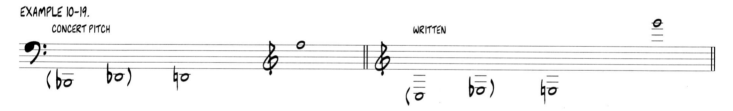

E was the accepted low note until the 1930s, when a low E♭ key was added. It is reasonable to expect E♭ to be the bottom note on all bass clarinets today. Many instruments have been constructed with a range extending down to low C. However, it would not be wise to expect this extension to be available.

Although the actual sounding range lies largely in the bass clef, all bass clarinet parts are written in the treble clef, which permits clarinetists to switch to bass clarinet and still use the same fingerings. The bass clarinet shares the same three distinct registers as the soprano. The chalumeau register is extremely rich and mellow and is very effective as a bass instrument in the ensemble. The throat register is thin and the upper register is slightly breathy and not as clear and bright as the soprano clarinet. The notes above G above the treble clef staff thin out considerably.

The same cautions that apply to the (soprano) clarinet should be observed when writing for inexperienced players on the bass clarinet. In school situations, there may be another consideration. The instrument might not be of top quality or may be poorly maintained; either of these conditions can make playing above the break difficult. Therefore, it would be wise to keep the part below the break. When combined with other instruments, effective bass clarinet parts can be written in this register.

The recommended practical written range for performers (doublers) at this level is as follows.

EXAMPLE 10-20.

Double Reeds

The three double reed instruments that will be discussed in reference to jazz arranging are the *oboe, English horn,* and *bassoon.* The fourth of these, the *contrabassoon,* is standard in the symphony orchestra, but its appearance in a jazz ensemble is unlikely. Though all of these instruments are an integral part of an orchestra, they are not common doubles for saxophonists. Players tend to take double reed instruments up after flute and clarinet, if at all. The primary reasons are that they are difficult to learn to play, and that embouchure maintenance and reed making are simply too time-consuming. Double reed instruments are more likely to be found in studio orchestra and recording situations.

The **oboe** is a non-transposing instrument and possesses the following written range.

EXAMPLE 10-21.

The registral characteristics of the oboe are in direct contrast to the flute. The lowest perfect fifth has a dense, nasal quality that can only be controlled at volumes of *mf* and above. This register should never be written at *p* or *pp.* The next octave and a half is the most effective range; here, the oboe is warm and reedy with good projection. Above high C, the tone thins out considerably and loses some of its characteristic tone quality. These notes are also difficult to control. A good practical range for the oboe is shown below.

EXAMPLE 10-22.

Because of its distinctive tone quality, the oboe is used primarily as a solo instrument in jazz. It is too assertive to be used effectively as an inner voice in sustained woodwind scoring. It can be used in combination with other woodwinds in unison, thirds, sixths, or octaves. Avoid exposed perfect fourths or fifths, because the oboe accentuates the bareness of these intervals. Because of the narrow opening in the double reed, it requires relatively little breath to play, so long passages are possible. However, frequent rests are still necessary to exhale stale air and replace it with fresh air.

The **English horn** is pitched in F and transposes up a perfect fifth.

EXAMPLE 10-23.

Its registral characteristics are similar to the oboe, but its tone is more delicate and less asser-tive. This allows it to combine with other instruments more successfully than the oboe. The first octave and a half is its most useful range. Above that, it begins to lose its personality and sounds like an oboe. It is normally used as a solo instrument and sounds best in slow, lyrical melodies.

A good practical range is as follows.

EXAMPLE 10-24.

The **bassoon** is a non-transposing instrument and possesses the following written range.

EXAMPLE 10-25.

Bassoonists are trained to read both bass and tenor clefs to avoid ledger lines, but the bass clef would probably suffice for a less-experienced player.

The bassoon is similar to the oboe in two respects: its low notes are almost impossible to attack softly, and its tone thins out in its high register. The first octave of the bassoon is strong and vibrant. The second octave is very expressive. In the third octave it becomes intense and reedy, but begins to thin out noticeably near the top of the range.

The bassoon would most likely be used as a solo instrument in a jazz setting. Since it does not project well, the accompaniment to any bassoon solo must be light. It blends well with other instruments and adds body to a line even though the other instruments absorb it.

A professional bassoonist is capable of playing the entire range of the instrument, but a safer practical range for the doubler or less-experienced player is as follows.

EXAMPLE 10-26.

The woodwinds are a very diverse group of instruments. While they may have certain features in common, each has its own unique timbral and registral characteristics, as well as its own individual dynamic curve.

By observing these peculiarities and taking into account the limitations of the players, it will be possible to write parts that are both accessible and musical. Always write for the player, not just the instrument.

Another important precaution to take is in reference to the fact that doublers need time to change from one instrument to another. Eight to ten seconds would be the minimum amount of time necessary to make the change. This change should be indicated immediately after the last note before the instrument change is to occur. The indications "to flute" or "to bass clari-net" should be written just above the staff.

EXAMPLE 10-27.

Also, if the new instrument is in a different key from the saxophone, enter the new key signature at the beginning of the first measure of music for the new instrument.

EXAMPLE 10-28.

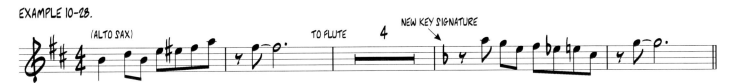

When switching back to saxophone, indicate the change in the same manner, using "to alto" immediately after the last note. Again, allow time for the change and enter the original key signature, if necessary.

EXAMPLE 10-29.

If the piece begins on an instrument other than the saxophone named at the top of the part, the name of that instrument should be entered above the first note it plays.

EXAMPLE 10-30.

BRASSES

Trumpet

In jazz, the B♭ trumpet is used exclusively because of its big, rich tone. It transposes up a major second.

EXAMPLE 10-31.

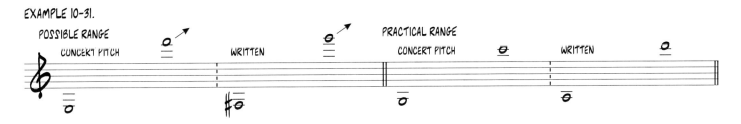

The upper limits of the trumpet's range are actually determined by the ability of the performer. Professional lead trumpet players are expected to have a consistent range up to F or G above high C. However, the majority of trumpet players do not fall into this category, and consequently, are not capable of playing these extremely high notes.

The trumpet has a natural dynamic curve, which means the higher the note, the more power and projection. The bottom three notes, F♯, G, and A♭ tend to be a bit dull and flabby. They do not balance well with higher pitches and tend to be covered by lower instruments playing in the same register. The A below middle C is a more practical bottom note in ensemble writing. But within this practical range (A to high D), almost anything is possible. The trumpet possesses a full dynamic range in all registers. Soft entrances on high notes are difficult but not impossible. Wide slurs are possible, but slurs wider than an octave are troublesome. More than one large leap in the same direction is difficult. Also remember that volume can affect flexibility. It is wise to avoid wide or awkward leaps at loud volumes. The trumpeter is most comfortable with scale passages and intervals that follow the overtone system.

Even though the trumpet is the lead voice in the ensemble, care should be taken not to overwrite for it. Frequent rests, even if they are brief, are necessary to keep the embouchure fresh. (This applies to the other brasses as well.)

Many trumpet players own instruments pitched in other keys, especially the C trumpet and the piccolo trumpet. Do not be persuaded to write for these trumpets in a jazz ensemble. Even if it might make high passages a bit easier (and that is debatable), the tone quality is totally uncharacteristic.

The **cornet**, also pitched in B♭ with the same range and transposition as the trumpet, was widely used in early jazz. But due to the increasing popularity of larger ensembles, the trumpet became the instrument of choice because of its greater carrying power. The cornet, with its softer, mellower tone, cannot compete with the trumpet at louder dynamic levels. Its use in recent years has been confined to small groups, where it functions effectively.

Flugelhorn

The flugelhorn was a mainstay of brass bands in the early twentieth century, but did not gain popularity in jazz until the 1950s. Now, most trumpet players double on flugelhorn. Because of its shape and bigger bell, it looks larger than the trumpet. However, it is pitched the same as the B♭ trumpet, transposing up a major second. Theoretically, it has the same range as the trumpet, but in practice this is not the case. Players normally use mouthpieces with deeper cups that make the low notes easy to produce and emphasize the warm, mellow tone, but make the high notes sound pinched and out of focus. A good practical range for the flugelhorn in ensemble writing is shown below.

EXAMPLE 10-32.

The flugelhorn is an extremely effective solo instrument in its middle register, and sounds best when played *mf*. At louder volumes it can sound strained. The tone of the flugelhorn in its first octave is very French horn-like. It blends with woodwinds well and when combined with trombones, the effect is warm and lush.

When changing from trumpet to flugelhorn or vice versa, observe the same rules set out previously in this chapter for the woodwinds. Allow at least five to eight seconds to make the switch; longer if the trumpet is muted.

Trombones

The **tenor trombone** is actually pitched in B♭. But, as is the case with most bass clef instruments, it is written in concert pitch and no transposition is necessary. In jazz writing, the tenor trombone is referred to simply as trombone. The sounding range is comparable to the trumpet, but one octave lower.

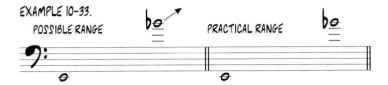

EXAMPLE 10-33.
POSSIBLE RANGE   PRACTICAL RANGE

Many trombonists have expanded the upper limits of the range considerably, but it is not wise to write above the given range, except possibly for solo passages.

Most trombonists today can read the tenor clef as well as bass, which eliminates a lot of ledger lines in high passages. This practice, however, has never been adapted in jazz scoring. Therefore, expect a lot of ledger lines in trombone parts; trombonists are accustomed to reading them. In fact, they prefer them rather than having the part written an octave lower with the designation *8va* above it.

The size of the bore and bell can affect the tone quality of the trombone significantly. Many prefer a smaller bore that has a bright, intense quality and is easier to play in the high register. Others use a larger bore that produces a fuller, darker tone. Lead players usually play smaller-bore horns because of their brighter, more compact sound; lower-part players prefer larger-bore horns for their rounder, more spread sound.

In its first octave and a half, the trombone is strong and fairly agile. However, many passages can be difficult in this range. This is because rapid alternation between extreme positions may be necessary and the fact that there are few alternate positions available in this register. The following passage would be impossible at fast, or even moderate speeds.

EXAMPLE 10-34.

From middle C upward, all of the notes can be played in one of the first three positions, which makes fast passages easier to execute. In order to write correctly for the trombone, the arranger needs to know the seven positions of the instrument and the overtone series of these notes.

The **bass trombone** is now a standard member of the jazz brass section. To improve flexibility in the lower part of the range and eliminate the necessity for using extreme positions, many performers choose a tenor trombone with an F attachment. This extra tubing also extends the lower range to B♭, and the larger bore makes the low notes quite strong. But the longer tubing also increases the distance between positions, so when the F attachment is used, there are only six positions.

EXAMPLE 10-35.

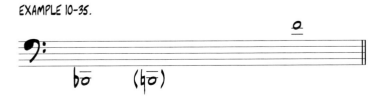

Notice that the low B natural is not available. Therefore a second set of tubing, called the E attachment, is sometimes added to make the B natural possible. An instrument with these two attachments, combined with a larger bore and bell makes a very effective bass instrument with a solid low register and very powerful tone. The ranges for the bass trombone are as follows.

EXAMPLE 10-36.

French Horn

The French horn is pitched in F and transposes up a perfect fifth.

EXAMPLE 10-37.

It has a wider range than the other brass and requires the use of both treble and bass clefs. The transposition is the same for both clefs.

To meet the range demands of modern horn music, all professional hornists play a double horn. This instrument has two sets of tubing: one in F and the other in B♭. This is not the arranger's concern. The part should be written in F and the performer will decide which set of tubing to use.

The lowest octave of the horn (from F♯ to F♯ in bass clef) has very little projection and is easily covered by other instruments. The most useful range is shown below.

EXAMPLE 10-38.

This is easily notated in the treble clef. The very high register (G to C) is brilliant and at loud volumes can produce a great deal of excitement. High trumpet lines are frequently doubled by one or more French horns an octave lower, with good effect. This places both instruments in a brilliant, assertive register.

EXAMPLE 10-39.

Because of the backward projection of the instrument and the covered sound produced by the hand over the bell, the horn does not compete successfully with the other brasses at volumes above *mf*. The accepted rule is that at dynamic levels above *mf*, two horns are required to match one trumpet or trombone. Proper miking, especially in the recording studio, can alleviate this situation.

An interesting effect accomplished on the French horn is the *stopped horn*, which is produced by inserting the right hand into the bell as far as possible. The effect is a sharp, nasal sound. It is usually used on single notes, occasionally on soft passages, but is especially affective on *sfz* attacks. The symbol is a "+" sign placed over the note. To resume normal playing, place an "o" over the note. Stopped notes should not be written below middle C.

It is important not to compare the written registers of the horn with the parallel written registers of the trumpet. When the trumpet is in its second octave, the horn is entering its third. At this point, the partials are very close together, making soft entrances and awkward leaps riskier on the horn than on the trumpet.

When horns are available they can be a very valuable middle voice in the ensemble. They blend well with all the brass and woodwind instruments and are effective on both melodies and countermelodies.

Tuba

The tuba is in concert pitch and sounds as written.

EXAMPLE 10-40.

Modern tubas are pitched in either B♭ or C, commonly referred to as *BB♭* or *CC*. The B♭ tuba is found more often in wind groups, and the C is more popular in orchestras. The choice of instrument is not the arranger's concern; parts are written in concert pitch with the player making the necessary transpositions.

Most modern tubas are equipped with a fourth valve that lowers the fundamental (either B♭ or C) a perfect fourth, extending the low register even further. A practical range for the tuba is as follows:

EXAMPLE 10-41.

However, most tuba parts in a jazz ensemble should be written within the following range.

EXAMPLE 10-42.

Here the tuba can match the other brass instruments in terms of agility, attack, and dynamic range. The tone quality in this range is round and mellow. It is less piercing than the bass trombone, but blends well with trombones and French horns.

Brass Mutes

There are mutes available for all brass instruments. A variety of mutes are available for the trumpet and trombone, but only *straight mutes* are used with the tuba, and the French horn uses a straight mute and sometimes another mute called a *brass mute*. And although mutes are made for the flugelhorn, they are almost never used. Therefore, the mutes discussed below apply only to the trumpet and trombone.

The **straight mute** is the most commonly used mute in symphony orchestras, but probably the least used in jazz. It has the widest dynamic range of all the mutes, from *pp* to *ff*. The straight mute possesses a crisp, pungent quality and is best utilized in staccato passages or punch chords. It can be used in sustained harmonies, or pads, but is not the best choice for slow, melodic passages. The metal straight is the overwhelming choice over the fiberboard or plastic varieties.

The **cup mute** produces a more muffled, rather nasal tone, with very little edge. The dynamic range is more limited than the straight mute. There are basically two types of cup mutes. One fits snugly against the bell and produces a muffled tone with almost no projection. It works best as a solo mute or in small ensembles. The other type has scalloped edges, which permits more air to escape. It has more bite and better projection and is the preferred choice in large ensembles. The cup is also a very versatile mute. It blends well with woodwinds and can be used in most types of melodic passages.

The **Harmon mute** is made of metal and has a stem in the middle that can be moved in and out or removed completely. The current trend is to play it without the stem. When the stem is removed, the sound is rather unfocused with an edgy, buzzing quality. Its unique sound makes it a popular choice of color for a solo trumpet, or for use in combination with other instruments, particularly saxophone and flute. It has very little dynamic range since all of the sound is forced through the small opening in the center. A large amount of air is necessary to produce a tone. The amount of air that a trumpeter would expend to produce an open *ff* would result in *mp* at best with a Harmon mute. This should be considered when writing dynamic markings for the Harmon. The trombone Harmon has a dull, tinny sound that most people find unpleasant. Trombones with cup mutes, or even straight mutes, are a better combination with Harmon-muted trumpets.

The **plunger** is actually the same as a plumber's plunger, without the stick. Its use as a muting device originated in jazz, but is finding its way into other types of music. The plunger is not as easy to play as it might seem. If it is not placed in precisely the right position in reference to the bell, the tone will break up. When it is placed tightly over the bell, a stuffy, popping sound is produced. The most common effect is the alternation of closed and open sounds. This is indicated by placing a "+" over the closed notes and an "o" over the open notes. While most trumpeters and trombonists are proficient with this "+ and o" maneuver, few are really adept at the subtle manipulations that are required to play an effective plunger solo. Many plunger soloists use a small straight mute called a **pixie mute** that, when inserted into the bell, makes the plunger easier to manipulate without the tone breaking up.

The **bucket mute**, when clamped over the bell, produces a soft, mellow tone with no edge. It has not yet gained universal acceptance, so not all players own one. Do not write for it unless you are sure that all the players have one. Practically the same effect can be achieved by simply instructing the players to play softly "in the stand."

Any photograph of a band from the thirties or forties will show that the **hat** was once standard equipment for brass players. Like the bucket, it can significantly reduce the volume and intensity of the sound without distorting it. It could also be held over the bell to muffle the tone like a plunger, or waved back and forth to achieve a "+ and o" effect. It is seldom used today.

When switching from either open trumpet to a muted one, fluegelhorn to an open or muted trumpet (and vice versa), or one mute to another, indicate the change in the same manner as woodwind instrument changes; immediately after the last note before the mute insertion or instrument change is to occur. The term "to Harmon" or "to cup" should be written just above the staff (the word "mute" is not necessary in these directions).

EXAMPLE 10-43.

If the switch involves a change from flugelhorn to muted trumpet, indicate both the trumpet and mute changes in the same instruction (i.e., "to trumpet w/ Harmon"). To discontinue use of a mute, write the word "open" after the last muted note.

EXAMPLE 10-44.

To specify a mute at the beginning of an arrangement, write the name of the mute over the staff just before the first entrance (i.e., "cup"). Allow the player a few seconds to insert or remove the mute. If the situation requires removing one mute and inserting another, more time is needed since the player has only one free hand. Brass players do not appreciate very fast mute changes that might result in either dropping the mute or denting the bell of the instrument.

A final word about the material in this chapter and the two that follow: One may be apt to treat this information as dry, and not grasp the full significance of its importance. Serious arrangers will soon realize that the only way to write successfully is by possessing a thorough knowledge of the instruments, and they should also make the acquisition of this knowledge an ongoing part of their education. The arranger who writes parts that are challenging but also accessible and musical, will command the respect and admiration of the players, and in the process, receive a better performance of the music.

CHAPTER 11
Large Ensemble Horn Sections

This chapter will explore the distinctive personalities of the saxophone, trumpet, and trombone as sections of the large jazz ensemble commonly known as the *big band*.

Saxophone Section

The saxophone section is the only one of the three groups that contains a full choir. It has grown in size through the years from its original orchestration of three parts (two altos and tenor) to today's traditional five parts (two altos, two tenors, and baritone; or soprano, alto, two tenors, and baritone). Some deviations on this arrangement that have occurred throughout jazz history include the sax sections of Woody Herman (four saxes: three tenors and baritone), Gerry Mulligan (four saxes: alto, two tenors, and baritone), Maynard Ferguson (four saxes: two altos, tenor, and baritone, or alto, two tenors, and baritone), Stan Kenton (five saxes: alto, two tenors, and two baritones), Bob Florence (six saxes: two altos, two tenors, and two baritones), Clare Fischer (six saxes: two altos, two tenors, baritone, and bass), as well as the sax sections for Broadway and Las Vegas show books (two altos, tenor, and baritone).

The range of the sax section from lowest instrument to highest exceeds three-and-a-half octaves with alto as the lead instrument, and four octaves with soprano as the lead.

EXAMPLE 11-1.

This large expanse permits this section to be harmonized easily with any voicing type, from close cluster voicings to spacious spread voicings.

EXAMPLE 11-2.

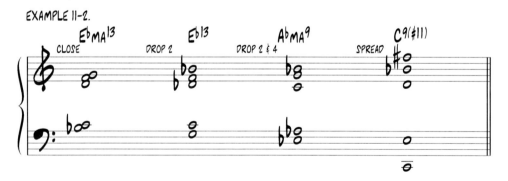

It is typically the most active horn section with the most virtuosic parts due to the relative ease with which the instruments can be played. Solis are typical for this section, ranging from lush ballads to notey, bebop-oriented lines.

Since there are traditionally five instruments in this section, solis can be written in several manners. Because these harmonizations involve like instruments, the timbre is always homogenous, no matter how far the voices are spread. The concept of four-note close-position voicings with doubled lead has existed since the swing era. The group Supersax re-popularized this sound in the seventies by performing harmonized versions of Charlie Parker's improvisations orchestrated in this manner.

EXAMPLE II-3.

TRACK 76
Part 1

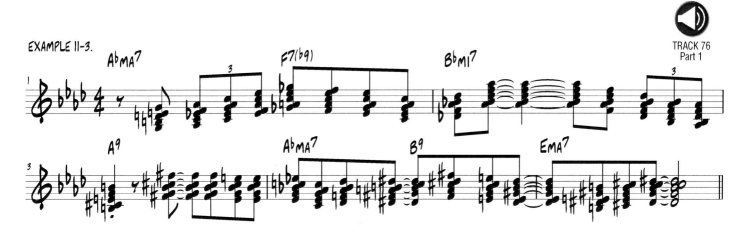

Other interesting textures can be created by using four-note drop-two or drop-two-and-four voicings with doubled lead, or five-note close drop-two or drop-two-and-four voicings.

EXAMPLE II-4.

TRACK 76
Part 2

Each of these works well for the saxophone section, assuming that the melody note is high enough to accommodate the more-open voicings.

As mentioned above, there are two options for the lead voice of the section: alto or soprano. Alto, the more traditional of the two, blends very well with the rest of the section because of its round sound and the fact that there are two of the same instruments present. The soprano has a lighter and brighter sound.

Since there are three or four different-pitched instruments in the sax section, unisons involving all five can be challenging to achieve due to the relatively small coincidence of unison pitches between the baritone and the alto or soprano. Baritone and alto share approximately one-and-a-half octaves of unison pitches, while baritone and soprano share one octave.

EXAMPLE 11-5.

If any line exceeds this range, there are three options. The first is to eliminate the instruments whose range is exceeded. In Example 11-6, letter A exceeds the baritone sax range midway through the phrase and would be written for altos and tenors only. In letter B, the line drops below the alto sax range at its midpoint and would be written for tenors and baritone only.

EXAMPLE 11-6.

TRACK 77

The second option is to dovetail the parts to accommodate the line. In the next example, the baritone begins the line and is joined by the tenors and then altos when it moves into each instrument's range. Notice that the tenor and alto entrances occur at the beginnings of phrase segments.

EXAMPLE 11-7.

TRACK 78
Part 1

The third option is to switch from unison to octaves to accommodate the out-of-range notes. This adds weight to the line. When transitioning between the two, make every effort to minimize awkward melodic movement. In the next example, the switch occurs at the beginning of the phrase segment in measure 3.

EXAMPLE 11-8.

TRACK 78
Part 2

Octaves are easily achieved in the sax section. One octave is typical and usually sufficient. The split can be made a number of ways with each resulting in subtle differences. The next four examples use the same melodic line at various transpositions to illustrate these options.

The first division places the top four saxes on the top note, while the baritone plays the bottom one. This provides a sufficient amount of weight to the line without being too ponderous.

EXAMPLE 11-9.

TRACK 79
Part 1

Another option puts the top three saxes on the top, while the second tenor and baritone play the bottom. This arrangement places a bit more emphasis on the lower note without overtaking the top. It is often used when the top note of a line lies consistently near the top of the tenor range where there is a possibility of intonation problems between the two tenors.

EXAMPLE 11-10.

TRACK 79
Part 2

These first two splits (Examples 11-9 and 11-10) are most commonly used as they retain focus on the top note. The next two splits place the emphasis on the bottom. One puts the top two saxes on the top note and both tenors and baritone on the bottom. This division often comes into play when a high-register line consistently exceeds the tenor range.

EXAMPLE 11-11.

TRACK 80
Part 1

The final possible split puts all the saxes except the top one on the bottom note. This places all the focus on the bottom note. This division is not common, but is sometimes used when the soprano is the lead voice of the section and the line exceeds the range of the alto.

EXAMPLE 11-12.

TRACK 80
Part 2

Two-octave splits are also possible in the sax section: altos (or soprano and alto) on the top note, tenors in the middle, and baritone on the bottom. However, this often produces an undesirably heavy sound. Nevertheless, it can be very effective when used on the final note or two of a line for emphasis.

EXAMPLE 11-13.

TRACK 80
Part 3

Alternate timbral possibilities are achieved in the sax section through the use of woodwind doubles. The bands of Duke Ellington and Glenn Miller popularized the sound of clarinet lead with the sax section (see below) and even five-part harmonized clarinet pads and solis were common in many of the bands of the era. Later, flutes and bass clarinet were added to the arsenal. Today, the most typical combination is that of two flutes (traditionally placed in the top two parts), two clarinets (traditionally placed in the third and fourth parts), and bass clarinet (traditionally placed in the baritone part), though all professional saxophonists are expected to play both flute and clarinet. Additionally, bass clarinet is expected as a standard double for baritone saxophonists.

There are several other combinations of these woodwinds that are of interest. Each produces a uniquely different sound. (The list below also contains the combination mentioned in the last paragraph for the sake of presenting a complete list.)

- Four or five flutes
- Four or five clarinets
- Four flutes and bass clarinet
- Four clarinets and bass clarinet
- One flute, three clarinets, and bass clarinet (or four clarinets)
- Two flutes, two clarinets, and bass clarinet (or three clarinets)
- Three flutes, one clarinet, and bass clarinet (or two clarinets)

Obviously, there are more woodwind choices than flute, clarinet, and bass clarinet. The other woodwinds that have been used in large ensemble writing include the piccolo, alto flute, oboe, English horn, and bassoon. (The bass flute as well as the E♭ soprano, alto, and contrabass clarinets, and contrabassoon have rarely, if ever, been used in jazz ensemble writing.) These instruments should never be written for without prior knowledge that there are saxophonists who not only own these instruments, but can also play them.

When writing for woodwinds, allow enough time for the player to switch from one instrument to another. For a more detailed discussion of this topic and how to indicate instrument changes, see chapter 10.

Two stylistic clarinet lead textures that were mentioned above are those associated with the Glenn Miller and Duke Ellington bands. In both situations, the clarinet lead is played in its *clarion* and *altissimo* registers. The Glenn Miller sound is written entirely in four-note close-position voicings with the lead voice doubled an octave below.

EXAMPLE 11-14.

TRACK 81
Part 1

Due to the higher melody notes and close-position voicing, this texture was played by clarinet, two altos, and two tenors because, in many cases, the bottom note of the voicing would exceed the baritone sax range. In this case, the baritone must either play lead clarinet or, if the lead alto plays lead clarinet, the baritone must play alto.

The clarinet lead texture created by Duke Ellington places the clarinet atop the rest of the section using five-note voicings without a doubled lead. These voicings are always in open position, often containing several fourths.

TRACK 81
Part 2

EXAMPLE 11-15.

In Duke's band, the second tenor always played lead clarinet, so the instrumentation for this texture involved clarinet, two altos, tenor, and baritone.

Trumpet Section

Like the saxophones, this section has also experienced growth throughout jazz history. During the transitional period from Dixieland to swing, the section was comprised of only two players. In the prime of the big-band era, there were traditionally three trumpets. Later, four became the norm, though many bands still used only three, such as Maynard Ferguson's Birdland Dream Band (not including Maynard) and Gerry Mulligan's Concert Jazz Band. In the 1940s, Woody Herman and Stan Kenton began using five trumpets, and contemporary bands such as Clare Fischer's, Bob Brookmeyer's New Art Orchestra, the Bob Florence Limited Edition, the WDR Big Band, the Danish Radio Orchestra, and the Stockholm Jazz Orchestra continue this concept. Since four is the prevailing number in most large ensembles, the examples below reflect this. Writing for five will be discussed briefly at the end of this section.

The trumpet section is written almost exclusively in close position, though occasionally a drop-two can be applied to eliminate a major second occurring between the top notes of consecutive voicings. This drop will lend more clarity to the melody by eliminating the second interval at the top.

TRACK 82
Part 1

EXAMPLE 11-16.

Drop-two voicings can also be applied to accommodate section players with limited-range capabilities.

TRACK 82
Part 2

EXAMPLE 11-17.

Section solis are least common in the trumpet section. This is due in part to the brightness of the horn as well as its range. Most trumpet solis are written with the melody in the upper register of the horn. This places all the parts in a comfortable range with no balance problems. However, if a four- or five-note voicing is retained when the melody nears middle C, the problem is not one of clarity, but one of projection. Here, the lower voices of the section will invariably be placed on notes that cannot be played loudly enough to balance up to the lead line.

EXAMPLE 11-18.

TRACK 83
Part 1

The solution is to reduce the voicing to two or three notes, or even to a unison.

EXAMPLE 11-19.

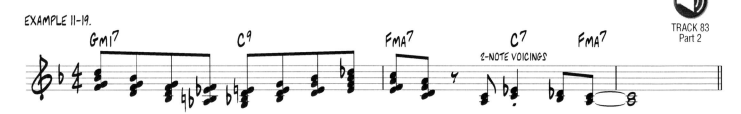

TRACK 83
Part 2

Generally speaking, the concept of harmonizing the trumpet section by itself is less common among today's arrangers. Classic trumpet solis such as Count Basie's "920 Special" and Woody Herman's "Apple Honey" sound dated by today's standards, partially due to their simple harmonizations. Even with the application of more complex harmonies, this concept has yet to be embraced. Instead, the section is more typically harmonized with the support of either or both of the other two horn sections. However, some great examples of modern trumpet soli writing can be found in Gordon Goodwin's "Count Bubba" and "Count Bubba's Revenge," and the harmonization of Clifford Brown's solo on "Cherokee" as performed by the GRP Big Band.

Since all the instruments in the trumpet section are pitched the same, unisons are obviously not problematic. However, considerations should be given to the lower-part players of the section. Even in professional groups, these players should not be expected to play extended passages above the staff. A general rule of thumb would be not to exceed a written C two octaves above middle C in these parts. The following example shows a line that would be considerably out of range for most trumpet section players.

EXAMPLE 11-20.

For less-experienced groups, this top note should be lowered, sometimes as far down as G atop the staff for middle and high school bands.

There are two practical ways to achieve an octave split. The most common option is to place the first and second parts on the top note and the other parts on the bottom one. This achieves the correct balance between the two pitches.

TRACK 84
Part 1

EXAMPLE 11-21.

A second option is used when the line is too high for all but the lead player. In this case, only the lead player plays the top note while the rest of the section plays the bottom one.

TRACK 84
Part 2

EXAMPLE 11-22.

The lowest trumpet can also play fluegelhorn while the rest of the section plays trumpet. This is done to bridge the timbral gap between the trumpets and trombones in lieu of a French horn. In many cases, this fifth part also functions as the lead voice of the trombone section.

TRACK 85

EXAMPLE 11-23.

Alternate timbral possibilities are achieved in the trumpet section in three ways. Since the sound of a trumpet emanates solely from the bell, the section can play with the bell into the stand. This softens the brassy qualities of the horn and is sometimes used as a substitute for a bucket mute or fluegelhorns. The fluegelhorn is the second timbral alternative. A section of four or five fluegelhorns, whether in unison or harmonized, offers a mellower option to the open trumpet. Lastly, other timbres can be accomplished through the use of mutes. The qualities of these were discussed in detail in chapter 10. An entire section playing the same type of mute can provide a welcome contrast to open horns, and sounds good whether in unison, octaves, or harmonized.

Different mutes can also be combined within the section with open trumpets, fluegelhorns, or other mutes. The section should be split equally between the two different sounds. The following are some typical examples of these combinations:

- Open trumpet and fluegelhorn
- Open trumpet and harmon mute
- Open trumpet and cup mute
- Fluegelhorn and harmon mute
- Fluegelhorn and cup mute
- Cup mute and harmon mute

These combinations should only be used for unisons or octaves.

Refer once again to chapter 10 for information on allowing enough time when changing instruments or mutes.

Trombone Section

The trombone section consists of a combination of tenor and bass trombones. The standard number of players is four, using either three tenors and one bass or two tenors and two basses. In the transitional period between Dixieland and swing, the tenor trombone remained a solitary instrument, adding only one more player, another tenor trombone, during the prime of the big-band era in the 1930s. Eventually, this number grew to three as the big band expanded, first with yet another tenor trombone, and then with a bass trombone. This switch from tenor to bass trombone as the third horn in the section contributed greatly to the depth of the section as well as the entire band. Finally, a fourth horn (a third tenor trombone), was added to the section, bringing the configuration to its current status.

Similar to the other horn sections, variations on the four-trombone section exist, both in the past and present day. In the mid forties, Stan Kenton introduced the jazz world to the five-member section, using four tenors and one bass. The five-trombone section never caught on as standard instrumentation. However, those bands that aspire to the Kentonian tradition use this format, sometimes using four tenors and one bass. Other combinations include three tenors and two basses; three tenors, one bass, and tuba; and two tenors, two basses, and tuba.

Aside from Stan Kenton, an accounting of trombone-section numbers that oppose the traditional four in the past fifty years include the GRP Big Band with one trombone, Maynard Ferguson's Birdland Dream Band of the fifties and Tadd Dameron with two, Gerry Mulligan's Concert Jazz Band, Buddy Rich, Woody Herman, and Dave Holland with three, and Stan Kenton with five.

All voicing types are possible for the trombone section. Spread and chorale voicings are exceptionally rich due to the round sound and range of the instruments.

EXAMPLE 11-24.

Close-position voicings are particularly effective when writing solis. The only possible hazard when harmonizing the trombone section is writing a voicing that is too low, thereby creating a muddy or ambiguous sound as shown in the next example.

EXAMPLE 11-25.

TRACK 86
Part 1

The solution, as with the other sections, is to reduce the voicing to just two or three lines or even a unison.

EXAMPLE 11-26.

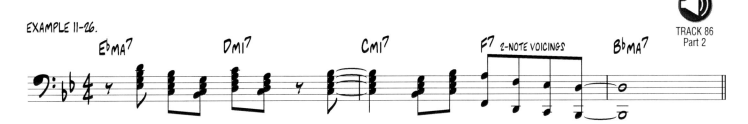

TRACK 86
Part 2

There is only one consideration when writing unisons for the trombone section, since they are all pitched the same. The bass trombone is usually written no higher than D above middle C (though many bass trombonists have the capability to play far above this note), so if the unison line extends consistently beyond this note, the section should either be split into octaves or the bass trombone should *tacet*. The next example shows such a case where the unison line changes to octaves to accommodate the notes out of range of the bass trombone.

EXAMPLE 11-27.

TRACK 87
Part 1

When writing octaves for the section, the most typical split places the tenor trombones on the top note and the bass trombone on the bottom. This works well for sections that use one bass trombone as well as those that use two. The section that uses three tenor trombones and one bass can also utilize the "two voices high, two voices low" split, provided the lower note doesn't extend too low for the tenor trombone.

TRACK 87
Part 2

EXAMPLE 11-28.

Due to the lower range of the instrument, another important concern when writing octaves for the trombone section is whether the lower note adds too much weight to the line, making it sound ponderous as in Example 11-29.

EXAMPLE 11-29.

The available alternate timbres for the trombone section include playing in the stand and the use of mutes. An entire section playing cup, plunger, or bucket mutes (again, the straight mute is rarely used) offers a few more colorations for the large ensemble. These sound good in all situations: unisons, octaves, and harmonized. Unlike the trumpets, the trombone section rarely combines open horns and mutes. Also remember that trombones need time to insert or remove mutes (see chapter 10).

Yet another color possibility for the trombone section, though not a common one, is the use of the baritone or euphonium. The conical bore of this horn provides a very round, spread sound that is better used when writing pads or music that is less rhythmic in nature. This sound was used as far back as the 1930s and 1940s in Claude Thornhill's band and recently on Don Sebesky's CD tribute to Bill Evans.

French Horn & Tuba

Although not considered standard instruments of the big band, the French horn and tuba have enjoyed recurring roles in the large ensemble throughout jazz history. In the big-band era, Claude Thornhill's band was well-known for its inclusion of two French horns and tuba in the ensemble. Both instruments were prominently featured on Miles Davis' *Birth of the Cool.* Tadd Dameron used a single French horn in his big band. Stan Kenton introduced the world to the concept of a fourth horn section in the large ensemble by adding four bell-front French horns, called *mellophoniums*, to his big band. Another innovative bandleader, Don Ellis, chose to replace the traditional trombone, section with a lower-brass section consisting of French horn, tenor trombone, bass trombone, and tuba. In the eighties, Rob McConnell included two French horns in his band, while the Mel Lewis Jazz Orchestra added one.

Though these horns have not gained a consistent role in the big band, it is important to understand why and how they are used in the large ensemble. Chapter 10 contains an in-depth discussion of the idiosyncrasies of both instruments. The following information is meant to supplement that.

The French horn, as a single instrument, is often used to bridge the timbral gap between the bright sound of the trumpet section and the round sound of the trombones. In addition to fitting into the middle of the brass section, it also works well as a lead voice atop the trombone section.

TRACK 88
Part 1

EXAMPLE II–30.

The French horn is also an effective solo instrument and combines well with woodwinds. However, due to the backward projection and the covered sound, one French horn cannot compete with a loud big band.

The tuba can provide a full, round sound at the bottom of the big band. Its presence as a bass instrument in the horn ensemble is unmistakable.

TRACK 88
Part 2

EXAMPLE II–31.

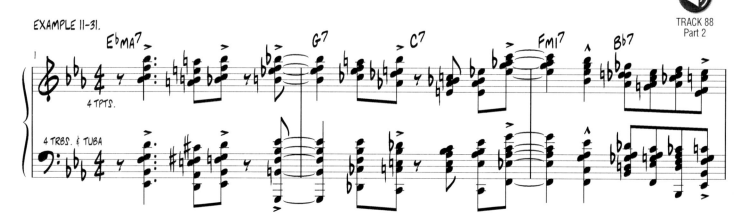

However, due to this tremendous sound, it should not play anything but bass notes/bass lines. If placed on any other notes, its sound will overtake the bassist and cause harmonic confusion. For this reason, it cannot merely be substituted for the bass trombone in all situations, because the bass trombone does not always play bass notes.

CHAPTER 12
Rhythm Section

The rhythm section provides both the harmonic and rhythmic foundation for any group. The instruments in this group include guitar, piano, bass, and drums. Some rhythm sections use either piano or guitar (and not both), based on the premise that their functions are similar and they could conflict with one another, especially in comping situations. However, these two instruments possess such unique qualities and orchestrational possibilities that there is an undeniable need for both in a complete rhythm section.

Too many arrangers tend to treat rhythm section writing as an afterthought. Failure to thoroughly consider all the available timbral possibilities may produce parts that contain little more than endless measures of chord slashes. An extreme example of this is the creation of a single, composite part for the entire rhythm section on one staff.

EXAMPLE 12-1.

Notice the absence of any textual cues as to what each specific instrument should be playing. All the decisions have been left to the players. Assuming this composite has been given to a guitar, piano, bass, and drum section, several questions immediately appear for each member:

- Piano and guitar: Are both of us comping at the same time? In measures 3–4, do I play the bass notes or tacet?

- Bass: Should I walk through the chord slashes or float the time? In measures 3–4, are these bass notes transposed for me or are they in concert pitch?

- Drums: Should I play time through this entire section, even through the rest in measure 5, or should it be treated as a break? In measure 3, should I just kick these figures or play time through them? In measure 4, should I play nothing, time, or a fill?

The other extreme presents the same one-staff composite part overflowing with cues.

EXAMPLE 12-2.

This example is also confusing as each player has to read all the cues to find the pertinent ones.

Though the idea of writing a single-staff composite rhythm section part is possible in a few situations, it shows a lack of creativity on the arranger's part and should rarely be considered.

Another shortcut takes the same information presented in Example 12-2 and places it on a grand staff.

EXAMPLE 12-3.

Though this spreads the information out so that the cues are much less crowded, it also creates rhythm section parts that are twice as long as they would normally be. This is another shortcut that should rarely be considered.

A head-to-head comparison of these two methods with a full score will clearly illustrate the importance of writing separate parts with detailed instructions for each instrument.

EXAMPLE 12-4.

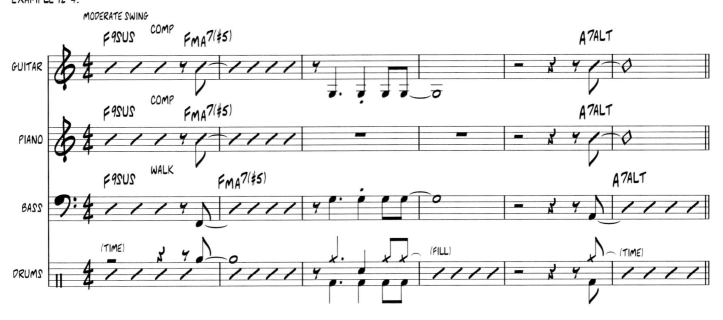

The general rule concerning rhythm section writing is to provide each player with the proper amount of information. In most cases, each part will be slightly different. The difficulty of the music and the ability of the players should dictate the amount of information provided on each part.

In addition to the information presented here, there are many books that explain the concepts specific to each instrument in greater detail. A listing of these can be found at the end of this chapter.

Piano

The piano, with a span of over seven octaves, has the widest range of any acoustic instrument.

EXAMPLE 12-5. PIANO RANGE

Staves

In most situations, the piano part is written on one staff, though it can be written on two, if necessary. If on one staff, it does not have to be written exclusively in either treble or bass clef; it can switch from one to the other to accommodate any specific notation.

EXAMPLE 12-6.

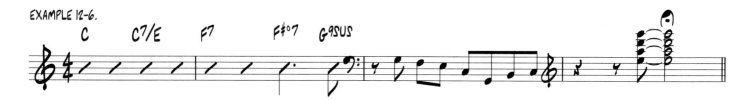

There are two situations that require a two-stave piano part:

- Notated chord voicings that span a large range require the second stave in order to eliminate an inordinate number of ledger lines.

EXAMPLE 12-7.

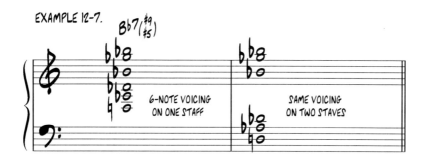

- Two entirely different lines may occur in each hand.

EXAMPLE 12-8.

A piano part can also switch from one to two staves at any time.

Generally speaking, piano voicings are best left to the pianist. However, these should be written out when specific voicings are desired or when writing music for beginning bands where the pianist needs assistance.

Types of Notation

There are six different notation possibilities for piano. They are listed below from most to least specific, followed by a description of what the pianist will do when presented with each notation type.

- **Single lines and fully-notated chords**: Everything is played exactly as written.

- **Top note of voicing with chord symbols**: Each note of the melodic line is played as a vertical sonority. Rhythms and chord qualities are played exactly as notated using the written line as the top note of the voicing. The type of voicing (close, open, or spread) is at the discretion of the pianist. The top line of the example below shows the two methods of indicating this. The first, and more common method combines the melodic line with chord symbols placed above, while the second includes an "x" notehead in addition to the melody note. The inclusion of this character helps to differentiate these vertical sonorities from a single line with chord voicings comped randomly beneath it (usually with the left hand as in Example 12-13). The second line of the example illustrates how this might be played, but that the type of voicing is ultimately left to the pianist.

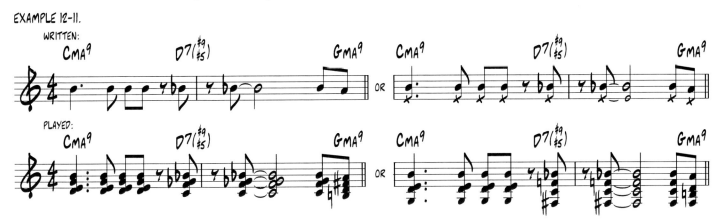

- **Chord symbols with rhythmic notation**: Each rhythm is played as a vertical sonority. Rhythms and chord qualities are played exactly as notated. The type of voicing, including the top note, is at the discretion of the pianist. The bottom line shows just two of many possibilities.

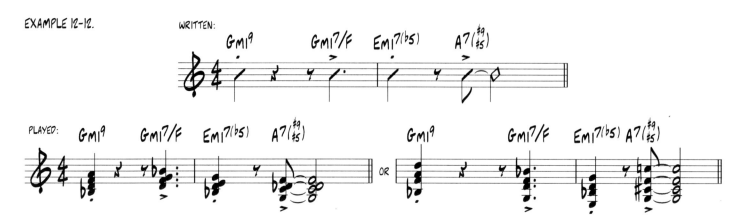

- **Single line with chord symbols**: This looks similar to lead sheet notation and is used when the pianist is playing the melody as a soloist. The basic melody line and chord changes are followed; however, the pianist is free to embellish the rhythms, harmonies, and texture (in other words, the melody does not have to be played as a single line in the right hand with chord changes comping in the left). This type of notation is also used in vocal arrangements and rubato instrumental solo passages, and in these cases, the melody line is indicated as a cue for the pianist and is not actually played.

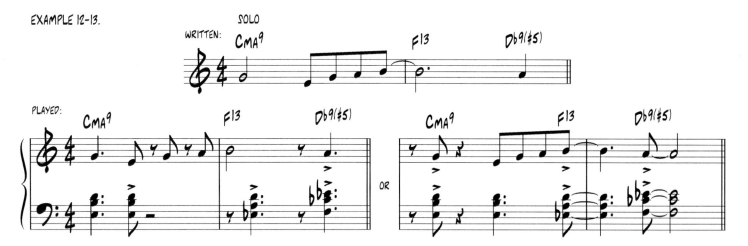

- **Chord symbols with slashes**: The pianist is free to improvise a rhythmic accompaniment (comp) using the indicated chords. The type of comp is dependent on the style of music.

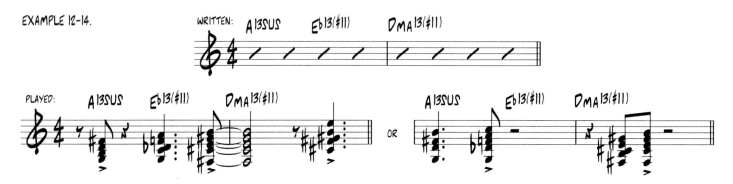

- **Combinations of any of the above**: Each type of notation is played as described above.

EXAMPLE 12-15.

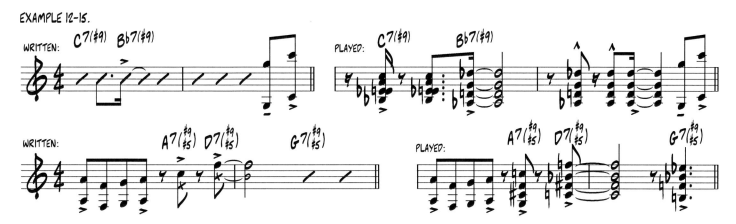

Chord densities usually vary within a chart. Detailed chord information should be provided when a horn section is playing specific sonorities or when thicker densities are essential to the style of the tune. The pianist should not embellish these further. Moreover, when the orchestration is dense and the harmonic rhythm is extremely quick (shout choruses are a good example of this), harmonic information should be omitted from the piano part in this section for three reasons:

- Due to the quick harmonic rhythm and chord density, the resulting part becomes difficult or impossible to play.

- A specific voicing has been orchestrated for the horns. Since a chord symbol does not provide a specific voicing, the pianist may clutter the ensemble's sound by playing a different voicing than the one already orchestrated.

- All the necessary harmonic information is being played by the horns. Piano voicings are redundant and unnecessary.

Basic chord qualities (no extensions and alterations) should be indicated in improvised solo sections involving only a soloist and rhythm section to allow for creativity. In these situations, the pianist is free to embellish chords to their logical density.

EXAMPLE 12-16.

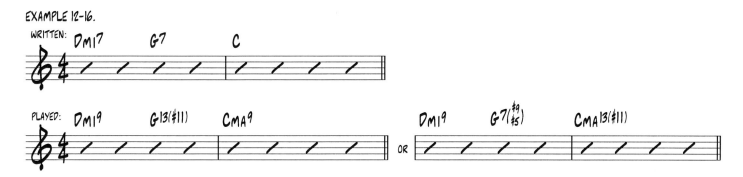

If a progression contains specific inner-voice movement, it should be notated within the slashes with the chord symbols above to clarify the desired line.

EXAMPLE 12-17.

The decision whether to notate specific rhythms or use slashes is dependent on each specific situation. Excessive use of rhythmic notation will hinder a pianist's creativity, but an insufficient amount may cause harmonic and rhythmic clashes. Consider each circumstance carefully before deciding which type of notation to use.

Guitar

The most important thing to know about the guitar is that it is a transposing instrument. It sounds an octave lower than written and transposes up that octave to concert pitch. A typical mistake is to disregard this transposition and write guitar parts that are an octave lower than desired.

EXAMPLE 12-18.

The range of the guitar is the sum of the ranges of all six strings. While the upper limits of each string are somewhat variable, a good rule of thumb is an octave plus a fifth. The next example first shows the open strings of the guitar followed by the (written) range of each string.

EXAMPLE 12-19.

The cumulative range of the six strings is:

EXAMPLE 12-20.

This three-and-a-half-octave range is more than any other instrument in the jazz ensemble except the piano, and encompasses most of the spectrum of the ensemble. However, it is always written in treble clef. It is not uncommon for guitar parts to contain notes both below and above the staff with several ledger lines. In extremely high passages, the use of the "8va" symbol is acceptable.

EXAMPLE 12-21.

Guitar parts employ the same six types of notation as the piano. Refer to the section on piano for descriptions and examples of these notations.

Too often, guitar parts contain only chord symbols and slashes. The guitar is such a remarkably versatile instrument that relegating it to merely interpreting chord symbols is a terrible waste. Despite being amplified, the guitar blends exceptionally well with all the instruments of the jazz ensemble. The two bottom strings are dark and somber; the middle two, mellow and rich; the top two, brilliant and penetrating. Interesting mixed colors can be obtained by combining the guitar with other instruments in unison. Or it can enrich a line by doubling it at the octave, either above or below. In single-line playing, the guitar is extremely agile, and in competent hands, has few limitations.

Guitar chord voicings are created in a different manner than the piano due to its tuning. Writing fully notated chords can be daunting at first. However, it is not necessary to be able to play the guitar in order to develop a comprehensive catalogue of idiomatic voicings. To formulate an initial concept of chord construction, visualize the tuning of the open strings (Example 12-19). They are tuned in perfect fourths, except for the major third between the second and third strings. It follows then, that voicings spaced in thirds and fourths are the most natural.

The following examples should be of assistance in beginning this process. All of the sample chords are constructed from C. They are in written notation, sounding an octave lower than shown.

- Four-note block voicings, which are comfortable on the piano, are difficult on the guitar, except on the four top strings. They are easiest to play in the upper register, where the frets are closer together. The following example shows some of the most useful block chords playable on the top four strings. The first seven of these constitute common chord types containing chord roots. They can either function as indicated or as rootless voicings (e.g., Cma7 can also be played as a rootless Ami9). The remaining three are intended for use solely as rootless voicings. One possible use is shown above each. The two notes at the end of the example indicate the possible range of all of these voicings. These notes represent the bottom note of the chord (i.e., the voicing indicated in the Cma7 chord could be used as a Cma7 with middle C as the bottom note, all the way up to top-line F as the bottom note).

EXAMPLE 12-22.

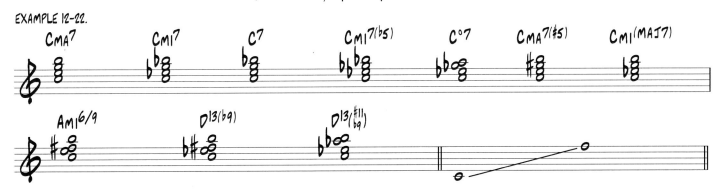

- Four-note drop-two chords are easily formed. The top four open strings form a drop-two Emi7.

EXAMPLE 12-23.

Below are drop-two voicings of the four common chord types (major, minor, dominant, and half diminished) in root position.

EXAMPLE 12-24.

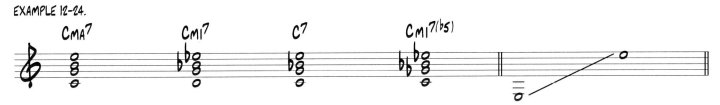

The inversions of these chords are also available. The following shows one example of this. Each chord is followed by two notes which indicate the lowest and highest possible bottom notes of each voicing (in this case, the seventh of the chord).

EXAMPLE 12-25.

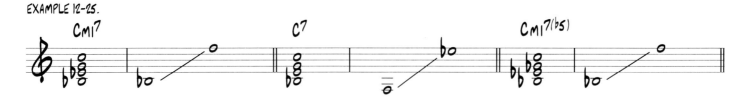

- Four-note drop-three chords are possible. The top five strings approximate a drop-three by deadening the fourth string. Skipping or deadening a string is common because it facilitates the use of wider intervals. Below are drop-three voicings of the four common chord types with their usable ranges.

EXAMPLE 12-26.

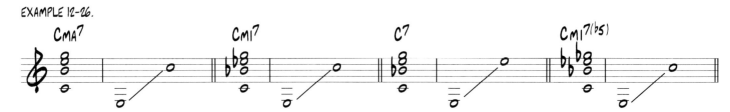

- Six-note chords are possible through the use of *barring* (one finger presses down on more than one string at the same time) and other techniques. These can also employ open strings and provide interesting sonorities. The following shows examples of both types. The ones using open strings are only playable as shown.

EXAMPLE 12-27.

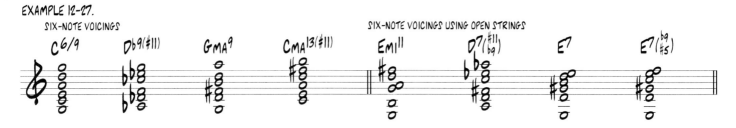

- There is a wide variety of available five-note chords. These are all playable within a few steps above and below the written C chords.

EXAMPLE 12-28.

- Some very interesting sonorities containing half steps and whole steps are possible. But these also involve open strings and are only available on certain pitches. The open string in the examples below is either E or B.

EXAMPLE 12-29.

When comping, guitarists frequently rely on two-note "cells" which are almost always guide tones. By adding an additional note above the cell, a variety of three-note chords can be constructed.

EXAMPLE 12-30.

With these cells (both two-note and three-note) as a foundation, another layer may be added above for additional tension. A choice of up to four different notes above each cell is possible.

EXAMPLE 12-31.

By combining all the possible choices for each layer above the two-note tritone cell, all forms of altered dominant ninth, eleventh, and thirteenth chords are available.

When scoring a tutti passage for large ensemble, a chordal guitar part is redundant. Single lines are more effective. But in a smaller group with two or three horns, a chordal guitar part can add considerable support. The following is an example of how the guitar might be used in such a setting to fill out the texture.

EXAMPLE 12-32.

TRACK 89

Bass

The bass is a transposing instrument, sounding one octave lower than written. Traditionally, both acoustic and electric basses have four strings tuned in perfect fourths. The example below shows the open strings and written and sounding ranges.

EXAMPLE 12-33.

Many orchestral bassists use a C attachment. This is an extension on the E string which makes all of the chromatic notes from the open E to the C below possible. This expanded range is shown in the next example.

EXAMPLE 12-34.

Most jazz bassists do not have this attachment, so be sure it is available before writing for it. If it is unavailable, another possibility is to ask the bassist to retune the E string. (This process is called *scordatura*). Most bassists would not object to doing this if it were for a good reason. The line in the following example could be played without jumping the octave by retuning the E string down to D. This could be done quickly with a few turns of the tuning peg.

EXAMPLE 12-35.

Due to the influence of many virtuoso performers (Jaco Pastorius, Jeff Berlin, etc.), many of today's electric basses are built with an extra one or two strings. Typically, one extra string is added at the bottom of the instrument and the second is added at the top. Assuming that each added string continues the perfect-fourth tuning, the range of the five-string bass is now extended downward by a fourth and the six-string instrument is expanded by a perfect fourth above and below, producing the following ranges:

EXAMPLE 12-36.

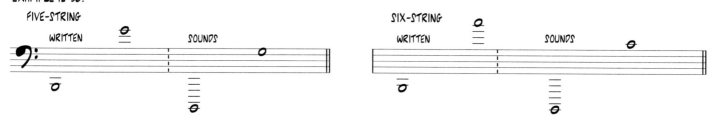

The principle of *scordatura* can also be applied to these basses, extending the possible downward range of the B string to an A.

Unless writing for a specific situation where arrangements will only be played by the same bassist, it is best to write within the confines of the original four-string tuning.

Types of Notation

There are only three types of notation found in bass parts. Again, they are listed from most to least specific with an explanation of what the bassist is expected to play when encountering each notation type.

- **Single lines**: Music is played exactly as written.

EXAMPLE 12-37.

- **Chord symbols with slashes**: The bassist is free to create a walking bass line or repetitive pattern using the indicated chords. The type of line or pattern is dependent on the style of music. The second line of the following example shows both a walking bass line and a repetitive pattern.

EXAMPLE 12-38.

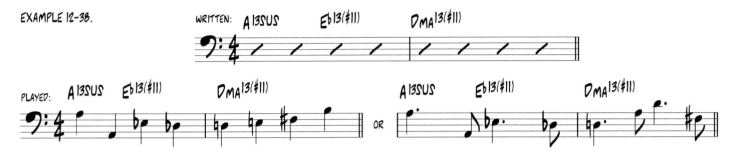

- **Combinations of both**: Each type of notation is played as described above.

EXAMPLE 12-39.

When the harmonic rhythm moves quickly, chord symbols should be omitted and written chord roots should be substituted. This will remove unnecessary information and clutter, as the bassist will most likely play chord roots in these situations anyway. This is shown in Example 12-40. Also notice that a note has been placed on the first beat of the third measure as the bassist is coming out of the written line and back to chord slashes.

EXAMPLE 12-40.

Walking bass lines are usually best left to the bassist. However, this task is sometimes unavoidable when writing shout choruses due to the dense, quickly moving harmonies associated with these sections. This, combined with the syncopations and anticipations found in jazz, and the downbeat orientation of a walking bass line, presents several quandaries for the arranger:

- When maintaining a walking bass line, is it more correct to place an upbeat chord's root on the downbeat before or after it?

- When working with successive, differently harmonized eighth notes, should the bass play all the roots? If not, which ones should be omitted?

- When should the walking bass line be abandoned in favor of writing identical rhythms with the horn ensemble?

In most shout-chorus situations, it is preferable to retain a walking bass line so as not to interrupt the time feel. The following three rules assume this.

1. When an upbeat horn chord is followed by a rest of any length, it should be considered an anticipation and its root should be placed on the following downbeat of the bass part.

TRACK 90
Part 1

EXAMPLE 12-41.

This information pertains *only* to the bass. If any horns are playing the roots of the chords discussed in this section, they should conform to the ensemble rhythm.

2. When an upbeat horn chord is preceded by a rest and followed by another chord, its root should be placed on the prior downbeat.

TRACK 90
Part 2

EXAMPLE 12-42.

3. When an upbeat horn chord occurs between downbeat chords, its root should be omitted from the bass line. The circled chords in the examples below denote these.

TRACK 91
Part 1

EXAMPLE 12-43.

There are occasional moments in a shout chorus where it is desirable to abandon a walking bass line in favor of playing the same rhythms as the horns. This is a subjective decision that places emphasis on those chords to which it is applied due to the interruption of the time feel. Thad Jones' music contains many of these wonderful moments. This technique can be effectively employed at phrase beginnings and endings, eighth-note passages where every note is harmonized with a different chord, or any other place where emphasis is desired.

TRACK 91
Part 2

EXAMPLE 12-44.

Though the above topic dealt specifically with swing eighths, these rules and suggestions can also be applied to all forms of straight-eighth music as well. In addition, they can be adapted for use in sixteenth-note oriented music by halving all the note values mentioned in the previous text.

Drums

Drum parts seem to be the most difficult for any arranger. The first problem arises when dealing with the proper location of particular drums and cymbals on the staff. Though every arranger has his own idea of symbology, the following is a chart that illustrates the typical staff placements and note-head types for each component of the drum set.

EXAMPLE 12-45.

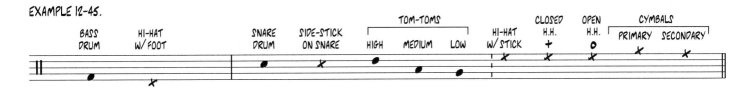

If there is ever any doubt as to whether a drummer will understand the arranger's intent, insert text describing exactly what is desired above the music at the points of concern.

The next issue concerns the stem directions for each component. There are four typical configurations:

1. Bass drum: stems down, all other instruments: stems up

2. Bass and snare: stems down, all other instruments: stems up

3. All drums: stems down, all cymbals: stems up

4. Foot-played instruments: stems down, hand-played instruments: stems up

Once a configuration has been established, it should be maintained throughout the arrangement. This text will employ the fourth configuration, as it is the one most commonly used by jazz publishers.

Types of Notation

There are four possible types of notation for drums. These are listed from most to least specific, followed by a description of what the drummer will play when encountering each notation type.

- **Fully-notated music**: Everything is played exactly as written.

EXAMPLE 12-46.

- **Slashes with rhythms written above or below the staff**: These rhythms indicate rhythm section or horn kicks. Rhythm section kicks are notated on first space F (treble clef), and horn kicks on top of the staff (G in treble clef). Both are written using traditional noteheads. A basic time feel is maintained while the amount of the given rhythmic information that will be played is at the discretion of the drummer.

EXAMPLE 12-47.

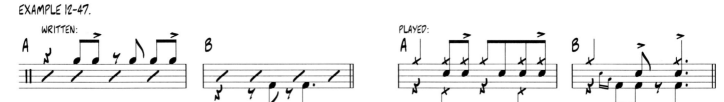

- **Time slashes**: In the drum part, the same slashes used for chords indicate a basic time feel. The type of pattern played is dependent on the style of music. In the following example, a typical swing feel is shown.

EXAMPLE 12-48.

- **Combinations of any of the above**: Each type of notation is played as described above.

EXAMPLE 12-49.

There are two methods of indicating extended amounts of time in a drum part. The first uses a series of one-bar repeats. The final measure of each set of repeats is always numbered so the drummer can keep track of the total number of measures to play. Other options include numbering the final measure of every line, or numbering every measure. One downside to this method is that the maximum number of repeat bars that can fit comfortably on a single line is usually no more than eight. Therefore, if thirty-two measures of time are to be indicated, the drummer's part will consist of four lines of one-bar repeats. This can look incredibly boring.

EXAMPLE 12-50.

The second method provides a more concise, less-cluttered look. The thick lines surrounding the textual phrase "Play # Bars" can take any form the arranger desires; the only constant is that it should fill the empty space around the phrase. With this method, there is no limit to the number of measures indicated per line; consequently the example cited above would only occupy one line instead of four. This makes it easier for the drummer to navigate the form of a tune or solo section.

EXAMPLE 12-51.

A detailed explanation of the creation of this type of extended time can be found in appendix 11.

It is essential to provide the drummer with the proper amount of rhythmic information. Look at the first two measures of "Anthropology" in the next example.

EXAMPLE 12-52.

This entire rhythm, if indicated for the drummer, contains more information than is necessary. An inexperienced player may try to play every note of this rhythm, making it impossible to maintain a time feel. The part should display a rhythm that indicates the natural accents of the line.

EXAMPLE 12-53.

There is also a possibility of giving too little information. In this case, the drummer has to either guess at the rhythms or just play time.

Another important job assigned to the drummer is that of setting up *figures*. This refers to a preparatory note (or series of notes) the drummer plays preceding a rhythmic ensemble figure. Regardless of a downbeat or upbeat, the final note of the setup always occurs on the prior downbeat as shown in the following examples. The setup note is circled in each.

TRACK 92

EXAMPLE 12-54.

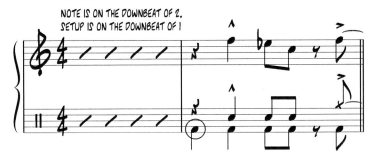

Vibraphone

The vibraphone is a non-transposing instrument written in the treble clef. It has a three-octave range.

EXAMPLE 12-55.

It is the only mallet instrument that produces a vibrato. This is done by a motor which turns paddles in the resonators. The speed of the vibrato can be varied or turned off completely. When it was first used in studio orchestras, the vibrato was extremely fast. The effect in early film scores from the 1930s was almost comical. With each generation of vibes players, the vibrato has gotten slower, until today the preference is no vibrato. This is the best situation for ensemble writing, because it results in a better blend with other instruments.

The vibraphone is also the only mallet instrument with a damper pedal. When the pedal is depressed it has a sustaining time of several seconds. When the pedal is off the tone sounds rather choked. But the pedal makes it an ideal jazz instrument. A skillful player can control the length of the notes and correctly interpret jazz articulations.

The tone is warm and mellow in the low register, becoming brighter and more metallic in the upper register. Like the guitar, it is very versatile and can blend with any instrument. It can also provide additional color by doubling melodic lines. In the low register, it can reinforce saxophones or trombones. The combination of vibes with trombones in cup mutes produces a velvety sound. In the middle register it works well with alto and trumpet, both open and muted. In the upper register, it can combine with flute, either in unison or octaves.

Solo playing is usually done with two mallets. With four mallets it can provide pads or comp behind soloists. Many performers today hold four mallets all the time so they can interject chords into their solo lines. Intervals of up to an octave between adjacent mallets are possible. This provides a wide range of chord voicings. Block, drop-two, drop-three, drop two-and-four, and spread voicings are all feasible.

In the 1960s, a wonderful texture was created by pianist George Shearing for his quintets. The piano played in four-part block voicing with the melody doubled at the octave; the vibes doubled the melody in the top octave while the guitar doubled the lower octave.

TRACK 93

EXAMPLE 12-56.

This texture has not been used much since, probably because it was so closely identified with Shearing. But the octave doubling of vibes and guitar on the melody could reinforce any combination of instruments in four- or five-part block voicing with good effect.

Miscellaneous Percussion

An in-depth discussion of all the other percussion instruments available to the arranger is far beyond the scope of this book. Aside from other pitched mallet instruments such as xylophone and glockenspiel, there are numerous instruments of indefinite pitch that are commonly used as auxiliary instruments in jazz ensembles, including claves, cowbell, maracas, shaker, tambourine, triangle, agogo bells, timbales, congas, and bongos. When writing for these instruments, it is best to leave the specifics to the players. It is only necessary to indicate three things on one of these parts: the type of groove, when to play, and when not to play. This is written in the same manner as a drum part, on a regular staff with a clef of indefinite pitch using time slashes.

EXAMPLE 12-57.

The only time it is necessary to notate anything other than this is when a specific rhythm is desired. The most-typical note placement for single instruments, such as tambourine or claves, is the third space. For those instruments that are in pairs, such as timbales or agogo bells, the note placements are the second space for the lower-pitched one and the third space for the higher. Regular or "x" noteheads can be used.

EXAMPLE 12-58.

Often, auxiliary percussion parts switch from one instrument to another within an arrangement. The same rules discussed in the last chapter regarding woodwind instrument and brass mute switching should be applied: allow enough time for the switch and use textual cues to indicate the switches.

EXAMPLE 12-59.

Also, when switching from an instrument of indefinite pitch to a pitched one, be sure to include the key signature, if necessary.

EXAMPLE 12-60.

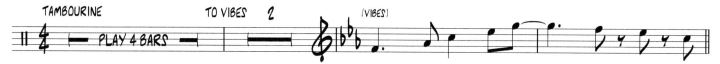

Resources

The following are some books that deal more specifically with the instruments of the rhythm section. Much of the information in them exceeds the needs of the arranger; however, each one also contains valuable insight that can be helpful when writing for these instruments.

Piano

The Chord Voicing Handbook by Matt Harris and Jeff Jarvis

The Jazz Piano Book by Mark Levine

Guitar

Joe Pass Guitar Chords by Joe Pass

Chord Melody Phrases for Guitar by Ron Eschete

Bass

The Bottom Line by Todd Coolman

Big Band Bass by John Clayton

Ray Brown's Bass Method by Ray Brown

The Evolving Bassist by Rufus Reid

Essential Styles For The Bassist by Tom Warrington

Drums

Essential Styles For The Drummer by Steve Houghton

The Jazz Drummer's Workshop by John Riley

Studio & Big Band Drumming by Steve Houghton

Latin Percussion

Poncho Sanchez Congo Cookbook by Poncho Sanchez

Vibes

Jazz Vibes: The Art and Language by Jon Metzger

PART III

Arranging Concepts

Chapters 13 through 15 contain the following topics:

- Arranging for the Small Ensemble
- Arranging for the Large Ensemble
- Arranging for Six and Seven Horns

These chapters present a comprehensive compilation of orchestration and arranging possibilities for groups ranging from two to fifteen horns.

CHAPTER 13
Arranging for the Small Ensemble

This chapter will explore the instrumental combinations and arranging options for small groups of various sizes. After a discussion of unison and octave doubling and the elements of an arrangement, the chapter is then divided into separate sections for two-, three-, four-, and five-horn groups. Each section includes instrument combinations, arranging options, historical references, and a sample arrangement.

Before beginning an arrangement, two important considerations must be addressed:

- The number and types of instruments to be used
- The possible ways the instruments can be combined

The list of available instruments in this chapter is limited to trumpet, trombone, and the saxophone family, as these have been the ones most often used in the small ensemble since the bebop era. However, many other instruments, such as flute, clarinet, bass clarinet, French horn, violin, and cello, have been successfully incorporated into the small ensemble. These are all effective solo instruments and provide interesting colors. But, when combined with brass and/or saxophones, problems of balance and blend arise. In terms of dynamic range and volume of sound, they do not match up well in all situations. The use of brass mutes can often alleviate this problem.

Piano, guitar, and vibes are non-sustaining instruments, and when combined with sustaining instruments, have other shortcomings. They cannot execute a crescendo or controlled decrescendo over a held note, nor are they fully capable of the many subtleties of articulation, such as a *sfz* attack. These instruments are used most effectively in fast moving passages where decay is not a factor.

Unison and Octave Doubling

When two instruments play in unison, they tend to cancel out each other's tone; the result is a new, mixed timbre. Each pairing of instruments creates its own color characteristics that should become a part of the arranger's tonal memory.

When writing for two or more instruments in unison, the first step is to compare their practical ranges to determine the *common range*. Take the lowest note of the highest pitched instrument and the highest note of the lowest pitched instrument; the interval between them is the common range. The widest common range would occur between two instruments in the same key and register.

EXAMPLE 13-1.

Instruments pitched a fourth or fifth apart have a smaller common range, but unison writing is still possible.

EXAMPLE 13-2.

The common range for instruments pitched an octave apart is smaller yet. Some interesting effects can be obtained, since it means placing the higher-pitched instrument in its low register and the lower-pitched instrument in its high register. However, writing entire melodies in this fashion is usually not feasible.

EXAMPLE 13-3.

Instruments pitched more than an octave apart would have very little range in common.

EXAMPLE 13-4.

When three or more instruments are combined in unison, the restrictions are compounded. As mentioned in chapter 11, the common range of a unison passage for soprano, alto, tenor, and baritone saxophones is one octave.

EXAMPLE 13-5.

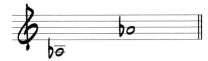

When unison is selected as the desired texture, but the range of the piece exceeds the range of one of the instruments, the best solution is to switch to octave writing. Always try to find the spot in the phrase where the smoothest transition from unison to octaves can be made. The passage in the next example is written for trumpet and alto, but at one point it goes beyond the alto range, so a change from unison to octaves is necessary.

EXAMPLE 13-6.

When instruments play in octaves, they retain much of their individual tone qualities. The doubling will add brilliance to the line if it is placed above the original, or add weight if it is placed below. Octave writing works best between two instruments pitched an octave apart. It is comparatively easy to find a key or range that is comfortable for both. Instruments pitched a fourth or fifth apart will have less success because of registral difficulties. One of them is likely to be placed in an uncomfortably high or low register. The following example shows such a passage written in octaves for trumpet and alto. It is first written in concert pitch, then transposed to show the problems incurred in the alto part.

EXAMPLE 13-7.

Here is the same passage written for alto and trombone. The key has been changed to place the alto in a comfortable range. But in so doing, the octave doubling in the trombone becomes uncomfortably low.

EXAMPLE 13-8.

Octave doubling between two instruments in the same key and register frequently poses problems. If one instrument is written in the middle register, the doubling may place the other in a very high or low register. Below is a passage where the flugelhorn is in a relaxed middle register, but neither octave doubling works very well for the soprano.

EXAMPLE 13-9.

One workable solution would be to lower the key, in this instance a perfect fourth. This places the flugelhorn in a lower, but still characteristic register and the soprano in a much more comfortable one.

EXAMPLE 13-10.

The same solution could be applied to the passage when written in octaves for the tenor saxophone and the trombone. The tenor, like the soprano, is capable of playing in a controlled manner in the upper register, as long as it is not too extreme.

EXAMPLE 13-11.

Combinations of unison and octave doubling using three or more instruments are also possible. The subtle textural nuances of brilliance, body, and weight can be regulated through the placement of the instruments in various octaves.

Elements of an Arrangement

There are four distinct elements of an arrangement:

- Melody
- Harmony
- Countermelody
- Accompaniment, or background devices

The synthesis of these elements is called *texture*. These textures, or arranging options, are categorized below according to the number of elements and the way in which they are combined.

Melody, the most important element, may be represented by a solo instrument, two or more instruments in unison, or two or more instruments in octaves. Octave doubling is not considered an addition of a new textural element. It is merely a widening of the vertical plane of sound.

A conventional view might argue that the addition of harmony to a melody does not constitute the addition of a new element. But the effect of a carefully planned harmony is so striking and powerful that it must be considered a separate element of musical expression.

When the melody is combined with a countermelody of an entirely different design, the listener's attention is constantly shifted from one line to the other. This establishes the two lines as separate elements.

The addition of accompaniment devices does more than just add density and complexity to the texture. The sustained coloristic effects of pads and the separate and distinct rhythmic ideas of punches contrast so successfully with the melody that they also become two distinct musical elements.

It will be assumed that all of the groups include a rhythm section. Even though it is more typical to use the rhythm section in such a way that it could be considered a separate element, it is to be thought of here in a strictly accompanimental role.

Two-Horn Arranging

Two-horn arranging became prominent during the bebop era because it proved to be the most effective setting for the intricate melodies of the period. This was, and remains, the most popular format for small groups beyond one horn and rhythm.

Instrument Combinations

Woodwind Combinations	Brass Combinations	Mixed Woodwinds and Brass
two sopranos, altos, tenors, or baritones	two trumpets	trumpet – soprano
soprano – alto	trumpet – flugelhorn	trumpet – alto
soprano – tenor	two trombones	trumpet – tenor
soprano – baritone	trumpet – trombone	trumpet – baritone
alto – tenor		soprano – trombone
alto – baritone		alto – trombone
tenor – baritone		tenor – trombone
		baritone – trombone

Arranging Options

One element

- One horn – melody
- Two horns – melody in unison

Two elements: melody and harmony

- one horn – melody; one horn – harmony

Two elements: melody and countermelody

- One horn – melody; one horn – countermelody

Historical References

Countless recordings have been made using this configuration, and it would be impossible to list all references. The following list contains some of the more significant artists and recordings. The text in parentheses indicates either specific musicians or recordings.

- Gerry Mulligan/Chet Baker (or Bob Brookmeyer, Clark Terry, Art Farmer)
- Cannonball Adderley Quintet
- Art Blakey & the Jazz Messengers
- Horace Silver Quintet
- Clifford Brown/Max Roach Quintet
- Miles Davis (recordings with John Coltrane and Wayne Shorter)
- Wayne Shorter (recordings with Freddie Hubbard and Lee Morgan)
- Brecker Brothers
- Dave Holland (*Points of View*, *Critical Mass*, and *Prime Directive*)
- Terence Blanchard/Donald Harrison Quintet
- Marc Copland Quintet
- Conrad Herwig (*New York Breed*)
- Randy Brecker (*In The Idiom* and *Live At Sweet Basil*)

The next example is an arrangement of "Bar Flies" for trumpet and tenor sax.

TRACK 94

This arrangement employs every possible option except one horn playing the melody. A1 is written in four-measure increments: the first four in unison, the second in octaves. A2 is in two-part harmony with contrary motion predominating. Letter B utilizes melody and countermelody. Measure 24 constitutes a point of convergence with the melody emphasized by a return to octaves. A3 is the most complex section, making use of most of the options within eight measures. Measure 25 begins in unison, measure 26 in harmony then countermelody, and measures 27–32 are in two-part harmony with all three types of motion. The first two measures of the Tag employ *quartal planing*. Measure 35 is in two-part harmony in thirds and sixths, culminating in an octave #11 on the downbeat of measure 36. This strengthens the final note of the melody.

Three-Horn Arranging

Three-horn groups can be traced back to early Dixieland. The most common texture in this style was improvised counterpoint, with the trumpet playing the melody, the clarinet playing a countermelody above, and the trombone playing a countermelody below. *Homophonic* textures (melody and harmony in the same rhythm) were also used. As improvised counterpoint gave way to written arrangements, homophonic textures assumed more prominence, as evidenced by the three-horn groups of the fifties and sixties. It is still a widely used format.

Instrument Combinations

Woodwind Combinations	Brass Combinations	Mixed Woodwinds and Brass
three altos, tenors, or baritones	three trumpets	trumpet – soprano – trombone
soprano – alto – tenor	two trumpets – flugelhorn	trumpet – alto – trombone
alto – tenor – baritone	three trombones	trumpet – tenor – trombone
soprano – tenor – baritone	two trumpets – trombone	trumpet – alto –tenor
two altos – tenor or baritone	trumpet – flugelhorn – trombone	trumpet – tenor – baritone
two tenors – baritone	trumpet – two trombones	trumpet – trombone – baritone
soprano or alto – two tenors		tenor – trombone – baritone
alto or tenor – two baritones		soprano or alto – tenor – trombone

Mathematically speaking, there are even more possible combinations than those listed above. The combinations presented here are either historical models or mentioned because of their effectiveness. For example, even though a combination of two sopranos and baritone is possible, it was not listed above due to its problematic range differences. The lists of four and five instrument combinations later in this chapter reflect a similar approach.

Arranging Options

One element
- Melody in unison
- Melody in octaves: one horn – top note; two horns – bottom note
- Melody in octaves: two horns – top note; one horn – bottom note
- Melody in two octaves

Two elements: melody and harmony
- Two-part harmony, melody doubled in unison, one octave above or one octave below
- Three-part harmony in close or open position

Two elements: melody and countermelody
- One horn – melody; two horns – countermelody in unison or octaves
- Two horns – melody in unison or octaves; one horn – countermelody

Two elements: melody and accompaniment devices

- One horn – melody; two horns – accompaniment devices

In addition, all the arranging possibilities for two horns are available. Here, one player does not play for purposes of relief or variety of color.

Historical References

The reappearance of Blakey, Silver, Adderley, and Holland in the following list is intentional, since all four leaders recorded a significant amount of material in the three-horn format as well as the two-horn format. Album names included from this point forward should be considered "must hear."

- John Kirby (classic three-horn group from the thirties; reissued on CD)
- Chet Baker Sextet
- Art Blakey & the Jazz Messengers (*Caravan, Ugetsu*)
- Horace Silver Sextet
- Cannonball Adderley Sextet
- Miles Davis (*Kind of Blue*)
- John Coltrane (*Blue Train*)
- Jazztet (Art Farmer/Benny Golson/Curtis Fuller)
- Herbie Hancock (*Fat Albert Rotunda, Sextant*)
- Dave Holland (*Seed of Time, Razor's Edge, Jumpin' In*)
- Mel Lewis (*Mellifluous, Lost Art*)
- Jerry Gonzalez & the Fort Apache Band

The next example is an arrangement of "Bar Flies" for trumpet, tenor sax, and trombone.

TRACK 95

EXAMPLE 13–13.

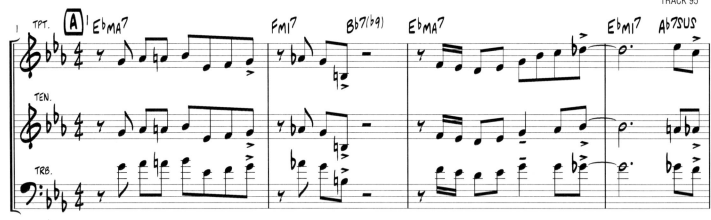

A1 begins with all three horns playing the melody in unison, then unfolds into three-part harmony in block voicing in measure 3. For the remainder of this section, the trumpet plays the melody alone with the other two horns playing punches and melodic fills. A2 begins with all three horns playing the melody, this time in octaves. Trumpet and tenor are on the top, trombone on the bottom. This configuration emphasizes the top octave with the trombone providing sufficient weight to the bottom. Measure 12 reverts to three-part block harmony. In measures 13–14 only the accented notes are harmonized with the approach notes in octaves. This technique adds further emphasis to the accented notes. Like the two-horn arrangement, this B section uses melody and countermelody. However, this time, the orchestration changes with the tenor playing the melody and the trumpet and trombone providing a harmonized countermelody. Measure 24 is again a point of convergence, harmonized in contrary motion. The first two measures of A3 continue in three-part harmony. Measure 27 begins in octaves and opens into drop-two voicings. Beginning in measure 29, tenor and trombone take over the melody in unison, then in harmony with predominantly contrary motion. This three-measure rest for the trumpet not only provides a brief respite, but its re-entry in the tag heightens the feeling of climax. The entire tag is written in harmony using drop-two voicings.

Four-Horn Arranging

This texture came about through the introduction of the saxophone into the ensembles of the twenties. Four-part improvised counterpoint became very difficult to manage unless it was carefully worked out. This led to more written arrangements and the homophonic texture again prevailed. Four-part, close-position voicing was a staple of saxophone writing during the big-band era of the thirties and became the model for four-voice writing of all types.

Instrument Combinations

Woodwind Combinations	Brass Combinations	Mixed Woodwinds and Brass
soprano – alto – tenor – baritone	four trumpets	trumpet – alto – tenor – trombone
two altos – tenor – baritone	two trumpets – 2 flugelhorns (or 3 & 1)	trumpet – tenor – trombone – baritone
alto – two tenors – baritone	four trombones	trumpet – alto – trombone – baritone
three tenors – baritone	two trumpets – two trombones	trumpet – alto – tenor – baritone
	flugelhorn – three trombones	two trumpets – alto, tenor or baritone – trombone
		trumpet – alto, tenor or baritone – two trombones
		alto – tenor – trombone – baritone

Soprano sax can be substituted for trumpet as a lead instrument anywhere in the third column. It can also be substituted for alto as a section instrument in the same column.

Arranging Options

One element

- Melody in unison
- Melody in octaves: two horns – top note; two horns – bottom note
- Melody in octaves: three horns – top note; one horn – bottom note
- Melody in two octaves: one horn – top note; one horn – middle note; two horns – bottom note
- Melody in two octaves: one horn – top note; two horns – middle note; one horn – bottom note
- Melody in two octaves: two horns – top note; one horn – middle note; one horn – bottom note

Two elements: melody and harmony

- Two-part harmony, two horns on each part, both parts in unison
- Two-part harmony, two horns on each part, both parts in octaves
- Two-part harmony, two horns on each part, a combination of unisons and octaves

- Three-part harmony in close or open position, one horn doubles bass figure
- Three-part harmony in close or open position, melody doubled in unison, one octave above or one octave below
- Four-part harmony in close or open position

Two elements: melody and countermelody

- Two horns – melody in unison or octaves; two horns – countermelody in unison or octaves
- Three horns – melody in unison or octaves; one horn – countermelody
- One horn – melody; three horns – countermelody (probable balance problems)

Two elements: melody and accompaniment devices

- One horn – melody; three horns – accompaniment devices
- Two horns – melody in unison or octaves; two horns – accompaniment devices

Three elements: melody, countermelody, and accompaniment devices

- One horn – melody; one horn – countermelody; two horns – accompaniment devices

In addition, all the arranging possibilities for two and three horns are available. Here, one or two players do not play for purposes of relief or variety of color.

Historical References

- Clifford Brown (*The Clifford Brown Ensemble Featuring Zoot Sims*)
- Benny Carter (*Further Definitions*)
- Quincy Jones (*This Is How I Feel About Jazz*)
- Shelly Manne (*Shelly Manne & His Men, Vol. 1*)
- Lennie Niehaus (*Vol. 5, The Sextet*)
- Freddie Hubbard (*Blue Spirits*)
- Sam Rivers (*Dimensions* and *Extensions*)
- Max Roach (*Percussion Bitter Sweet*)
- Thelonious Monk (*Monk's Music*)
- Dave Pell Octet
- Gerry Mulligan Sextet (*Introducing the Gerry Mulligan Sextet*)
- Charles Mingus (*Mingus Ah Um* and *Mingus Dynasty*)
- Oliver Nelson (*The Blues & the Abstract Truth* and *More Blues & the Abstract Truth*)
- Bud Shank & Trombones (*Cool Fool*)
- Archie Shepp (*Four for Trane*)
- Gil Evans (*Into the Hot*)
- Paquito D'Riviera (*Return to Ipanema*)
- Marcus Roberts (*Deep in the Shed*)
- Don Grolnick (*Nighttown and Weaver of Dreams*)
- Horace Silver (*Hardbop Grandpop*)

The next example is an arrangement of "Bar Flies" for trumpet, alto sax, tenor sax, and trombone.

EXAMPLE 13-14.

In two- and three-horn writing, the possibility of timbral variations is limited. Beginning with four horns, these options increase. At A1 of Example 13-14, tenor and trombone play this entire section in unison. At A2, trumpet and alto assume this role an octave higher, with the tenor and trombone playing punches and melodic fills. In the B section, a single horn (the alto) takes over the melody while the other three horns provide background support. In measure 24, emphasis is provided through a somewhat reverse approach, with only the low horns stating this phrase in unison. At A3, the first two measures are in two-part harmony, with each part doubled at the unison. Measure 27 begins in unison and spreads into four-part drop-two voicings. This is the first time in this arrangement where four-note vertical sonorities are used. Beginning in measure 29, the first two phrase segments are harmonized with the accented notes in four-part drop-two and the approach notes in two parts. The third phrase segment is harmonized entirely in drop-two. The melody in measure 32 is played by alto, tenor, and trombone in two parts using contrary motion. The tag is harmonized in four-part drop-two voicing, with the final note spreading to drop-two and three. The infrequent use of this texture up to this point lends greater impact to the climax.

Five-Horn Arranging

The earliest prototype was the five-saxophone writing of the big-band era. Much of this was four-part close-position voicing with melody doubled an octave lower. But many of the Duke Ellington compositions of this period were actually five-part arrangements. This texture is still widely used in saxophone writing as well as for groups with mixed instruments.

Instrument Combinations

Woodwind Combinations	Brass Combinations	Mixed Woodwinds and Brass
soprano – alto – two tenors – baritone	five trumpets (any combination of trumpets and flugelhorns)	trumpet – alto – tenor – trombone – baritone
two altos – two tenors – baritone	five trombones	trumpet – soprano – alto – tenor – baritone
soprano or alto – two tenors – two baritones	three trumpets – two trombones	two trumpets – two saxes – trombone
soprano or alto – three tenors – baritone	two trumpets – three trombones	two trumpets – two trombones – sax
	flugelhorn – four trombones	soprano – alto – tenor – trombone – baritone

Arranging Options

One element

- Melody in unison
- Melody in octaves: three horns – top note; two horns – bottom note
- Melody in octaves: two horns – top note; three horns – bottom note
- Melody in octaves: four horns – top note; one horn – bottom note
- Melody in two octaves: one horn – top note; two horns – middle note; two horns – bottom note
- Melody in two octaves: two horns – top note; two horns – middle note; one horn – bottom note
- Melody in two octaves: two horns – top note; one horn – middle note; two horns – bottom note

Two elements: melody and harmony

- Two-part harmony, three horns – melody; two horns – harmony, both parts in unison
- Two-part harmony, two horns – melody; three horns – harmony, both parts in unison
- Two-part harmony, two or three horns on each part, both parts in octaves
- Two-part harmony, two or three horns on each part, both parts in a combination of unisons and octaves
- Four-part harmony in close or open position – melody doubled in unison, one octave above or one octave below
- Five-part harmony in close or open position

Two elements: melody and countermelody

- Three horns – melody in unison, one or two octaves; two horns – countermelody in unison or octaves
- Two horns – melody in unison or octaves; three horns – countermelody in unison, one or two octaves
- One horn – melody; four horns – countermelody in unison, one or two octaves (probable balance problems)

Two elements: melody and accompaniment devices

- One horn – melody; four horns – accompaniment devices
- Two horns – melody in unison or octaves; three horns – accompaniment devices
- Three horns – melody in unison, one or two octaves; two horns – accompaniment devices

Three elements: melody, countermelody and accompaniment devices

- One horn – melody; one horn – countermelody; three horns – accompaniment devices
- Two horns – melody in unison or octaves; one horn – countermelody; two horns – accompaniment devices
- One horn – melody; two horns – countermelody in unison or octaves; two horns – accompaniment devices

In addition, all the arranging possibilities for two, three, and four horns are available. Here, one, two or three players do not play for purposes of relief or variety of color.

Historical References

- Tadd Dameron (*Fontainebleu*)
- Gerry Mulligan (*Songbook*)
- Lennie Niehaus (*Vol. 2, Zounds!* and *Vol. 3, The Octet, pt. 2*)
- Supersax (All recordings)
- Phil Woods (*Rights of Swing* and *Evolution*)
- Rod Levitt (*The Dynamic Sound Patterns of the Rod Levitt Orchestra*)
- Tower of Power (All recordings)
- Anthony Wilson (*Adult Themes*)
- Randy Brecker (*34th & Lex*)
- Joe Lovano (*52nd Street Themes* and *Streams of Expression*)

A five-horn arrangement of "Bar Flies" can be found in Chapters 17–22 where it is used as a primary example.

About Color Possibilities

As shown in previous chapters, it is possible to write music without reference to any particular instrumentation. But as the aural memory is developed and expanded, music will more frequently be composed with specific colors and textures in mind. At this point, it is critical not to lapse into a predictable mold and continually rely on a few familiar textures. It is only through continuous experimentation that an awareness of the inexhaustible means of expression that are available will be developed.

The following chart shows a typical four-horn group with color possibilities for each player. By randomly drawing lines from one player to another, almost two-hundred color possibilities emerge.

Player 1	Player 2	Player 3	Player 4
trumpet	alto sax	tenor sax	trombone
flugelhorn	soprano sax	flute	trb. w/cup mute
tpt. w/cup mute	flute	clarinet	trb. w/bucket mute
tpt. w/harmon mute	clarinet	bass clarinet	

In addition to the obvious top-line combination of trumpet, alto, tenor, and trombone, the following are three other combinations among many that would provide excellent color varieties.

- Flugelhorn, soprano, bass clarinet, and trombone w/bucket mute
- Trumpet with cup mute, clarinet, flute, and trombone w/cup mute
- Trumpet with Harmon mute, flute, tenor, and trombone with bucket or cup mute

CHAPTER 14
Arranging for the Large Ensemble

The large ensemble presents a vastly larger number of possible textures and concepts than the small ensemble, from unisons to very complex contrapuntal passages. The initial focus of this chapter is on *tutti* (the simultaneous use of all the instruments of an ensemble) arranging concepts. This section will deal with homophonic writing and the construction of vertical sonorities for full ensemble, followed by a discussion of those techniques that involve more than one layer of activity. The remainder of the chapter will explain non-tutti concepts as well as other interesting timbral possibilities. The examples in this chapter will utilize four trumpets, four trombones, and five saxophones. Deviations from this setup will also be discussed.

Tutti Concepts

One Element: Homophonic Voicings

The building of tutti chords always begins with the brass section. It is essential that the brass voicings contain complete, well-balanced chords. The techniques already learned for four- and five-part writing will provide an excellent foundation for brass choir voicing. For example, four-part block voicing can be easily adapted for a full brass section through a device called *double block voicing*. This is constructed from the top down by first scoring the four trumpets in block voicing with the melody in the top voice. These notes are then doubled an octave lower in the trombones. The result is a compact four-part texture with a surprising amount of intensity.

TRACK 97
Part 1

A slightly different texture can be achieved by using a drop-two voicing in the trombones. This creates a lower center of sound and a more resonant quality. The doubled lead in the first trombone retains the focus on the melody.

TRACK 97
Part 2

The simplest way to complete either of these voicings is to double the top four saxophone parts in unison with the trombones.

TRACK 97
Part 3

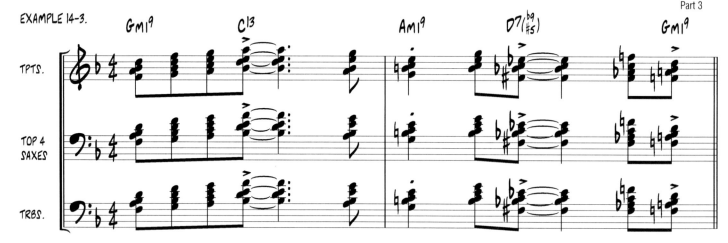

The only exception to this would be if the first trumpet line was consistently low—fourth line D or lower. In this case, to avoid sounding bottom heavy, the brass section would revert to double block voicing, while the top four horns of the saxophone section would be placed across the trumpets and trombones. In some cases, the first alto might even double the first trumpet.

There are two options for the baritone sax. The first is to double the melody just below the trombones, which would result in four instruments playing the melody in three octaves. This is not excessive, as a strong focus on the melody is one of the main reasons for using this voicing.

TRACK 98
Part 1

Much of the big-band music of the forties and fifties relied heavily on this texture, as did the great Sammy Nestico/Count Basie charts of the sixties. It is still an appropriate voicing for fast-moving ensemble passages and music that does not require six- and seven-note harmony.

Another option for the baritone sax is to play roots on the bottom of the chord. This provides a great deal of emphasis and is suitable for passages which contain only two or three notes per measure.

TRACK 98
Part 2

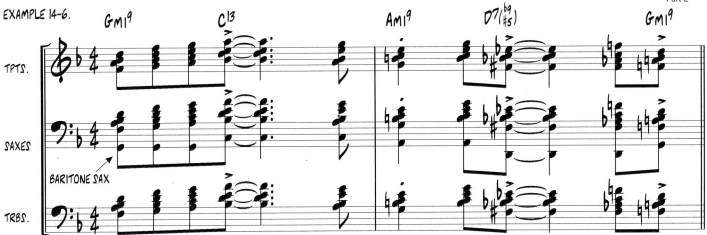

EXAMPLE 14-6.

Double block voicing provides an easy transition to large ensemble writing. Its overuse can make an arrangement sound one-dimensional. It is best employed sparingly in combination with the other available voicings. With the emphasis in contemporary arranging on increased dissonance and more complex textures, drop and spread voicings have been found to be more suitable. Most contemporary eight-part brass voicings consist of five-note chords with octave doubling of three notes. These five-part chords establish the basic tension level, with six- and seven-note chords added for additional tension.

The following is a general procedure for harmonizing brass section chords which works for all of these types of voicings.

1. **Enter all of the available information** about the passage, including the chord progression and the lead trumpet line in the correct register.

EXAMPLE 14-7.

2. **Complete all of the necessary harmonic preparation**: chord substitutions, alterations and extensions, harmonization of nonharmonic tones, and tonicization.

EXAMPLE 14-8.

3. **Enter both guide tones in the trombone staff.** This is essential to ensure that each trombone chord makes complete harmonic sense.

EXAMPLE 14-9.

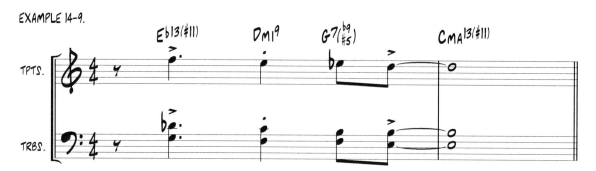

4. **Add the two remaining trombone notes.**

EXAMPLE 14-10.

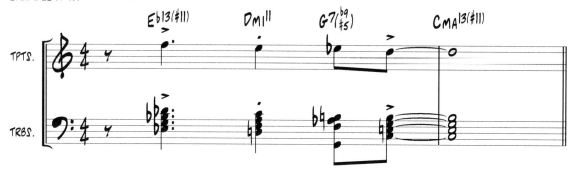

5. **Complete the trumpet section harmonization.** The choice of notes will depend to some degree on the selected trombone notes. The trumpet voicings should sound good as an entity, but unlike the trombones, do not have to contain the guide tones; they are more apt to play color or altered tones.

EXAMPLE 14-11.

The above process is correct, but too general for the novice. There is a need for separate, more specific guidelines for the construction of the individual trumpet and trombone section voicings that combine to form brass section voicings. A discussion of these follows, starting with the trombone section.

The placement of the guide tones in Example 14-9 is the most logical choice, but not the only one. Some circumstances might necessitate the inversion or separation of the guide tones. The following are some alternate guide-tone placements.

EXAMPLE 14-12.

No matter where they are placed, trombone section voicings should *always* contain the guide tones.

There are several options for the addition of the remaining two notes:

- Add both basic tones. (The third chord in this example has only one basic tone because of the altered fifth.)

EXAMPLE 14-13.

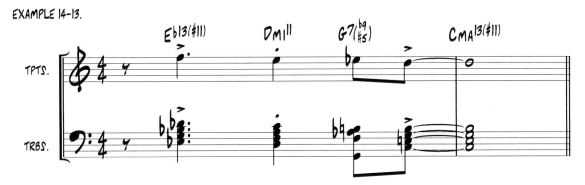

The following example shows all of the possible trombone voicings which contain both guide tones and both basic tones. Each chord type begins with high, tight voicings, and progresses to wider drop and spread voicings.

EXAMPLE 14-14.

- Add one basic and one color or altered tone.

EXAMPLE 14-15.

Notice that this resulted in the first trombone doubling the first trumpet line. This is often a desired effect and not something to be arrived at by accident. But other solutions are possible with this option. The next example shows all of the trombone voicings with one basic tone and one color tone for the first chord only. They also begin with high, tight close-position voicings, and progress to more expanded drop and spread voicings.

EXAMPLE 14-16.

• Add two color or altered tones.

EXAMPLE 14-17.

Here are all of the possibilities for the first chord only, presented in the same sequential fashion.

EXAMPLE 14-18.

9TH AND 13TH

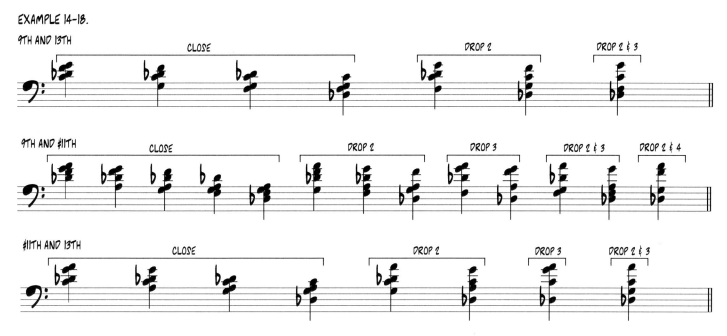

9TH AND #11TH

#11TH AND 13TH

There are still other approaches to adding the remaining two trombone notes to the existing guide-tone placements found in Examples 14-9 and 14-12.

- Double the trumpet melody an octave lower and place it in the first trombone part above the guide-tones.

EXAMPLE 14-19.

- Use the top guide tone as the first trombone part. Then add a color tone either between the guide tones or under them.

EXAMPLE 14-20.

- Invert the guide tones and add a color or basic tone. This third note could appear above or below the guide tones.

EXAMPLE 14-21.

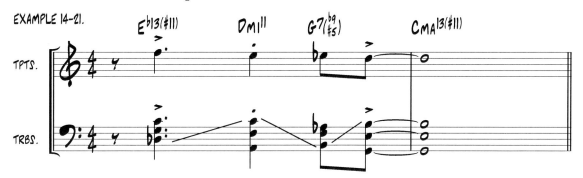

These voicings could then be completed by adding the roots in the fourth part.

A variant of this would make use of a combination of both basic tones in the fourth trombone part to make the line smoother.

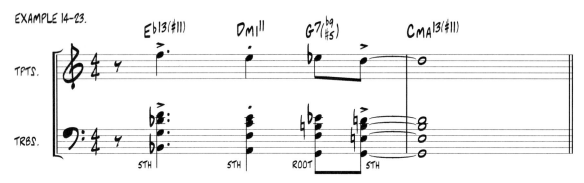

Trombone voicings should be created carefully as they establish the harmonic foundation for the horn ensemble. Once the initial voicing of a phrase has been established, the possibilities for the entire ensemble diminish greatly.

The following are two options for the completion of brass-section trumpet voicings.

1. Complete the harmonization by adding three different pitches below the first trumpet line within the octave. These note choices affect the overall tension of the voicing, which could be mild as two guide tones and two basic tones, or as sharp as four altered or color tones. The voicings in the next example contain a high tension level because of the predominance of color and altered tones.

For every voicing, there are numerous possibilities. To illustrate this, the next example shows four alternate trumpet voicings for the final chord that contain four different pitches.

EXAMPLE 14-25.

2. Double the lead trumpet an octave lower and add two pitches between these two notes. The result may be either triadic or non-triadic. If triadic, and the voicing contains color or altered tones, a polychordal effect is achieved when played with the trombone voicing. Both triadic and non-triadic examples are shown below.

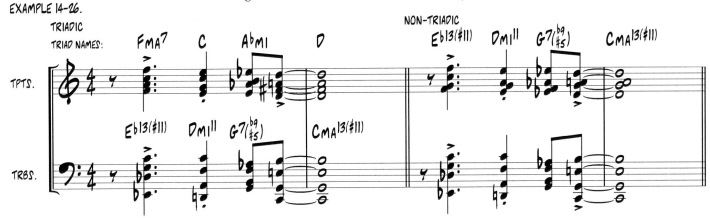

EXAMPLE 14-26.

All the options presented above can stand alone as brass-section voicings. These will be integral later in the chapter when multilayered concepts are presented. However, in order to complete this discussion of homophonic tutti ensemble voicings, the saxophone section must be incorporated. This can be accomplished by following these guidelines:

*   They should impart the full meaning of the chord. Each voicing should contain all guide tones, most typically at the bottom.

*   Avoid doubling pitches within the section as this can upset the balance of the chord.

*   Double the guide tones in unison with the trombones when possible, rather than an octave higher. This will place the saxophones either in the middle or near the bottom of the brass chord, depending on the range of the trumpet melody.

*   Half-step dissonances or clusters sound best in the middle of the voicing rather than the top or bottom.

*   In high trombone voicings where the fourth trombone is not playing the root, it is acceptable for the baritone sax to take over this function. In fact, there are times when the baritone can perform this function more easily than the bass trombone and provide a welcome variety in texture.

Next is a final, complete homophonic tutti harmonization of the passage examined in this chapter so far. This is only one of several possibilities.

TRACK 99

EXAMPLE 14-27.

The four-note phrase used in the above examples was chosen because it was easy to harmonize. This is due to the fact that it contained stepwise movement in the middle register, and all four melody notes were either color or altered tones. Experience has shown that this is rarely the case. The following melody, with its wide leaps, extremes of range (both high and low), and predominance of basic and guide tones, is more challenging to harmonize.

EXAMPLE 14-28.

One possible harmonization for this is presented below.

TRACK 100

EXAMPLE 14-29.

This melody contains ten leaps of a fifth or greater. The challenge is to lessen this movement in as many voices as possible, which can be done in several different ways. In the trumpet section's pickup note, a two-note voicing was chosen over a four-note voicing. In most of the remaining trumpet chords, the voicing type was changed from block to drop-two or vice versa. The wide leaps were lessened in the trombone and sax sections by reducing their size in the lead lines throughout, or by retaining the same voicing in consecutive chords.

Though many possible homophonic voicing types are available in any given situation, each arranger may have favorites that are used consistently. This vocabulary is attained only through personal experimentation.

The choice of voicing type is dependent on the following factors:

- **Melody placement**: Higher-pitched lead-trumpet notes allow for higher lead trombone and saxophone notes. Inversely, lower lead-trumpet notes restrict the possibilities for the lead trombone due to the chance of overlapping pitches between the lower trumpets and higher trombones.

- **Note length**: Short notes may not allow enough time for extremely low bass trombone notes to speak.

- **Tempo**: Generally speaking, eighth notes at fast tempos should be voiced tighter than those at slower tempos.

- **Harmonic placement**: Cadence points can usually be voiced in a more spread fashion.

- **Dramatic effect**: Sudden leaps up or down would result in wider or closer spacing between voices.

- **Desired density**: Tight voicings containing seconds as opposed to spread voicings with few or no seconds.

- **Voice leading**: Proper voice leading should be maintained within the individual lines even as voicing types change.

Due to its impact, the homophonic voicing is the most commonly used tutti arranging texture. However, no matter how harmonically and/or rhythmically interesting it may be, this sound can become tedious if used exclusively for more than eight measures or so. Several other possibilities for tutti arranging are discussed in the next section.

Two Elements: Saxophone Section Against the Brass Section

The second most serviceable texture for full horn ensemble pits the saxophone section against the brass section. As mentioned in chapter 11, the saxophone section is the only group in the big band that comprises a full choir. When the trumpet and trombone sections are combined, they form a brass choir. Each group has the capability to play powerful unison or octave lines as well as widely spread harmonizations.

This configuration involves the concepts of melody and countermelody or melody and any number of accompaniment devices. For the sake of clarity, one group is usually in unison or octaves, while the other is in harmony. The possible combinations are as follows:

- Saxes – unison or octave melody; Brass – unison or octave countermelody

EXAMPLE 14-30.

TRACK 101
Part 1

- Brass – unison or octave melody; Saxes – unison or octave countermelody

TRACK 101
Part 2

EXAMPLE 14-31.

- Saxes – harmonized melody; Brass – unison or octave countermelody

TRACK 102
Part 1

EXAMPLE 14-32.

- Brass – harmonized melody; Saxes – unison or octave countermelody

EXAMPLE 14-33.

TRACK 102
Part 2

- Saxes – unison or octave melody; Brass – harmonized accompaniment

EXAMPLE 14-34.

TRACK 103
Part 1

•   Brass – unison or octave melody; Saxes – harmonized accompaniment

TRACK 103
Part 2

EXAMPLE 14-35.

It is possible to harmonize both elements in any of the above combinations. However, extra care must be taken when choosing to do so because these combinations often involve moments where one line is static while the other is active, resulting in a harmonic clash. These momentary clashes will not present a problem as long as the active line does not pause on a note whose harmonization differs from that of the static note.

TRACK 104
Part 1

EXAMPLE 14-36.

If this does happen, an undesirable clash occurs as shown in the next example.

TRACK 104
Part 2

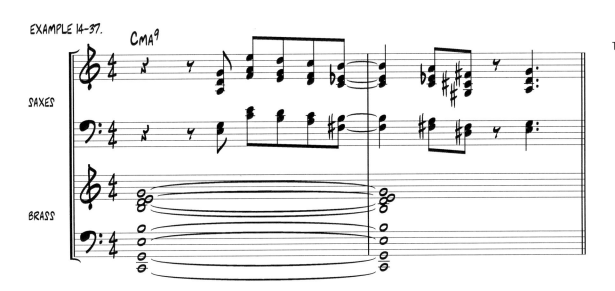

Another way to divide the horn ensemble into two groups is by pitch.

- Alto saxes with trumpets; tenor and baritone saxes with trombones

- Alto and tenor saxes with trumpets; baritone sax with trombones

The tenor saxes can be placed in either group because their range falls in the middle of the horn ensemble. This type of cross-section writing creates two groups that possess the timbral attributes of both reeds and brass in each group. When combined with the melody and countermelody/accompaniment combinations mentioned above, this concept can provide a fresh alternative to the well-worn compartmentalized "brass versus saxes" idea.

TRACK 105

Three Elements: Melody, Countermelody, Accompaniment

This is the most active of the typical tutti arranging concepts. For the sake of clarity, the melody and countermelody are written in unisons or octaves, while the accompaniment is always harmonized. This combination can be arranged any number of ways, with the most typical consisting of each horn section taking one of the three roles.

TRACK 106
Part 1

EXAMPLE 14-39.

Similar to the alternative orchestration mentioned in the last section, these elements can also be written across sections, usually according to pitch.

TRACK 106
Part 2

EXAMPLE 14-40.

Four or More Elements

This mainly contrapuntal concept can be found in the contemporary large ensemble writing of Bob Mintzer, Jim McNeely, and many others. It is difficult to describe in detail as each composer has his/her own unique way of creating it. The following are some of the qualities this type of writing may possess:

- It can consist solely of a series of highly rhythmic lines, legato lines, or combinations of both.

- Lines are sometimes orchestrated across sections, creating a series of small groups within the large ensemble horn section.

- Because of the complexity of the intersecting lines, this kind of writing is most often linear, with only occasional harmonization.

- A repetitive or non-repetitive accompaniment figure played by the rhythm section and/or a group of wind instruments may provide the basis for this type of writing with the contrapuntal lines placed atop it.

- It can be an additive process with each line being introduced separately or all lines may begin at the same time.

- Each line may contain spaces so that the other lines can be heard, creating a kind of composite idea.

The following are two examples of this kind of writing. The first excerpt contains five elements, while the second contains four. The lines in both examples enter one at a time, starting with the bass line and moving upward.

EXAMPLE 14-41.

EXCERPT FROM "LATER THAT SAME DAY" BY MIKE TOMARO
SAMBA

Non-Tutti Concepts

Combination of Two Sections

The next set of instrument groupings combines two of the three horn sections using homophonic writing. One such pairing that has already been discussed is trumpets with trombones. There are two other possibilities: saxes with trombones and saxes with trumpets. Once again, reeds are combined with brass, but these groupings possess slightly different timbral attributes than those mentioned above.

The sax section/trombone section combination contains a majority of lower-pitched horns and possesses a muscular sound when written in unisons and octaves.

TRACK 109
Part 1

TRACK 109
Part 2

Though lead alto can play up to A♭ two octaves above middle C (and soprano as high as lead trumpet), mid-range lines are most effective for this grouping. The dynamic level is typically written no louder than *mf*, facilitating a balance between the lead trombone and lead saxophone. Also, due to the trombone's inability to play extremely fast lines in the low register, slower tempos or lines that are less "notey" are best.

There are several ways to harmonize this configuration using four-note voicings with four different notes.

• Block or drop-two voicings with the sections in unison

TRACK 110
Part 1

• Double-block voicing in octaves with the saxes on top, trombones below

TRACK 110
Part 2

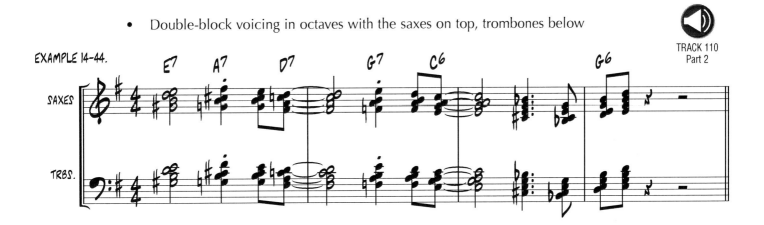

• Saxes in block voicing, trombones an octave below using drop-two

EXAMPLE 14-45.

In all of these situations, the baritone sax can either double the melody an octave below, or play chord roots beneath the trombone section (there's more information to follow regarding integrating the baritone sax with the trombone section for yet another option). On the track, the baritone doubles the melody on the first example, and plays the chord root on the second. Example 14-46 shows both of these options.

EXAMPLE 14-46.

Going beyond four-note voicings, the sax section/trombone section combination can also be harmonized using five, six, and seven notes. These can be written in close position to achieve a cluster effect or open to gain greater breadth and less tension. The orchestration of these voicings is a bit more complex due to the unequal distribution of notes between all the horns. Typically, the two sections are interlocked and some notes are judiciously doubled at the unison or octave.

EXAMPLE 14-47.

The combination of the saxophone and trumpet sections offers many different options. Here, the majority of the instruments are higher pitched, but the lower horns can balance with them for purposes of octave doubling. Unison passages extending beyond A♭ above middle C are not possible because of the range of the baritone. The composite sound of these two sections is much less round than the sax/trombone configuration due to the reedy quality of the saxes and edgier sound of the trumpets. For this reason, the dynamic level is usually *mf* or louder because soft passages, though possible, are not within the character of this combination. Due to the agility of these instruments, fast rhythms at quick tempos are possible.

TRACK 113
Part 1

EXAMPLE 14-48.

Because of the large composite range of the saxophone section and the even higher range of the trumpets, more types of harmonizations are possible.

- Four-note double-block voicing in octaves with the trumpets on top, and the top four saxes below

TRACK 113
Part 2

EXAMPLE 14-49.

- Trumpets in block voicing and saxes an octave below using drop-two or drop-two and four

EXAMPLE 14–50.

TRACK 114
Part 1

As before, in these two situations, the baritone is placed either on the melody an octave below or at the bottom of the ensemble on chord roots.

The saxophone section/trumpet section combination can also be written exactly like the brass section, with the saxes taking the notes that would normally be played by the trombones. Here, the baritone would always be placed at the bottom on the chord root.

TRACK 114
Part 2

EXAMPLE 14–51.

There is a timbral variation of this grouping that involves the sax section playing flutes while the trumpet section inserts harmon or cup mutes or plays flugelhorns. Unisons are possible, provided the line lies in a comfortable range for both sets of instruments. Typically, the flutes are the most problematic in this situation. However, since they are in unison, the line can usually project well enough to balance with the trumpets. If it lies consistently below the staff, the only way to balance the two sections is to amplify the flutes. The result is a composite of both sections, with the degree of edginess dependent on the trumpet muting or use of the flugelhorn.

TRACK 115
Part 1

EXAMPLE 14-52.

Octaves are also very useful, with the flutes on the top and the trumpets on the bottom.

TRACK 115
Part 2

EXAMPLE 14-53.

It is also possible to split the octaves within each section, resulting in a more homogenous sound.

TRACK 116
Part 1

EXAMPLE 14-54.

A possible problem exists with the ability of the bottom flutes to balance up to the bottom trumpets. If this type of octave doubling is desired, it may be best to use alto flutes or clarinets instead of flutes on the bottom octave. (Track 20, part two demonstrates the clarinet option.)

TRACK 116
Part 2

EXAMPLE 14-55.

This combination can be harmonized in two ways: block voicing doubled at the unison or doubled at the octave. When doubled at the unison, the sound is an amalgam of the flutes and whatever trumpet color is used. Balancing the flutes and trumpets may be an issue if the harmonization places the bottom flutes in their lower range.

TRACK 117
Part 1

EXAMPLE 14-56.

Block voicing doubled in octaves results in a clearer, more piercing sound due to the high, two-octave expanse between the two sections. The flutes play the top octave, which places them in their middle and high registers, while the muted trumpets or flugelhorns play in their middle register. In this arrangement, balance is rarely a problem and the color of both of the instruments is easily discernable.

TRACK 117
Part 2

EXAMPLE 14-57.

Addition of Two or More Instruments from One Section to Another

This concept enables the use of voicings with more than four notes to be played by any one section by adding instruments in the same pitch range or of similar timbre. There are two typical combinations, both using the trombone section as the foundation. The first adds both tenor and baritone saxes. These horns can either envelop the trombone section with the tenors above and the baritone below, or interlock with it, allowing each voicing to produce a slightly different sound. When the saxes envelop the trombone section, the sound of the saxes predominates.

EXAMPLE 14-58.

TRACK 118
Part 1

When intermingled, the trombone sound is dominant.

EXAMPLE 14-59.

TRACK 118
Part 2

Since there is a relatively small number of six- and seven-note chords, there is a good possibility that two or three notes will be doubled at the unison or in octaves in either situation.

The second combination adds two flugelhorns atop the trombone section. The timbre of both sets of these instruments is similar and sounds homogenous when blended. This grouping works well when writing pads. Again, pitches may be doubled at the unison or octave.

TRACK 119

EXAMPLE 14-60.

The Addition of a Single Instrument to Another Section

The final four combinations presented in this chapter either increase the density of a voicing, provide additional color, or both.

- Baritone sax with trombone section: This can be accomplished in two different ways. The first places the sax on the chord root with the four trombones above. The baritone adds an edgy quality to the bottom of the section.

TRACK 120
Part 1

EXAMPLE 14-61.

The second places the baritone inside the section directly above the bass trombone. Here, the overall sound of the section remains unchanged with the baritone providing only density to the harmony. The baritone is capable of balancing with the trombones at all dynamic levels.

TRACK 120
Part 2

EXAMPLE 14-62.

- Bass clarinet with trombone section: The bass clarinet is always placed beneath the section on chord roots. Its warm, mellow sound does not have the ability to project as well as the baritone sax. Because of this, it works best at softer dynamic levels. The combination of bass clarinet and trombones in cup mutes is especially effective. Note that in the next example, flutes and muted trumpets are also present.

TRACK 121

EXAMPLE 14-63.

- Flute (or piccolo) with trumpet section or brass choir: The function of this combination is purely for additional color and works well with any combination of mutes or flugelhorns. A single flute is either placed in unison with the lead trumpet or an octave above. At the unison, its color blends with the trumpet. When placed an octave above, its sound is more assertive. Count Basie's band used both the flute and piccolo in this manner to great effect. In the following example, the flute is written an octave above the lead trumpet.

TRACK 122

EXAMPLE 14-64.

The piccolo can often be substituted for the flute. When sounding an octave above, its sound is assertive, yet lighter than the flute. When sounding two octaves above, it is placed in its most brilliant register and projects over the section at any volume. It is never placed in unison with the lead trumpet as this would place the instrument in its lowest octave, which has very little projection.

- Flugelhorn or trumpet with sax section: The trumpet can either double the lead saxophone or function as the lead voice in a six-part soli. This combination offers an interesting alternative to the traditional five-part saxophone soli.

TRACK 123

Alternate Instrumentations

As history has shown, there have been many deviations from the standard setup; enough to merit a brief mention of each one and its idiosyncrasies.

When writing for **five trumpets**, there are three possible configurations:

- Five different notes in close or drop-two voicing: The fifth note will most likely result in a cluster voicing. These voicings are most resonant when the cluster is in the middle or bottom. If the cluster occurs at the top of the voicing, it may be desirable to drop the second voice an octave to retain focus on the top note.

- Four different notes with doubled lead in the fifth part

- Four different notes in a drop-two voicing with doubled lead in the fourth part

When writing for **three trombones**, there are two possible configurations:

- When bass trombone is playing chord roots, there is a gap between the second and third trombones that is usually filled by the baritone saxophone.

- When they are closely spaced, the baritone saxophone takes over the function of playing chord roots.

The use of **five trombones** would necessitate the use of five trumpets for the sake of balance. The added trombone would probably be another bass trombone. This would result in a thicker texture in all registers, with the center of sound dependent on the placement of the lead trombone.

A section consisting of only **four saxophones** negates the use of doubled lead. Solis can be written in either block or open voicings. Historically, the purpose of using **six saxophones** has been to lower the center of sound. The added saxophone is either baritone or bass.

Resources

The following is a list of some important large ensembles. It is recommended you listen to as many of them as possible:

Woody Herman Big Band

Stan Kenton Big Band

Johnny Richards Big Band

Buddy Rich Big Band

Maynard Ferguson Big Band

Gerry Mulligan Concert Jazz Band

Miles Davis/Gil Evans Collaborations

Thad Jones/Mel Lewis Jazz Orchestra

Mel Lewis Jazz Orchestra

Vanguard Jazz Orchestra

Bob Mintzer Big Band

Bill Holman Big Band

Clayton-Hamilton Jazz Orchestra

Bob Brookmeyer's New Art Orchestra

Maria Schneider

Bob Florence Limited Edition

WDR Jazz Orchestra

Danish Radio Orchestra

Stockholm Jazz Orchestra

This list is by no means complete; it is meant to be a point of departure.

CHAPTER 15
Arranging for Six and Seven Horns

A study of arranging for six and seven horns is more apt to be a result of experiences in large ensemble writing rather than from an expanded concept of arranging for four and five horns. Several contemporary writers, including Bill Holman, Don Sebesky, Rob McConnell, and Jim McNeely, have found that writing for smaller ensembles of this type provides a valuable outlet. Far from being merely expanded combos or "little big bands," these groups can develop their own distinct personalities. The textural and harmonic possibilities for six and seven horns will be discussed separately.

Instrumentation

The makeup of a six-horn group would most likely be one of two configurations:

- Three brass (two trumpets, one trombone) and three saxophones (ATB, ATT, or TTB)

- Four brass (two trumpets, two trombones) and two saxophones (AT, AB, TT, or TB)

The makeup of a seven-horn group would most likely be:

- Four brass (two trumpets, two trombones) and three saxophones (ATT, ATB, or TTB)

French horn would be an interesting substitute for trumpet or trombone. Bass trombone is a valuable asset in a group with two trombones. Of course, all the woodwind doublings and mute combinations discussed in earlier chapters are possible as well.

The addition of a sixth or seventh horn offers several advantages over five-horn writing:

- There is more flexibility when writing backgrounds.

- Unison writing with like instruments is expanded to include two trumpets and two trombones as well as two or three saxophones.

- Section writing: three or four brass or three saxophones is feasible.

Tutti Concepts

While groups of this size cannot achieve the sonic impact of a large ensemble, they can duplicate virtually all of the harmonic vocabulary. In Example 15-1, each chord (or each measure) consists of three columns of chord voicings. The left column contains a sampling of chords voiced for eight brass and five saxophones (with saxophone notes in brackets). The middle column shows a reduction for seven horns, and the right column, a reduction for six.

EXAMPLE 15-1.

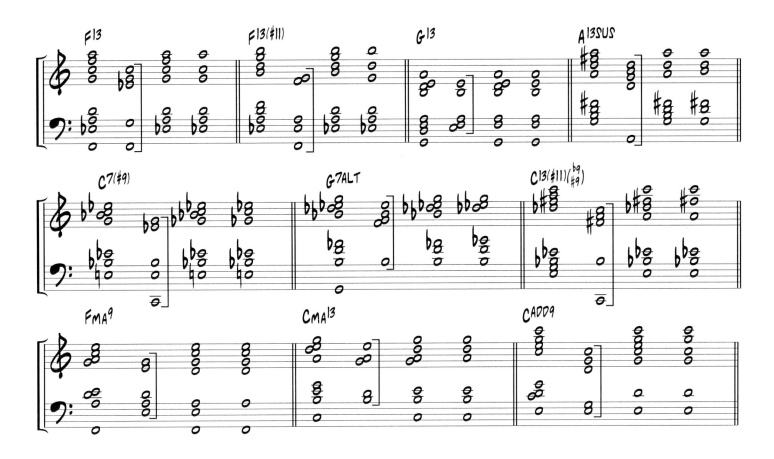

In the six- and seven-note chord reductions, the root and fifth are frequently omitted to retain the maximum number of color tones and achieve the desired level of tension.

The effectiveness of voicings with roots in the bottom voice depends on whether or not the instrumentation contains a true bass instrument—either a baritone sax or bass trombone. Both the tenor trombone and tenor saxophone are capable of playing bass notes on occasion, but neither would be desirable in extended passages.

One Element: Homophonic Voicings

Analysis of large ensemble tutti passages will show that most are harmonized in four, five, or six parts, with unison and octave doubling.

Six-horn ensembles would have the following options:

- Four-part harmony with octave doubling of two notes

TRACK 124
Part 1

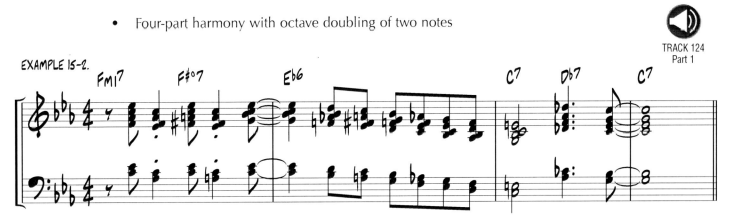

• Five-part harmony with octave doubling of one note

TRACK 124
Part 2

EXAMPLE 15-3.

• Six-part harmony

TRACK 124
Part 3

EXAMPLE 15-4.

Seven-horn ensembles would have the following options:

• Four-part harmony with octave doubling of three notes

TRACK 125
Part 1

EXAMPLE 15-5.

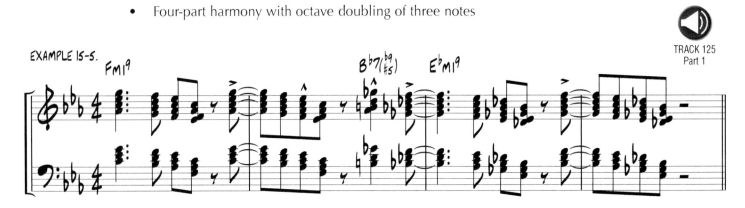

- Five-part harmony with octave doubling of two notes

TRACK 125
Part 2

- Six-part harmony with octave doubling of one note

TRACK 126
Part 1

- Seven-part harmony

TRACK 126
Part 2

Two Elements: Melody and Countermelody or Accompaniment

In six-horn groups, unisons or octaves are very powerful. The traditional "saxophones against brass" antiphony can be easily emulated in a group with three brass and three saxophones.

EXAMPLE 15-9.

Though not essential, either element could be reinforced with guitar or piano.

Harmonized accompaniment devices such as pads and punches require a minimum of three horns in order to balance effectively with the remaining three horns that are playing the melody. In groups containing four brass and two saxes, the four brass could adequately provide a background for the saxophones.

EXAMPLE 15-10.

But in the reverse situation, one of the trombones should be relegated to playing the role of a third saxophone.

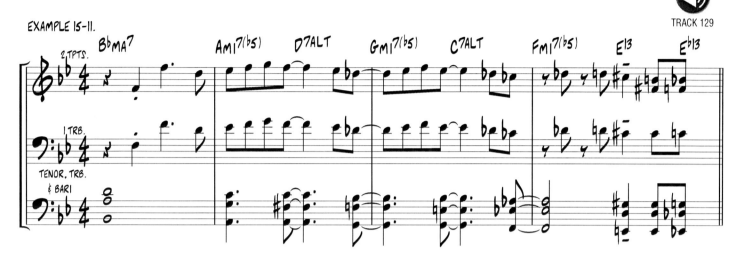

In seven-horn groups, the additional horn eliminates the limitations posed above. It can be added to either element without seriously affecting the balance between melody and countermelody or melody and accompaniment.

Three Elements: Melody, Countermelody, and Accompaniment

In a six-horn group with four brass and two saxophones, the three elements can be divided equally.

However, if one of the elements contains punch chords, the reinforcement of piano and/or guitar to this device is essential.

EXAMPLE 15-13.

TRACK 131

The seventh horn alleviates this problem, and three elements can be attained solely with the horns.

EXAMPLE 15-14.

Four Elements

The combination of four elements can only be achieved with six horns by integrating the rhythm section. In the next example, three of the four elements are unison lines while one is harmonized. The harmonized line is played by piano and guitar to allow for doubling of the unison lines in the horns.

TRACK 132

EXAMPLE 15-15.

The addition of the seventh horn permits a redistribution of the elements so that the line that was played above by piano and guitar can be reinforced by horns.

EXAMPLE 15-16.

Non-Tutti Concepts

Any of the three-horn sections can be augmented by the addition of one or more horns from another section, or by combining sections. These are valuable for creating stronger unisons, fuller harmonies, and textural variety. However, it is a mistake to use them in an attempt to duplicate the sound of a large ensemble. Six or seven horns cannot produce the massed effects and sheer volume of an eighteen- or twenty-piece ensemble. The focus should be on more transparent textures and the exploitation of the unique color combinations within the ensemble. The next example shows one possibility of unique color combinations.

TRACK 133

EXAMPLE 15-17.

An ensemble of this size should be thought of as a group of soloists, each with the dual role of soloist and member of the ensemble. It is also important to write for the individual, not just the instrument. By exploring the special qualities of each player, the arranger can create a unique personality for the entire group. This soloistic attitude, combined with the awareness that every note counts, makes it possible to achieve a level of performance that is rarely obtained in a large ensemble.

The following is a list of some important reference recordings for six- and seven-horn groups:

Six-Horn Groups

Miles Davis (*Birth of the Cool*)

Bill Kirchner Nonet (*Trance Dance*)

Joe Roccisano (*Leave Your Mind Behind* and *The Joe Roccisano Nonet*)

Joe Lovano (*52nd Street Themes* and *Birth of the Cool Suite*)

Seven-Horn Groups

Rob McConnell (*Thank You Ted*, *The Rob McConnell Tentet*, and *Music of the Twenties*)

Zoot Sims (*Hawthorne Nights*, arrangements by Bill Holman)

Jim McNeely (*Group Therapy*)

Gerry Mulligan Tentet (*The Original Gerry Mulligan Tentets and Quartets*)

Thelonious Monk (*The Thelonious Monk Orchestra at Town Hall*)

PART IV

The Arrangement

Chapters 16 through 22 discuss the preliminary planning stages involved in the creation of an arrangement as well as its component parts:

- Introduction
- Melody Chorus
- Interlude
- Solo Chorus with Backgrounds
- Shout Chorus and Recapitulation
- Ending

Each chapter culminates in a critique of two full-length arrangements; "Bar Flies" for small ensemble and "Charming William" for large ensemble. Full scores for both of these charts can be found in appendix 7. Chapter 23 explores new trends in jazz arranging and composition through the examination of music by four contemporary writers: Jim McNeely, Bob Brookmeyer, Don Grolnick, and Maria Schneider.

CHAPTER 16
Planning an Arrangement

Once a piece has been selected and the arranging possibilities determined, the arranger must use all his/her knowledge and experience to write an arrangement that is both creative and original. The piece must be analyzed to determine ways in which the various elements may be reconceived to achieve this goal. Listed below are the most important aspects that should be scrutinized carefully, and about which conscious choices should be made.

- Choice of Key
- Choice of Style and Tempo
- Choice of Meter
- Melodic Paraphrase
- Reharmonization

Choice of Key

Ensembles/General considerations

This is one of the critical early decisions that must be made. The so-called "standard key" should never be chosen automatically unless there is a very good reason. One such reason might be a tune that is difficult to play or has an involved chord progression. Many of John Coltrane's tunes fall into this category. When instrumentalists have spent a considerable amount of time mastering a piece in its original key, they may not appreciate the challenge of having to play it in another key. Just having to play an intricate melody in an unfamiliar key could be needlessly problematic. However, a piece with an uncomplicated melody and difficult chord progression, such as "Cherokee," could be set in another key and then followed by a modulation to the original key for the improvisation.

The range of a piece is not determined solely by the key, but rather the interval from the lowest note to the highest. Two pieces in the same key may have entirely different ranges. Here are five pieces, all in the key of B♭, with their respective ranges.

EXAMPLE 16-1.

Most standards and bebop tunes fall into this approximate range (higher-pitched instruments and voices would refer to the treble clef version; lower pitched, bass clef).

EXAMPLE 16-2.

American popular songs usually encompass the range of a tenth or eleventh. Instrumentals may have a slightly wider range.

In the majority of situations, the selection of the proper key entails the concurrence of two factors: the range of the piece, and the instrument(s) or voice selected to play it. The way to bring these two factors into agreement is to use a kind of sliding scale:

- If the key of the piece is fixed, select an instrument whose range most closely matches the range of the piece.

- If the choice of instrument(s) or voice is fixed, move the key up or down so that its range fits comfortably into the practical range of the selected instrument or voice.

Solo Voice or Instrument

Voice

The key for a vocal arrangement should never be selected without consulting the singer. Even if the *tessitura* (the most comfortable vocal range) of the singer is known, his or her style and unique qualities must be taken into account. And the song itself may have its own peculiarities, such as:

- Emphasis on high or low registers
- Repeated or sustained high or low notes
- Unusually long phrases
- Unsingability of certain vowel sounds in the high register

Most female jazz singers are altos, while most male singers are baritones. The approximate ranges for these voices are as follows.

EXAMPLE 16-3.

The standards from the thirties to the sixties are written in keys that usually fall in the male range. More contemporary pop and rock songs are not so easily classifiable.

Trumpet

When writing a solo for the trumpet, the registral intensity must be taken into consideration. The song "Tenderly," for example, is a favorite among trumpet players. The original key is E♭. But a low B♮ occurs three times—in measures nine, eleven, and twenty-five—and is held for three beats on each occasion. This note, when transposed for trumpet, is a low D♭: the worst note on the instrument. It is out of tune and difficult to project. Raising the key one whole step to the key of F would eliminate this problem and place it in a brighter register.

Trombone

Standard keys are generally too low for the trombone. Although their ranges fall within the practical range of the instrument, the first octave of the trombone is not the most expressive. Nor is it the most agile, due to the lack of alternate slide positions. Pieces like "Groovin' High" and "Confirmation" would be extremely difficult to play in their original settings. Beginning with Tommy Dorsey in the 1940s, trombonists have been pushing the upper limits of the trombone higher and higher. The top range of many contemporary artists extends above the treble clef. Some trombonists are likely to claim that key is not an issue; if the original key is selected, they will simply play it an octave higher. However, be aware of the changes in registral intensity that will occur. These extremely high-register notes can often sound pinched and strained. This can alter the character of a melody, particularly a ballad. The instrument may simply not be able to project the warmth and elegance that the piece demands in that register.

A much wiser course would be to raise the original key a fourth or fifth and place it in this general range:

EXAMPLE 16-4.

Alto sax

The middle and upper registers of the alto sax are the most preferred for solo playing. But a song like Duke Ellington's "In a Sentimental Mood" could pose problems. It begins with six eighth-note pickups ascending to a high E, which is held for five beats. This event occurs three times in the song. While this note is within the practical range of the instrument, sustaining it for five beats at full volume can produce a shrill, almost whiny quality that could negate the intended effect.

Tenor sax

The wide practical range of the tenor sax easily accommodates most standard keys. But registral characteristics must be taken into account, as well as the stylistic preferences of the performer. When playing a classic tenor-saxophone vehicle like "Body and Soul," some may prefer the warm, dark sound of the low register while others might choose the lighter, brighter, upper register. The piece could be played in either octave, although the higher version would involve the extreme upper limits of the range. Unless the arranger has a specific register in mind, the best solution in most cases would be to write the melody in its original octave and leave the choice of register up to the performer. But raising the key a fourth or fifth would be a viable alternative.

Baritone sax

The baritone sax has surprisingly few limitations and can be an excellent solo instrument, as long as the low extremities are avoided. These can sound gravelly and, although effective for bass lines and ensemble parts, may not be suitable for solo playing.

Choice of Style and Tempo

Arrangers have had a fondness for stylistic permutations since the 1930s, when a passion was developed for "swinging the classics." Melodies were borrowed not only from symphonic and operatic works, but from every conceivable genre. The practice continues to the present time; here are some of the most frequently used stylistic transformations:

- **Ballad to bolero, bossa nova, or medium swing feel**: A ballad can also be transformed into a samba by doubling the note values; a thirty-two measure piece becomes a sixty-four measure piece.

- **Fast swing to samba or other fast Latin groove**: Another option is to retain the swing feel and decrease the tempo. Double-length tunes (like many of Cole Porter's) can be reduced by halving the note values; a sixty-four measure piece becomes a thirty-two measure piece.

- **Standard to Afro-Cuban**: Many jazz standards are adaptable to Afro-Cuban rhythms, particularly the mambo.

- **Bebop to funk**: highly syncopated bebop tunes (like "Moose the Mooche") can easily be converted to funk tunes. Most tunes can be written in a funk style by syncopating its melody.

Sometimes arrangements can be written in two or more different styles, starting in one style and switching to another. These changes can either take place from chorus to chorus or within the chorus itself. A typical example of the first type is an arrangement that is written in a funk style in the first chorus and then switches to swing in the second. The second type is exemplified in Bronislau Kaper's "On Green Dolphin Street," which traditionally alternates between Latin in the A sections and swing in the B sections.

Choice of Meter

Meters other than 4/4 and 3/4 were seldom used in early jazz. But after the successful experiments by Dave Brubeck in the sixties and the Don Ellis Orchestra in the seventies, the use of complex meters, metric modulation, meter changes, and time signature alteration became important tools for the arranger.

Metric modulation involves changing tempo through the extension or diminishing of the value of the basic time unit. A well-known example of this is Dave Brubeck's "Blue Rondo Ala Turk" where three eighth notes of the 9/8 time signature equal one quarter note of the 4/4 blues.

Meter change refers to a momentary insertion of a different meter. A good example can be found in the analysis of Don Grolnick's arrangement of "What Is This Thing Called Love?" in chapter 23.

Time signature alteration was explained in detail in chapter 1. Below is a review of the options discussed there:

- Converting 4/4 to 3/4 using a 1:1 ratio
- Converting 4/4 to 3/4 using a 1:2 ratio
- Converting 3/4 to 4/4 using a 1:1 ratio
- Converting 3/4 to 4/4 using a 1:2 ratio
- Converting 4/4 to 5/4 or 7/4 using a 1:1 ratio
- Converting 4/4 to 5/4 or 7/4 using a 2:1 ratio
- Converting 4/4 to 7/8 by subtracting 1/2 beat from the end of each measure

Melodic Paraphrase

Chapter 1 contains everything needed to know about melodic paraphrasing. The decisions to be made here are whether or not it is needed, and if so, how much. Chances are that an arrangement that involves changes of style and/or meter will also require some melodic paraphrasing. Only straightforward adaptations of jazz tunes are unlikely to need this kind of treatment. However, don't hesitate to apply some personal touches to even the most sacred of jazz standards. Use caution so as not to alter rhythmic and melodic figures that make up the essence of the piece. It would be very difficult, for example, to re-rhythm a piece like "Straight, No Chaser" without seriously jeopardizing its integrity.

Reharmonization

This is the most effective way for an arranger to place a personal stamp on an arrangement, especially a ballad. Arrangers often employ more reharmonization at slower tempos because the ear has more time to absorb complex harmonies. A lot of time and patience is required to develop a knack for reharmonization. Here are some suggested ways for the inexperienced arranger to become involved in the process:

- Start with turnarounds—those cadential progressions that occur at the ends of phrases and sections of a piece. Binary (ABAC) and ternary (AABA) forms have two or three places for turnarounds, not to mention the final cadence that must be altered to connect choruses.

- Expand existing tonicizations from simple secondary dominant chords into two- or three-chord progressions.

- Look for new areas for possible tonicizations. Some scale tones and scale fragments are more easily approached from the flat side of the tonality; others are more accessible from the sharp side, while some are responsive to either treatment.

- Learn as many alternate progressions for blues and "rhythm" changes as possible. Portions of these may be applied to other tunes as well.

Decisions on all of these aspects need to be made before much writing can be done. One exception might be reharmonization; this can be an ongoing process. A first attempt at reharmonization might be satisfactory. However, through experimentation or necessity, alternate harmonies may be later discovered.

Formal Structure of the Arrangement
General Characteristics

Once the decisions on tempo, meter, style, harmonization, and instrumental possibilities have been made, the focus should be on the various component parts that make up the arrangement. Early jazz arrangers developed a format that mimics the classical *Sonata-Allegro* form. This gradually became standardized during the big-band era and still serves as the basic model. The main components, listed with their classical counterparts, are as follows:

- Introduction
- Setting of the melody (exposition)
- Improvisation section (development)
- Ensemble, or "Shout" section (continuation of development)
- Restatement of the melody, in part or whole (recapitulation)
- Ending (coda)
- Other features, such as interludes, sendoffs, and additional ensemble or soli passages may be inserted.

This format has proven to be remarkably flexible and resilient, and has served arrangers well for decades. But due to changes in styles and the mere presence of the creative process, ways are being sought to alter or manipulate the format. Many have had remarkable success in doing so, even to the extent of creating entirely new forms. These efforts should provide a source of constant study and inspiration for serious writers. However, for the novice, it is best to become familiar with the established format before seeking ways to manipulate it.

Specific Forms

This focus on formal arrangement must necessarily lead to a short discussion of form. Several passing references have been made concerning it in previous chapters, but preparations for writing a full arrangement would not be complete if the role of form in the organization of musical ideas was not examined.

The basis of form is repetition. Repetition is necessary to enhance aural retention. But excessive repetition leads to monotony; monotony can only be relieved by variety. Therefore, all good melodies contain contrasting ideas. The form of a piece is determined by the way in which these contrasting elements are arranged. A given number of themes can be arranged in only so many ways. This is why the formal arrangement of the majority of jazz compositions falls into one of three categories: *binary, ternary,* or *blues*. Even contemporary composers who prefer *through composition* to the traditional forms still rely heavily on repetition and contrast. The reason for the continued reliance on these traditional forms is that they have been found to be aesthetically satisfying. But the persistence of these forms should not be looked upon as being restrictive. Within these frameworks, infinite variety is possible. Just as no two pieces are exactly alike, no two forms are identical.

The form of a piece does not determine its length. All these forms are very flexible. The standard blues is twelve measures long. But twenty-four measure blues are common, and there are contemporary examples of blues ranging from eight to thirty-two measures.

Binary and ternary forms are normally thirty-two measures long. But there are many sixteen and sixty-four measure examples. Conceivably, with the addition of extra repeats, internal structural deviations and extensions, practically any length is possible.

An overwhelming proportion of jazz and popular works are structurally composed of three parts. The "concept of statement – departure – recapitulation" **ternary** structure has proven to be the most aesthetically satisfying of all musical forms. Given the normal repeat of the first section, the ternary form has evolved into a thirty-two measure form consisting of four eight-bar phrases. This may be represented by the letters AABA.

The **binary** form consists of two more or less equal halves and is designated by the letters ABAB', or ABAC, depending on the amount of deviation from the original B section in the final phrase. Unifying elements are stressed in the A section. It usually consists of a four-bar phrase that is repeated sequentially. The first eight measures of "Just Friends," "Airegin," and "My Romance" are examples of this sequential treatment. Contrast in the B section is achieved not only thematically, but through a modulation to a closely related key, usually the dominant. The two halves of a binary form can never be exactly alike because of this change of tonal center. The final B (or C) must cadence in the original key.

The classic twelve-bar **blues** form consists of three four-measure phrases, with the first two thematically linked. It may be represented by the letters aa'b. "Now's the Time," "Blue Monk," and "Blues Walk" are representative of this type. Many blues are more through-composed and have three dissimilar phrases: abc. "Billie's Bounce," "Blues for Alice," and "Chi-Chi" fall into this category.

Form and orchestration

Form and orchestration are inextricably linked, but the relationship can be a complex one at times. It might be expected that the most efficient orchestration is one that reinforces the unifying and contrasting elements of the music. This is usually true, but not always. Sometimes orchestration is treated as a separate element and the two work independently of each other. The ramifications of this relationship between form and orchestration will be discussed in detail in the succeeding chapters.

The Full-score Setup

One more task remains before the actual writing begins: creating a full-score setup for the instrumentation to be used.

After the score layout has been prepared, the first question is "Where do I begin?" One obvious answer might be "at the beginning," but it may not be the correct one. In fact, most arrangers do not begin with the introduction. So much time has already been spent deciding on the various ways of treating the piece, and so the next logical step could be the actual setting of the melody. After that, the creative process should take over and the path of least resistance should be followed. The Introduction, Ending, and Shout Chorus often require the most original composition and may have to wait until later. Backgrounds for the improvisation section are less demanding from a compositional standpoint and might be the next undertaking. With many arrangers, melodic and rhythmic ideas develop more easily than harmonic ones. If that is the case, write them down and keep going; they can be harmonized later. The more prolonged the inspirations are, the more spontaneous the music will sound. Additional material—interludes, send-offs, etc.—can also be inserted later.

Another question that could be asked at the outset is "How long should the arrangement be?" Length, from a purely creative standpoint, should never be an issue; only the limits of the arranger's imagination will hinder this. But sometimes external factors can play a role in determining the length of an arrangement. Here are some instances:

- **"Head" chart**: This is the most basic of all arrangements, consisting of a setting of the melody, followed by improvisation and a recapitulation of the melody. Every good arranger has written head charts at some time or other. They serve a multitude of purposes and can form the basis for a full-blown arrangement at a later time.

- **Vocal arrangement**: Singers usually have definite ideas about the length of an arrangement, especially if it is to be part of a stage presentation. One thing they do not enjoy is standing around doing nothing during extensive improvisation or ensemble passages (unless they are involved in the improvisation). Length of introductions and endings may also be determined by specific situations. Long ones are necessary for entrances and exits, but if the singer is already onstage, they may be very short.

A beginning arranger rarely possesses the ability to visualize an arrangement in its entirety. A more feasible approach would be to deal with the component parts (Introduction, Melody Chorus, Interlude, Solo Chorus, Shout Chorus Ending) separately and then connect them into a meaningful whole. The next six chapters discuss each of these components in detail and suggest ways of combining them to form a complete arrangement.

CHAPTER 17
The Introduction

Introductions establish the mood for the entire arrangement. Paradoxically, they can be created at any time during the writing process. Some wait until the entire chart is written to compose the introduction; others will not proceed until the introduction is complete. The moment of inspiration will vary for each arrangement.

If one chooses to compose the introduction before arranging the first chorus, the decision-making process discussed at the beginning of chapter 16 regarding key, style, and meter will have to be completed. The only other aspect discussed in that chapter that will affect the introduction is reharmonization. The extent of reharmonization of the melody will directly influence the harmonic complexity of the introduction.

Development Strategies

This section illustrates some possible options for developing an introduction for an arrangement.

Improvised piano chorus, with or without rhythm section accompaniment

This was a trademark of Count Basie's band in the thirties and continues as a viable way to begin an arrangement.

Final four or eight measures of the tune

The existing melody could be orchestrated or a new one could be created on the chord changes. This presentation of the existing melody was overworked on vocal charts during the big band era and can easily sound trite unless skillfully crafted.

Orchestration or variant of an historical introduction

Two introductions on standard tunes that have remained closely associated with them are Charlie Parker's "Star Eyes" and Dizzy Gillespie's "All the Things You Are." However, present use of these verbatim goes against any arranger's better judgment. Here's how the intro to "All the Things You Are" could be reworked.

EXAMPLE 17-1.

Interlude as introduction

Dizzy Gillespie's "Night in Tunisia" contains an interlude that was originally only heard before the first solo break. It was later used between all solos and there is no reason it couldn't be used as a point of departure for an introduction. An arranger-composed interlude could also be placed at the beginning of a chart.

Motivic development

This is a staple of every composer/arranger. This process involves the manipulation of the unique elements in a composition. Motives can be taken from any place in the tune. There are three possible types of motivic development that can be used singularly or in combination: harmonic, melodic, and rhythmic.

- **Harmonic**: John Coltrane's "Giant Steps" is comprised of three tonal centers spaced a major third apart. The introduction in the next example states the tonic chord of each tonal center. These chords are intentionally placed out of order to accommodate the movement into the body of the tune. Rhythmic elements were also introduced.

TRACK 135
Part 1

EXAMPLE 17-2.

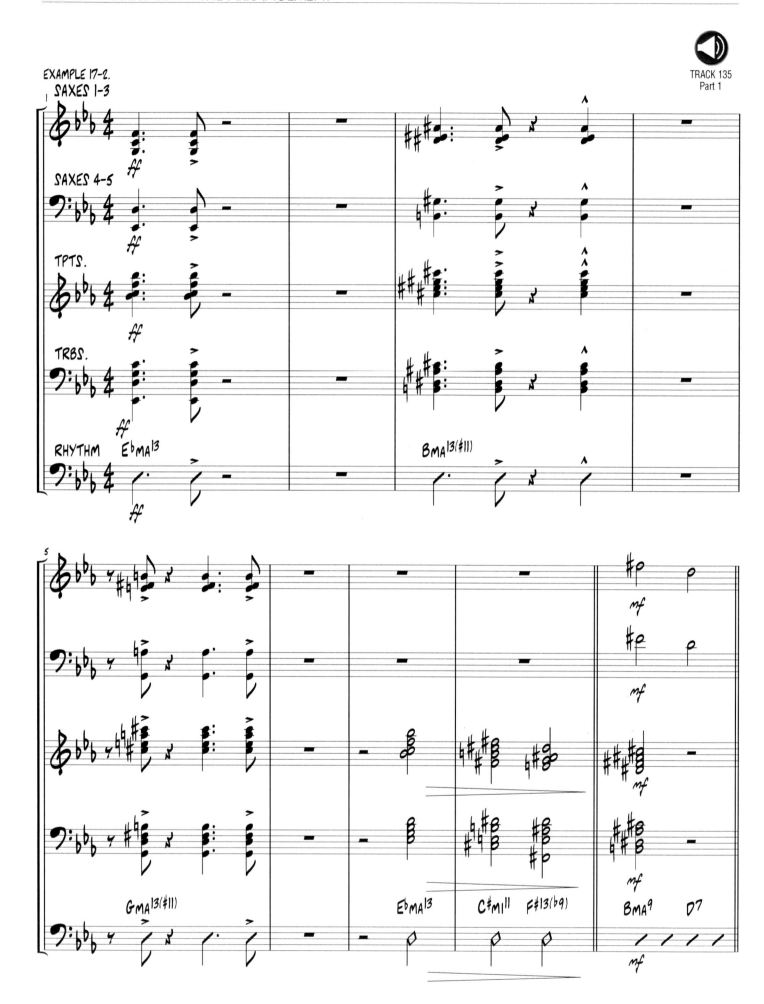

- **Melodic**: The first two notes of "Day in, Day Out" comprise a rising whole step. This interval is developed sequentially and used as the basis for this introduction. The melody is harmonized using major triads which, when combined with the bass line, create tension through contrary motion.

TRACK 135
Part 2

EXAMPLE 17-3.

When using the initial motive, the idea should not be overstated to the extent that it renders the opening of the first chorus anticlimactic. Motives taken from later in the form offer a more subtle approach. The introduction to "Let It Snow" is an example of this. The chosen motive occurs at the end of the A section. The three-time repetition of the title constitutes a descending scale that is harmonized using parallel 13th chords with altered 9ths and suspended chords.

EXAMPLE 17-4.

TRACK 136

- **Rhythmic**: In the following introduction, the distinctive rhythmic patterns of "Straight, No Chaser" were isolated without regard for melodic contour. New melodies were created from these motives and were paired with their mirrors. Each motive ends with a vertical sonority derived from the intervals of each melody. These motives are separated by drum fills, resulting in a total of twelve measures, alluding to the blues form.

TRACK 137

EXAMPLE 17-5.

Rubato

The "stolen time" characteristic known as *rubato* can take shape in a number of ways. The simplest use of rubato may take place in a solo feature known as the *cadenza*. This could range from a free-form improvisation without a tonal center to a specified set of chords.

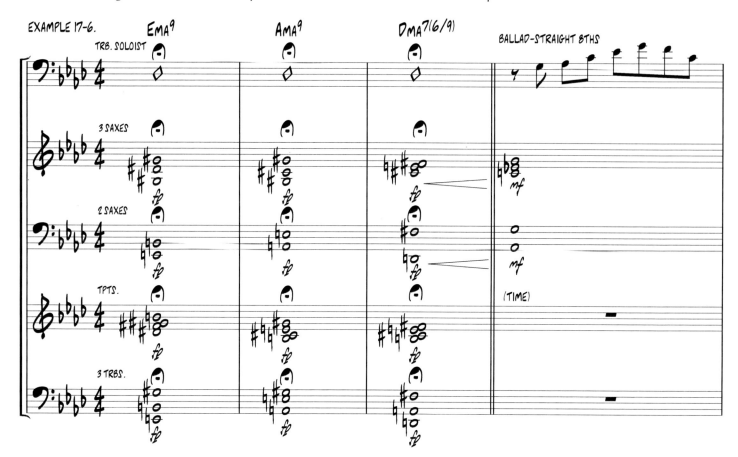

Another form of a rubato introduction involves a pianist or guitarist playing a section (verse, first "A," bridge, etc.) of the tune unaccompanied. Many vocal arrangements begin in this fashion.

Quotations of other music

These could include other tunes by the composer or tunes with the same word or subject matter. For example, an arrangement of Antonio Carlos Jobim's "One Note Samba" might contain quotes from any of his other compositions. This idea, though enticing at the outset, could easily backfire if the references are so obscure or convoluted that no one recognizes them.

Originally composed material that establishes the character of the tune

Some great examples of this can be found in the arrangements of Marty Paich ("My Old Flame"), Bob Brookmeyer ("Willow Weep for Me"), Jim McNeely ("Yesterdays," "In a Sentimental Mood," "In the Wee Small Hours") and Slide Hampton ("Inner Urge").

Pedal Tones

A *pedal tone* is a note sustained through various changes of harmony. The commonly used scale degrees for pedals are dominant and tonic. Dominant pedals are the best choice for intros as they are anticipatory in nature and help to set up the passages that follow. Tonic pedals are more passive in nature. Dominant pedals may occur in any voice, but tonic pedals are almost always in the bass. The pedal by itself creates a static situation. It does not have to be merely a long, sustained note; it can be broken into various rhythmic patterns as in the following example.

EXAMPLE 17-7.

Other notes may be added to the pedal so that it can attain some melodic significance.

EXAMPLE 17-8.

Many diverse expressive values can result, depending on what happens above the pedal tone. In the following example, a feeling of reflection is achieved through the use of long note values and mild dissonances.

TRACK 138
Part 1

EXAMPLE 17-9.

The next example projects much more tension and excitement by employing shorter note values and sharper dissonances.

TRACK 138
Part 2

EXAMPLE 17-10.

Vamps

These define tonality through repetition as well as establish the groove. *Vamps* are comprised of any number of chords using functional or nonfunctional harmonies, or a combination of both.

The most common vamps containing functional harmony are shown below.

One-Chord Vamps

One-chord vamps typically consist of the repetition of the tonic chord. There are three chord qualities that can function as one-chord vamps:

- Major: all extensions are usable.
- Minor: all extensions and alterations are usable except for mi7(♭5).
- Dominant: all extensions, suspensions, and alterations are usable except for those altered chords containing flatted ninths or raised fifths. These chords do not function as tonic chords.

There is a danger of monotony when using a single chord for an entire introduction. In order for this type of vamp to be effective, the melodic ideas and orchestration must compensate for the inherent sameness of a single chord. The next example incorporates five different elements into an eight-measure vamp over a single chord. This was designed to be a background for a high-register piano solo, creating a sixth element.

TRACK 139

EXAMPLE 17-11.

Two-Chord Vamps

Two-chord vamps are usually one or two measures in length. The allotted space is typically divided equally between the two chords. The following are the most often-used harmonically functional two-chord vamps. The chord qualities and alterations have intentionally been omitted as there are many possible combinations of major, minor, and dominant chords.

- I–V
- I–♭II
- I–IV
- I–♭VII
- I–VII

Three- and Four-chord Vamps

Like two-chord vamps, three- and four-chord vamps are usually one or two measures long, depending on tempo. The tonic chord always occupies half the space of a three-chord vamp, while four-chord vamps divide the space evenly. The next example shows the most typical three- and four-chord vamps containing functional harmony.

- I–II–V
- I–IV–V
- I–♭VI–V
- I–VI–II–V
- III–VI–II–V
- I–♭III–♭VI–♭II

Nonfunctional Harmony Vamps

Next are some common vamps employing nonfunctional harmony. Those with root movement retain the same chord quality. It is the exact transposition that makes this type of vamp appealing.

- Same Root: due to the lack of root movement, this vamp is dependent on changing chord qualities (Cma9–Cmi9).
- Minor Seconds: these may be transposed either direction, up or down (Cma9–Bma9 or Cma9–D♭ma9).
- Major Seconds: either direction (Cma9–B♭ma9 or Cma9– Dma9).
- Minor Thirds: either direction (Cma9–Ama9 or Cma9–E♭ma9).
- Major Thirds: either direction (Cma9–Ema9 or Cma9–A♭ma9).
- Tritone: (Cma9–G♭ma9).

As discussed previously in the section on pedal tones, the establishment of the vamp is only the first step to writing an introduction of this type. Further melodic and rhythmic elements must be added.

No Introduction

It is also possible to begin an arrangement with no introduction. The selection of this option often requires some type of initial gesture, whether subtle or dramatic. For instance:

- Presentation of the melody without its harmony: this could be a single instrument or two playing the melody without accompaniment. Two brilliant examples of this are Bob Florence's "Straight, No Chaser" and Bill Finegan's "C Jam Blues" where, in both cases, Mel Lewis begins by approximating the melody on the drum set. Another example of this is Miles Davis' recording of "Oleo" where he plays all three A sections of the tune without accompaniment.

- Use of *broken* or *stop time* (see chapter 20, p. 319): tunes like "Speak Low" have been traditionally played in this manner.

- Use of a single chord to set up the melody: Thad Jones' "Little Pixie II" begins with a muted brass chord that precedes the opening saxophone soli.

Combinations

Many of the above options may be combined. For example, any type of motivic development could be combined with rubato and/or pedal tones.

The linkage between the introduction and the first chorus is of paramount importance; the melody should sound as if it is an outgrowth of the introduction. The effective connection of the two should be seamless, not as if one part was haphazardly pasted onto the other.

Conclusion and Analysis

From this point forward, the small ensemble arrangement of "Bar Flies" and the large ensemble arrangement of "Charming William" will be discussed in detail. The full scores for these arrangements may be found in appendix 7.

Bar Flies

TRACK 164

The introduction to the five-horn arrangement of "Bar Flies" stemmed from two sources: Charlie Parker's "Star Eyes" (the progression on which "Bar Flies" is based) and the initial descending major second of this melody. The primary feature of Bird's intro was a bass line on which he and Miles Davis improvised. The seven notes of this line were retained, but re-rhythmed with additional material added. This obscures the original line to the point where most listeners would not even be aware of this homage. This source of inspiration is nonetheless important to the arranger. The second idea—the descending second—was harmonized using parallel dominant thirteenth chords. Since these did not effectively establish the tonality, a ninth measure containing a dominant chord was added to bring it into focus.

Charming William

TRACK 167

The introduction for the large ensemble arrangement of "Charming William" is comprised of two separate sections, creating a sort of "double introduction." This was a necessity due to the abundance of activity in the initial thirty-two measures. A cool-down period was essential before proceeding to the statement of the melody. The two distinct progressions also foreshadow the solo sections found later in the chart.

The first section uses an additive process, based on a I-VI-II-V-III-VI-II-V vamp. All the chords were altered to set up a high tension level. The trombones and bass enter first with a rhythmically diverse statement of the progression. It is intentionally sparse to accommodate a second line. The trumpet section was chosen for the second entrance because of its contrasting register. The goal here was to create a line that would stand on its own, but would also produce a complete statement when combined with the trombones. To heighten the tension, the trumpet section was voiced in clusters.

The subsequent two saxophone lines were constructed to be rhythmically compatible with the existing brass lines. The decision to write unison lines was intentional; to add any further harmonic complexity could result in cacophony. They were voiced in octaves to give them the necessary emphasis to balance with the brass. The first line, played by alto, tenor, and baritone, begins in measures 17–18 with a brief quote of "Billy Boy." The remainder is freely composed on the B$\flat$ half-whole diminished scale. The final line, played by soprano, tenor, and guitar, is also freely composed with little regard for the chord changes. This literally sends the introduction "over the top." It ends with an upward sweep in measure 32, culminating with a B$\flat$ dominant suspension on the downbeat of measure 33.

The second section of this intro is eight measures in length. It is a two-chord vamp played only by the rhythm section. These two chords form the basis for the reharmonization of the melody that follows.

CHAPTER 18
Melody Chorus

Most arrangers begin an arrangement with a setting of the melody. In this case, the decision-making process discussed in chapter 16 regarding key, style, meter, reharmonization, and extent of melodic paraphrase will have to be completed at this point.

The next task is to create an arrangement that balances repetition and contrast through the use of changing colors and textures. First, determine how the repetitions within the form are to be treated. Repeated sections generally require a change of orchestration; subsequent ones are usually more fully orchestrated. The principle of small to large, or simple to complex, works best.

Ternary Form

The ternary form (AABA) presents the biggest challenge. Here the A theme is heard three times, two of them occurring consecutively. The temptation is to simply put a repeat around the first A, as it is usually printed in fake books. Although this can be a workable solution with some of the material being played the second time only, it is always better to write it out. This makes it possible to vary any of the musical elements, not just add to the existing ones. The following are some of the many ways the first two A sections may be varied:

- First time: melody, second time: countermelody
- First time: melody, second time: solo with accompaniment
- First time: melody, second time: harmonized melody with new paraphrase
- First time: harmonized melody, second time: harmonized new paraphrase of melody. The melody has been stated in its most obvious form in the first A. The second A allows for a freer interpretation that may only go as far as an occasional reference to the original melody.
- First time: harmonized melody, second time: melody with countermelody
- First time: harmonized melody, second time: solo with accompaniment

Contrast is inherent in the B (bridge) section. New harmonies and thematic material are introduced. Movement to other key areas is common. The best procedure here is to reinforce these new, contrasting elements with changes in color and texture, rather than continuing with previously used ones. A sub-climax frequently occurs near the end of this section.

Since the final A is separated from the other two by the bridge, it is possible to reintroduce some material from the first or second A. But a simple repeat of one of the previous A sections is insufficient. It is best to save a surprise or two for the final A. This is often the most heavily orchestrated, because of the possibility of a subclimax in this section. If a lighter texture were chosen for the start of the section, a change to a fuller one would be necessary to create a sense of finality.

Binary Form

Most of the comments about ternary form will apply to the other forms as well. Binary form, with its two balanced halves and contrasting themes, does not require as many changes of texture as ternary form. It is possible to maintain the same basic texture throughout the first half with only slight changes or additions. With the repeat of the second A, however, a new and usually fuller texture is required. Most binary pieces have a subclimax near the end of the last phrase.

Blues and Shorter Forms

In blues and other short forms, one repeat with a change of texture in the second chorus is the norm. Again, small to large is the best approach. Refer to the section on ternary forms for suggestions on how to vary the repetition.

Three statements of a blues are possible, but the first would have to be very sparsely orchestrated. For instance:

- First chorus: one unaccompanied solo instrument
- Second chorus: two instruments (i.e., muted trumpet and flute) with a bass line
- Third chorus: melody with countermelody or accompaniment devices

The Final Phrase

Regardless of form, in the final phrase it becomes necessary to think beyond the first chorus, as what happens next will largely determine how this phrase will be orchestrated. If this decision has not been made, the final phrase should not be completed until it has. There are basically three options:

- A chorus of improvised solos with backgrounds: this is the most frequent choice.
- Another ensemble chorus: this would be a more likely choice with a larger ensemble because of the greater variety of textures available.
- An interlude: this consists of original material outside the form of the piece, designed to set up the next event (See chapter 19).

Regardless of which option is chosen, an important detail to be considered is the occurrence of the final cadence. Most commonly, this occurs on the downbeat of the next-to-last measure. In thirty-two-measure forms, this would be the downbeat of measure thirty-one. If the final note is anticipated by one half-beat, this leaves two full measures for a solo break or written instrumental material.

EXAMPLE 18-1.

Pieces that end in the last measure are less common; some that do include "Night in Tunisia," "Dat Dere," "Epistrophy," and "Oleo."

One-measure breaks are generally not as effective as two-measure breaks. However, at slow tempos, one measure may be enough to adequately prepare the next event. In fact, many ballads such as "In a Sentimental Mood," "'Round Midnight," "Lush Life," and "Prelude to a Kiss" end on the last measure.

Solo Break and Solo Section

A solo break is usually unaccompanied, but some orchestration may occur, as long as it does not interfere with the soloist and maintains the feel of a break. Some possibilities to accompany the solo instrument include:

- Drum fill

TRACK 140
Part 1

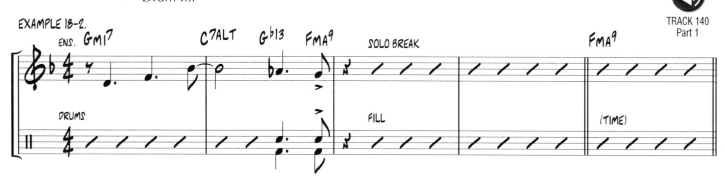

- Sustained or repeated bass note

TRACK 140
Part 2

- Rhythm section turnaround

TRACK 141
Part 1

- Orchestrated turnaround

EXAMPLE 18-5.

If there is no solo break, a melodic fill must be created that will move the music into the next section.

A setting for solo instrument presents some unique challenges. The task here is to create the desired mood and let the soloist do the rest. Subtle changes in color and texture should provide variety without inhibiting the soloist.

The primary focus is usually on the solo instrument throughout the first chorus. A two- or four-bar instrumental passage can sometimes be inserted without interrupting the continuity. This works best with melodies that contain short, repeated motives. The question then arises as to whether the soloist should play a harmony part in the ensemble passage. When a large ensemble is involved, the answer is definitely not. In smaller groups, the decision is based on each particular situation. But if it is decided that it is necessary to include the soloist to achieve the desired ensemble texture, it should be clearly marked in the solo part.

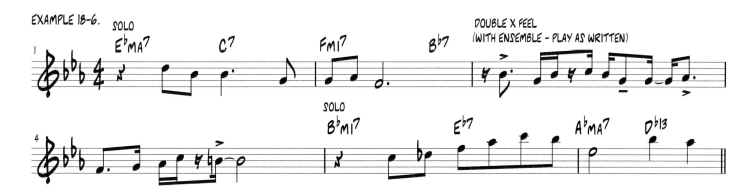

EXAMPLE 18-6.

It is sometimes appropriate for the soloist to play a written lead part with the ensemble for a few measures. The best place to do this is at the beginning of a phrase. Such a change of role occurring in the middle or near the end of a phrase will sound intrusive. Once again, this should be marked on the solo part.

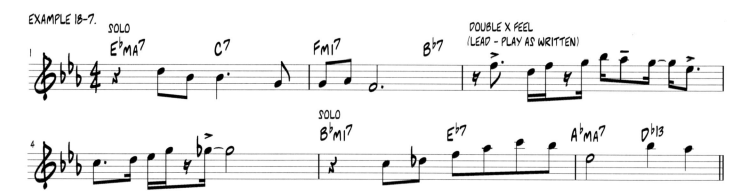

The most frequently used background devices in ballad arrangements are pads and slow-moving countermelodies. At faster tempos, a combination of pads and punches is effective.

Always resist the temptation to overwrite backgrounds. Those that contain involved reharmonizations or intricate patterns of punches can force the soloist to stay very close to the written melody. This is not necessarily a bad idea; it is, however, one that requires careful crafting.

Conclusion and Analysis

Finally, keep in mind that this is only the first chorus of the arrangement. Much of the drama and excitement will come later. Don't use up every idea in the first chorus. Experience will develop the ability to think in terms of larger segments and to apply the principles of unity and variety in terms of a whole arrangement.

These thoughts are implemented in the first chorus of the arrangement of "Bar Flies." The goal was to use as many two-, three-, four-, and five-horn combinations and arranging techniques as possible. It was also the intent in this chorus to use five-note sonorities sparingly, reserving them for later portions of the chart. The result is a constant flow of ideas, creating a seamless interwoven texture.

Bar Flies (See appendix 7, p. 412 for the full score.)

The first seven measures of letter A maintain a two-part texture, with trumpet and alto playing the melody in unison and tenor and trombone providing a countermelody. This is the only section of this chorus that retains a single texture. The eighth measure is harmonized in four parts, strengthening the cadential progression.

TRACK 164
0:11

Letter B begins in three-part harmony and expands into five parts by the fourth note, then continues in this manner to the end of the phrase. The second phrase is anticipated by a three-note pad played by the lower three horns with trumpet and alto playing the melody in thirds. The phrase ends in five parts. The third phrase (mm. 22–24) has trumpet, alto, and trombone in three parts with tenor and baritone providing punches at the ends of the phrase segments. The lower four horns continue with a harmonized countermelody. The three-note cadence in measure 25 is harmonized in five parts.

TRACK 164
0:21

The trumpet plays the melody through letter C. A countermelody is played by the alto (and sometimes guitar) with the lower three horns providing harmonic support for both elements. The subclimax at the end of this section is achieved with all the instruments playing in octaves.

TRACK 164
0:30

Letter D begins with trombone and baritone in unison. In measure 35, the tenor joins them to create a pad, which supports the trumpet and alto melody in thirds. The remainder of this phrase is in five-part harmony. The trumpet is omitted in the next phrase in favor of the alto on the melody. The lower three horns provide harmonic support. In measure 40, the baritone sets up the final phrase segment.

TRACK 164
0:40

Trumpet once again takes over the melody in the tag, with the lower horns playing a pad beneath. The last phrase begins in octaves and ends in five-part open voicings. This provides momentum for the first soloist, negating the need for an interlude.

TRACK 164
0:50

Charming William (See appendix 7, p. 444 for the full score.)

The original form of the tune "Billy Boy" kicks off the exposition (letter E), and is comprised of four, four-measure phrases. As is the case with all short forms, one statement of the melody is insufficient; this arrangement contains two. Because of the non-jazz nature of the tune, all elements have been freely interpreted.

TRACK 167
0:52

The form has been elongated by extending the ends of the second and fourth phrases by two measures. The third phrase and first two measures of the last phrase (letter F) have been truncated to 3/4. The two melody statements are separated by a four-measure passage.

A feeling of bitonality persists throughout. The entire melody is in C. The vamp in the first phrase is in B♭; the second phrase moves to A♭. Relief from the static pedal is provided in the third phrase by faster harmonic rhythm. The fourth phrase begins with a II-V in C (the only reference to the original key), but cadences in G♭. The ensuing four-measure passage re-establishes the B♭ pedal. The only difference between the two statements is the harmonization of the third phrase.

The exposition begins with the pickup to letter E, with saxophones playing the melody in octaves. The trombones enter at the end of the second phrase and provide harmonic support in the third phrase. This initial statement ends with octave saxes and rhythm. The four-measure passage beginning in measure 61 that separates the two statements re-establishes the B♭ pedal and is reinforced by the brass.

TRACK 167
1:23

The second rendering of the melody (letter G) is multilayered and contains increased rhythmic activity. The saxes continue with the melody, this time in two-part harmony. The trumpets provide a countermelody, while the trombones maintain the accompaniment established in the four-measure insert.

The third phrase (letter H) is homophonic in texture. The use of the full ensemble and increased harmonic rhythm and complexity all combine to create the first climax of the arrangement. The fourth phrase concludes with saxes in two parts with the brass echoing.

TRACK 167
1:37

The exposition is followed by a twelve-measure transition into the solo section beginning at Letter I. The B♭ pedal is restated with the saxophones playing a new line above. The brass section enters in the fifth measure with previously stated material. The transition concludes with a four-measure ensemble send-off in 3/4 (m. 93) for the first soloist.

TRACK 167
1:49

CHAPTER 19
Interlude

The continual cycling of a song form, though standard practice in jazz, can become monotonous. One of the most commonly used devices to provide relief is the *interlude*. This is a passage of original material written outside the form that connects major sections of an arrangement. It can be placed between the following sections:

- The melody and first improvised solo section
- Two different solo sections
- A solo section and shout chorus or other development section
- A shout chorus and recapitulation

Interludes are not necessary features of an arrangement. In fact, most arrangements do not contain interludes of any kind. However, when in need of a temporary change of musical scenery, they can be very effective.

Interludes usually interrupt the flow of the groove through the use of breaks, repetition of two- or four-measure rhythmic phrases, or pedals. They are typically eight measures in length, but can be as short as two measures and as long as sixteen measures or more. The following shows some examples of interludes found in big band and jazz standards:

- "Cottontail" by Duke Ellington: four measures; occurs between the melody and Ben Webster's solo.
- "Groovin' High" by Dizzy Gillespie: seven measures; occurs between Slam Stewart's and Dizzy's solos.
- "I Mean You" by Thelonious Monk/Coleman Hawkins: four measures; occurs between each soloist.
- "In the Mood" by Joe Garland: two interludes: the first is four measures and occurs between the tenor and trumpet solos, the second is two measures and occurs between the trumpet solo and the recapitulation.
- "In Your Own Sweet Way" by Dave Brubeck (found on Miles Davis's *Workin' with the Miles Davis Quintet*): eight measures; occurs between every chorus.
- "A Night in Tunisia" by Dizzy Gillespie: sixteen measures; occurs between the melody and the first soloist. Dizzy's big-band arrangement contains a second interlude that is eight measures long that occurs between the last soloist and the shout chorus.
- "Round Midnight" by Thelonious Monk (found on Miles Davis's *Round About Midnight*): three measures; occurs between the melody and John Coltrane's solo.
- "Seven Steps to Heaven" by Victor Feldman (found on Miles Davis's *Seven Steps to Heaven*): the eight-measure introduction serves as an interlude between each soloist.
- "Take the 'A' Train" by Billy Strayhorn (1941 version): four measures; occurs between the muted trumpet solo and the saxophone send-off at the key change.

Functions

Interludes may serve many functions:

- Provide a climax for a song that does not contain one: Tunes like "A Night in Tunisia" and "Woody'n You" that are repetitive or sequential, contain no natural climax. An interlude could be inserted at the end of the form before proceeding to the solo section to supply one.

- Break up the continual repetition of a chord progression by supplying contrasting harmonic material for improvisation: The interlude of "In Your Own Sweet Way" accomplishes this brilliantly.

- Relieve the tension of a complicated progression: An interlude comprised of one or two chords can provide this relief and allow the improviser to concentrate momentarily on the melodic aspects of the improvisation. A great example is in John Coltrane's "Moment's Notice."

- Create a springboard for a soloist: In this situation, the interlude usually ends in a solo break.

- Provide an opportunity for modulation to a new key.

Characteristics

Though there are no detailed guidelines governing the construction of an interlude, there are several typical characteristics:

- Its melody may be derived from existing thematic material or freely composed, almost generic in nature, with no particular link to the tune's melody or harmony.

- It can be a partial or complete restatement of the introduction. This is a simple, yet effective, way to create an interlude.

- It can control the mood of an arrangement through an increase or decrease in tension. This can be accomplished through melody, harmony, or orchestration.

- It can be a series of repetitions of a two- or four-measure phrase. These can be exact or transposed versions of the original, typically in increments of half steps, whole steps, minor thirds, or major thirds.

Conclusion and Analysis

Bar Flies (See appendix 7, p. 412 for the full score.)

TRACK 165
0:51

The purpose of the interlude at letter J is to separate the two solo sections. The ideas were derived from the introduction; both are variants on the originals (see chapter 17). There is a constant feeling of upward movement, achieved through transposition, melodic movement, and orchestration. It can be broken down into three segments. The harmony in the first two measures is transposed up a minor third in the third and fourth measures. In terms of orchestration, the Interlude begins with three horns, then four, then five. The final five notes are harmonized in contrary motion and set up a two-measure solo break.

Charming William (See appendix 7, p. 444 for the full score.)

TRACK 168
0:59

The interlude at letter S also separates two solo sections and is intended to create a fresh start for the trumpet solo. It is sixteen measures long, consisting of an ascending bass line and descending melody that decrescendos to its end. This effect is enhanced by the lightened orchestration beginning in the ninth measure.

CHAPTER 20
Solo Chorus with Backgrounds

Improvisation is a crucial element in the developmental phase of an arrangement. Beginning with the earliest written charts, designated sections for improvised solos were included. Due to the three-minute restriction on early recordings, these solos were usually limited to eight or sixteen measures and were tightly integrated with the ensemble sections. This format persisted throughout the big-band era. As recording technology improved in the fifties, arrangements became longer and so did the solo sections. In the sixties, Thad Jones and his contemporaries introduced the concept of extended solos. In this setting, the soloist was given free reign to create a multi-chorus solo. Sometimes more than one soloist was given the opportunity for extended improvisation. In these situations, the combined length of the solo sections probably exceeded the length of the written sections.

This practice is still prevalent today, but by no means predominant. Many contemporary arrangements contain solo sections of specific length. But whatever the ratio between solo and ensemble, it must be decided by the arranger. The balance between written and improvised passages is important.

At this point in the planning of an arrangement, a dichotomy in the thought process occurs. Throughout the introduction and setting of the first chorus, a certain pace and mood has been established which must be maintained. However, in the solo section, the primary focus should be on the soloist, and in order to create a generative situation, the arranger must think like a soloist. Many of the great writers were, and are, great soloists. Certainly they all have studied what the great soloists have done, that is, how they build their solos, how they interact with background material, etc. Only in this way can a setting be fashioned which will allow the soloist the greatest freedom and opportunity to be creative.

Overall Organization

Before any writing takes place, three decisions concerning the overall organization of the solo section must be made:

- Selection of chord progression
- Choice of soloist(s)
- Length of solo section

Selection of Chord Progression

In many arrangements, the chord progression decided upon for the original setting of the piece is continued in the solo section. But this is not always the case. Here are some situations that might require a reworking of the harmony:

- An involved reharmonization was created for the first chorus. While it may have been effective there, it might be too complicated or restrictive for the soloist. When the progression is too involved, the soloist may become so preoccupied with making the changes that it will be difficult to construct a meaningful solo. The following is an example of an extensive reharmonization of "I've Got It Bad" that has been simplified to a more accessible progression for the soloist.

EXAMPLE 20-1.

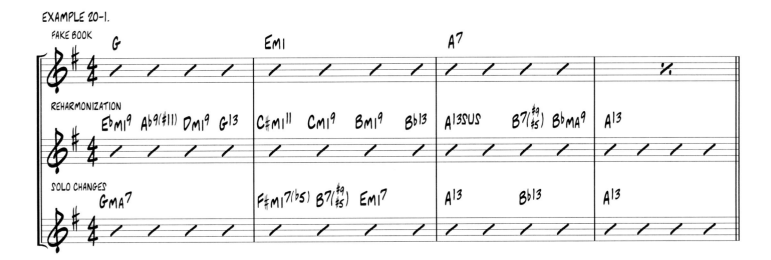

- Another good reason for simplifying changes is to allow the rhythm section more opportunities for personal interpretation. An examination of several Thad Jones arrangements will illustrate this. Compare the rhythm section progression in the first chorus with those in the solo section.

- The piece contains chord progressions (or even meter changes) that would be a hindrance to the soloist. In cases like this, there are three choices:

  - Retain the original setting.

  - Make some modifications, such as eliminating or revising the problem areas.

  - Create a new, simplified solo format. Arrangements of "Tell Me a Bedtime Story" and "Red Clay" have successfully employed this kind of treatment.

Afro-Cuban pieces, regardless of the amount of complexity in the chord progression, traditionally include a solo section called a *montuno*. A typical montuno is either two or four measures in length and is repeated ad infinitum, with or without backgrounds. The simplest montuno is constructed on a Mixolydian scale, with the root of the dominant-seventh chord acting as a kind of stationary pedal.

EXAMPLE 20-2.

The next example shows four common montuno progressions. They may be used in both major and minor keys.

EXAMPLE 20-3.

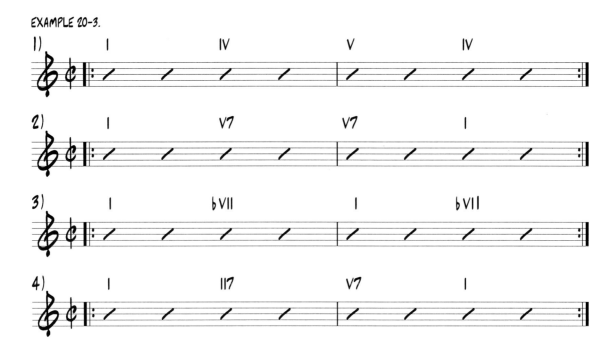

Contemporary collaborations of jazz harmony and Latin rhythms have produced more complex progressions.

EXAMPLE 20-4.

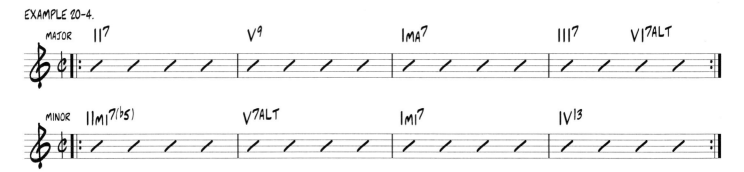

Montunos can appear in conjunction with the regular solo changes and be placed either before or after them. They provide relief from formal restrictions and allow the soloist and rhythm section to concentrate on other musical elements.

Choice of Soloist(s)

The instrumentation and textures used in the arrangement thus far will probably suggest a particular instrument as the preferred solo voice. Or, it may be decided to open this section to include any or all instruments. This decision will affect the manner in which this section is organized.

The simplest solution is to designate one soloist and place the chord changes in that part and write backgrounds for everyone else. If two soloists are decided upon, the changes should be placed in both parts. In a small group, it may be necessary to write the same background notes in both solo parts to retain the desired fullness. The changes would then be placed above these figures. The following example shows both options.

EXAMPLE 20-5.

If the section is open for all to solo, the changes must be written in every part. The only exception would occur when the progression is a commonly known one (blues, rhythm changes, modal tunes, etc.).

The solo section should close with a first and second ending. However, if there is more than one soloist, the chorus will be repeated many times, so the numbers "1" and "2" will be confusing. The following shows a better way to designate multiple repeats.

EXAMPLE 20-6.

To avoid having to skip over internal repeats, everything should be written out. In a ternary form, write out the first two A sections. In binary forms, *never* use the eight-measure first and second endings. This practice, which is often used in fake books, can only lead to confusion.

Length of Solo Section

It is rare in contemporary arrangements to allow a soloist only one chorus, except in slow ballads. Therefore, it is strongly recommended that a separate solo chorus containing only chord changes for the rhythm section and designated soloists be placed in front of the background chorus. This first chorus should be enclosed with repeat signs and the indication "On Cue" or "Backgrounds On Cue" placed at the beginning of the background chorus. This extra chorus offers distinct advantages: it makes extended solos more manageable, control of background entrances easier, and avoids the problem of having to write the changes over the backgrounds (this can get quite messy, especially in trombone parts containing a number of ledger lines). A typical cluttered-looking trombone part in this situation might look like this:

EXAMPLE 20-7.

Since the changes have already been written in the first chorus, it is not necessary to repeat them. Simply indicate that the soloist is to continue through the background chorus.

In earlier times when music was handwritten, arrangers were reluctant to spend extra time and paper writing out a separate chorus of changes. This was especially true if they had to copy their own parts. But time-saving short cuts invariably result in more rehearsal time. Today, with music notation software, presenting this extra chorus involves only a simple copy and paste.

Writing the Backgrounds

Now that the solo format has been established, attention can be focused on the backgrounds themselves. The chief purposes of a background are to:

- Establish or maintain a mood.

- Stimulate the soloist.

- Add rhythmic vitality.

- Provide orientation for the formal and harmonic elements.

The first decision in this part of the process involves the placement of the backgrounds in conjunction with the song form. In situations where each soloist will take multiple choruses, the backgrounds should encompass an entire chorus, entering in the initial measures of the form. When only one chorus is to be played by each soloist, the point where the backgrounds enter is dependent on tempo. In ballads, they typically come in after eight measures (assuming the form is thirty-two measures), with the possibility of entering after only four measures or as late as sixteen. At faster tempos (again using the thirty-two measure format), they typically enter after sixteen measures.

Even though the center of attention is the soloist, the arranger can still influence the general mood and energy levels of this section through the types of backgrounds chosen. Listed below are the most frequently used types of backgrounds, categorized from the least invasive to the most invasive:

- Pad: sustained with long note values

- Single line with little rhythmic complexity

- Punch chords: one or two per measure

- Riff-oriented punch chords

- Rhythmically complex, nonstop lines

- Two layers: combination of line, pad, or punch chord

- Two independent lines

With the number of instruments available in a large ensemble, orchestrating backgrounds should not be a problem. Here, a rule of thumb might be to use instruments of contrasting colors and registers to help highlight the soloist; woodwinds behind a brass solo, brass behind a woodwind solo, low instruments behind a high soloist, etc. But the key word is "behind." Always think of backgrounds as being behind a soloist, not above or below.

In smaller ensembles, flexibility in the solo section is of primary importance. A single-line background written in all the parts is the simplest solution. Two-note punch chords are another alternative. These dyads should be included in all parts, written with stems up and stems down.

EXAMPLE 20-8.

They can also be used in conjunction with unison or octave lines. But chords with more than two notes would require experienced players to figure out which note to play at any given time.

Sendoffs

One excellent way to heighten the tension level at the beginning of a solo section is through a device called a *sendoff*. When used, it is the very first event in the solo section. It may be as long as four measures or as short as a single note. The following are some typical sendoffs written for the brass section.

EXAMPLE 20-9.

TRACK 142

A sendoff does not require extra measures; it is a part of the form. In a two-chorus solo format, it occurs at the beginning of the first chorus, with instructions to "Play first time only" or "Play at the beginning of each solo."

A sendoff can be prepared by a written ensemble passage or a drum break at the end of the first chorus or interlude, as in the next example.

TRACK 143

EXAMPLE 20-10.

Rhythm Section Solos

Writing backgrounds for rhythm section soloists requires special attention. In many situations, the most preferable option is no backgrounds at all. The absence of horn sonorities provides relief (both aural and physical), and makes the horn entrance in the next section more effective. Here are some guidelines for each instrument:

- **Bass**: Use only the most subtle, sparse textures in a soft dynamic range. Muted brass or woodwinds with punch chords or mid-range, close-position pads are effective.

- **Piano**: Due to the piano's harmonic capabilities, harmonized pads would be redundant and intrusive. Use only slow-moving unison lines, dyads, or punch chords.

- **Guitar**: Like the piano, the guitar's chordal capabilities tend to make pads redundant. The guitar can be a bit more assertive than the piano and offers more leeway in choice of textures and dynamics.

- **Drums**: Open drum solos are less common today as many drummers prefer to solo on a given structure, such as the form of the piece. In this case, punches, pads, and unison lines may be written for the horns and the rest of the rhythm section. The following example shows the initial eight measures of a sixteen-measure drum solo that is scored for trombones, baritone sax, and rhythm section.

TRACK 144

EXAMPLE 20-11.

Double-Time

The practice of using double-time in the second chorus of a ballad became common in the small groups of the fifties and was soon incorporated into ensemble writing. In spontaneous small groups, the choice of whether to use it or not rested with the rhythm section. But in orchestrated settings, the decision must be made by the arranger so that the background figures have the proper double-time feel.

There are two ways to notate double-time:

- Retain the original quarter-note pulse and create the double-time feel by writing figures in short note values. This would be indicated on the parts as "Double-Time Feel."

- Actually double the tempo. Here the quarter note is moving at twice the speed of the previous section. This would be marked "Double-Time."

The choice of which method of notation to use depends on the level of experience of the group and the intricacy of the written figures. The first method entails writing a lot of small note values—eighth and sixteenth notes. These are complicated to read and it can be difficult to retain the proper swing feel.

EXAMPLE 20-12.

The second method is easier to read and is better for inexperienced players. Here is how the previous example would look if written in actual double-time.

EXAMPLE 20-13.

If it becomes necessary to notate double-time in the rhythm parts, here are some suggestions:

- The double-time feel is set in motion by the drummer playing his high-hat twice as fast. The accompanying top cymbal or brush patterns would play a skipping, two-beat pattern.

EXAMPLE 20-14.

- The piano or guitar would use a more staccato, offbeat comping pattern.

EXAMPLE 20-15.

- The bass pattern is critical. If the bass retains the same quarter-note pulse (with a few fills), the result will be a two-beat feel, twice as fast. The effect of this would be a rather relaxed one.

EXAMPLE 20-16.

- If the bass walks twice as fast, the drummer would complement this with a traditional ride cymbal pattern and the result would be a much more energetic, insistent feel.

EXAMPLE 20-17.

The transitions in and out of double-time can be sudden or gradual. Sudden ones create a dramatic effect. If a gradual transition is desired, the rhythm section can begin easing into double-time a few beats before the chorus begins. This could also be accompanied by an ensemble figure. If this passage involves short note values, it would be wise to indicate "Swing 16ths" on the parts.

TRACK 145
Part 1

EXAMPLE 20-18.

A smooth transition from double-time back into the original time is best accomplished through a gradual elongation of the figures to suggest a gradual slowing down.

TRACK 145
Part 2

EXAMPLE 20-19.

Finally, if using the second method, avoid writing a figure that has two different types of notation as in the following example.

EXAMPLE 20-20.

Stop-Time

This is one of the oldest devices in jazz and is still used occasionally. It is a discontinuous rhythmic accompaniment for a soloist. In its simplest form, a punch chord is played on the downbeat of every measure, or every other measure. More complex forms can be created through a combination of downbeat and upbeat punch chords. In the next example, the drummer is the soloist.

TRACK 146
Part 1

EXAMPLE 20-21.

An even more sophisticated version would be to vary the figures as to length and point of entry.

TRACK 146
Part 2

EXAMPLE 20-22.

To maintain a stop-time feel, a minimum of two beats should be retained between figures at slow or medium tempos. In faster tempos, more space is necessary.

As an alternative to a whole chorus of stop-time, there are ways of combining stop-time with regular time. Due to the equal separation of the A sections in a binary form, there are two options. The normal procedure is to have the stop-time on the A sections. The opposite is also possible, with the stop-time occurring in the B sections, assuming the chord progression accommodates this reversal. There are even some progressions such as "On Green Dolphin Street" that work either way. Here are two rhythm section sketches for a horn solo using both formats.

EXAMPLE 20-23.

The ternary form, with its three A sections, presents a different situation. Since these occupy twenty-four measures of the form, one type of time will predominate. Employing stop-time in the B section will provide only a momentary contrast, while using it in the A sections will make it the prime feature of the chorus. A great example of stop time in the A sections is the Count Basie septet recording of "Lester Leaps In."

A multi-chorus solo section could conceivably begin with stop-time, but should not end with it; it works best somewhere in the middle.

Trading Fours

The concept of *trading fours* is a well-established tradition in small-group playing. Whether between pitched instruments or pitched instruments and drums, the format is the same; each soloist exchanges four-measure improvisations while maintaining the harmonic form. Even during drum solos, where the rest of the rhythm section rests, the form remains intact. The alternation of phrases can also include trading twos and eights (and sixes, in a twelve-bar blues).

This device can be easily adapted for any sized ensemble and any soloist, with the arranger assuming the role of one of the soloists, typically the first. These orchestrated passages may be harmonized, but unison ensemble lines are also very effective. In a large ensemble, one section could play the lines, with the others providing background support. Any instrument could assume the role of soloist opposite these orchestrations. In the following example, the arranger (composed horn parts) "trades fours" with a guitar soloist.

TRACK 147

EXAMPLE 20-24.

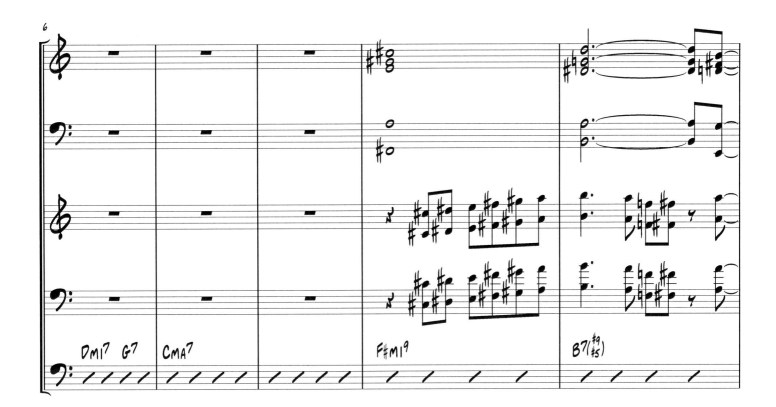

This procedure could be reversed, with the soloist or drummer playing the leading role and the ensemble following. This format would not work if it leads into another ensemble section. It would be awkward for the ensemble to play the last four measures and then go directly into a shout chorus.

Another variant is to trade fours using the sections of the ensemble: saxes versus brass, or trumpets versus trombones. This format would have limited possibilities in a small ensemble.

TRACK 148

EXAMPLE 20-25.

Multiple Solo Sections

One of the disadvantages of having only one solo section is that repeated hearings of the same background figures and changes can disrupt the momentum of the arrangement, placing the band into a sort of holding pattern. The best way to avoid this is to write two or more separate solo sections. Of course this means writing more background material, but the results will be worth the effort.

One way to accomplish this without writing any additional material is to simply reorchestrate the existing backgrounds. For example, use brass behind a saxophone solo and then do the reverse for the second solo. Or use high-pitched instruments for the first solo and low-pitched instruments for the next. Bob Florence successfully employed this technique in "Be-Bop Charlie" and "Funupmanship."

Another solution would be a reharmonization. This could involve new harmonies or the simplification of the existing changes. These are often placed over a pedal. Jim McNeely's "Off the Cuff" is an excellent example of this.

Modulating to a different key can provide a solution to the problem that occurs when the two solo instruments have different tessituras. For instance, the key of D♭ might be suitable for an alto saxophone solo, but F might be more comfortable for the trombone. It can also provide heightened interest, as in the case of Woody Herman's recording of "Four Brothers," where the first two saxophone solos are in A♭ and the last two move to F.

A final option is to change the whole feel of the arrangement. This could be accomplished by using double-time or half-time. A meter change or switching from straight-ahead time to funk or Latin might be appropriate. A complicated progression might be replaced by a montuno or a modal setting. In Bob Mintzer's "Acha," the tenor solo is based on the changes of the tune, while the trombone solo that follows is written solely on a two-chord montuno.

It is usually best not to juxtapose the two solo sections. They should be separated by at least an interlude or modulatory passage. Extended ensemble passages or saxophone solis are interesting options.

Conclusion and Analysis

Bar Flies: First Solo

TRACK 165
0:09

There are two separate solo sections in this tune, the first for the horns beginning at letter E, and the second for the rhythm section (piano, guitar, or bass) beginning at letter K. The first set of backgrounds is preceded by an entire chorus of chord changes in all the horn parts. This allows the greatest flexibility as to the choice of soloists. The backgrounds beginning at letter F (track 165, 0:09) are intended to be played behind either the tenor or trombone. They are written in four-part harmony with the tenor and trombone notes identical. The text indicates that if one of these instruments is not soloing, the written notes should be played. The three A sections of the form contain shorter note values with more space between them. The bridge has contrasting longer phrases. All four sections possess a minimum of ideas, each repeated with some variation.

Bar Flies: Second Solo

TRACK 166
0:07

There is a change of color in the second section (letter K) using flute, bass clarinet, tenor, and muted brass. It would have seemed an obvious choice for all three saxophones to switch to woodwinds, resulting in either two flutes and bass clarinet, or flute, clarinet, and bass clarinet. The decision not to use a second flute was due to the fact that this choice would have placed both the second flute and trumpet in uncomfortably low registers. The clarinet could have successfully substituted for the tenor.

The four-measure rest at the end of this set of backgrounds (measure 160) is a typical amount of time at this tempo to change instruments and remove mutes. No time was provided at the beginning of this section for this, as it was assumed that multiple choruses would be played and there would be at least one full chorus to complete the instrument and mute changes.

Unlike the first solo section, there is no separate chorus of changes for the soloists as this would be redundant for the rhythm section. The two endings contain identical changes, the difference between the two being the crescendo in the "To Continue" ending. This is crucial to raise the dynamic level for the shout chorus that follows.

Charming William: First Solo

TRACK 168
0:09

This arrangement also contains two solo sections (letters J and T) separated by an interlude. The first is for soprano saxophone, the second for trumpet. Both begin with a full chorus scored for the soloist and rhythm section alone, enclosed in repeats. This allows for multiple choruses before the entrance of the backgrounds. Each contains distinctive harmonic and rhythmic elements. These contrasting characteristics help to sustain interest.

The first solo begins in measure 97 with eight measures of soprano and drums. It follows an ensemble send-off and provides a bridge to the solo changes that begin in measure 105. The chorus is thirty-eight measures long with the form A-B-A-C-tag. The rhythmic feel is mainly broken time, similar to the groove established in the melody chorus. The harmony is based on the three two-chord vamps taken from the melody chorus. These consist predominantly of slash chords with the bass providing a strong pedal feel. Both A sections are a B♭ pedal, the B section is an A♭ pedal, and the tag is a G♭ pedal. The C section contains four measures of slash chords written in contrary motion and two measures of a functional II-V progression.

The backgrounds enter in measure 143 and are through-composed. The changes in orchestration coincide with the sections of the form, clearly defining them. The full orchestration in the tag creates a climax for the end of the soprano saxophone solo.

Charming William: Second Solo

TRACK 169
0:19

The trumpet solo begins in measure 197 (letter T) and conforms to the original sixteen-measure form of the song. The harmony is functional, centering on the key of B♭. To alleviate the monotony of the constant cycling of this progression, every other chorus modulates up a minor third to D♭. This two-key format creates the illusion of a thirty-two measure form. The time feel is straight ahead with a walking bass line.

The backgrounds help delineate the two key areas. In the B♭ section (letter V), a single idea is carried throughout each section, first by the saxes, then by the trombones. The D♭ section (letter X) contains a combination of shorter figures and punch chords. The trumpets are used sparingly throughout in order to heighten the impact of the impending shout section. This solo section concludes with a two-measure dominant pedal which sets up the shout chorus.

CHAPTER 21
Shout Chorus and Recapitulation

The shout chorus and recapitulation, though separate sections of an arrangement, are inextricably linked. The *shout chorus* is unquestionably the focal point of the arrangement. It is here that the main climax will occur, putting the whole arrangement in perspective. It offers the best opportunity for arrangers to display their creativity, as shout choruses are ideally comprised solely of original material.

Recapitulation involves either a full or partial restatement of the melody. Though not essential to a jazz arrangement, this unifying concept has been a feature of western music since the eighteenth century. The decision as to whether to include a recapitulation is a critical one. After the extensive departure through a variety of developmental sections, a return of the melody may be necessary to create a sense of completion. However, there is also a possibility that a complete restatement of the melody, whether verbatim or rearranged, would be redundant. A better choice might be a partial recapitulation or none at all. This decision is an aesthetic one and each arrangement will provide its own solution.

A shout chorus can present a formidable challenge for those with no background in composition. The next few paragraphs contain some general thoughts on how to approach this task.

Always think rhythmically. In a shout chorus, syncopated figures should take precedence over long strings of eighth notes. Sometimes just creating a strong rhythmic framework will stimulate the formation of melodic ideas.

Creating the Melody

Because composition can be a very elusive process, let nothing get between the initial creative spark and its ultimate fruition. When a good idea comes, no matter when or where, find a way to write it down as no one has an inexhaustible supply of good ideas. Always use the instrument on which you are the most proficient; or, better yet, sing. Do not use the piano. It is a valuable tool for checking voicings and finding new sonorities, but it can hinder melodic creativity, especially if technical proficiency is lacking. In fact, it might not be a good idea for pianists to create at the keyboard; they may be apt to inject pianistic idioms into a melody that is intended to be played by wind instruments. Improvise a line and record it; then transcribe it. Examine it and keep all, some, or none of it.

While composing the melody for the shout chorus, it is important to consider the instrumentation, especially the lead voice. The range of this instrument and the size of the ensemble, among other factors, will determine the specific range in which it must be written. Ideally, the imagination should have free rein. But there is nothing as frustrating as writing a good melody only to find that it does not work in the selected key. The appropriate range for a lead line in a shout chorus is dependent on the size and ability level of the group. Generally speaking, the larger the ensemble, the higher the range. For smaller groups, E♭ (above middle C) up to B♭ (or C) in the treble clef is a good location to center the melody (see Ex. 21-1). For large ensembles, B♭ up to E♭ (or F) is more suitable, provided that the lead trumpet possesses this range.

EXAMPLE 21-1.

In any case, the melody should only touch on the highest pitches, not center on them.

One possible solution to this dilemma of placing the lead voice in the proper range is to modulate to another key. But this may cause problems later on. For instance, if a partial recapitulation is planned, it may be awkward to modulate back to the original key in the middle of the form. If so, this necessitates writing an entire shout chorus in the new key.

Formal Considerations

The smallest amount of original material necessary to create a shout chorus is eight measures. This holds true regardless of form. This concept is illustrated below using blues, ternary, and binary forms.

Blues

Many blues are organized formally into three four-measure phrases: A-A'-B. In the A section, measures 1–2 are tonic-oriented; 3–4 move toward IV. In A', measures 5–6 are subdominant in quality; measures 7–8 prepare the final cadence. The B section is cadential; ii7-V7-I, followed by a turnaround. "Blue Train," "Tenor Madness," "Mr. P.C.," and "Blues Walk" are good examples of this.

The easiest way to write a melody that will work for both A and A' is to use only the common tones between the harmonies in the corresponding measures of the two phrases.

TRACK 149
Part 1

EXAMPLE 21-2.

Another approach that allows more creative freedom is to write a four-measure phrase and make the necessary alterations to accommodate the chord progression in A'.

TRACK 149
Part 2

EXAMPLE 21-3.

Finish with a contrasting four-measure melody for the B section which cadences in the eleventh measure of the form (starting in the third measure of Ex. 21-4). The result would be a riff-like melody.

TRACK 149
Part 3

EXAMPLE 21-4.

Though not necessary, it is common practice to recapitulate this form. Some choices include:

- Instead of composing a final four-measure phrase, insert the final four measures of the melody. By itself, this may be too short. If so, other options are to repeat the entire chorus or repeat the final phrase twice. (See chapter 22 for information on tagging the melody.)
- Repeat the melody once or twice using the original orchestration. This decision is dependent on the tempo of the arrangement. An interesting variation, provided that the original choruses were orchestrated from small to large, is to repeat them in reverse order.
- Repeat the melody once or twice with a new orchestration.

Ternary

In a ternary form (AABA), the eight-measure A section typically consists of two contrasting but complimentary four-measure phrases which form a complete idea. "My Old Flame," "Chelsea Bridge," and "Prelude to a Kiss" are constructed in this manner. The juxtaposition of the first two A's requires different cadences: the first A would end in a turnaround, the second in a complete cadence. So instead of eight measures of original music, it would probably involve writing ten measures. The next example shows a shout chorus composed on the first two A sections of a jazz tune in ternary form.

TRACK 150

EXAMPLE 21-5.

At this point, several options are available which do not involve writing any additional original material:

- Recapitulate the second half of the first chorus.
- Write an instrumental or rhythm-section solo for the bridge, with or without background figures, then recapitulate the last A section of the first chorus.

- Use the A section of the shout, preferably with some variation or change of orchestration, to complete the chorus. This may be followed by a complete recapitulation of the first chorus or a coda.

All that remains to have a complete shout chorus is to write an original bridge.

Binary

In a binary form (ABAB), the A section differs somewhat from its ternary counterpart: there is no final cadence and it is open-ended leading directly to the B section. Sequential passages, both melodic and harmonic, are common. These sequences may occur within the phrases or between them, making them more complimentary than contrasting. "My Romance," "Just Friends," and "Airegin" demonstrate examples of this. Since there are only two A sections in a binary form instead of three, and they do not appear consecutively, there is less chance of monotony. In this situation, it is possible to begin with only two measures of music and repeat them, making the pitch alterations to accommodate the changing harmonies. In a few instances, the harmonic movement can sustain interest for eight measures, but four measures are usually enough. At this point, the arranger should either write a rhythmic or melodic variant on the previous motive, or write a new, complimentary motive for the second phrase. The following example illustrates both approaches. In the first version, measures 5–8 are a melodic variant on measures 1–4. The second version is through-composed.

TRACK 151

EXAMPLE 21-6.

There are two options available for completing the shout chorus with only eight measures of original material:

- Write an instrumental or rhythm section solo for the B section, with or without background. (In a large ensemble, a sax soli might be a good choice.) Then recapitulate the last half of the melody chorus.

- Repeat the previously composed A section of the shout, either in its original form or with some variation or change of orchestration. A rhythm section solo or sax soli would complete the chorus. This may be followed by a complete or partial recapitulation of the melody chorus or coda.

The B and C sections are never identical. The B always centers on a dominant half cadence, while the C ends on the tonic. The melodies of the two sections would never have more than four to six measures in common. Therefore, a minimum of ten to twelve measures is usually necessary to complete the form. In the following example, the two sections have five measures in common, requiring six additional ones, totaling eleven.

EXAMPLE 21-7.

TRACK 152

These are admittedly very tentative first steps. Subsequent attempts would involve a greater amount of original material until entire shout choruses, even through-composed ones, become routine.

Five-Step Compositional Sequence

These steps show a gradual evolution of a shout chorus from a melodic paraphrase with no reharmonization to a completely original melody and harmonization. "Billy Boy" was chosen because its short form allows each concept to be sustained throughout. Longer forms would necessitate the use of a variety of techniques. Many of these, such as section solis and unison passages, may not utilize the entire ensemble.

Step One

This is nothing more than a paraphrase of the melody with background figures.

- Write a paraphrase of "Billy Boy" for the saxophone section.
- Write complimentary figures for the brass section.
- Harmonize both sections, when appropriate.

EXAMPLE 21-8.

TRACK 153

A successful paraphrase can be accomplished with only a few devices, if they are used creatively. In example 21-8, the following were used:

- Syncopation (mm. 2, 4, 10, 13).
- Rhythmic anticipation and delay (mm. 2, 4, 8, 10, 11, 13, 14).
- Nonharmonic tones, specifically, upper and lower neighbors, changing tones, and passing tones (mm. 1, 3, 5, 7, 14, 15).
- Added tones (mm. 3, 6, 8).
- Repeated tones (m. 9).

The brass figures are a combination of punches, fills, and pads. The punches and fills occur mostly during long notes and rests in the melody. They function as a reaction to the saxophone figures rather than in a setup role. The trombones provide variety with a countermelody in m. 9 and a pad in measures 13–15. Some of the figures begin in unison and end in harmony; this adds emphasis to the final syncopated note.

The reharmonization of the melody is minimal. It is a III7-VI7-II7-V7 progression appearing three times. There is one passing chord, the Fm7 in measure 12. Half-step planing occurs in measure 3. A tritone substitution for the dominant appears in the final cadence (m.15). The saxophones are written in five-part harmony, using predominantly drop-two and drop-two-and-four voicings. Contrast in texture is achieved by alternating unison passages with harmonized ones. Each of the first three phrases begins in unison before breaking into harmony. Momentum is enhanced by not placing the chord roots in the baritone sax. The only roots that appear are at the half-cadence in measure 8 and the final cadence.

The brass voicings are consistent: trumpets are in close position and the trombones are in spread formation with the bass trombone playing the roots. There is a strict adherence to the placement of both guide tones immediately above the root (in the second and third trombones). The only exceptions are in measure 10 where there are two different positions of the same chord and the stepwise progression in measures 11–12.

Because of the emphatic climax in measure 15, the arrangement could actually end there. The many references in the paraphrase to the original melody might make even a partial recapitulation of the first chorus redundant.

Step Two

In this step, the primary goal is to move away from melodic paraphrase and write a more original melody. This does not represent a radical departure. The melody is still diatonic and contains several references to the original. The texture is almost entirely homophonic.

EXAMPLE 21-9.

Example 21-9 is more characteristic of a shout chorus for the following reasons:

- There are fewer running eighth notes and more emphasis on offbeat accents.

- The lead trumpet part is consistently higher.

- The drummer is more involved: the big fill in measures 7–8 with smaller ones in measures 10 and 13 help sustain the relentless rhythmic drive while providing breathing room for the horns.

The harmonic framework is essentially the same as the previous version. But tension is heightened through:

- Chromatic alterations occur in the inner parts (the melody is still diatonic except for a few blue notes at the end).

- Half-step planing (measures 1, 6, 8, 9) and diatonic parallelism (measures 4, 5, 11) are employed.

- Tritone substitutions (measures 2, 6, 8, 12) help smooth out the bass lines in the bass trombone and baritone sax.

The harmonic complexity of this shout chorus resulted in the need for a more specific bass part in some sections. Consequently, this part contains both written lines as well as chord symbols. Also, due to the rapid movement and complexity of the harmonies, the piano was eliminated through most of this shout chorus, because if it was written out with all the chord substitutions and anticipations, it would be nearly impossible to play. It is used only in the places were harmonic underpinning was necessary.

Step Three

This melody is the same as the previous one, but the texture is entirely different. The brass voicings are essentially the same but a unison or octave saxophone countermelody has been added. Some editing was done to the brass melody in measures 2, 3, and 10 to provide more space for the countermelody. The shorter saxophone fills are written in octaves, but the longer one in measures 7–8 was harmonized for greater strength.

EXAMPLE 21-10.

TRACK 155

Step Four

This version presents a total departure from the original melody and harmony. The melody is very chromatic and bears no thematic relationship to the original. The basic harmonic framework is still recognizable only through the dominant half cadence in measures 7 and 8 and the authentic cadence at the end. The reharmonization supports the chromatic melody by including a large number of chromatic passing chords. The texture of the horn ensemble is homophonic and harmonized as a brass choir. The saxophones provide reinforcement in the middle register. The guide tones are doubled in unison for greater clarity.

EXAMPLE 21-11.

TRACK 156

The bass part is fully written out in order to bring the complex chord progression into focus.
The walking bass works in the first eight measures, but would cause too many momentary
dissonances in the last eight. The syncopated line ensures the clarity of the harmonies. Also,
the piano is eliminated entirely in this version.

Step Five

This represents the most complex version of a shout chorus. It consists not only of the free harmonization presented in step four, but also includes the addition of a saxophone counter-melody, similar to the concept presented in step three. This shout chorus was chosen for use in the full-length arrangement of "Charming William." For further descriptive analysis of this music, refer to the end of this chapter. The full score for this shout chorus is in appendix 7 beginning at measure 261.

Other Approaches

The term, "shout chorus" originated in the big band era and referred to the section that followed the solos. It was almost always loud and high and scored for the full ensemble. This expression has persisted to the present day and has become more generic in nature, referring to any section that involves the entire horn ensemble, no matter what the volume or range. This could appear anywhere in the arrangement. Aside from the standard shout chorus formats explained in detail earlier in this chapter, there are several other approaches.

- **Horn ensemble without rhythm section accompaniment**: This could employ any of the tutti concepts discussed in chapter 14. It provides relief for both the listener and the rhythm section players.

TRACK 157

EXAMPLE 21-12.

• **Softer, mid-range, homophonic ensemble**: The softer dynamic can create either a
feeling of relaxation or anticipation.

EXAMPLE 21-13.

TRACK 158

- **Unison (or octave) tutti line**: This relatively simple technique is actually quite effective. The line can also be harmonized at significant points, as shown in measures 7–8 of the following example. The occasionally harmonized chords provide interest as well as points of focus.

EXAMPLE 21-14.

TRACK 159

- **Two or more unison (or octave) lines**: All lines should have equal importance and not be accompanimental.

EXAMPLE 21-15.

Because of the variety of these approaches, the term, "shout chorus" may seem inappropriate. A more common phrase used to refer to any of these is "ensemble chorus."

Recapitulation

As mentioned at the beginning of this chapter, the recapitulation creates a sense of completion to an arrangement. It should not be thought of as a way to avoid writing complete shout choruses. The recapitulation may consist of a full chorus, half chorus, final section of the song form, or the last half of this section. It is not inherent that the material be repeated verbatim through the entire recapitulation; it can be re-orchestrated. Additionally, the music could be reorganized. For instance, the three A sections of the ternary form provide sufficient material that any parts of these could be manipulated to create a fresh variant without writing any new music.

A return to the original melody may be achieved through the placement of the terms *D.S. al Fine* or *D.S. al Coda* above the final measure of the section preceding the recapitulation.

EXAMPLE 21-16.

D.S. al Fine: This requires no extra writing and results in an exact repetition of the melody. The amount of recapitulation is determined by the placement of the sign. In other words, the nearer the *D.S.* is placed to the beginning of the melody chorus, the longer the recapitulation. The sign is placed above the first measure of the recapitulation. The *Fine* is placed above the final note of the melody.

EXAMPLE 21-17.

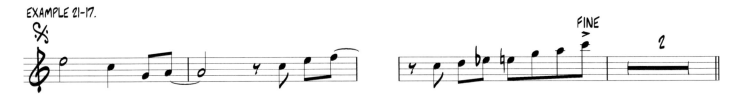

D.S. al Coda: When an exact repetition of the entire melody or the abruptness of a *D.S. al Fine* is deemed unsatisfactory, a *Coda* sign becomes necessary to allow for re-arrangement of the remainder of the melody. The *D.S.* is placed in the same manner as above. The *Coda* sign is placed at the end of the last measure of exact recapitulation and appears above the staff (sometimes the term *To Coda* is also placed directly in front of the sign). This directs the player to the final section of music. Another *Coda* sign is placed atop the first measure of this section. The equivalent of at least one staff should separate the *Coda* from the main body of music (sometimes the *Coda* is place on a different page).

EXAMPLE 21-18.

In those rare instances where the arrangement has no introduction, the term *D.C.* (which means "back to the head" or "beginning") replaces *D.S.* (which means "back to the sign") in the above terms.

The decision as to whether any of these signs are used or the recapitulation is copied out is dependent on two factors: if the exact recapitulation consists of a relatively small number of measures, it should be copied to the end of the arrangement; in longer arrangements, if the use of a sign would result in awkward page turns, the music should again be copied.

If an exact recapitulation is desired and if the music directly preceding it is in a different key, a modulation back to the original key will be necessary. Traditionally, a return to the original key is inherent in a recapitulation, but is not absolutely essential. In the case of a difficult melody, such as a bebop head, playing the tune in another key may be problematic. An exact recapitulation in the new key (necessitating a transposition of the original music) is possible only if the two keys are within a minor third. If they are any further apart, problems of range, sonority, and tessitura would most likely occur. Even within the minor third interval, occasional problem areas may appear that require re-orchestration. Because of the likelihood of these problems, it is best to consider re-arranging the recapitulation if it is in any key other than the original.

Bar Flies

TRACK 166
0:49

The melody of this shout chorus beginning at letter O is through-composed with no thematic repetition. The use of five-part homophonic scoring was deliberately curtailed throughout the rest of the arrangement to increase its effectiveness in this section. Approximately two-thirds of the thirty-six measure form is written in this manner. Variety was achieved through the use of two other textures. The turnarounds at measures 172–173 and 180–181 are written in two parts with the trumpet, alto saxophone, and guitar imitating the low horns. After its first two measures, the remainder of letter R (m. 192) employs melody and accompaniment. The melody is scored in combinations of unisons and thirds. The final two measures contain the only reference to the "Bar Flies" melody. The homophonic passages are all written in five-part harmony with the guitar doubling the trumpet an octave below. In keeping with the suggested trumpet range for the small ensemble, the top note of the trumpet melody is concert A♭.

Charming William

TRACK 169
1:04

The sax line over the A♭ pedal in measure 259 provides the impetus for the shout chorus which begins at letter Z. The impact of this shout chorus is due to the combination of the homophonic texture, dense harmonies, and the highly rhythmic nature of the melody. The first six measures are homophonic. The next two (measures 267–268) break the horn ensemble into two sections with harmonized brass and an octave saxophone countermelody. The homophonic texture immediately resumes at letter AA and continues for three measures. The remaining five measures return to the brass-versus-saxophones format used earlier. The downward movement of the brass and saxophone lines along with the lessening dynamics set up the recapitulation that follows. Further analysis of melodic and harmonic details of the shout chorus can be found in step four of the five-step compositional sequence.

TRACK 169
1:34

The recapitulation presents the melody in a much more subtle fashion than the original two statements. This is designed to provide relief from the sustained high levels of dynamic and harmonic tension present in the shout chorus. It begins at letter BB with a metrically compressed 3/4 version of the vamp originally stated at letter D. The melody is carried through the entire final chorus by the trombone section, initially in unison. Harmon-muted trumpets and mixed woodwinds provide a veiled backdrop. In the second half of the chorus, the rhythm section drops out, leaving the trombone chorale to carry the remainder of the recapitulation.

CHAPTER 22
Ending

The structural plan of *Exposition–Development–Recapitulation* has been widely used in many styles of music because it creates a satisfying sense of balance and symmetry. But in many jazz arrangements, this recapitulation does not occur. If it is felt that some sense of completion is necessary, an ending (or *coda*) can provide this opportunity.

Although arrangements are seldom written sequentially, the ending is usually the last part to be written. This is because an examination of the arrangement as a whole is necessary to determine how much additional material, if any, is needed to bring the piece to a complete and satisfying conclusion.

It is important that the length and complexity of the ending be in proportion to the arrangement as a whole. In shorter arrangements, the proper feeling of finality may be accomplished within the form itself. Longer, more elaborate arrangements may require newly written material which is extraneous to the basic form.

Another important consideration is what musical and expressive values need to be represented in the coda. For example, is there a need for an increase or decrease in dynamic tension? Faster pieces generally require an increase in tension, while slower pieces tend to end in a calm, reflective manner. If the climax has just occurred in the shout chorus, the ending may be a continuation or reaffirmation of it, or merely provide a postscript. But if there is a recapitulation of all or part of the original setting of the piece, then another climax may be necessary to affirm the proper feeling of finality.

When the length and complexity of the coda has been established, a decision must be made as to what form the ending will take. The number of approaches to writing an ending is incalculable, so an exclusive generalization is impossible. However, there are several devices that have found a permanent place in every arranger's repertoire. The remainder of the chapter will be devoted to a discussion of the various techniques that are commonly found in a coda, and how they may be employed to express the desired musical values.

Cadential Formulas

The primary purpose of any coda is *cadential* (closing or conclusionary). In shorter arrangements, the most economical solution employs the final cadence of the first chorus as the final cadence of the arrangement, providing it is sufficiently strong. The concept of the *D.S. al Fine* was explained in detail in the previous chapter. This results in an abrupt ending. A more emphatic one could be achieved by placing a hold over the last note.

EXAMPLE 22-1.

This has become common practice in most fake books and small ensemble arrangements, but is not recommended due to the possibility of confusion. A clearer way is to extract the last few measures to form a coda.

EXAMPLE 22-2.

Still more emphasis can be achieved by rewriting the final cadence so that it ends on a higher pitch, with or without a fermata.

EXAMPLE 22-3.

In some instances, the above approaches are adequate, but a reworking of the final cadence would provide even more emphasis and a stronger feeling of conclusion. The focus will first be on the final note and its approach. Some questions should be asked, such as should it be:

- Long or short?
- Loud or soft?
- High or low in pitch?
- Harmonized with consonant or dissonant harmony, or in unison?
- Fully orchestrated, or dissolve into a single note, or instrument?
- Approached in tempo, or preceded by a ritardando, fermata, or caesura?

The answers to these questions will help determine how the approach to the final note will be treated and how much new material is needed.

Extended Cadences

The search for new and fresh cadential formulas is a never-ending one. The problems in this quest stem from countless years of stereotyped formulas that have created an expectation of certain qualities of tension and release. The solution is to create new melodic and harmonic passages which are fresh sounding, but also have these requisite qualities.

A frequently used device is the *deceptive cadence*, in which the tonic chord is replaced by another. There is a myriad of possibilities, and Example 22-4 shows a typical song ending with some substitutes for the tonic chord in the key of C.

EXAMPLE 22-4.

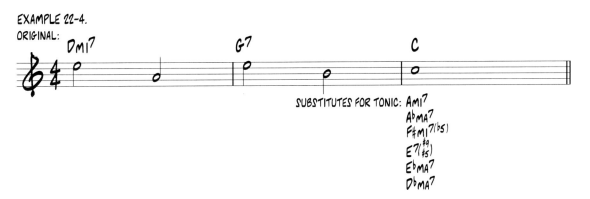

Once the cadence has been interrupted, the substitute chord may be followed by one or more additional chords, before the final tonic is reached. Again, the choices are numerous; here is one possibility in the key of C:

EXAMPLE 22-5.

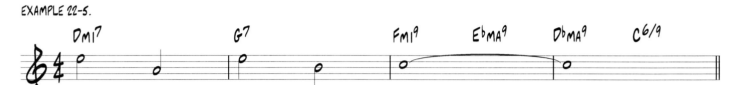

All of the chords in Example 22-5 are on the flat side of the tonality. These contribute to the feeling of calmness and repose, while delaying the final tonic. But it is also possible to use harmonies from the sharp side of the tonality.

EXAMPLE 22-6.

Another way to extend the final cadence is to follow the tonic chord with one or more additional chords, and then return to the tonic chord one final time.

EXAMPLE 22-7.

These create a suspended or unfinished feeling. But since the final tonic was already sounded, this additional bit of drama can be refreshing.

Cadenza

The *cadenza* had its origins in the eighteenth-century classical concerto. The purpose was to provide the soloist with an opportunity to display technical mastery. In jazz, the purpose is much the same. It is found most often in ballad arrangements that feature a soloist, and is placed near the end. The cadenza is usually preceded by a short ritardando and a held chord, typically a dominant or dominant preparation. The cadenza can range in scope from a brief epilogue to an extended, dazzling technical display that is improvised by the soloist.

In fast pieces, the drummer is the soloist most often chosen to perform a cadenza. The extended drum solo at the end of a fast piece was popularized during the big-band era by Chick Webb, Gene Krupa, and Buddy Rich. Thad Jones successfully integrated the drum cadenza into some of his arrangements, like "Greetings and Salutations." Here the extended cadenza is punctuated by a series of held chords.

A variation on the standard rubato cadenza on fast pieces also made its appearance in the big-band era. Here the soloist improvised in tempo, accompanied by the drummer. The prototype of this kind of free improvisation was Benny Goodman's "Sing, Sing, Sing." Jim McNeely's updated version of the same piece serves as a contemporary example.

Tags

The *tag* ending has been a long-standing technique in improvised combo arrangements, and has become a staple of written ones as well. It provides a more extensive elaboration or elongation of the final cadence. The name suggests that it is a kind of appendage added to the end of the basic form. But actually, there are two kinds of tags: those that are inserted before the final tonic chord and those that occur after it. The following examples demonstrate both concepts. For illustration purposes, 22-8 shows a typical cadence in a thirty-two measure form:

EXAMPLE 22-8.

The purpose of the first kind of tag is to delay the appearance of the final tonic chord in measure 31 by repeating measures 29–30 two times, adding four extra measures to the form.

TRACK 161

EXAMPLE 22-9.

Literal repeats can be tiresome, so some variation is desirable. One solution is to transpose the first repeat upward to a new pitch level, then return to the original in the second repeat. The most frequently used transpositions are a minor second, major second, and minor third.

TRACK 162

EXAMPLE 22-10.

The variation process can involve other elements of the music, such as melody, harmony, rhythm, register, and orchestration.

TRACK 163
Part 1

EXAMPLE 22-11.

In the second type of tag, the final cadence is completed, but the tonic is immediately followed by a chord (or chords) that set up a repetition of the cadence.

TRACK 163
Part 2

EXAMPLE 22-12.

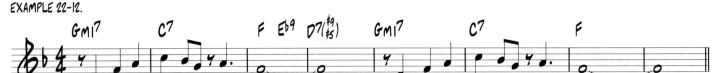

While the first type of tag traditionally withstands several repetitions, the second can quickly become tiresome due to the repeated sounding of the tonic, so it is usually repeated only once. But this repetition can be much more emphatic through the use of variation and/or extension.

Pedal Tones

The use of *pedal tones* was discussed previously in connection with introductions and interludes. In those situations, the dominant pedal was the best choice. It is anticipatory in nature and helps to set up the passages that follow. In an ending, different expressive values are required—those of finality, calmness, and repose. For these purposes, the tonic pedal works best. Dominant pedals may occur in any voice, but tonic pedals, especially in endings, are almost always in the bass. They can be introduced on the final tonic chord, serving as an extension of the cadence.

Vamps

The construction of *vamps* was also discussed earlier in chapter 17, but a few remarks concerning their use in endings are necessary. A vamp should not be inserted merely to prolong an ending; it should serve a definite purpose. That is, to convey a specific musical or emotional effect. To achieve this, the emphasis will most likely be on the control of tension; either a gradual increase leading to a climax, or, conversely, a gradual relaxation leading to minimal activity. Tension can be controlled through a variety of means: volume, pitch, dissonance, texture, density, etc.

An arrangement rarely ends with a vamp. Additional material, however brief, is needed to create a convincing conclusion. One notable exception is the so-called "fade-out" ending. It has been in vogue for a long time in jazz and pop music and is still considered a viable option. It is a sort of romantic concept, since the absence of completion requires the listener to imagine the final resolution. Also keep in mind that it is much less effective in live performance than on recordings.

Reintroduction of Previously Stated Material

There are times when a moment of inspiration from within the arrangement is so striking that it bears repetition. The restatement of this material could impart the sense of completion normally provided by the recapitulation. It could come from the main melody, introduction, interlude, or shout chorus. In arrangements of broader scope, the treatment of this material could evolve into an additional development section.

Bar Flies

The ending to "Bar Flies," beginning at letter S, utilizes the concept of restated material. Here, the first four measures of the introduction become a springboard for a dialogue between trumpet and alto saxophone at letter T. After several repetitions, the remaining horns enter at letter U to provide support. At the end of the dialogue, the introduction is restated at letter V in its entirety, and ends with a dissonant cluster chord.

Charming William

The coda begins at letter EE with the return of the final two-chord vamp from the original melody (mm. 57–58), still in 3/4. Final statements are made by harmon-muted trumpets and mixed woodwinds. At measure 319, the rhythm section concludes the arrangement with a continuation of the vamp, gradually diminishing to *pp*. This effect is enhanced by the gradual reduction of notes in the bass and piano.

CHAPTER 23
Where Do We Go from Here?

The great jazz arrangers of the past seventy-five years have developed a mature tradition that has produced hundreds of successful arrangers throughout the world. The prominent contemporary ones are all rooted in this tradition and affirm the continuity of it. But jazz, like any art form, must be able to adjust to change, or be in danger of becoming obsolete. The last twenty-five years has seen a steady acceleration in the rate of change, particularly in arranging. The chief contributing factor is the emergence of the arranger/composer.

The concept of arranger/composer began with Jelly Roll Morton and Don Redman in the 1920s. The swing era produced many memorable original pieces in which the composition and the arrangement were inseparable. "One O'Clock Jump," "In the Mood," "String of Pearls," "Take the 'A' Train," and "Clarinet Ala King" are but a few examples. In the fifties, Horace Silver, Benny Golson, and Oliver Nelson wrote pieces for small ensembles that were not just tunes, but full-blown arrangements. Thad Jones, Bob Brookmeyer, and Gerry Mulligan later adapted the concept to the contemporary large ensemble. The trend continued to accelerate until it became the predominant force. The act of jazz arranging has become inseparable from the act of composition. Both the composition and its setting unfold as one cumulative process.

An examination of current trends in jazz arranging might lead one to consider some of the traditional techniques discussed in this book irrelevant. In the never-ending quest for innovation and originality, young arrangers are often tempted to abandon traditional methods. But the truly successful ones do not espouse innovation without justification. Rules are not broken just for the sake of breaking them, but rather adapted to meet their needs. The aim of this final chapter is to assist in establishing the proper connection between the traditional elements and the works of contemporary composer/arrangers. An examination of some of their compositions and arrangements will help illustrate this. It is advised you obtain original recordings and scores of the pieces discussed through your local library or music retailer.

Organic Composition

An approach embraced by many contemporary composers is that of *organic composition*. This concept is based on the extensive development of one or more motives. Instead of a fully developed theme, the composer begins with a single germinal idea and then subjects it to rhythmic, intervallic, and harmonic manipulation. This becomes the unifying device throughout an entire piece.

Bob Brookmeyer's Composition "Celebration Two And"
(from the CD *New Works* recorded by Bob Brookmeyer's New Art Orchestra; Challenge Jazz: CHR 70066)

This remarkable ten-minute composition is based entirely on a single rhythmic cell (♩. ♪♩).

Several variants of this motive are heard throughout the piece. Some are used for melodic construction while others appear as background material. They are subjected to development, combined with interesting harmonies and shifting tonalities, then shaped into four- and eight-measure phrases which gradually evolve into longer melodies.

As is generally the case with this type of composition, the original motive's significance is only established during the developmental process. The opening statement of this piece is played by two keyboards, with drums filling between the motives. It employs two variants of the original motive.

EXAMPLE 23-1.

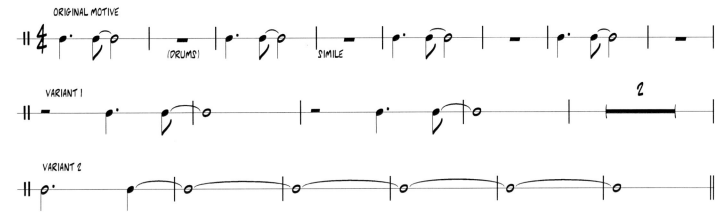

The augmentation of the second variant imparts a strong cadential feeling. Brookmeyer employs this variant several times throughout the piece.

The second statement is an extended passage played by the brass, based on the original motive. Once again, the drummer fills between motives and is later joined by the baritone saxophone soloist. The melodic scheme of this section is essentially based on the idea of a rising first interval followed by a descending second one, strongly suggesting the feeling of a four-measure phrase. Later, the original motive and first variant are combined to form a three-measure phrase.

EXAMPLE 23-2.

At 2:30, the second note of the original motive is extended to form a four-measure phrase. This becomes the basis for an ABA form with the key arrangement F-A♭-F. The melody is played by the two soloists—baritone sax and valve trombone—and answered by the ensemble.

EXAMPLE 23-3.

At 3:25, the original version of the motive provides the foundation for a lyrical interlude in F, which is used to introduce two long improvisational sections; first the baritone sax, then the valve trombone. The four variants of the original motive are used as background material for the soloists.

EXAMPLE 23-4.

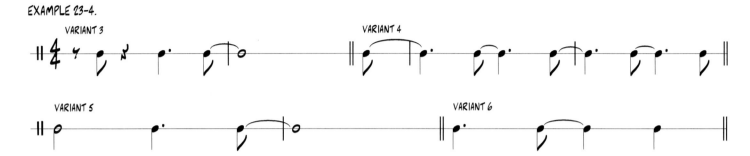

The success of this piece is due largely to the skillful and imaginative manipulation of the motive. But another important reason the piece is able to sustain interest with such a limited amount of material is that the listener's attention is constantly shifted from the ensemble to the soloists. During the improvisational sections, the motivic material is used mostly for backgrounds and is not the primary focus.

The organic construction of this piece precludes an exposition and recapitulation of the theme. The climactic ensemble shout chorus is replaced by several smaller subclimaxes. But there are still many traditional elements:

- Drum intro
- Interludes
- Solo breaks
- Stop-time
- Improvised solos with backgrounds
- Collective improvisation
- Trading fours
- Coda – including an extensive cadenza

Flexible Song Forms

When conceiving original thematic material for an extended jazz composition, the current trend is to avoid the standard song forms with symmetrical phrases and well-defined cadences. The preference is for shorter, more flexible melodies that are capable of expansion or development. They are frequently open-ended, which, when combined with strong transitional material and modulatory passages, gives a strong feeling of continuity and a free-flowing succession of ideas. There is also a decided preference for more contrapuntal textures.

Jim McNeely's "Extra Credit"

(from the CD *Lickety Split* recorded by the Vanguard Orchestra; New World Records: 80534-2)

"Extra Credit" consists of six themes alternating with five modal (ii7-V7) interludes. The first four provide solo space while the fifth serves as an ensemble shout. McNeely calls this a "moving rondo." In the classical rondo, a main theme is alternated with other themes: ABACAD, etc. In "Extra Credit," the A theme is heard only at the beginning and the end. The other themes are presented sequentially with solo interludes: ABC-interlude-BCD-interlude, etc.

The themes vary in length: B, C, D, and E are sixteen measures, A is longer, and F is much shorter. Each progresses smoothly to either the next theme or one of the solo interludes. The absence of strong cadential action creates a continuous flow.

One of the most interesting features is the way themes C, D, and E are introduced as background material behind the soloists. In subsequent appearances, they are more fully orchestrated and become part of a more complex texture, frequently accompanied by one or two countermelodies.

The organization of the themes ultimately determines the form of a rondo. But despite the predominance of composed material, traditional jazz elements still abound:

- Continuous focus is on the drummer.
- Several open solo sections exist, based on ii7-V7 and modal harmonies.
- Mainstream jazz rhythms and idioms keep the music swinging.
- There is a predominance of regular four- and eight-measure phrases.
- A traditional shout chorus takes place after the last solo.

This recording also has many other excellent examples of Jim McNeely's compositions. The accompanying booklet contains short analyses of all the music by the composer.

Decomposition

It is understandable that the way in which composers have treated standards and compositions by other jazz composers has also undergone a metamorphosis. This process, sometimes referred to as "decomposition" or "recomposition," goes far beyond melodic paraphrase and reharmonization. The piece is reduced to its barest fundamentals—melodic motives, rhythmic figures, harmonic skeleton, formal elements—and is subjected to extensive development and transformation. The composer decides which elements to control and to what extent, while exerting at least minimal control over others. Some elements may be manipulated at one point, and others at another time. Rarely are all elements manipulated at one time. The relationship of the final result to the original can be tenuous at best. In fact, the piece might never appear in its original form. The focus is more on how the arranger transforms the elements to give the work its own identity rather than on the piece itself. It is important to remember that in order to fully appreciate what has taken place, one must know the piece in its original form. The following are brief analyses of two excellent examples of this process.

Don Grolnick's Arrangement of "What Is This Thing Called Love"
(from the CD *Nighttown* recorded by Don Grolnick; Blue Note: CDP 0777 7 98689 2)

This thirty-two bar AABA song by Cole Porter is done as a slow mambo. In the A sections, rhythm, meter, harmony, and form undergo extensive reworking. Only the melody remains recognizable. The first A section is shortened from eight to five measures. Measures four, seven, and eight are eliminated. Measure two is in 3/4, and measure three is in 2/4. The cadence at the end of the phrase has been eliminated. Only the first measure is unchanged.

The second A is similar in form to the first, but the melody and harmony are reworked so that there is a cadence in B major.

The B section consists of eight measures in 4/4, but only the first three measures bear any melodic or harmonic relationship to the original. Starting in measure 4, there is an obvious quote of Harold Arlen's "The Man That Got Away."

The first three measures of the final A section are the same as the first. In the final four measures, there is a series of seven dotted-quarter notes metered as three measures of 3/4 and one of 3/8. This sets up a metric modulation in which the dotted-quarter note equals the half note ($\bullet\cdot = \bullet$) to begin the improvisation section.

Below is a rhythmic diagram of the first chorus.

EXAMPLE 23-5.

The composer does not impose any restrictions on the soloists in the improvisation section; the form and changes are close to the original. Grolnick does include some background figures which contain veiled references to the original melody. At the end of the drum solo, the drummer executes the metric modulation in reverse ($\bullet = \bullet\cdot$) to set up the recapitulation of the first chorus.

To complement this unusual treatment of a standard, many traditional elements are present.

- Formal scheme: Intro-head-solo section-recapitulation-ending
- Extended solos with backgrounds
- Drum solo

Maria Schneider's Arrangement of "Giant Steps"
(from the CD *Coming About* recorded by the Maria Schneider Jazz Orchestra)

In this recomposition of the John Coltrane classic, the melodic contour and form are close to the original. Rhythm, meter, and harmony are manipulated.

The exposition consists of two choruses of the sixteen-measure form. They are alike in meter and rhythm, but different in harmonic treatment. The original key changes are obscured in the first chorus through the use of chromatic planing. The melody is harmonized with one chord, called a *cell*, which is transposed to the different melodic pitches. In the second chorus, the planing is still evident, but the key changes are brought more into focus.

In measure fifteen of the second chorus, an *elision* (a shortening or overlapping of two formal elements) occurs. The turnaround is eliminated and replaced by an eight-measure repeated vamp, which sets up the improvisation section. The following example shows a rhythmic and metric diagram of the first two choruses.

EXAMPLE 23-6.

As in Grolnick's arrangement, the soloists are presented with the original form and chord changes. Other traditional elements are present:

- Overall scheme: Intro-head-interlude-solo section-ensemble shout-recapitulation-ending
- Extended solos with backgrounds
- Stop-time
- Send-offs
- Interlude

Since each piece of contemporary music offers its own unique solution for combining new techniques with traditional values, the only way to gain real insight is through repeated listening and detailed analysis of many compositions and arrangements. The reader is strongly urged to use the following list of composers and arrangers as a starting point.

Bob Brookmeyer	Bob Mintzer
Bill Holman	Vince Mendoza
Clare Fischer	Maria Schneider
Michael Abene	John Hollenbeck
Jim McNeely	Anthony Wilson

APPENDICES

APPENDIX 1
Enharmonic Spelling and Rhythmic Notation

In the days of pencil and paper arranging, the music copyist was responsible for respelling notes and simplifying rhythms that were written awkwardly by the arranger. Since the advent of music notation software, many arrangers have taken on this auxiliary task. Too many writers merely input the parts and print, without even a cursory examination of the individual parts. Consequently, the parts are much more difficult to read than they should be. Since the commercial musician is expected to play his part perfectly the first time, it is the responsibility of the copyist to facilitate this in every way possible. This appendix contains guidelines pertaining to enharmonic spelling and rhythmic notation that should aid the arranger/copyist in the creation of more clearly readable parts and scores.

Enharmonic Spelling

Enharmonic tones are those that have the same pitch but are spelled differently. Every note of the chromatic scale can be spelled two different ways; some can be written three ways if double sharps or flats are used.

When writing scores and parts, situations concerning the proper spelling of chromatic tones are constantly arising. The important thing is that the arranger makes the correct choices, not the music notation software, as it is not equipped to do so. The goal is not only to be theoretically correct, but to make the individual parts as readable as possible. In many situations, relying on the key signature or invoking the scale of the key of the moment will help determine the best option. The remainder can be resolved by following two simple rules:

1. **Always use as few accidentals as possible**.
   This can be accomplished by using sharps for ascending chromatic passages and flats for descending ones.

EXAMPLE A1-1.

   When flats are used in ascending passages or sharps in descending ones, they have to be canceled out, resulting in twice as many accidentals.

EXAMPLE A1-2.

   In keys other than C, the natural sign may replace sharps in flat keys and flats in sharp keys.

EXAMPLE A1-3.

Also notice the use of the F♯ in the flat key and the B♭ in the sharp key in the previous example. These eliminate the need for extra accidentals, making the music easier to read.

But following this rule rigidly may mean using double flats or sharps as well as unfamiliar spellings like E♯, F♭, B♯, and C♭.

EXAMPLE A1-4.

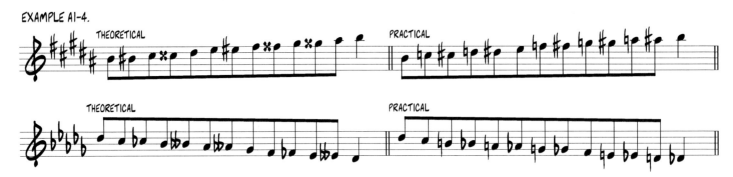

This can create some undesirable augmented and diminished intervals that are difficult to comprehend, both melodically and harmonically. Here are some of those unacceptable intervals extracted from the previous example.

EXAMPLE A1-5.

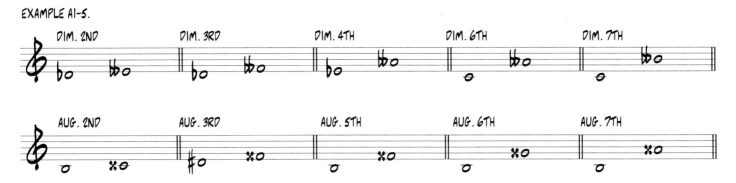

The best solution would be to change them enharmonically to a more recognizable interval. Correctness should always be balanced with practicality. Here are the intervals from A1-5, notated in a more practical way.

EXAMPLE A1-6.

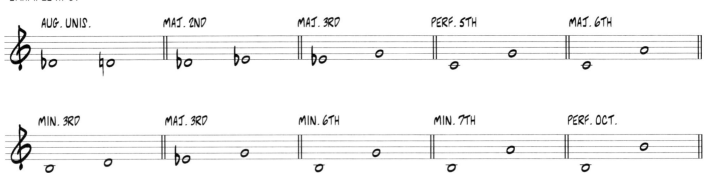

2. **Retain as many familiar patterns as possible**.

These include scales, scale segments, and chord arpeggios. Facility in sightreading requires the ability to grasp several notes at one time rather than reading note to note. Recognizing familiar patterns facilitates this process.

In the following example, some familiar groupings have been obscured due to incorrect note spelling.

EXAMPLE A1-7.

When these are enharmonically corrected, the B♭ minor scale segment and the E♭ major triad are easily recognizable.

EXAMPLE A1-8.

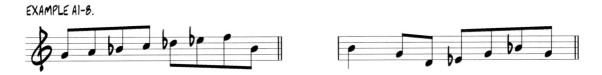

The diminished-seventh chord presents a unique situation for enharmonic spelling. This chord is only found diatonically as a vii°7 in minor. It most frequently precedes a minor chord in cadential or tonicizing situations. Because of its symmetric construction of minor thirds, there are only three of them. This means that each can, through enharmonic spelling, be found in four different keys. The following example shows each of the three chords in four different keys, with the correct spelling. (Note that the key of each chord is indicated above, not the root name.)

EXAMPLE A1-9.

The interval between the root and seventh is a diminished seventh, which is enharmonic with a major sixth. Occasionally the seventh may need to be respelled to avoid a double flat or sharp. But when the diminished seventh is functioning as a vii°7, it should always be spelled with the leading tone as the root and change the seventh enharmonically if necessary for easier recognition. In example A1-9, the two notes with an X above them should be respelled enharmonically.

Dilemmas may arise when selecting a key for performance. Suppose the choice was between G♭ and F♯ major. The pianist might not have a preference. The bass and guitar would probably prefer the sharp key, because of the tuning of their open strings. But if transposing instruments are involved and the key of F♯ was selected, two or three additional sharps would be added to their transposed parts. This would result in *theoretical* keys of eight or nine sharps. In this instance, G♭ is the only correct choice.

Internal modulations in a piece can also be problematic. Many of these move to the flat side of the original tonality, such as "flat three" or "flat six." In sharp keys, this does not present a problem. But if the modulation was to "flat six" of the key of D♭ (as in the bridge of Horace Silver's "Ecaroh"), this would result in a theoretical key of B♭♭. The obvious solution is to write it in A major, even though it obscures the original key relationship.

Confusion can occur when progressing to or from a remote key. Contemporary improvisational materials contain countless examples of ii7-V7-I7 progressions where the ii7-V7 are in a sharp key and the I7 is in a flat key, or vice versa. It is best to select the appropriate tonic key and then make the preceding chords and melodies correspond.

Sometimes the correct spelling is not the most practical one as in the next example, where the second, third, and fourth parts have chromatic tones generated by the chord spelling.

EXAMPLE AI-10.

These parts would be more easily read if they were written the following way:

EXAMPLE AI-11.

Another solution is to use no key signature. Pieces like "Invitation," "Very Early," and "Tones for Joan's Bones" depart so quickly and frequently from the original key that canceling out the original key signature requires as many accidentals as having no signature at all.

Another aid related to enharmonics is the *cautionary* or *courtesy* accidental. These are accidentals that are not musically necessary, but lessen the possibility of misplayed notes. There are three situations where the use of cautionary accidentals can eliminate any possible confusion. An "X" has been placed above each note that includes a courtesy accidental.

    1.   Notes within the measure

EXAMPLE AI-12.

    2.   Notes across the bar line

EXAMPLE AI-13.

    3.   Octaves within or across the measure

EXAMPLE AI-14.

Traditionally, cautionary accidentals are written parenthetically; however common practice today in commercial music is to write them without parentheses. In some situations, these accidentals may appear as many as two or three measures later. Never hesitate to use cautionary accidentals if there is any question as to the correct pitch.

Rhythmic Notation

Eighth-Note Oriented Music

In eighth-note oriented music, the most fundamental rule regarding proper rhythmic notation in 4/4 and 2/2 is the maintenance of a visual subdivision of the measure. In other words, the reader should be able to see two equal halves of a measure at all times. This particularly pertains to note values shorter than a dotted quarter; longer values (whole, dotted half, and half notes) should be written in their most concise form. Specifically, it applies to quarter and dotted quarter notes that lie astride the visual subdivision. Here are some common violations of this rule followed by their corrected versions.

EXAMPLE A1-15.

The following examples contain dotted quarters that do not fall in the middle of the measure. These should also be written in their most concise form.

EXAMPLE A1-16.

The most common figure found in jazz is the eighth-quarter-eighth syncopation. Since the quarter note is played short in this rhythm, as it should be in jazz, there is an ongoing controversy regarding the correct notation of this figure. Since there is no prevailing opinion on this, all the following versions of this figure are acceptable, provided that a staccato or "cap" articulation is placed atop the quarter note.

EXAMPLE A1-17.

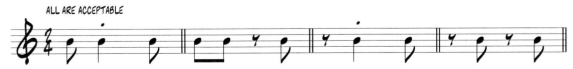

One version found in older music that is no longer acceptable occurs when this figure extends over the bar line. No articulation was ever used, and the tied eighth was intended to be played short. Even when a staccato is placed over the tied eighth, this is still confusing and should never be written. Instead, use of a rest on the downbeat is acceptable.

EXAMPLE AI-18.

It is common practice to place a staccato articulation over a downbeat quarter note rather than write it as an eighth note followed by an eighth rest.

EXAMPLE AI-19.

It is improper in jazz and commercial music to place a staccato articulation over any note longer than a quarter.

EXAMPLE AI-20.

An unusual situation persists concerning the usage of the staccato articulation on notes shorter than a quarter (in swing-feel tunes). Tunes such as "Hi-Fly," "Doodlin'," and "Blues March" contain eighth-note passages where the downbeat notes are to be played short. (This figure can also be found in many shuffles.) These are usually written as dotted eighths and sixteenths, and are articulated as shown in the next example. There are also three other notation possibilities for this figure, presented in order of preference.

EXAMPLE AI-21.

Generally speaking, the beaming of eighth notes should reflect the time signature. In 4/4, eighths can be beamed in groups of two, three, and four. When beamed in groups of two or four, they must be whole beats, not parts of beats. In groups of three, the beamed notes must be preceded by a downbeat eighth rest.

EXAMPLE AI-22.

*THESE EXAMPLES ARE CONSIDERED INCORRECT BECAUSE THE LAST EIGHTH NOTE BEFORE EACH REST WOULD NORMALLY BE NOTATED AS A STACCATO QUARTER NOTE.

In 3/4, the above rules for 4/4 apply as well. Additionally, groupings of five and six eighth notes are also permissible. When beamed in groups of five, the beamed notes must be preceded by a downbeat eighth rest. Factors such as accents, dynamics, and melodic contour will help determine the manner in which the notes are grouped.

EXAMPLE A1-23.

Dotted quarter rests should not be used in any time signature where the quarter is the pulse (2/4, 3/4/, 4/4, etc.). They are only to be used in those time signatures where the dotted quarter is the pulse (6/8/, 9/8, 12/8, etc.).

EXAMPLE A1-24.

Sixteenth-Note Oriented Music

In sixteenth-note oriented music, the rule regarding the visual subdivision of a measure is appended to include the visual maintenance of the beat. In the following examples, the beat has been obscured in the incorrect versions. Corrected versions follow.

EXAMPLE A1-25.

The sixteenth-eighth-sixteenth version of the syncopation shown in Example A1-17 is also a point of contention. Since no consensus has been reached, all of the following versions of this figure are acceptable, provided that a staccato articulation is placed atop the eighth note.

EXAMPLE A1-26.

In fact, the concept of the staccato-articulated eighth note is common practice in sixteenth-note oriented music.

EXAMPLE A1-27.

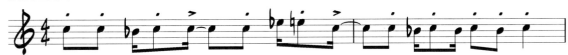

In extremely syncopated passages such as the ones shown below, the use of staccato eighth notes is essential as it makes any passage more readable.

EXAMPLE A1-28.

The beaming of sixteenth notes should reflect the beat. Sixteenths can be beamed in groups of two, three, and four. When beamed in groups of four, they must occur within a whole beat. In groups of three, the beamed notes must be preceded by a downbeat sixteenth rest. In groups of two, the beamed notes can be placed anywhere within the beat, provided that the accompanying rests maintain the integrity of the beat.

EXAMPLE A1–29.

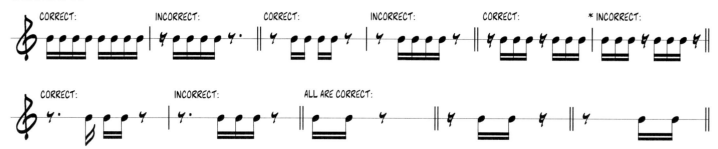

* This example is considered incorrect because the last sixteenth note before each rest would normally be notated as a staccato eighth note.

Combinations of sixteenth and eighth notes and rests can also be beamed as long as they do not exceed one whole beat. Any rests surrounded by notes can also be contained within the beaming.

EXAMPLE A1–30.

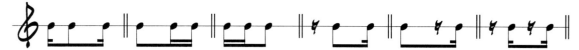

Dotted-Quarter-Note-Pulsed Music (6/8, 9/8, 12/8)

In all of these meters, visual maintenance of the pulse is essential. Except for the dotted half, notes or rests should not exceed the dotted quarter. Half notes and half rests are never used. The next example shows all the possible combinations of figures contained within the beat:

EXAMPLE A1–31.

An interesting exception to this is the *hemiolia* (*hemiola*), which has existed in Spanish, Mexican, and Latin-American music for centuries. It is based on the formula of three beats against two and is notated contrary to the dotted-quarter pulse.

EXAMPLE A1–32.

The beaming of eighth and sixteenth notes and rests should reflect the dotted-quarter pulse at all times.

EXAMPLE A1-33.

Miscellaneous

When writing in the more uncommon compound meters such as 5/4, 7/4, and 9/4, the combinations of figures and the beaming of eighth notes should always reflect the internal subdivisions.

EXAMPLE A1-34.

In jazz and commercial music, the release of a note is just as important as its attack, and contributes to the rhythmic precision of the music. Whether a downbeat or upbeat release is desired, it should be clearly indicated. This can be accomplished in three ways:

EXAMPLE A1-35.

Slurs, as a phrase indicator, have long been a component of jazz and commercial music. In recent years, their use has diminished to the point where much of today's music does not contain any. One situation where a slur can be helpful is to indicate internal movement within a sustained chord. In the following example, second measure, the top staff sustains a single note while the bottom staff changes with the chord. The slur indicates that the two notes should be played as smoothly as possible so that a prominent attack is avoided.

EXAMPLE A1-36.

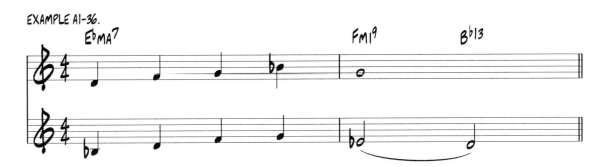

APPENDIX 2
Unacceptable Minor-Second Dissonances

This appendix covers minor-second dissonances that are to be avoided when writing multiple-note voicings.

Major Chords

- When the root of the chord is the top voice, do not use the major seventh. The closest usable pitches are the major sixth and the natural fifth. The major sixth is often used as a substitute for the major-seventh guide tone when creating major-chord voicings with the root on top.

EXAMPLE A2–1.

- When the natural fifth of the chord is the top voice, do not use the lowered fifth. The closest usable pitches are the natural third (most typical) and the natural fourth (only used in a 4-3 suspension).

EXAMPLE A2–2.

Minor Chords

- When the third of the chord is the top voice, do not use the natural ninth. The closest usable pitches are the root, the major seventh (minor chord with major seventh), and the minor seventh.

EXAMPLE A2–3.

- When the minor seventh of the chord is the top voice, do not use the natural thirteenth. The closest usable pitches are the natural fifth (used in most situations) and the raised fifth (mi7 chord with a ♯5).

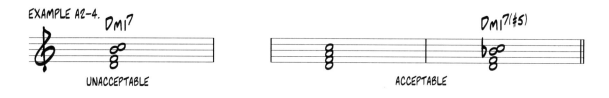

EXAMPLE A2–4.

Half-Diminished Chords

- When the minor third of the chord is the top voice, do not use the natural ninth. The closest usable pitches are the root and the minor seventh.

EXAMPLE A2–5.

- When the diminished fifth of the chord is the top voice, do not use the natural eleventh. The closest usable pitch is the minor third.

EXAMPLE A2–6.

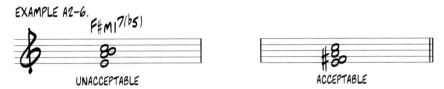

Dominant Chords

- When the natural fifth of the chord is the top voice, do not use the lowered fifth. The closest usable pitches are the natural fourth (this creates a suspended dominant chord) and the natural third.

EXAMPLE A2–7.

- When the seventh of the chord is the top voice, do not use the natural thirteenth. The closest usable pitches are the raised fifth (used in an altered dominant chord) and natural fifth.

EXAMPLE A2–8.

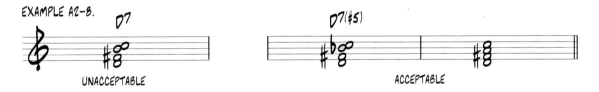

- When the lowered ninth of the chord is the top voice, do not use the root. The closest usable pitch is the minor seventh.

EXAMPLE A2–9.

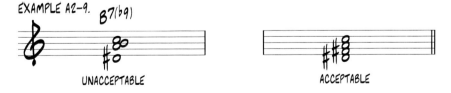

- When the natural ninth of the chord is the top voice, do not use the lowered ninth. The closest usable pitches are the root, the minor seventh, and the natural thirteenth.

EXAMPLE A2–10.

- When the natural thirteenth of the chord is the top voice, do not use the raised fifth. The closest usable pitches are the natural fifth and the lowered fifth.

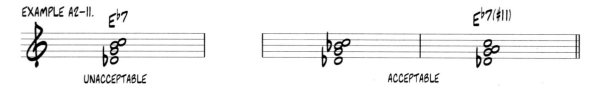

Fully-Diminished Chords

- When the root of the chord is the top voice, do not use the major seventh. The closest usable pitch is the diminished seventh.

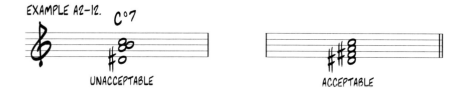

- When the minor third of the chord is the top voice, do not use the natural ninth. The closest usable pitches are the root and the major seventh.

- When the diminished fifth of the chord is the top voice, do not use the natural eleventh. The closest usable pitch is the minor third.

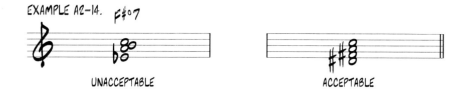

- When the diminished seventh of the chord is the top voice, do not use the lowered thirteenth. The closest usable pitch is the diminished fifth.

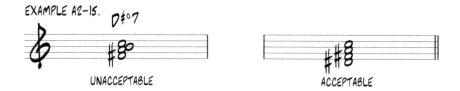

APPENDIX 3
Sequence of Chord Tension and Density

The list below exhibits a generally accepted sequence of tension and density for each chord type. It is arranged from mildest to sharpest. The introduction of major and minor seconds and tritones into a close-position voicing is responsible for the increase in tension, while the number of color tones and alterations constitutes its density.

Major Chord

This uses the Ionian or Lydian scale (the following notes replace or are added to the notes of the basic triad).

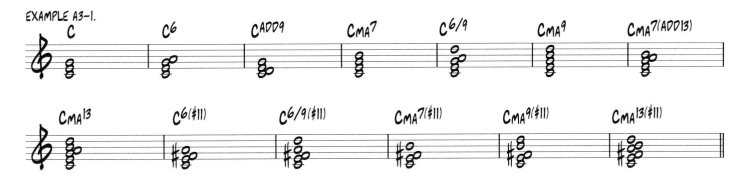

Dorian-Minor Chord Functioning as ii Chord or Tonic

The Dorian scale is used (the following notes are added to the basic triad).

Melodic-Minor Chord Functioning as Tonic

This uses the melodic-minor scale (the following notes are added to the basic triad).

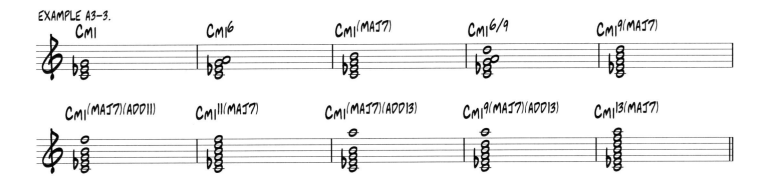

Half-Diminished Chord

The Locrian or Locrian #2 scale is used (the following notes are added to the basic half-diminished 7th chord).

EXAMPLE A3–4.

Unaltered Dominant Chord

This uses the Mixolydian or Lydian dominant scale (the following notes replace or are added to the notes of the basic dominant-seventh chord). Here, the raised eleventh functions as a natural extension in the chord due to the inability to use the natural eleventh in any situation other than suspended dominant chords.

EXAMPLE A3–5.

Suspended Dominant Chord

The Mixolydian scale is used (the following notes are added to the basic suspended dominant-seventh chord).

EXAMPLE A3–6.

Altered Dominant Chord

This uses the whole tone, Mixolydian ♭6, altered, or half-whole-diminished scale (the following notes replace or are added to the notes of the basic dominant-seventh chord).

EXAMPLE A3–7.

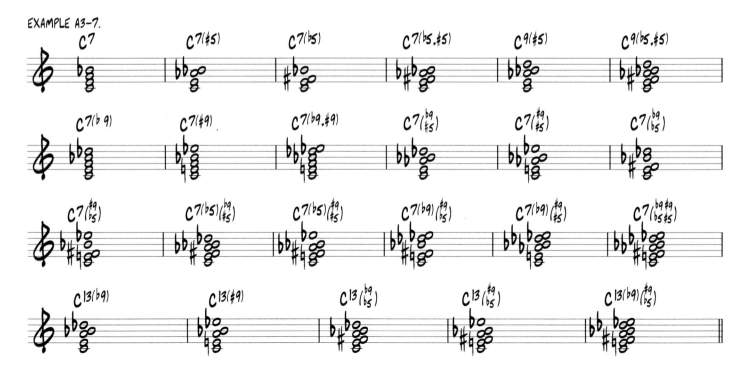

Fully-Diminished Chord

The whole-half-diminished scale is used (the following notes are added to the basic fully-diminished seventh chord).

EXAMPLE A3–8.

APPENDIX 4
Compendium of Four-Note Close-Position Voicings

This compendium shows most of the possible voicing combinations containing all applicable guide tones for all scale tones with a "C" root. They are presented in order of tension, from least to most tense. In order to hear a complete voicing, each must be played with a chord root.

MAJOR CHORDS

DORIAN-MINOR CHORDS (MINOR II OR TONIC QUALITY) CONTAINING A 6TH OR MINOR 7TH

MELODIC-MINOR CHORDS (TONIC QUALITY) CONTAINING A MAJOR 7TH

HALF-DIMINISHED CHORDS

UNALTERED DOMINANT CHORDS

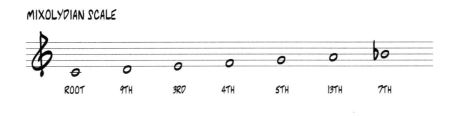

EXTENDED OR ALTERED DOMINANT CHORDS

13TH ON TOP

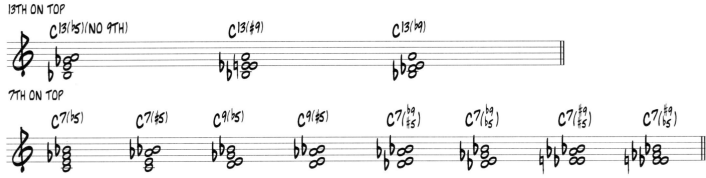

FULLY-DIMINISHED CHORDS

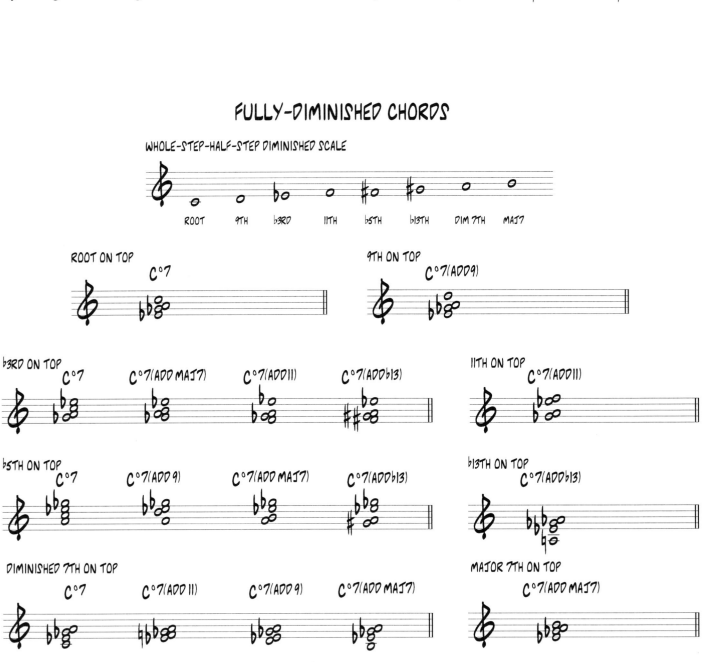

APPENDIX 5
Compendium of Three-Note
Close-Position Voicings

This compendium shows all the possible voicing combinations for all scale tones with a "C" root. Those listed first are complete as they contain all necessary guide tones. The specific chord they constitute is indicated by the chord symbol above. The remainder of the voicings are incomplete and contain varying combinations of basic, guide, and color tones. All voicings must be played with a chord root.

MAJOR CHORDS

5TH ON TOP

DORIAN-MINOR CHORDS (MINOR II OR TONIC QUALITY) CONTAINING A 6TH OR MINOR 7TH

MELODIC-MINOR CHORDS (TONIC QUALITY) CONTAINING A MAJOR 7TH

HALF-DIMINISHED CHORDS

UNALTERED OR EXTENDED DOMINANT CHORDS

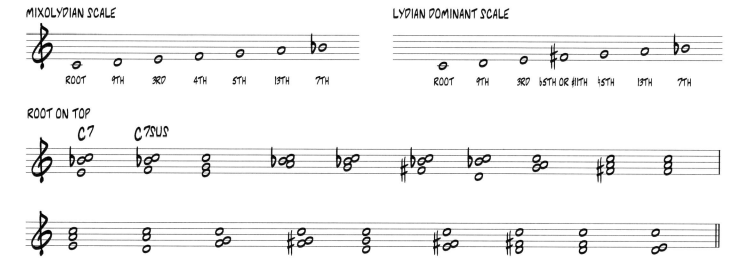

ALTERED DOMINANT CHORDS

13TH ON TOP

FULLY-DIMINISHED CHORDS

WHOLE-STEP-HALF-STEP DIMINISHED SCALE

11TH ON TOP

♭5TH ON TOP

♭13TH ON TOP

DIM. 7TH ON TOP

MAJ 7TH ON TOP

APPENDIX 6
Compendium of Five-Note Close-Position Voicings

This compendium shows all the possible voicing combinations for all scale tones with a "C" root. All voicings must be played with a chord root. Due to the frequent appearance of seconds, many should also be revoiced to an open position so that the harmonic properties of each voicing may be heard more easily.

DORIAN-MINOR CHORDS (MINOR II OR TONIC QUALITY) CONTAINING A 6TH OR MINOR 7TH

HALF-DIMINISHED CHORDS

UNALTERED DOMINANT CHORDS

13TH ON TOP

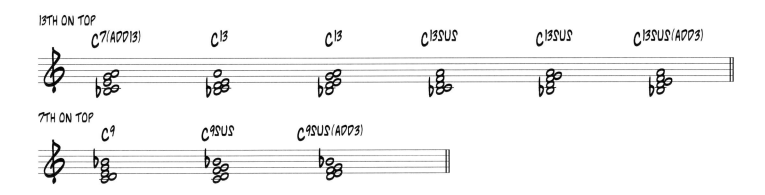

ALTERED DOMINANT CHORDS

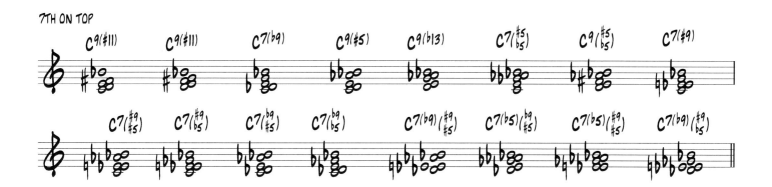

FULLY-DIMINISHED CHORDS

APPENDIX 7
"Bar Flies" and "Charming William" Full Scores

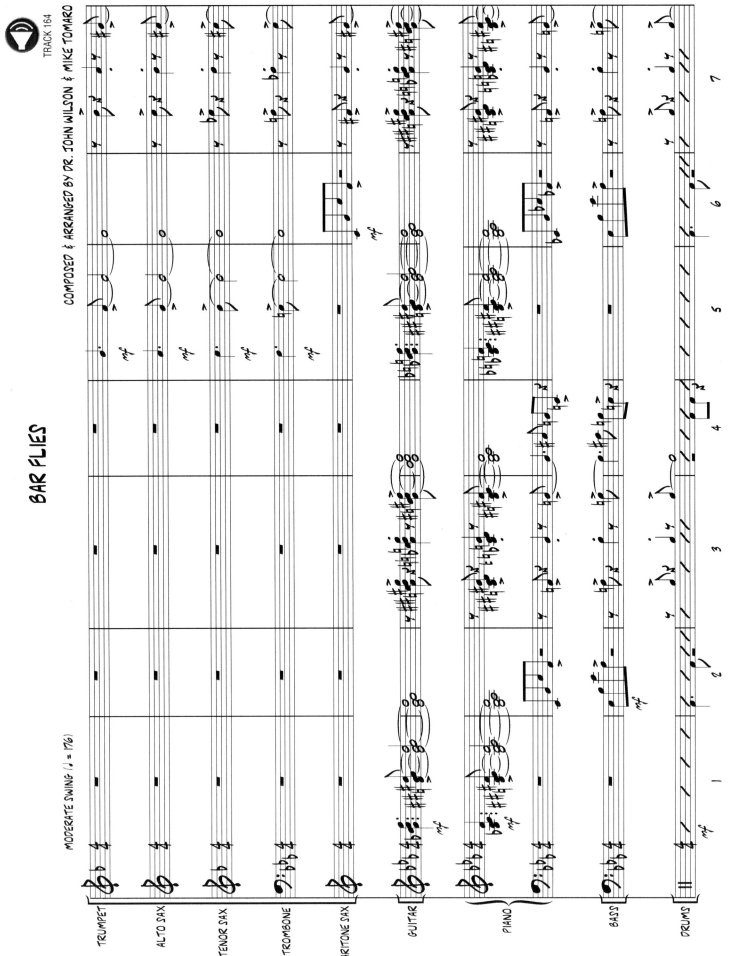

BAR FLIES

COMPOSED & ARRANGED BY DR. JOHN WILSON & MIKE TOMARO

TRACK 164

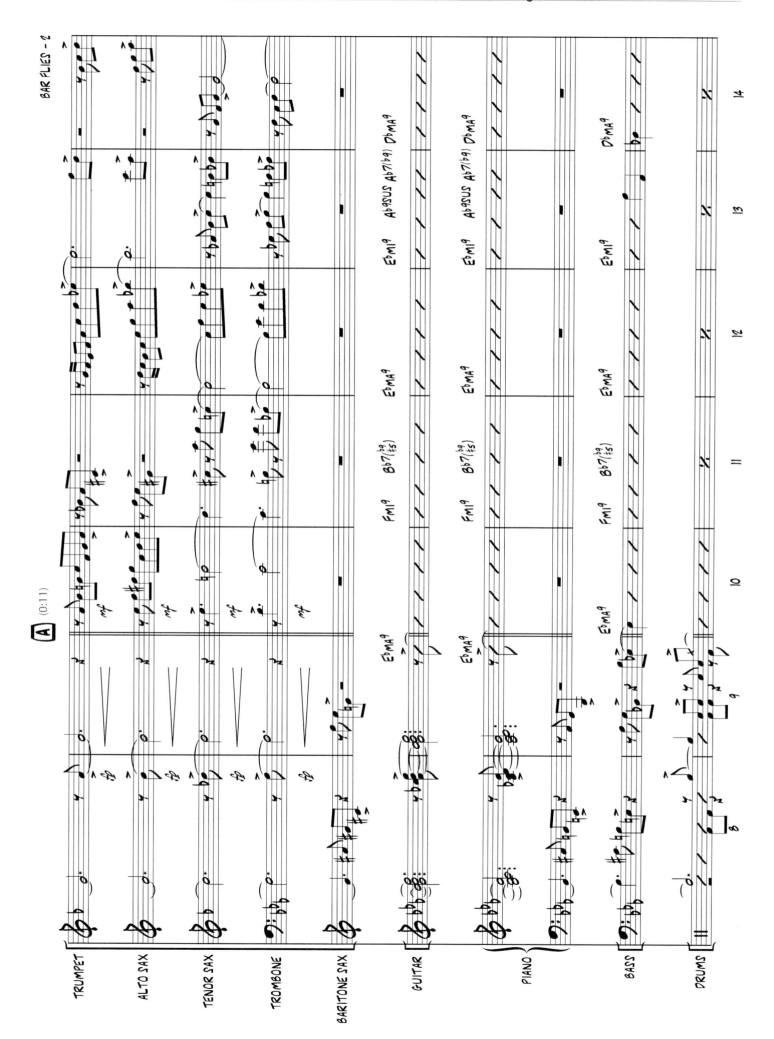

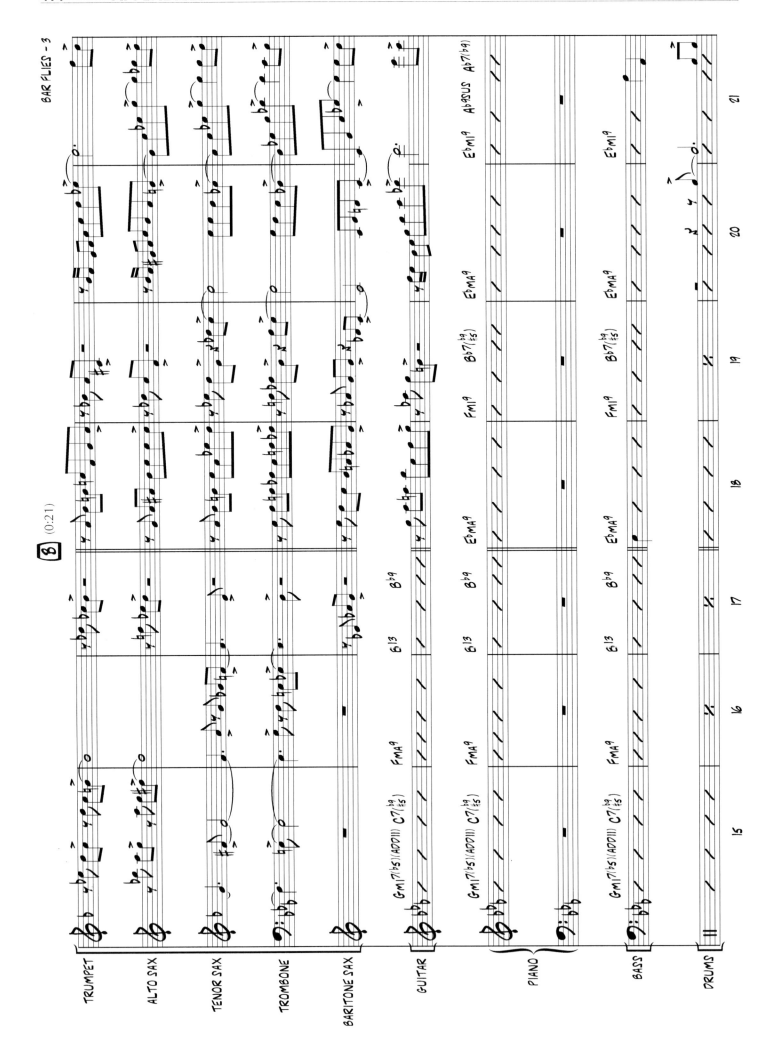

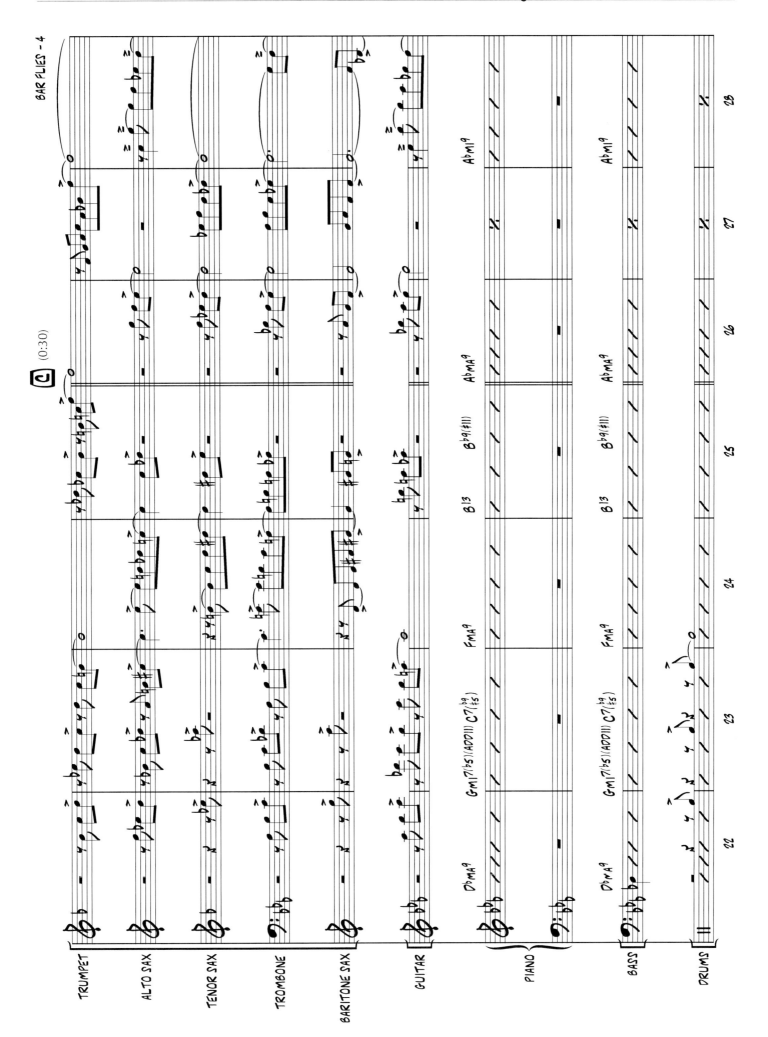

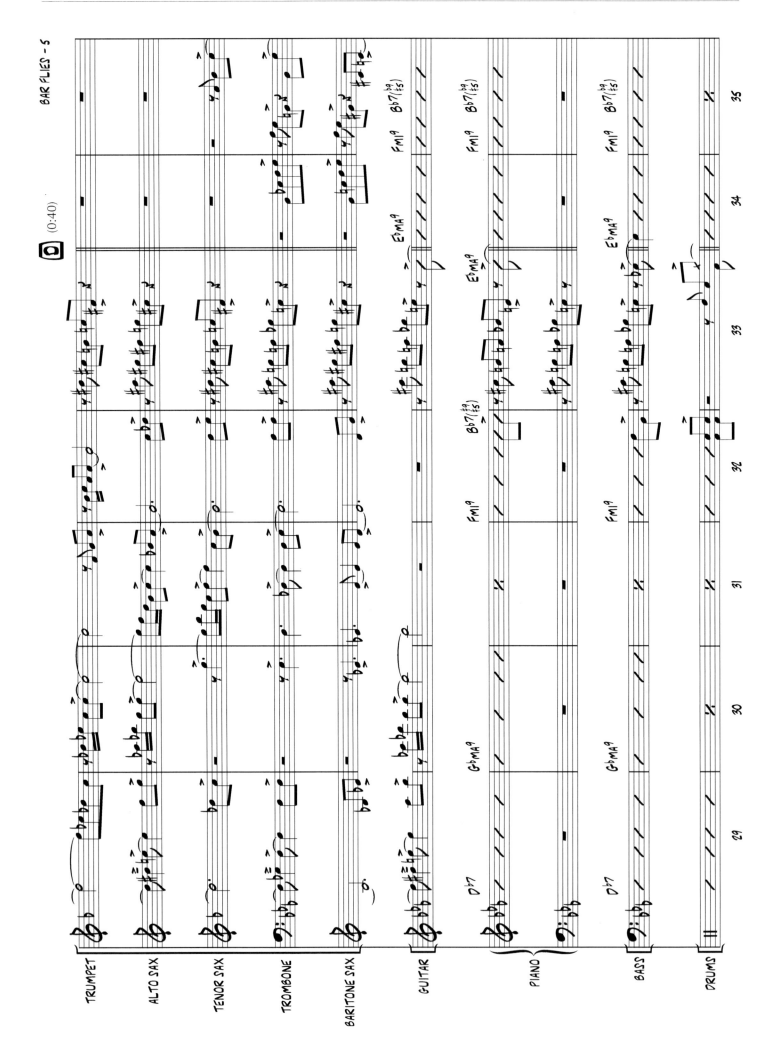

BAR FLIES - 7

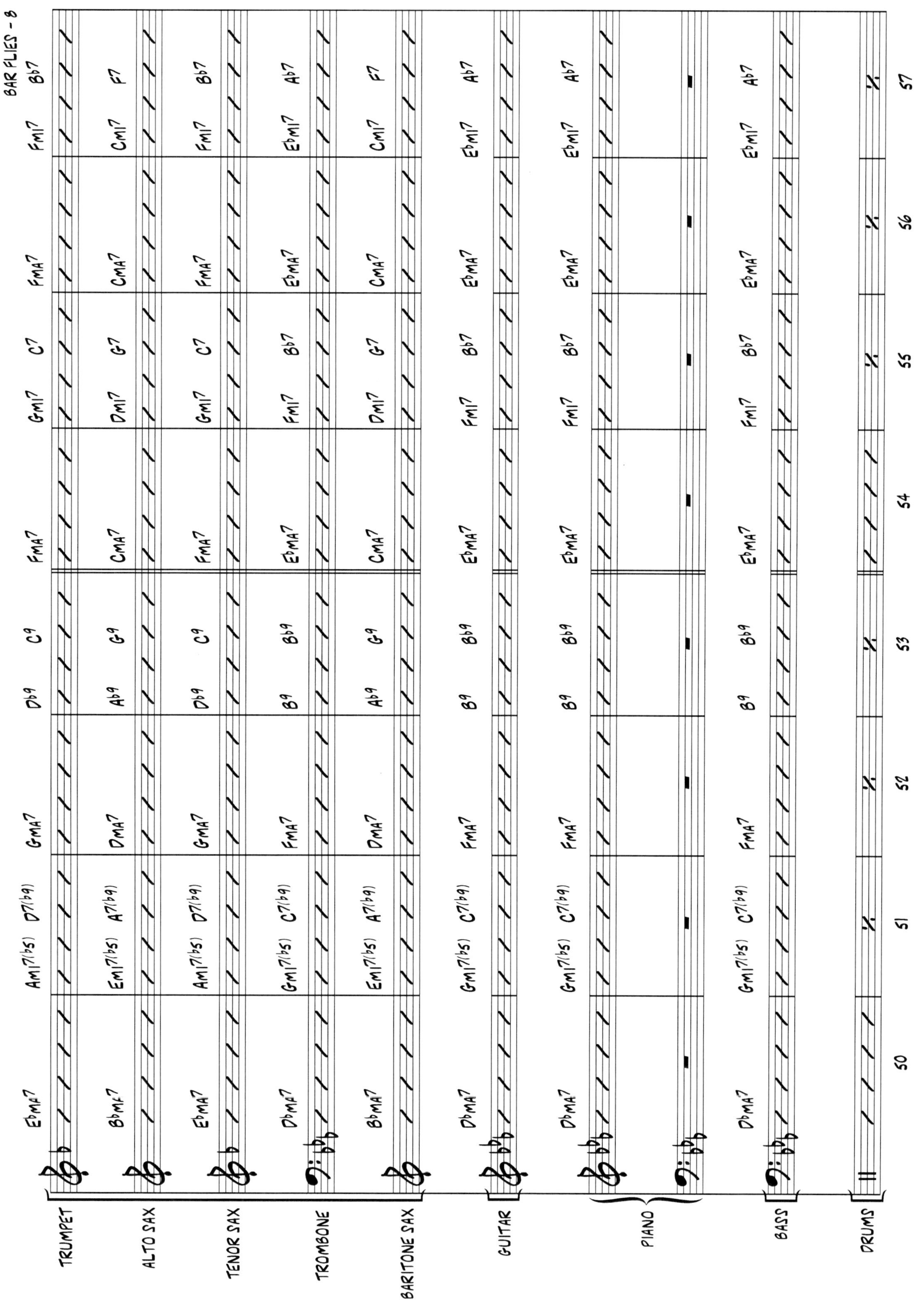
BAR FLIES - 8
TRUMPET
ALTO SAX
TENOR SAX
TROMBONE
BARITONE SAX
GUITAR
PIANO
BASS
DRUMS
50
51
52
53
54
55
56
57

BAR FLIES - 9
TRUMPET
ALTO SAX
TENOR SAX
TROMBONE
BARITONE SAX
GUITAR
PIANO
BASS
DRUMS
E♭MA7 Ami7(♭5) D7(♭9) GMA7 Cmi7 F7 B♭MA7 B♭mi7 E♭7
B♭MA7 Emi7(♭5) A7(♭9) DMA7 Gmi7 C7 FMA7 Fmi7 B♭7
E♭MA7 Ami7(♭5) D7(♭9) GMA7 Cmi7 F7 B♭MA7 B♭mi7 E♭7
D♭MA7 Gmi7(♭5) C7(♭9) FMA7 B♭mi7 E♭7 A♭MA7 A♭mi7 D♭7
B♭MA7 Emi7(♭5) A7(♭9) DMA7 Gmi7 C7 FMA7 Fmi7 B♭7
D♭MA7 Gmi7(♭5) C7(♭9) FMA7 B♭mi7 E♭7 A♭MA7 A♭mi7 D♭7
D♭MA7 Gmi7(♭5) C7(♭9) FMA7 B♭mi7 E♭7 A♭MA7 A♭mi7 D♭7
D♭MA7 Gmi7(♭5) C7(♭9) FMA7 B♭mi7 E♭7 A♭MA7 A♭mi7 D♭7
58 59 60 61 62 63 64 65

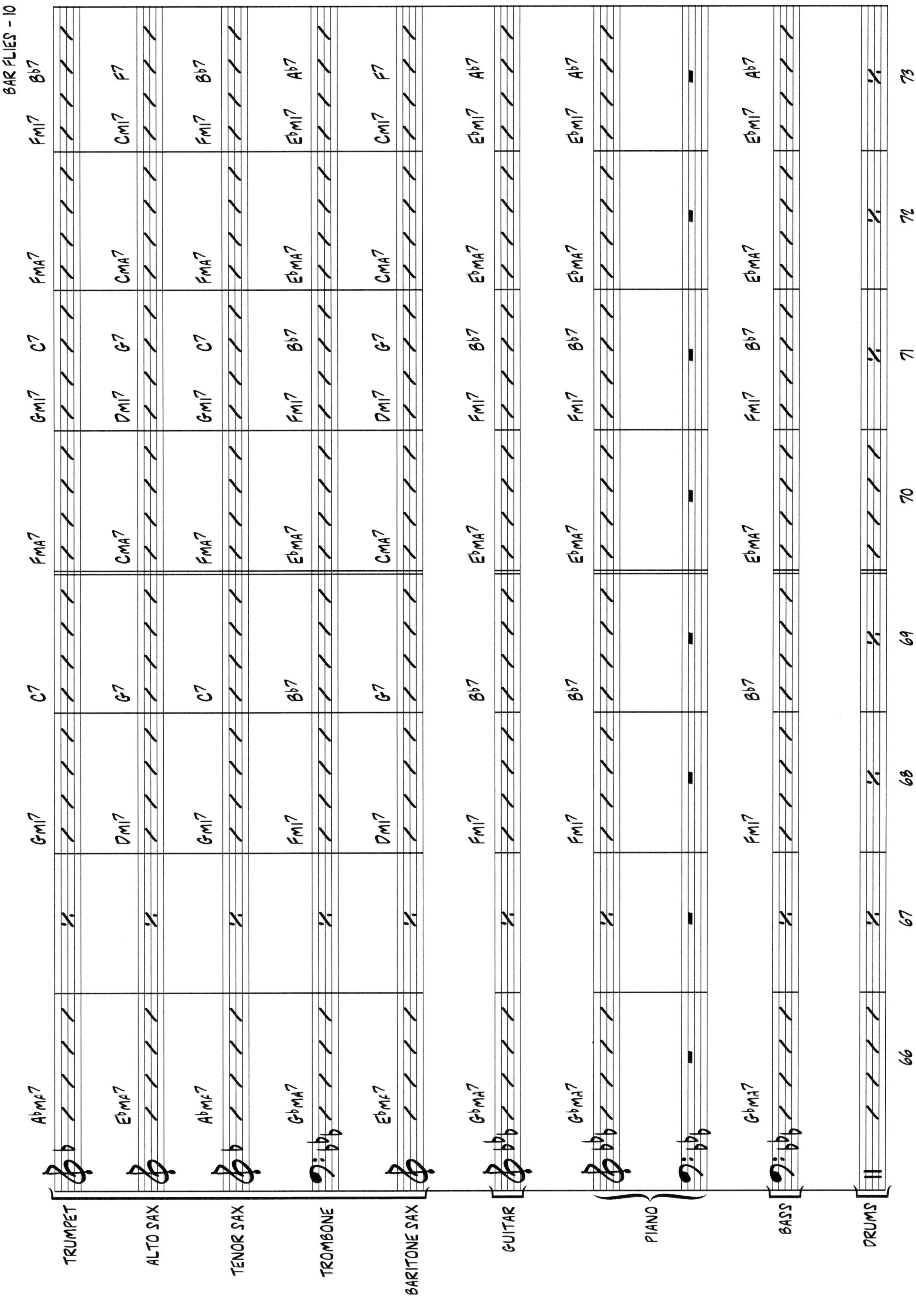
BAR FLIES - 10
TRUMPET
AbMA7 GMI7 C7 FMA7 GMI7 C7 FMA7 FMI7 Bb7
ALTO SAX
EbMA7 DMI7 G7 CMA7 DMI7 G7 CMA7 CMI7 F7
TENOR SAX
AbMA7 GMI7 C7 FMA7 GMI7 C7 FMA7 FMI7 Bb7
TROMBONE
GbMA7 FMI7 Bb7 EbMA7 FMI7 Bb7 EbMA7 EbMI7 Ab7
BARITONE SAX
EbMA7 DMI7 G7 CMA7 DMI7 G7 CMA7 CMI7 F7
GUITAR
GbMA7 FMI7 Bb7 EbMA7 FMI7 Bb7 EbMA7 EbMI7 Ab7
PIANO
GbMA7 FMI7 Bb7 EbMA7 FMI7 Bb7 EbMA7 EbMI7 Ab7
BASS
GbMA7 FMI7 Bb7 EbMA7 FMI7 Bb7 EbMA7 EbMI7 Ab7
DRUMS
66 67 68 69 70 71 72 73

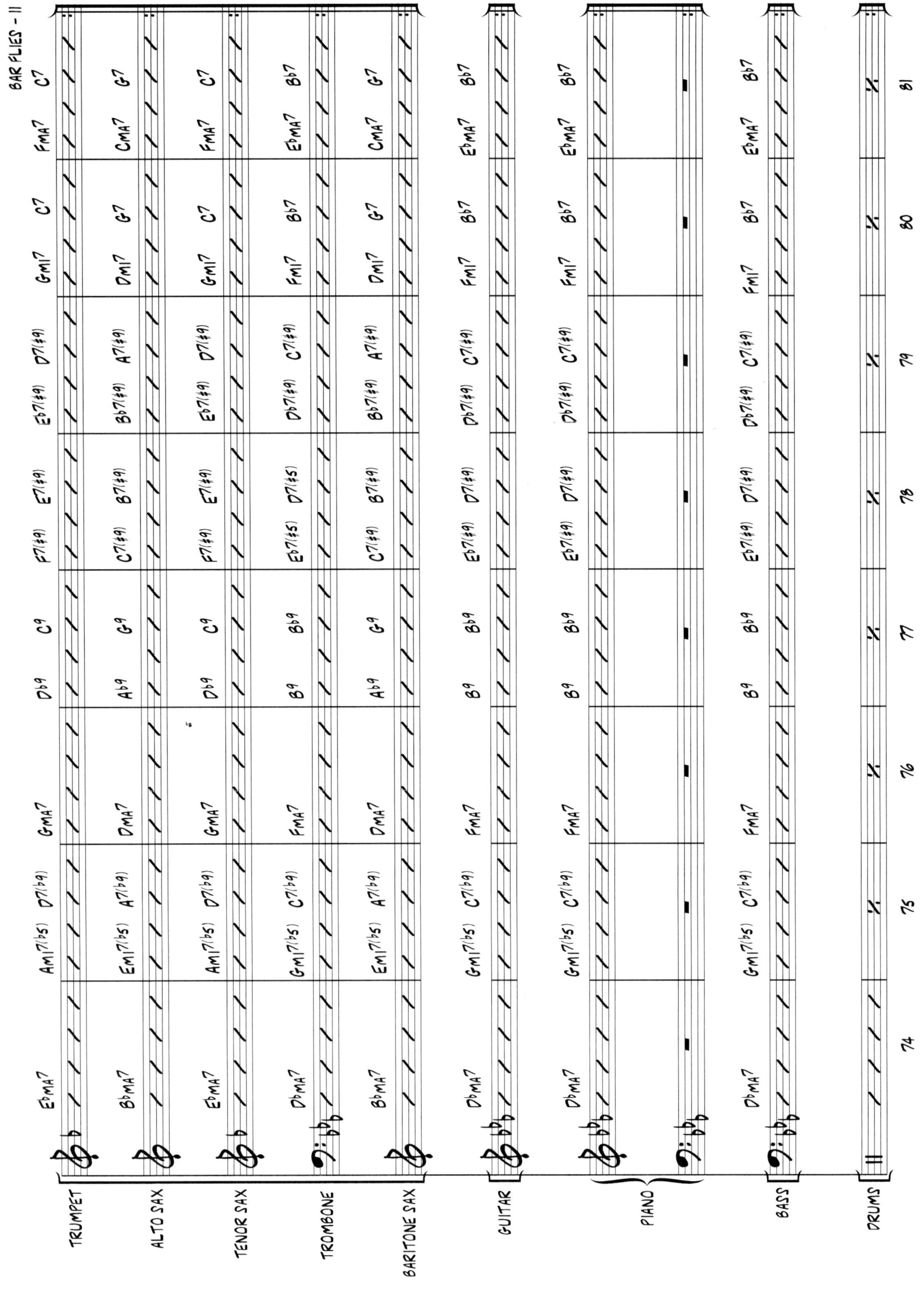
BAR FLIES - II
TRUMPET
EbMA7 | AMI7(b5) D7(b9) | GMA7 | Db9 C9 | F7(#9) E7(#9) | Eb7(#9) D7(#9) | GMI7 C7 | FMA7 C7
ALTO SAX
BbMA7 | EMI7(b5) A7(b9) | DMA7 | Ab9 G9 | C7(#9) B7(#9) | Bb7(#9) A7(#9) | DMI7 G7 | CMA7 G7
TENOR SAX
EbMA7 | AMI7(b5) D7(b9) | GMA7 | Db9 C9 | F7(#9) E7(#9) | Eb7(#9) D7(#9) | GMI7 C7 | FMA7 C7
TROMBONE
DbMA7 | GMI7(b5) C7(b9) | FMA7 | B9 Bb9 | Eb7(#5) D7(#5) | Db7(#9) C7(#9) | FMI7 Bb7 | EbMA7 Bb7
BARITONE SAX
BbMA7 | EMI7(b5) A7(b9) | DMA7 | Ab9 G9 | C7(#9) B7(#9) | Bb7(#9) A7(#9) | DMI7 G7 | CMA7 G7
GUITAR
DbMA7 | GMI7(b5) C7(b9) | FMA7 | B9 Bb9 | Eb7(#9) D7(#9) | Db7(#9) C7(#9) | FMI7 Bb7 | EbMA7 Bb7
PIANO
DbMA7 | GMI7(b5) C7(b9) | FMA7 | B9 Bb9 | Eb7(#9) D7(#9) | Db7(#9) C7(#9) | FMI7 Bb7 | EbMA7 Bb7
BASS
DbMA7 | GMI7(b5) C7(b9) | FMA7 | B9 Bb9 | Eb7(#9) D7(#9) | Db7(#9) C7(#9) | FMI7 Bb7 | EbMA7 Bb7
DRUMS
74 75 76 77 78 79 80 81

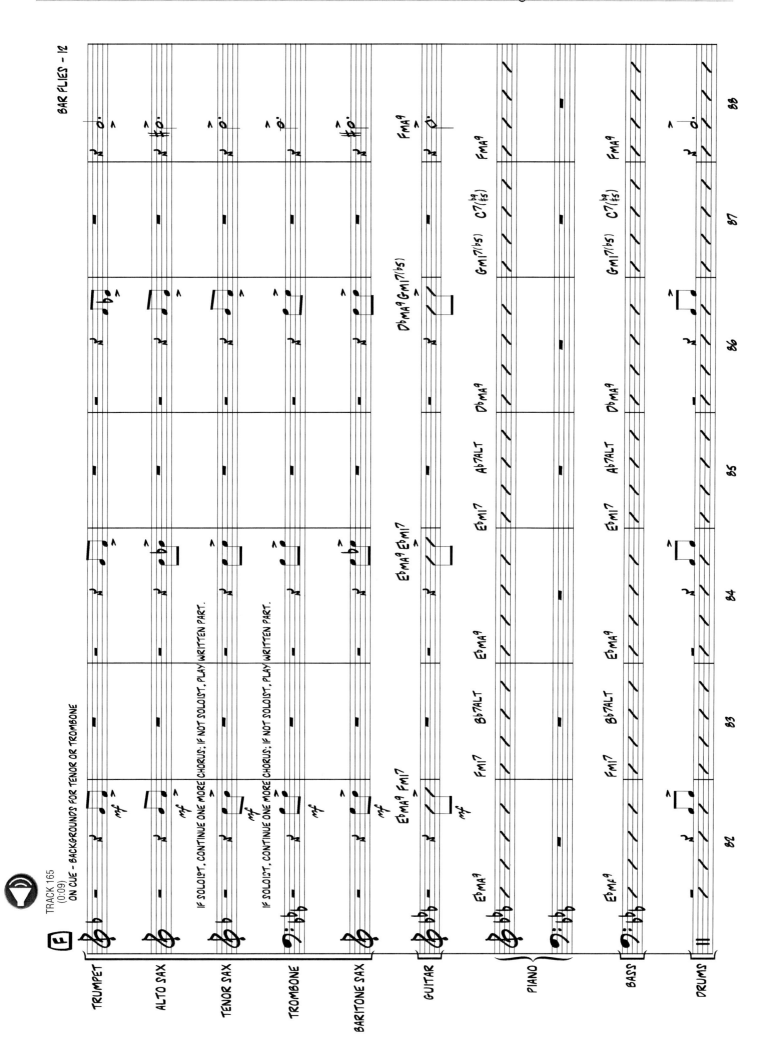

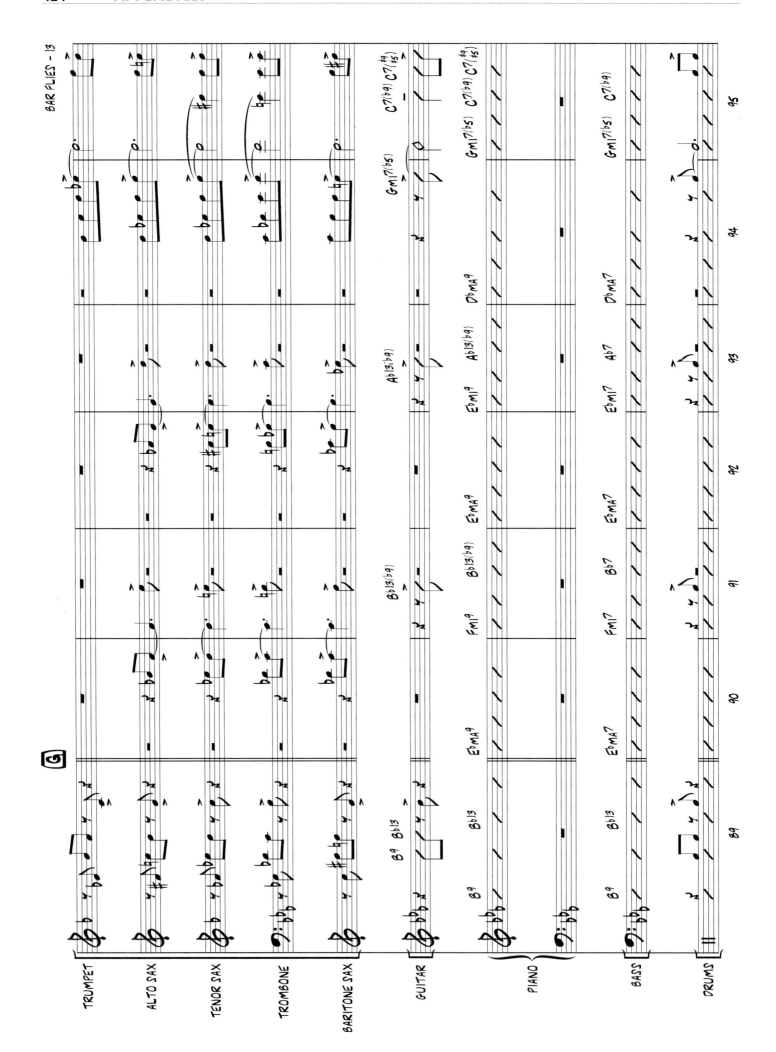

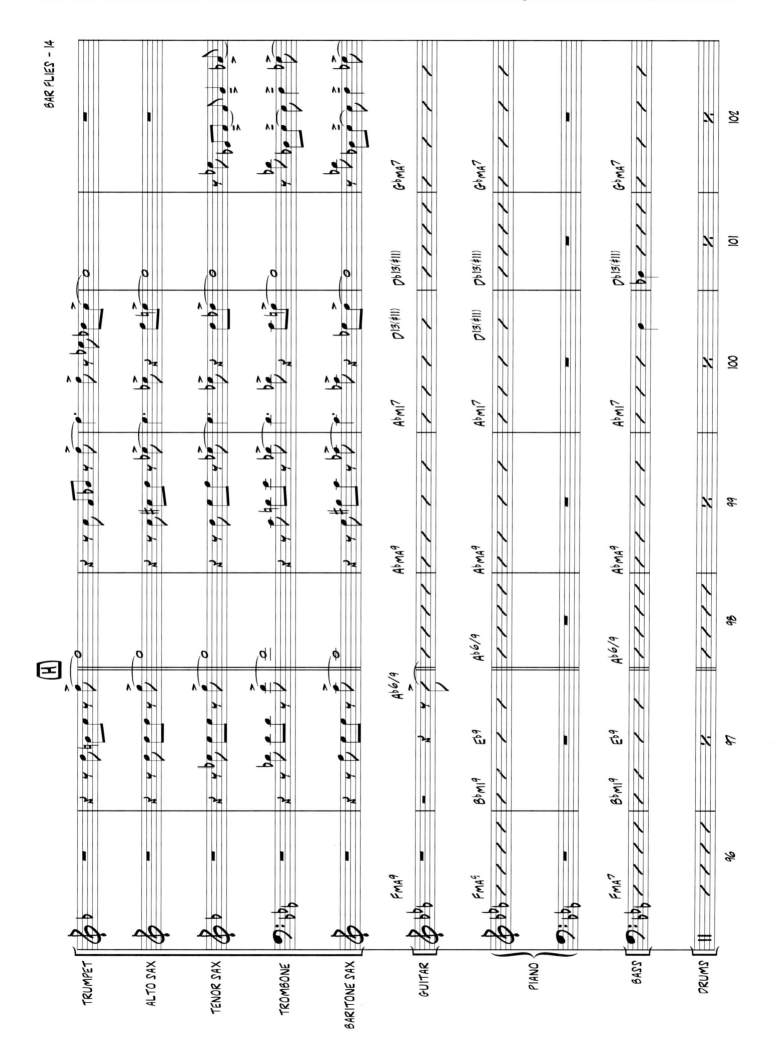

BAR FLIES - 15
I
TRUMPET
ALTO SAX
TENOR SAX
TROMBONE
BARITONE SAX
GUITAR
PIANO
BASS
DRUMS
FMI7
Bb13(b9)
EbMA9
Eb6/9
FMI7
Bb13(b9)
EbMA9
Eb6/9
EbMI7
Ab13(b9)
103
104
105
106
107
108
109

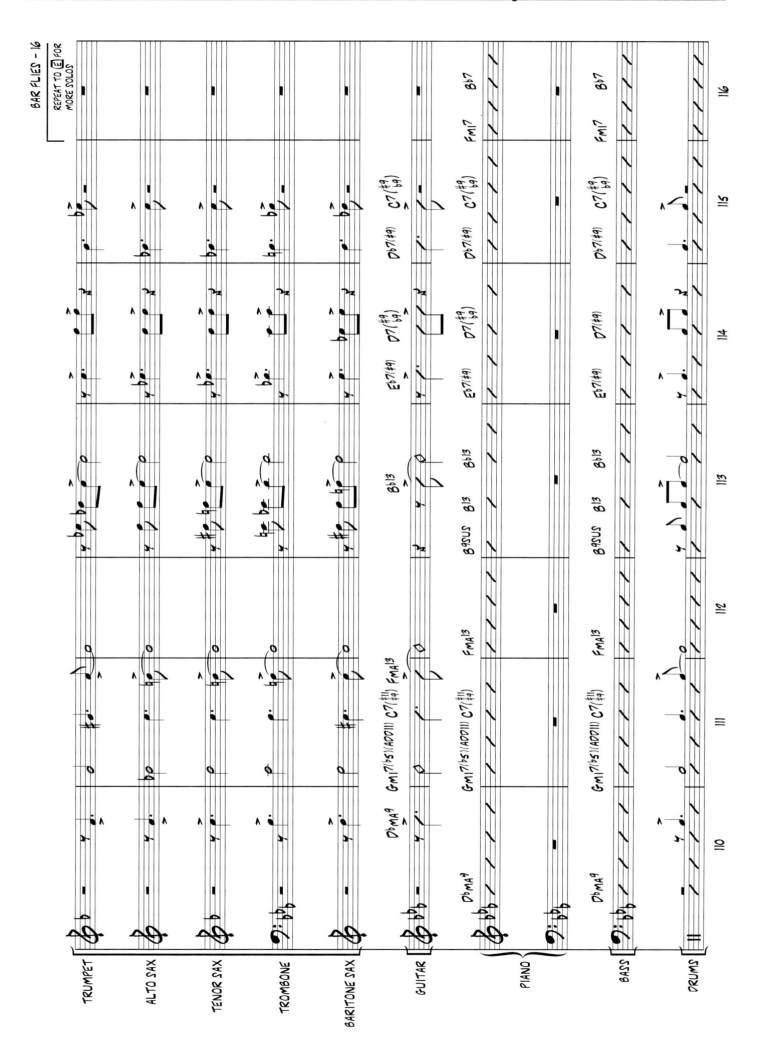

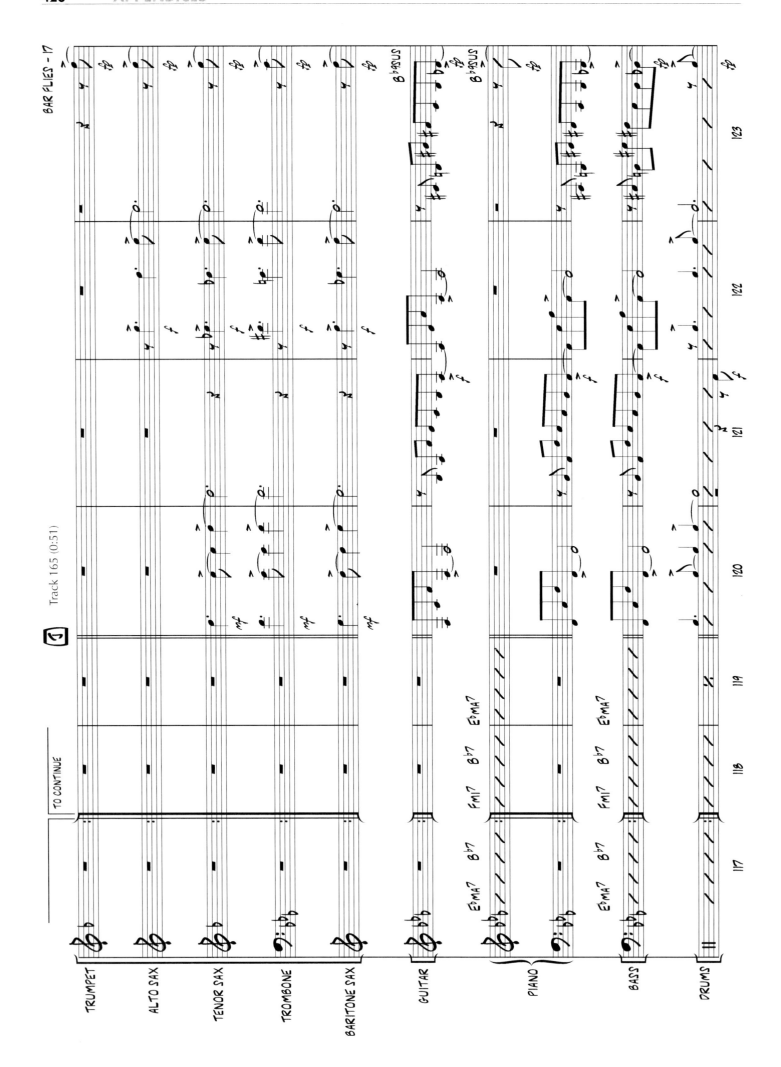

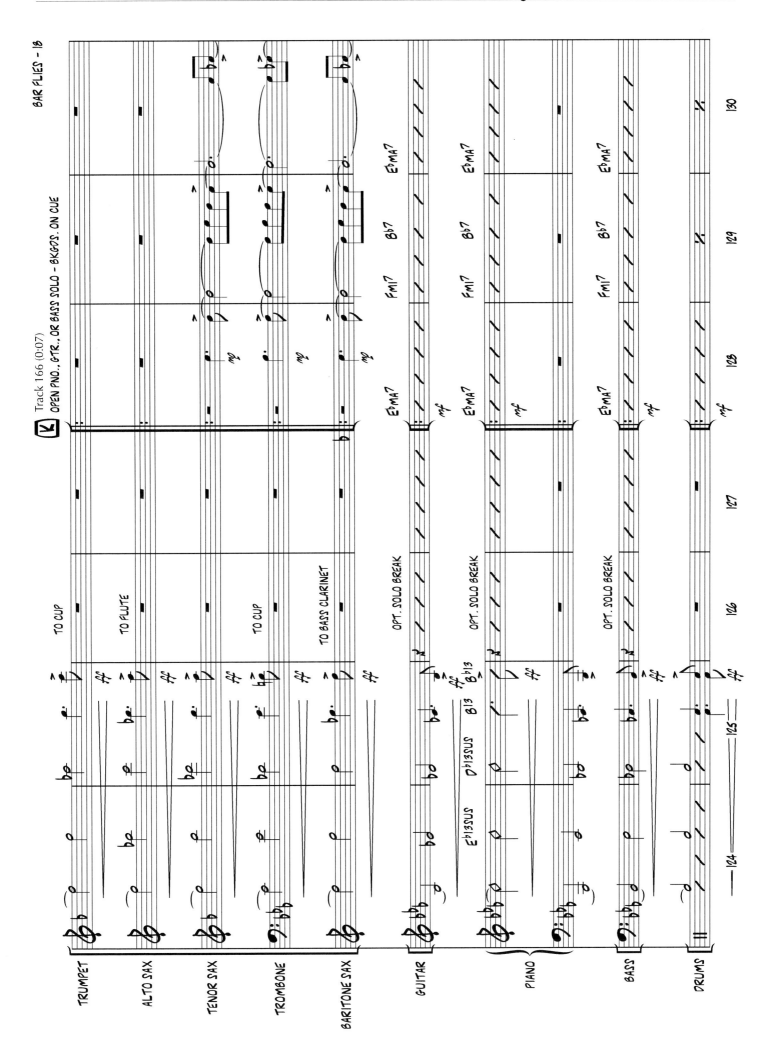

BAR FLIES - 19
TRUMPET
ALTO SAX
TENOR SAX
TROMBONE
BARITONE SAX
GUITAR
PIANO
BASS
DRUMS
LEAD
L
E♭MI7 A♭7 D♭MA7 GMI7(♭5) C7(♭9/♯5) FMA7 B9 B♭9 E♭MA7 FMI7 B♭7
131
132
133
134
135
136
137

BAR FLIES - 21
TRUMPET
ALTO SAX
TENOR SAX
TROMBONE
BARITONE SAX
GUITAR
PIANO
BASS
DRUMS
Abmi7
Db7
Gbma7
Fmi7
Bb7
145
146
147
148
149
150
151

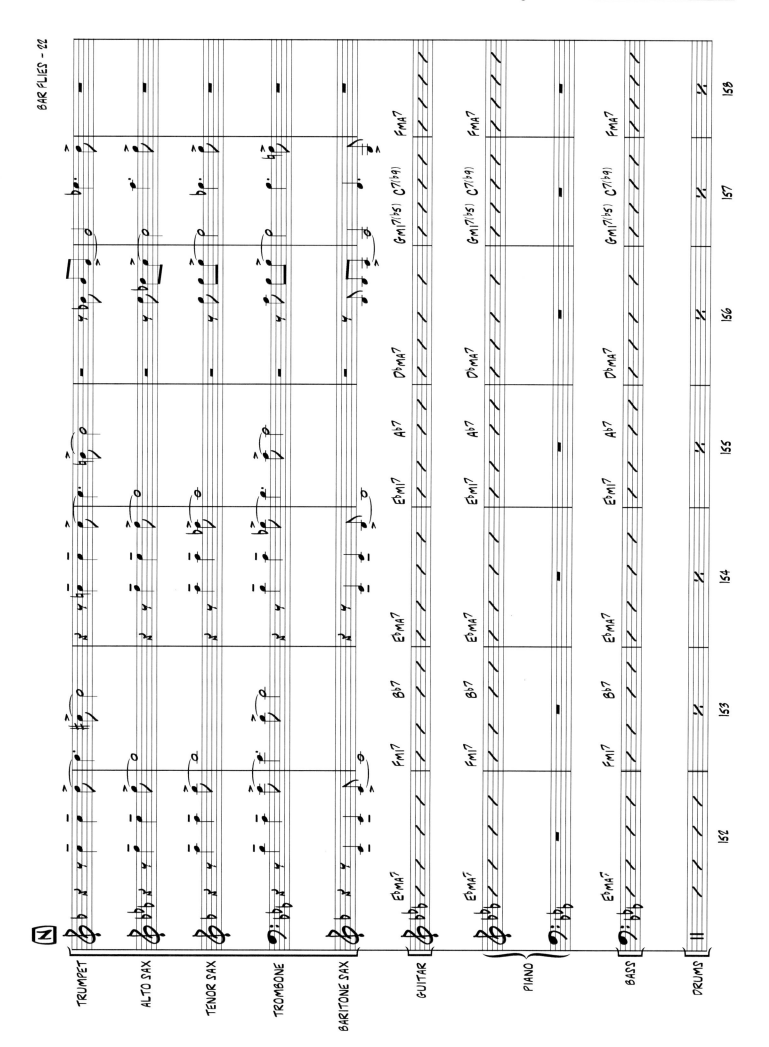

BAR FLIES - 23
REPEAT TO K FOR MORE SOLOS
TO CONTINUE
OPEN
TO ALTO
OPEN
TO BARITONE
TRUMPET
ALTO SAX
TENOR SAX
TROMBONE
BARITONE SAX
GUITAR
PIANO
BASS
DRUMS
B9 Bb9 Eb7(#9) D7(#9) Db7(#9) C7(#9) Fmi7 Bb7 EbMA7 Bb7 Fmi7 Bb7 EbMA7 Bb7
SET UP SHOUT CHORUS
159 160 161 162 163 164 165

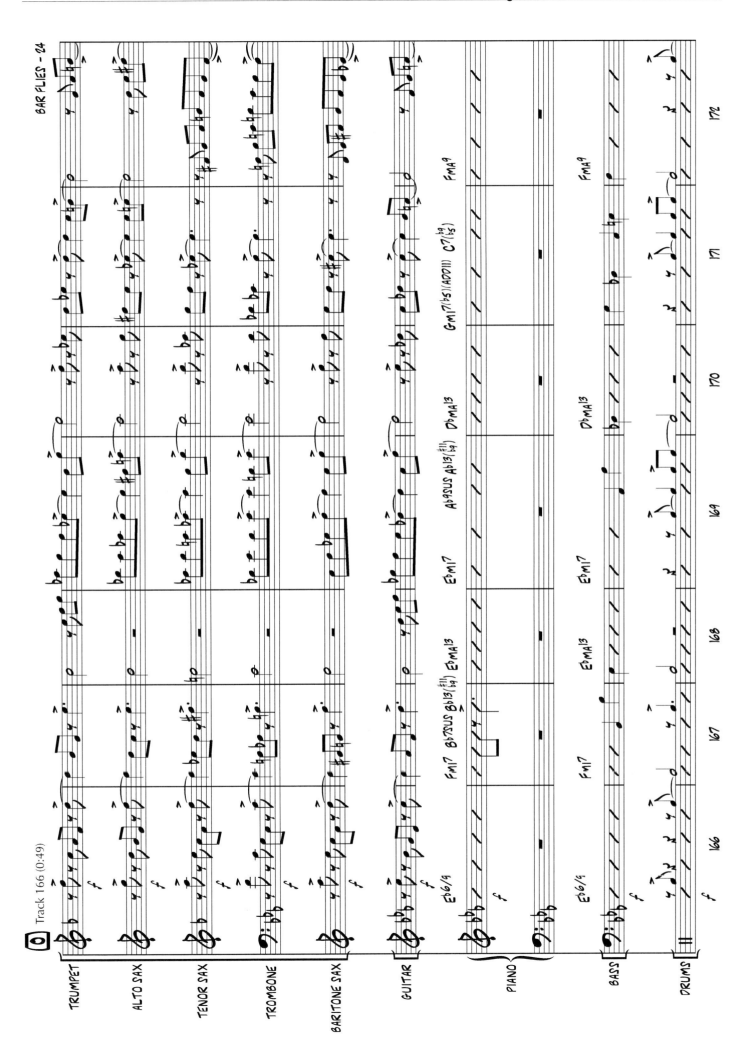

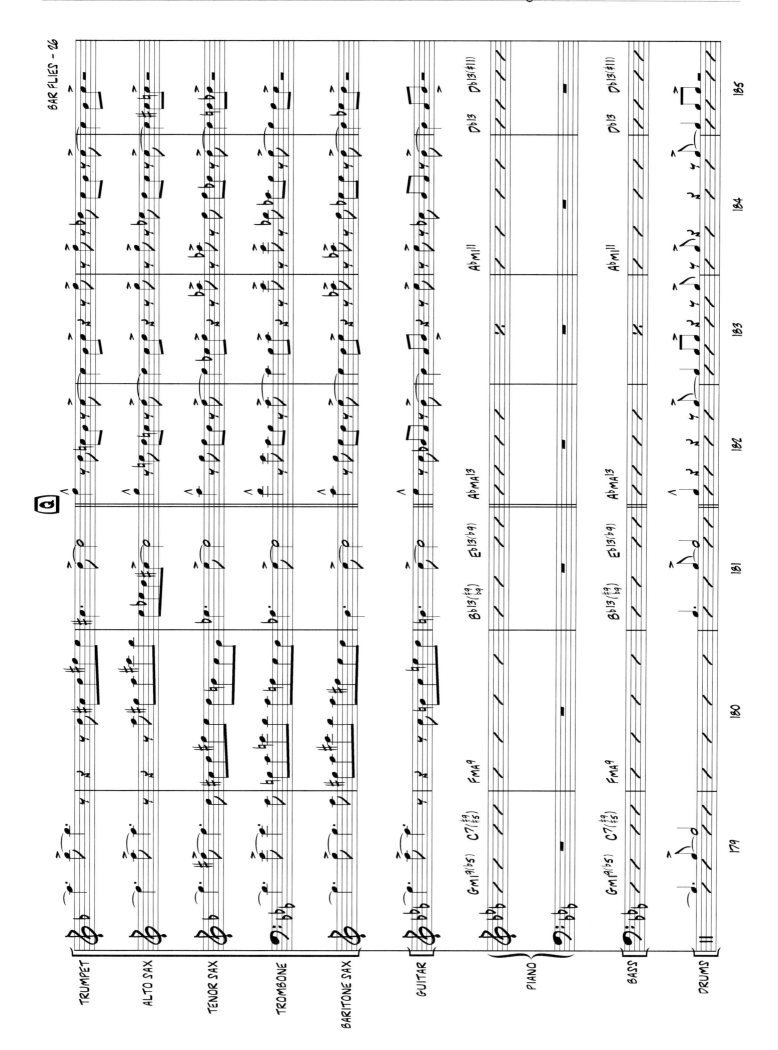

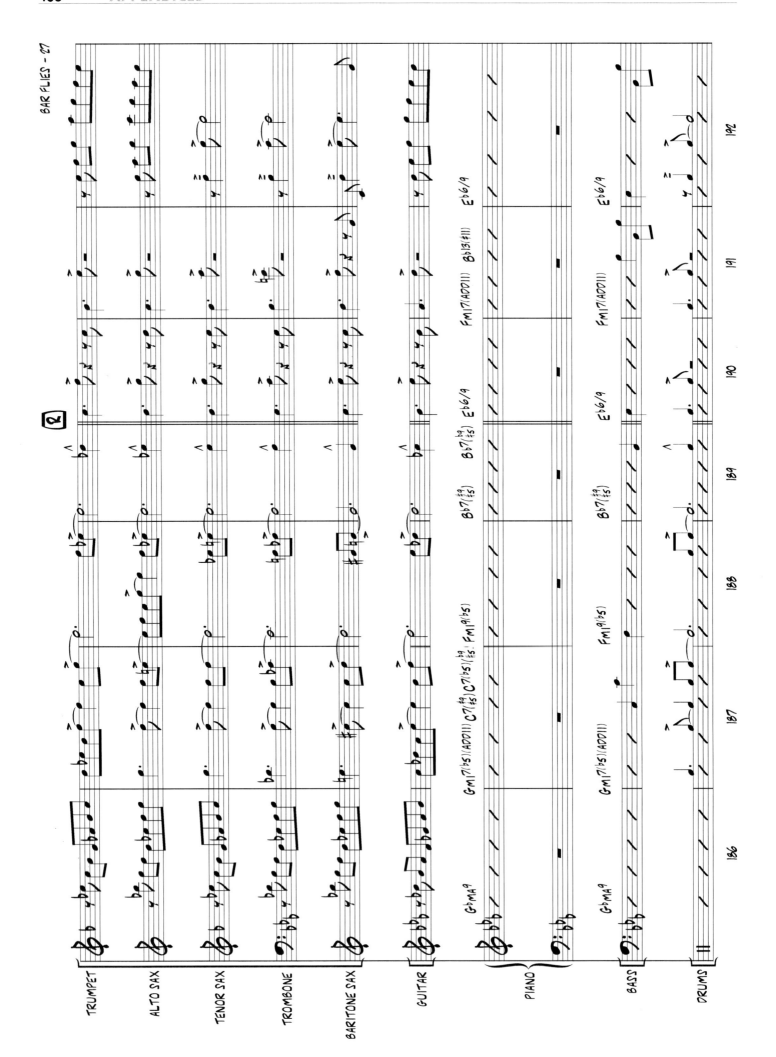

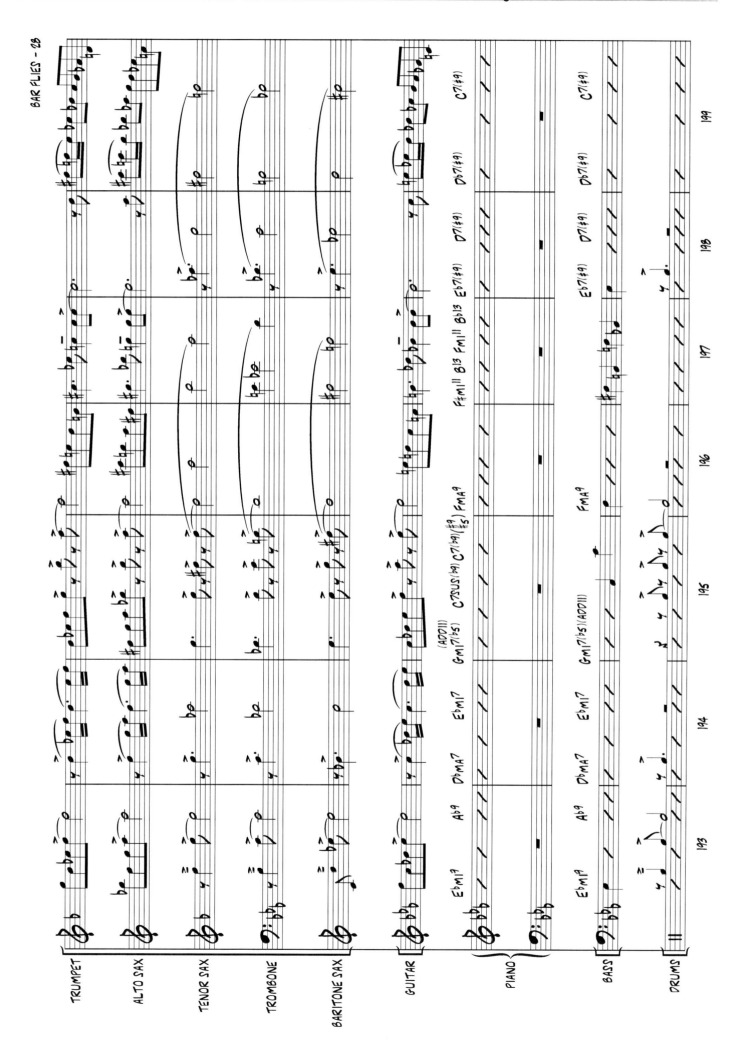

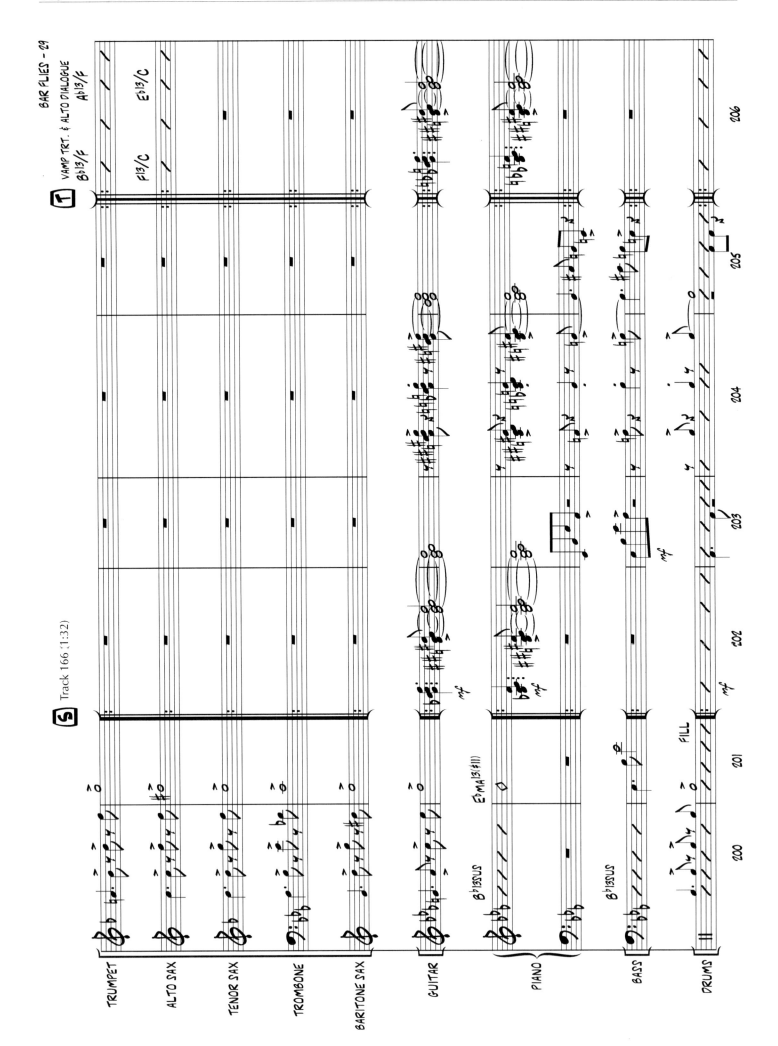

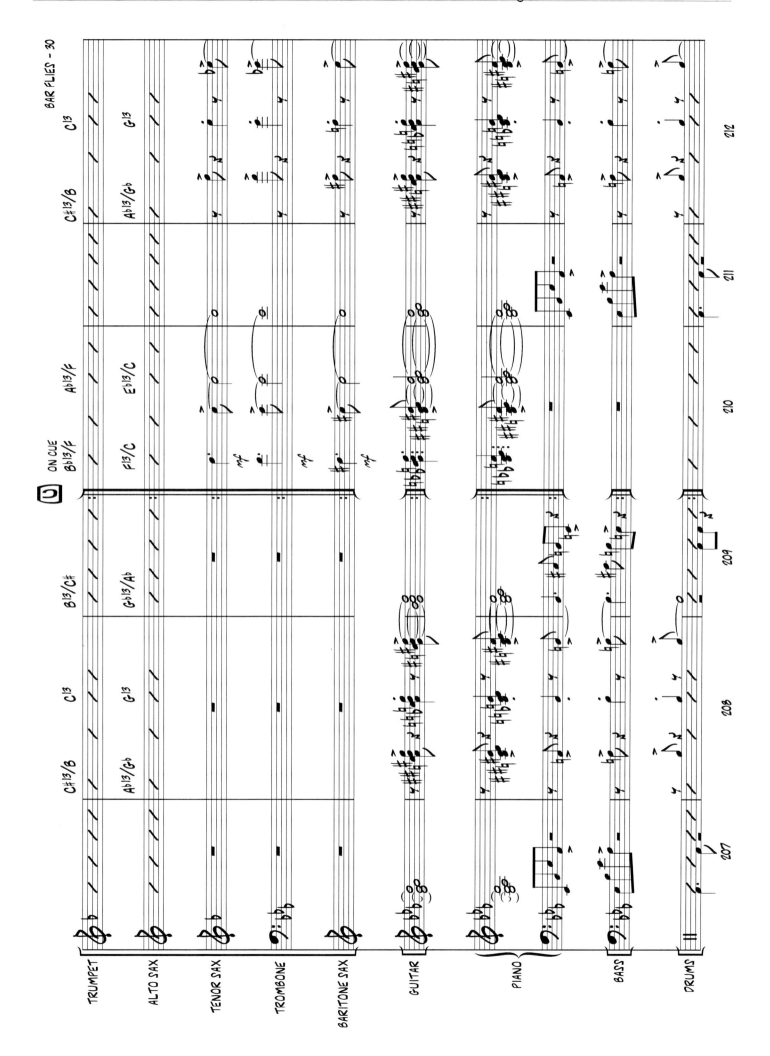

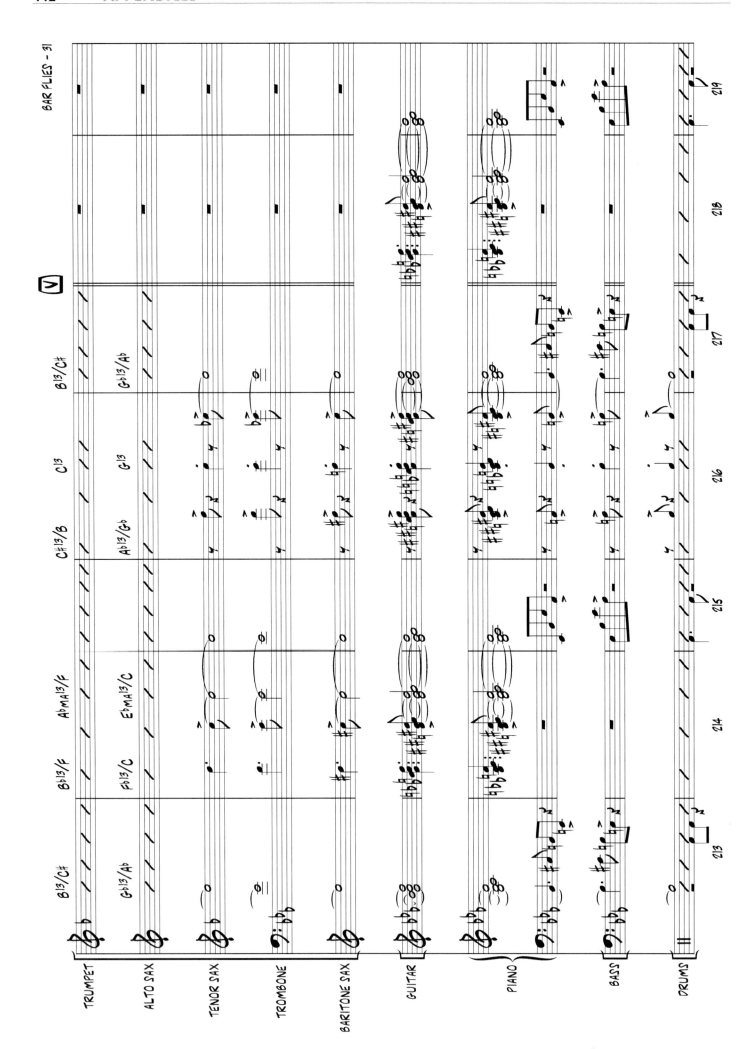

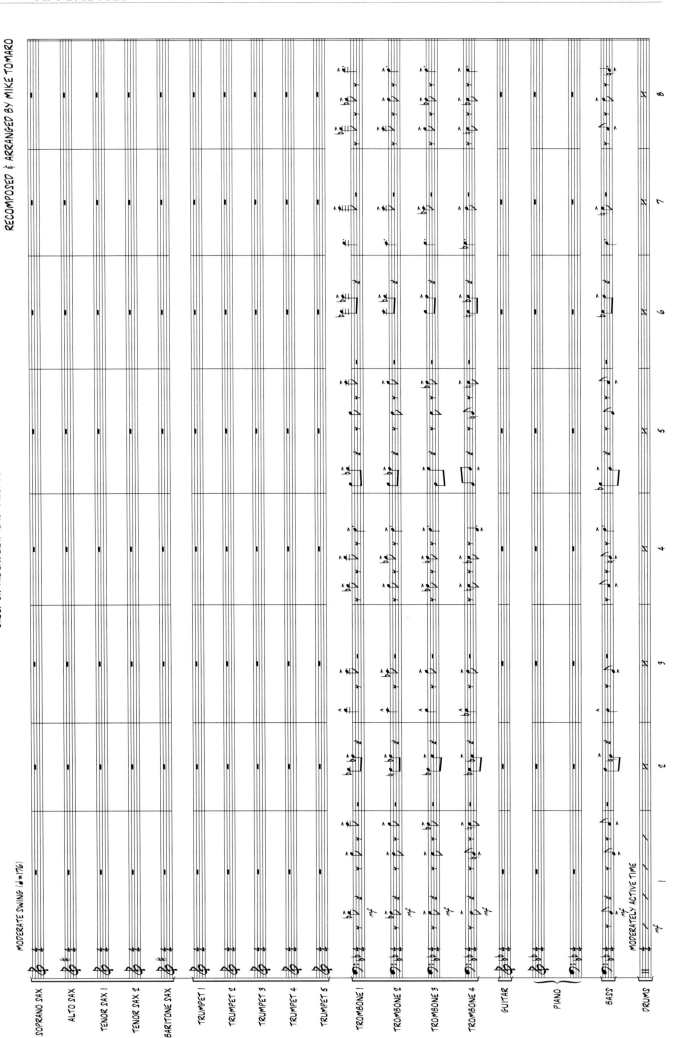

CHARMING WILLIAM

BASED ON THE ENGLISH TUNE "BILLY BOY"

RECOMPOSED & ARRANGED BY MIKE TOMARO

TRACK 167

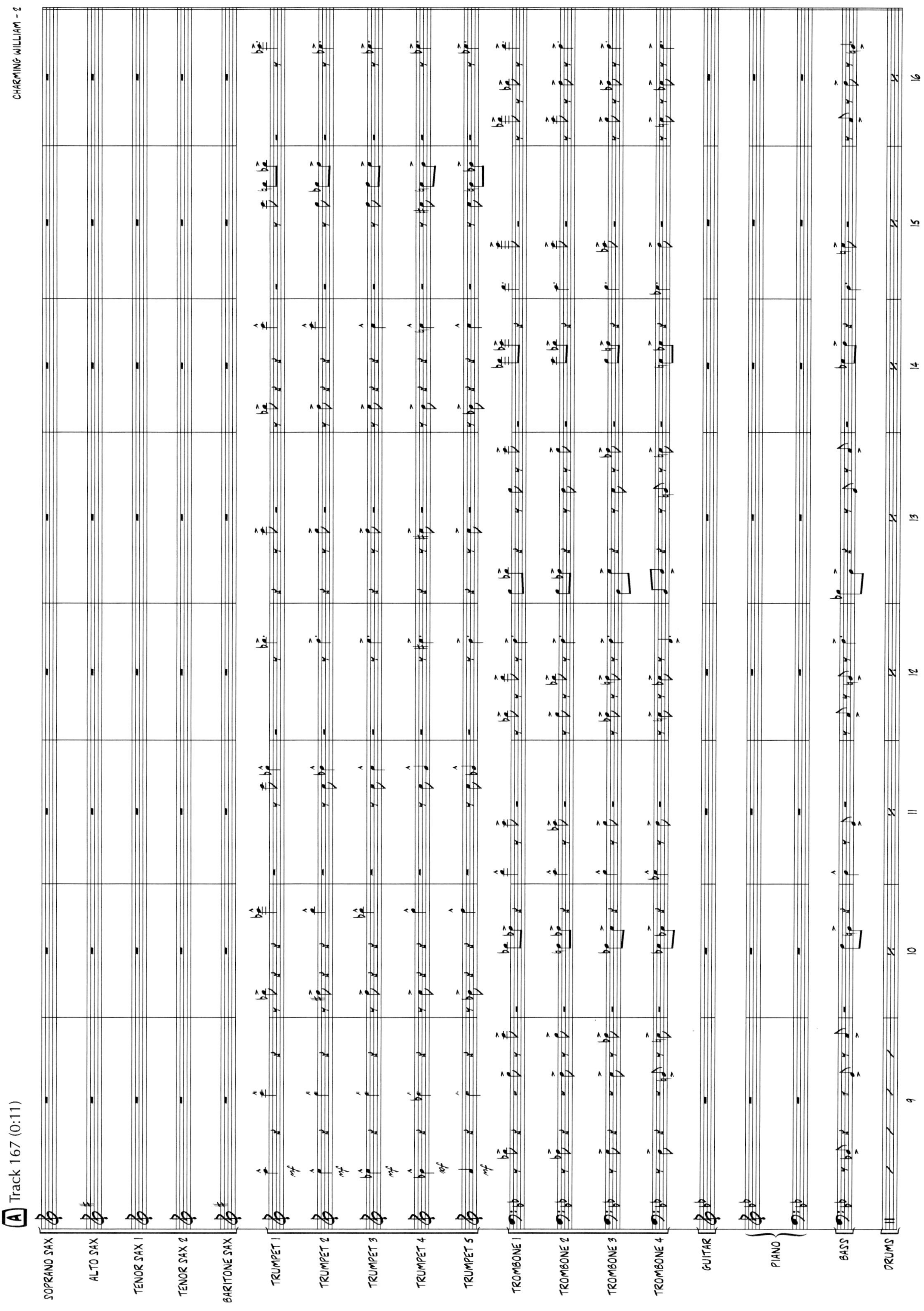
CHARMING WILLIAM - 2
A Track 167 (0:11)
SOPRANO SAX
ALTO SAX
TENOR SAX 1
TENOR SAX 2
BARITONE SAX
TRUMPET 1
TRUMPET 2
TRUMPET 3
TRUMPET 4
TRUMPET 5
TROMBONE 1
TROMBONE 2
TROMBONE 3
TROMBONE 4
GUITAR
PIANO
BASS
DRUMS
mf
9
10
11
12
13
14
15
16

Track 167 (0:21)

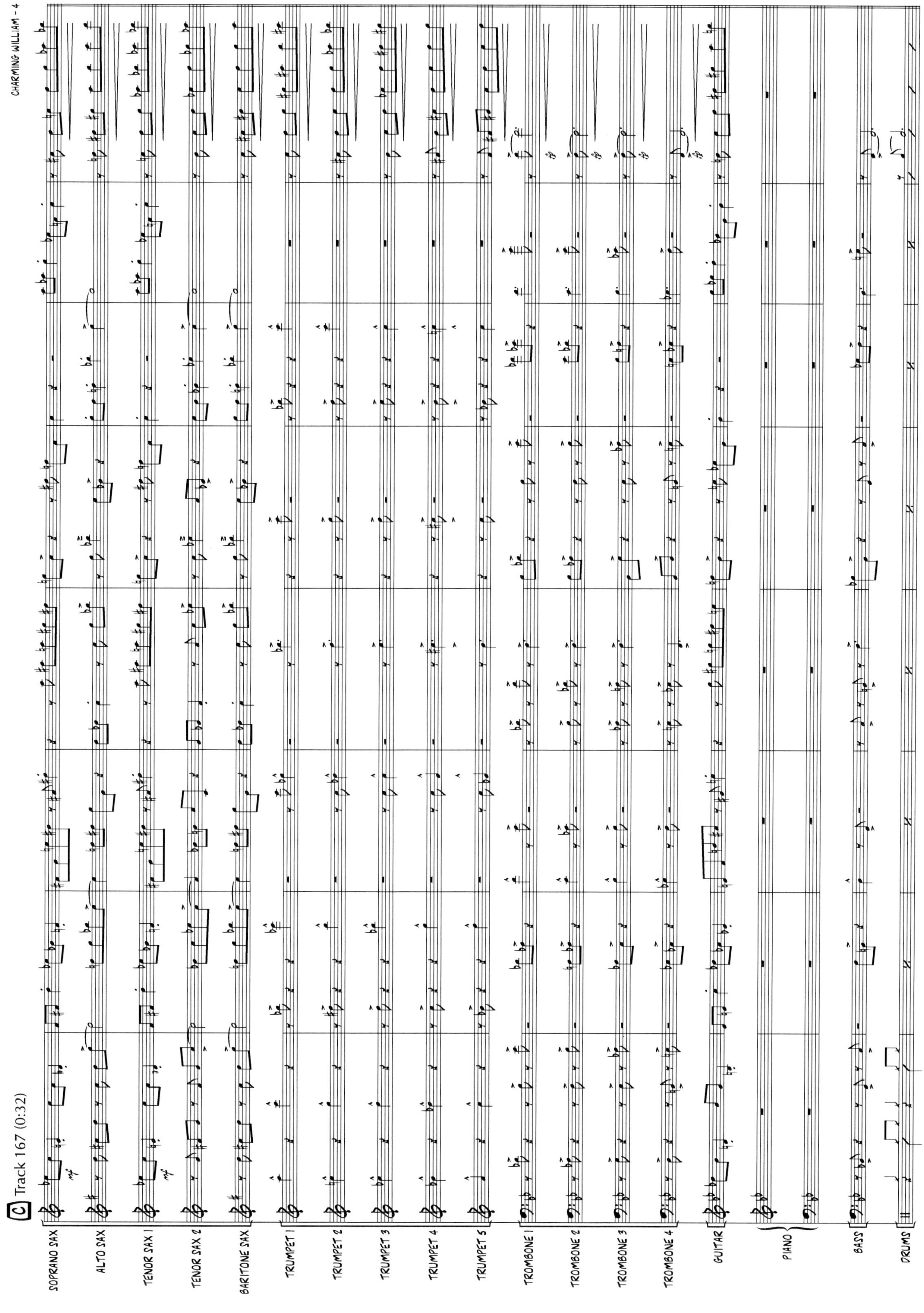
CHARMING WILLIAM - 4
C Track 167 (0:32)
SOPRANO SAX
ALTO SAX
TENOR SAX 1
TENOR SAX 2
BARITONE SAX
TRUMPET 1
TRUMPET 2
TRUMPET 3
TRUMPET 4
TRUMPET 5
TROMBONE 1
TROMBONE 2
TROMBONE 3
TROMBONE 4
GUITAR
PIANO
BASS
DRUMS
25
26
27
28
29
30
31
32

CHARMING WILLIAM - 5

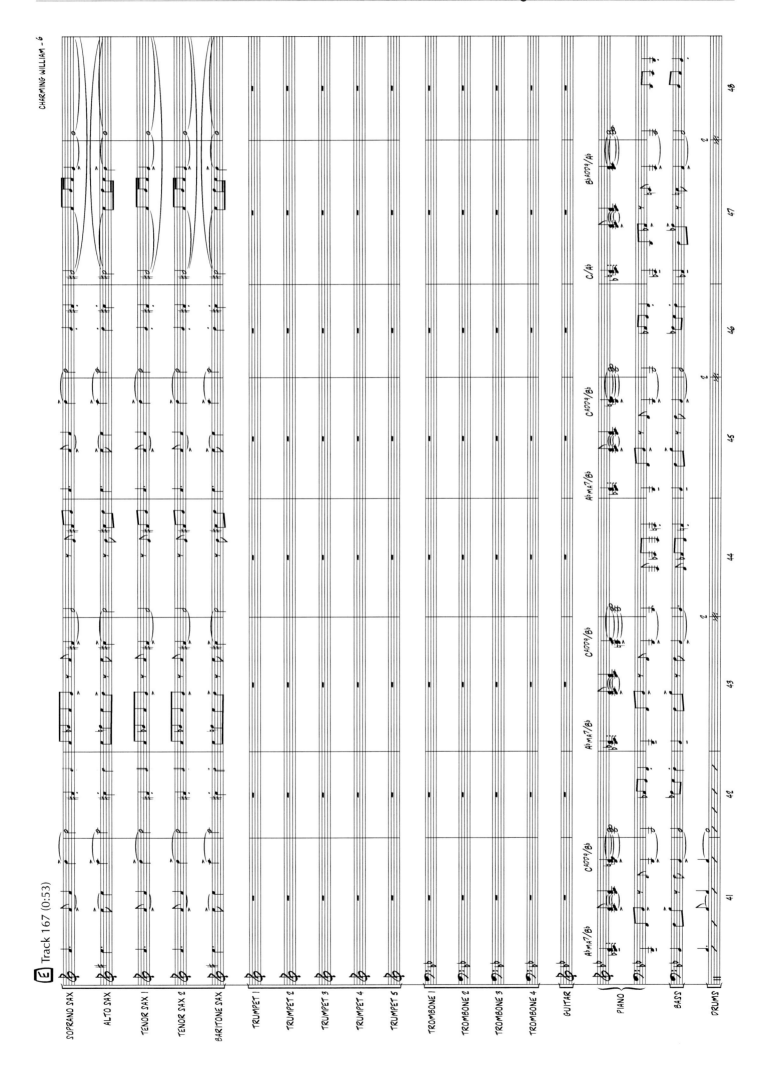

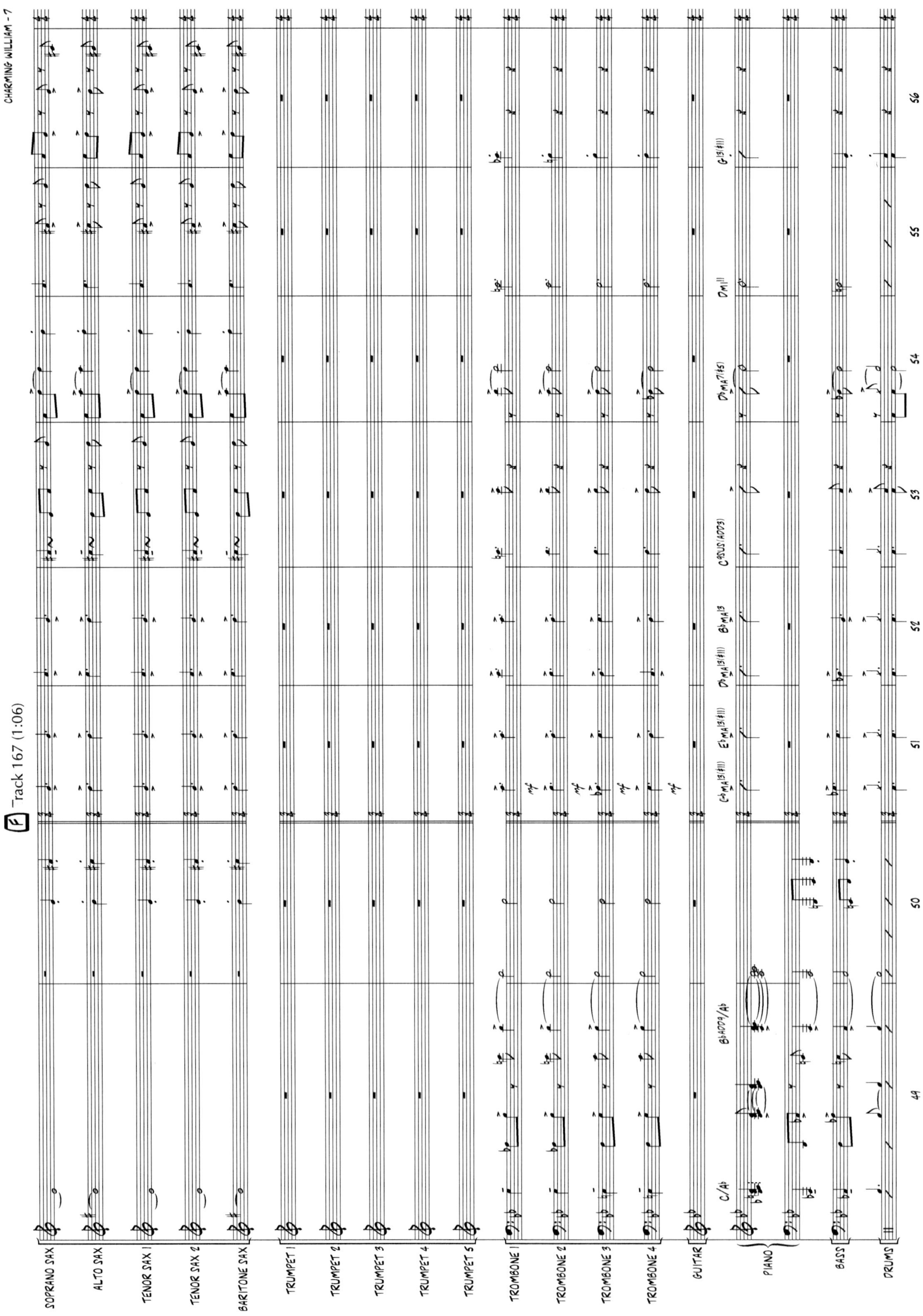
CHARMING WILLIAM - 7
F
Track 167 (1:06)
SOPRANO SAX
ALTO SAX
TENOR SAX 1
TENOR SAX 2
BARITONE SAX
TRUMPET 1
TRUMPET 2
TRUMPET 3
TRUMPET 4
TRUMPET 5
TROMBONE 1
TROMBONE 2
TROMBONE 3
TROMBONE 4
GUITAR
PIANO
BASS
DRUMS
C/Ab
BbADD9/Ab
EbMA13(#11)
DbMA13(#11)
BbMA13
C9SUS(ADD3)
DbMA7(#5)
DMI11
G13(#11)
49
50
51
52
53
54
55
56

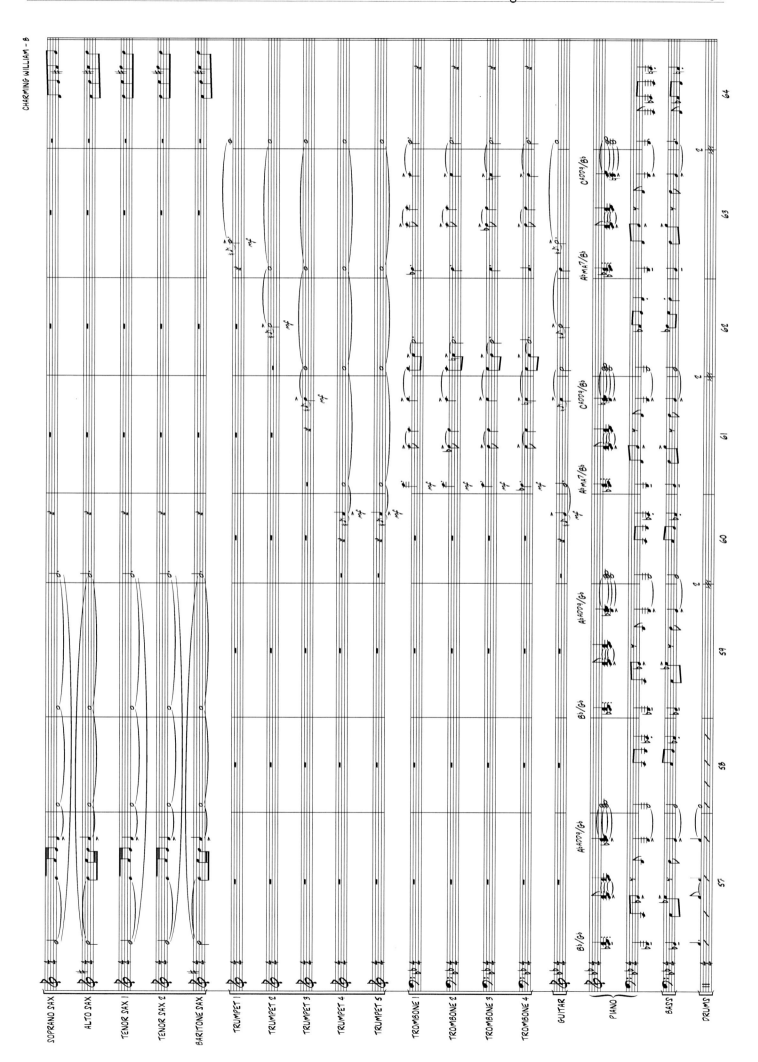

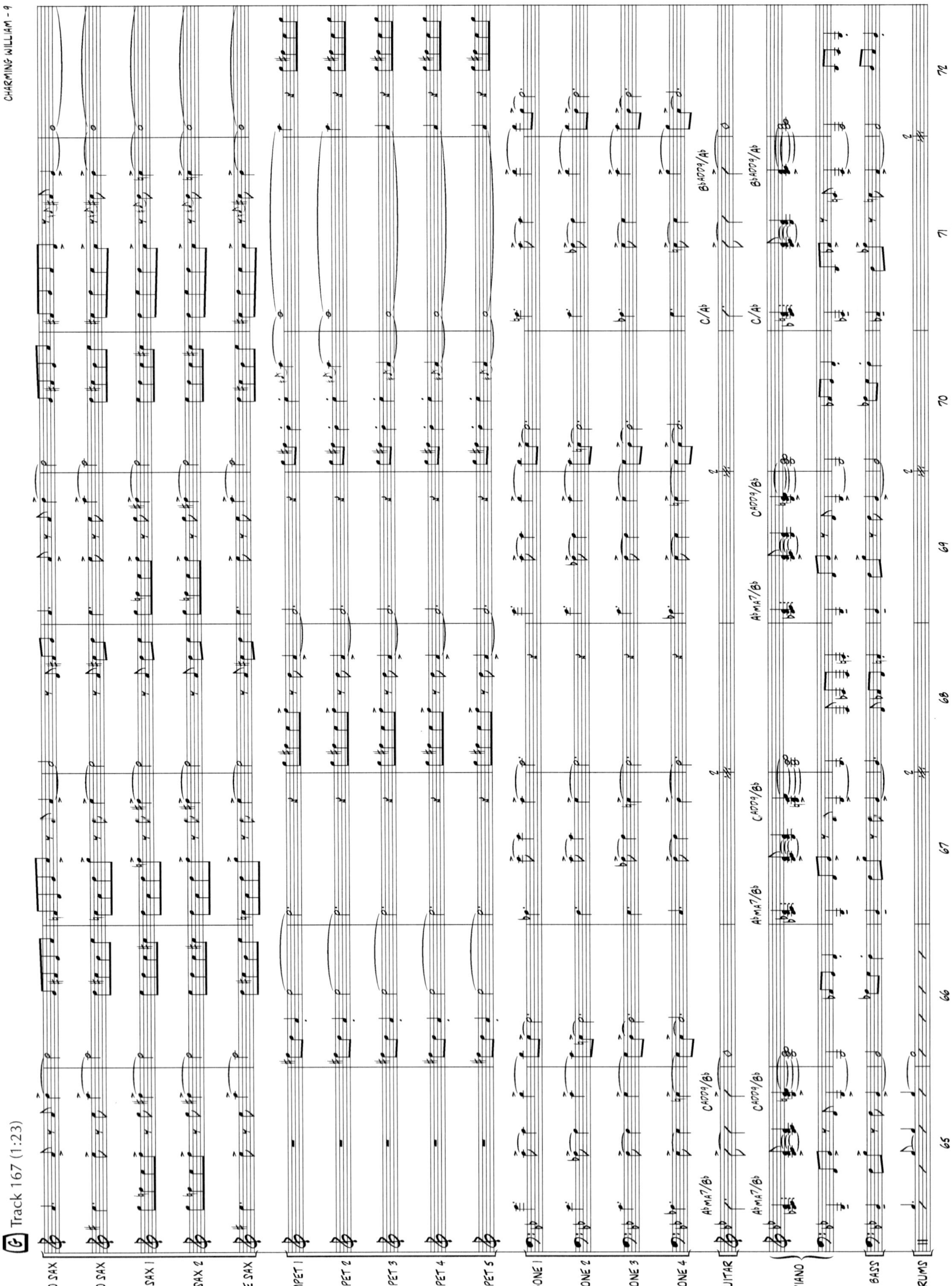

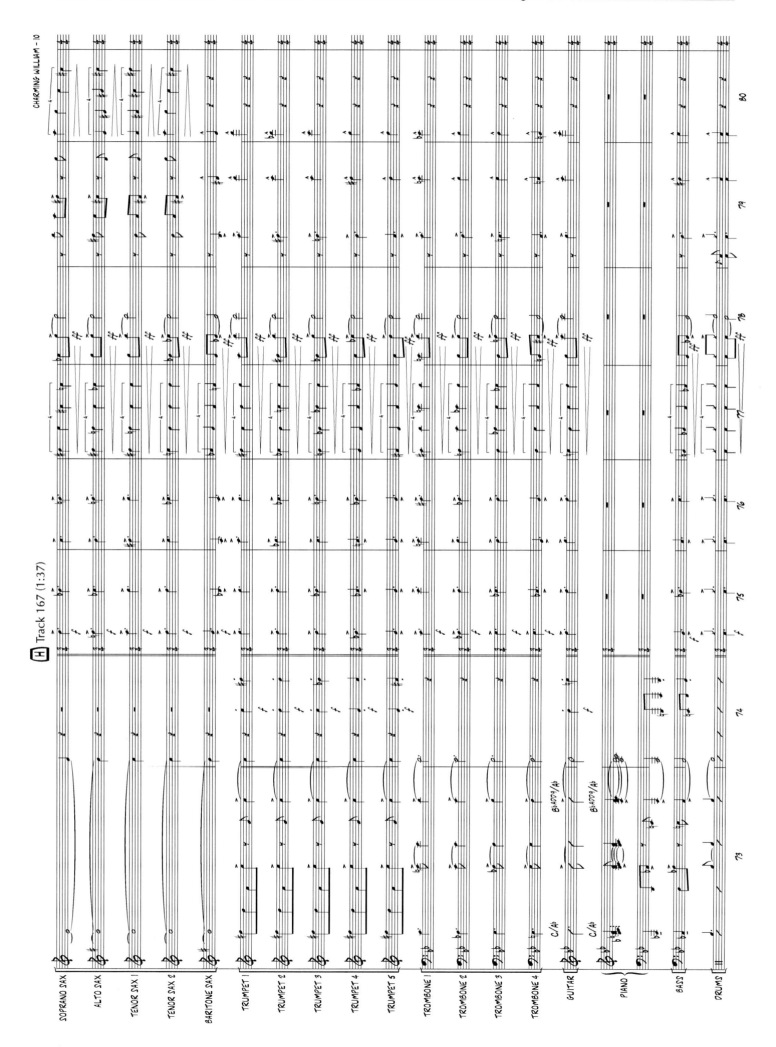

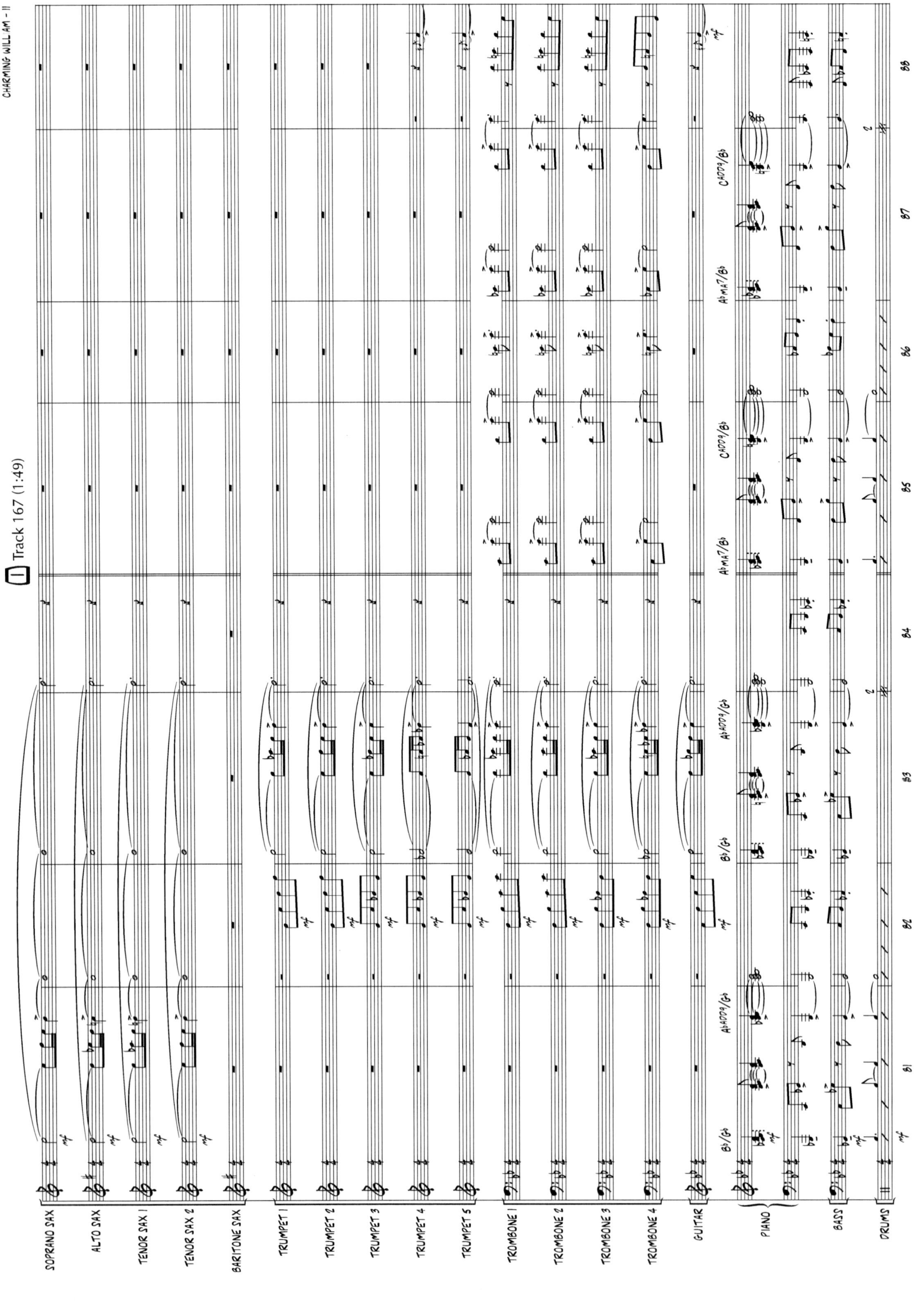

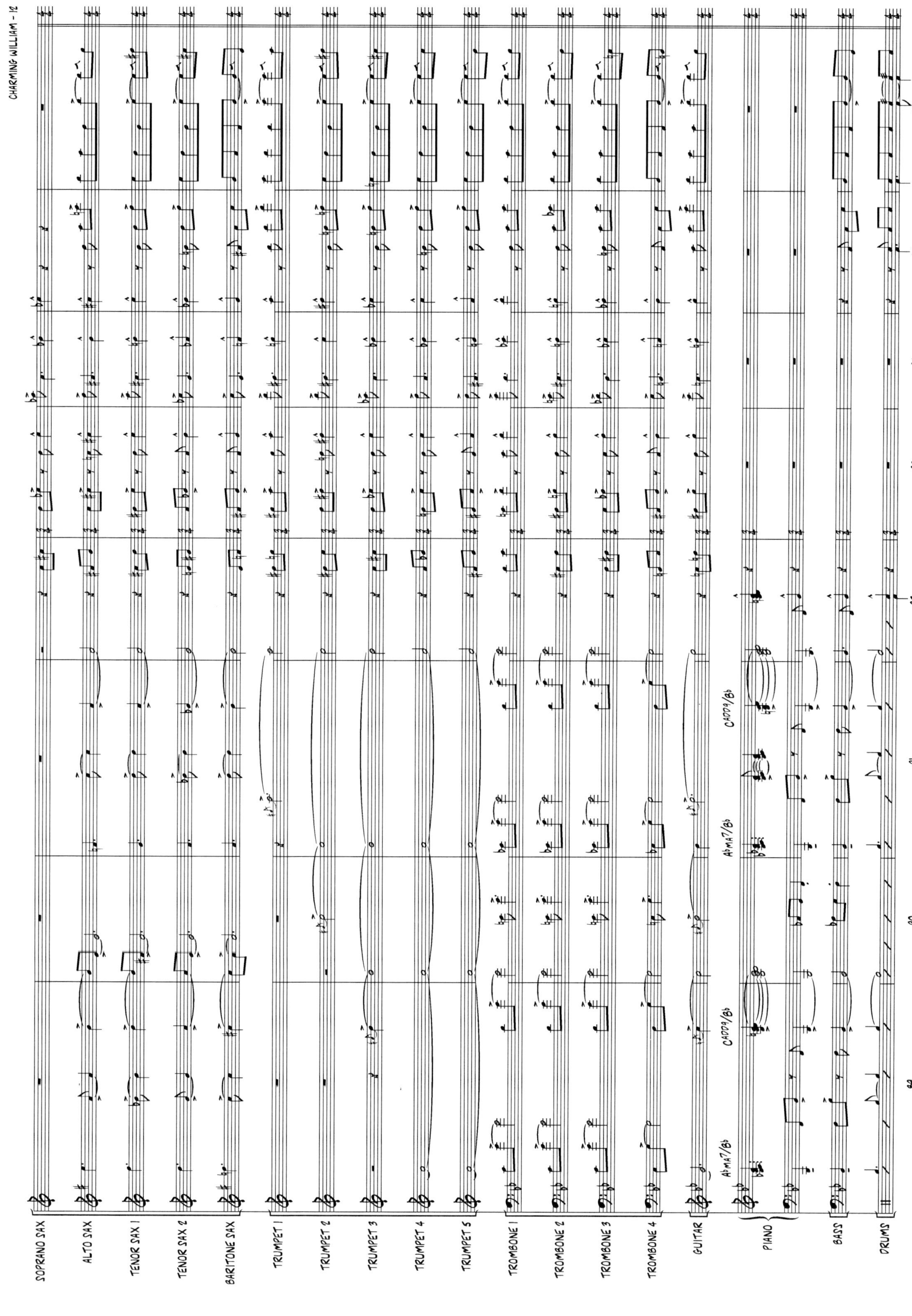

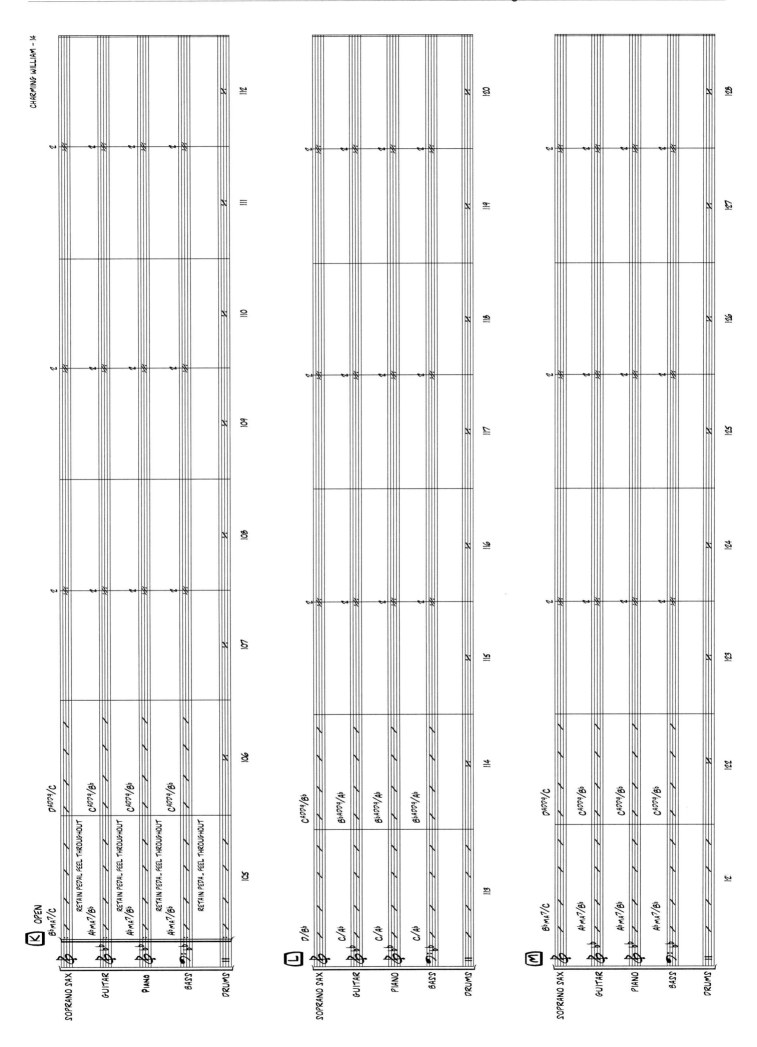

Charming Will Am - 15

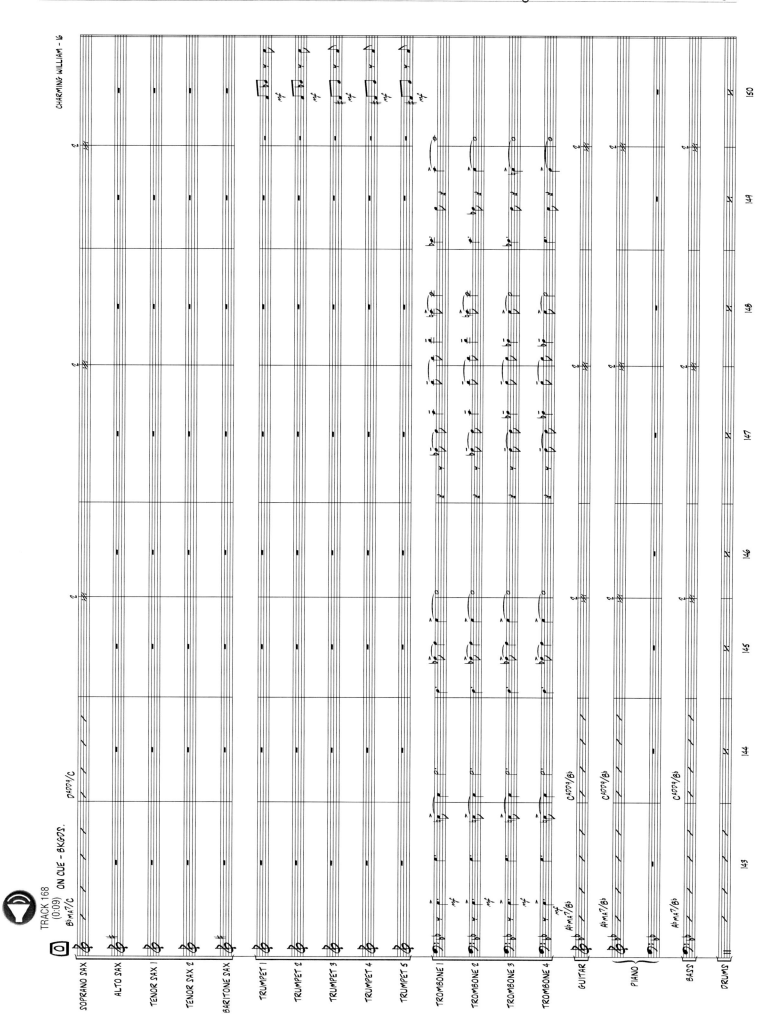

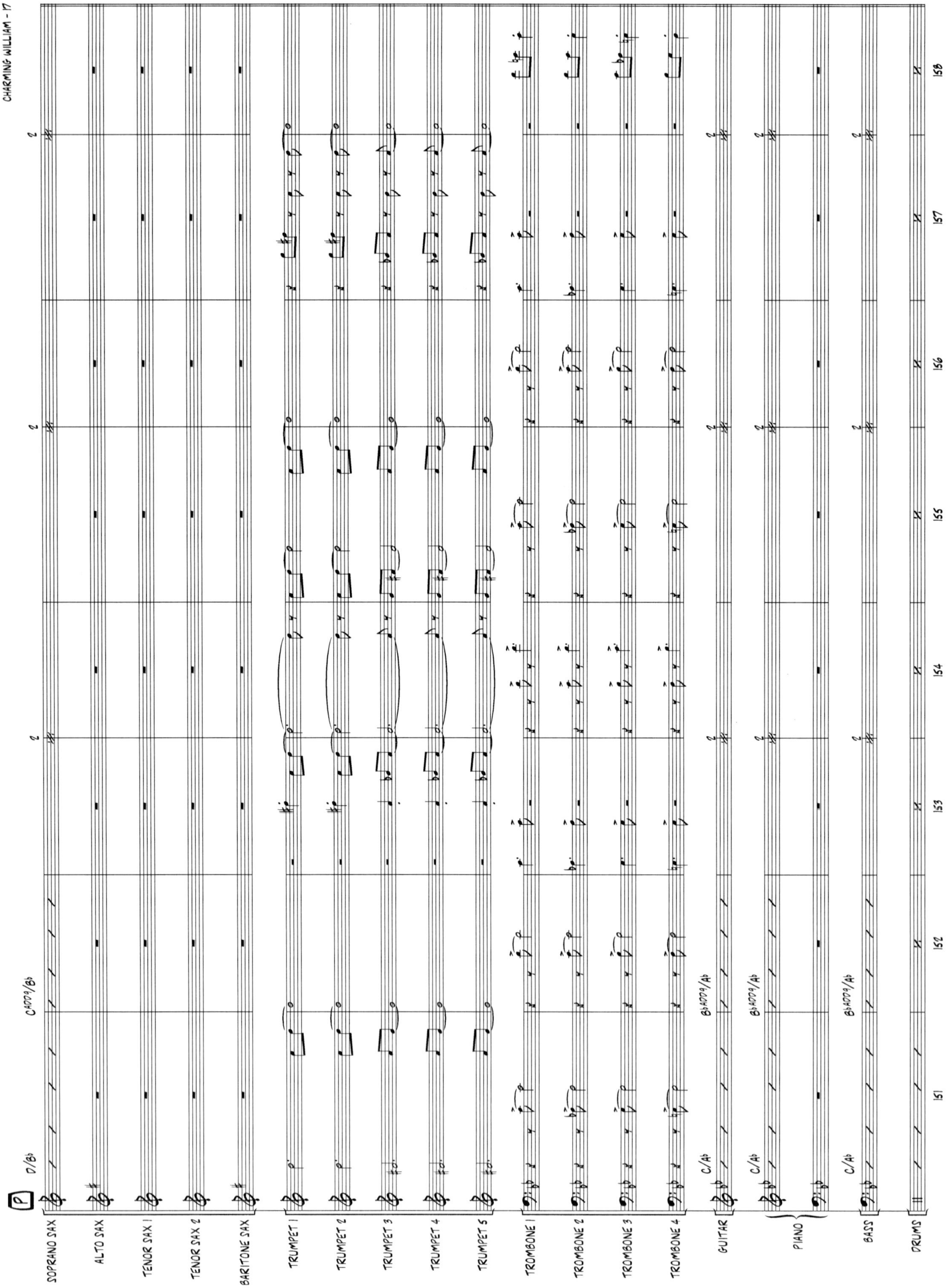

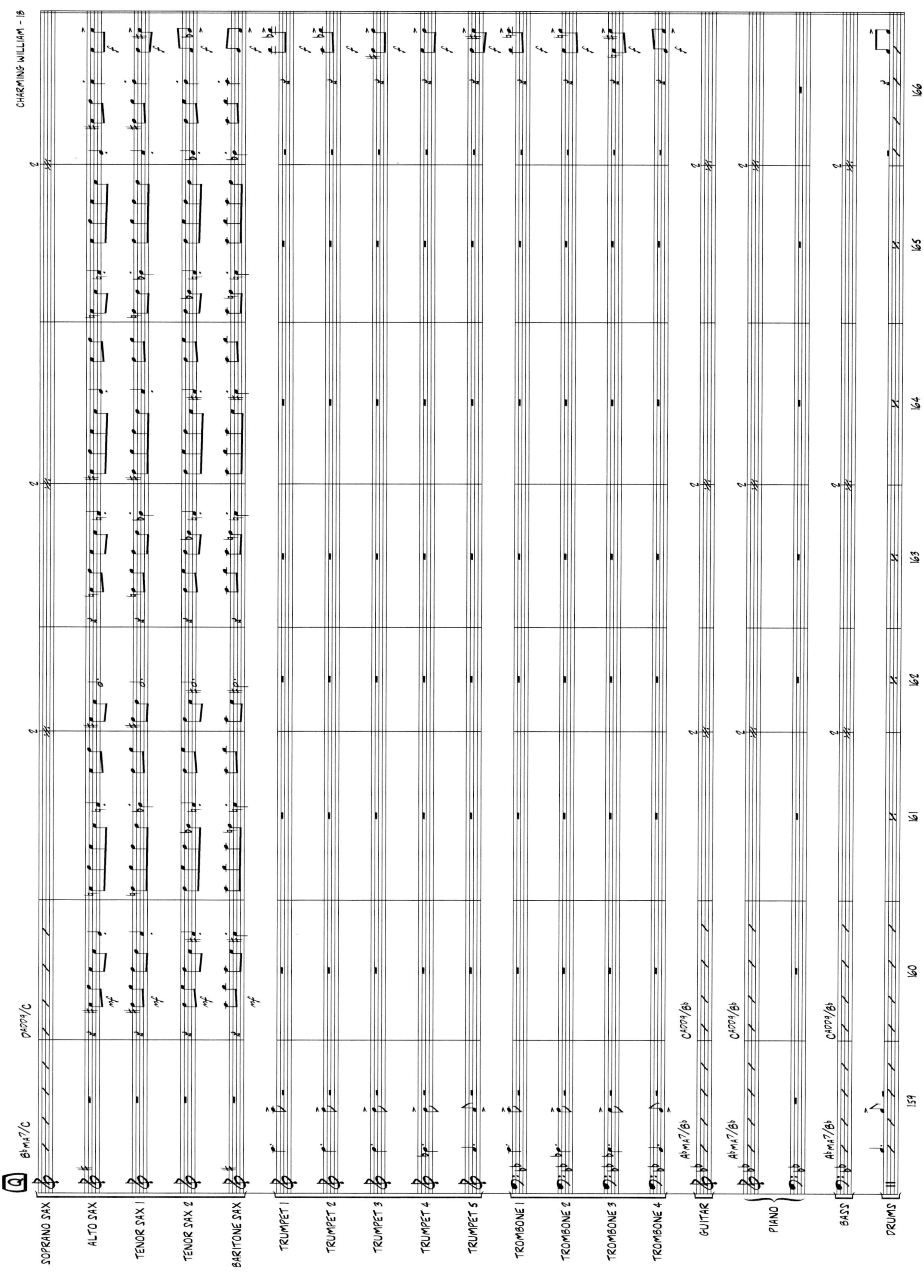

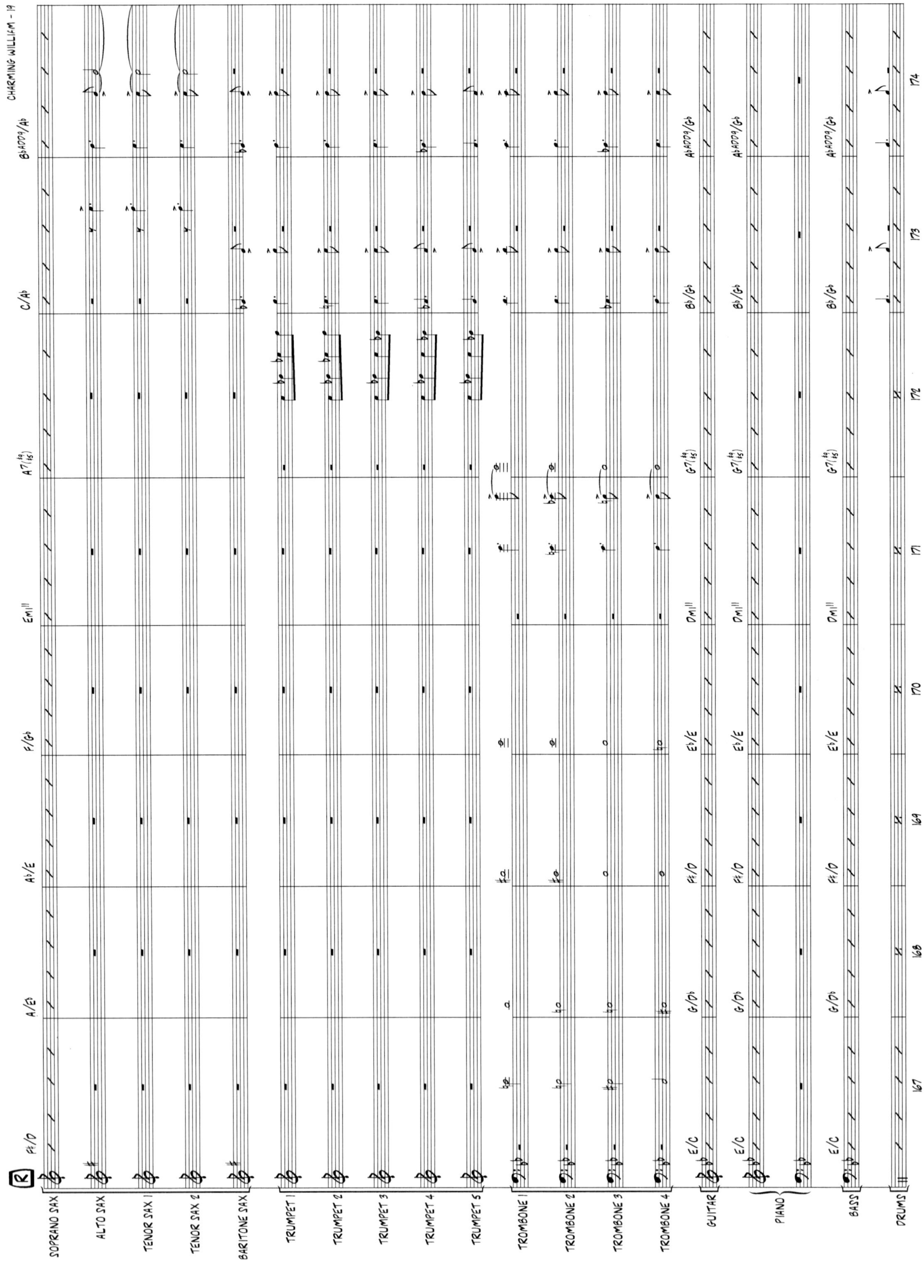

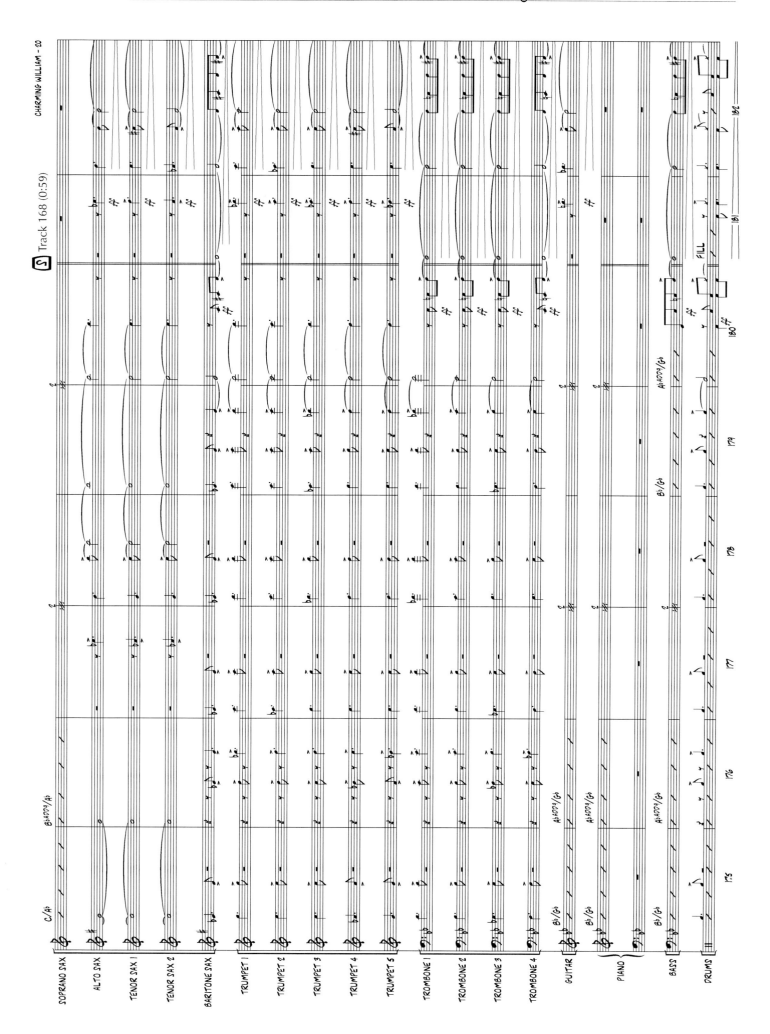

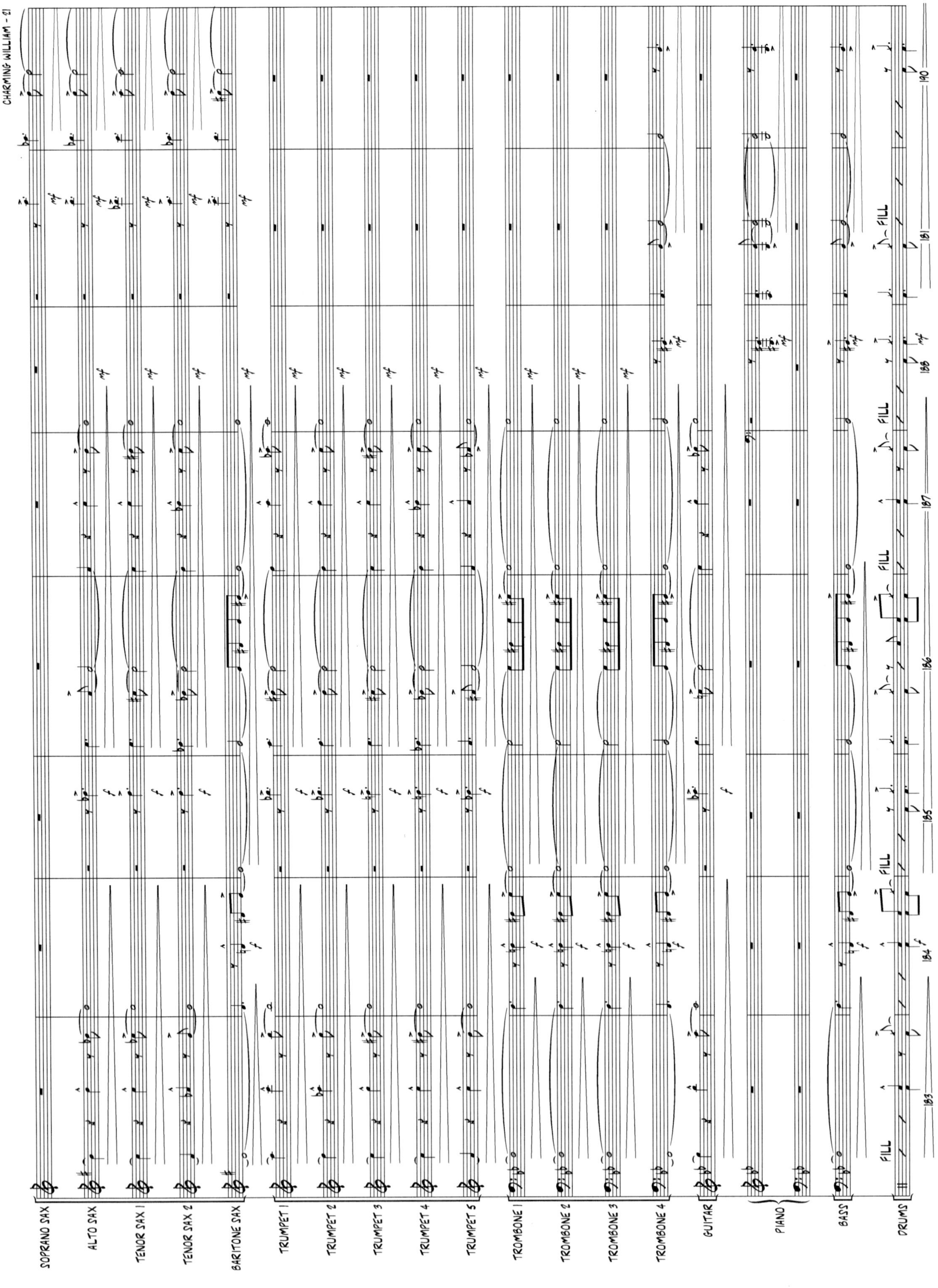

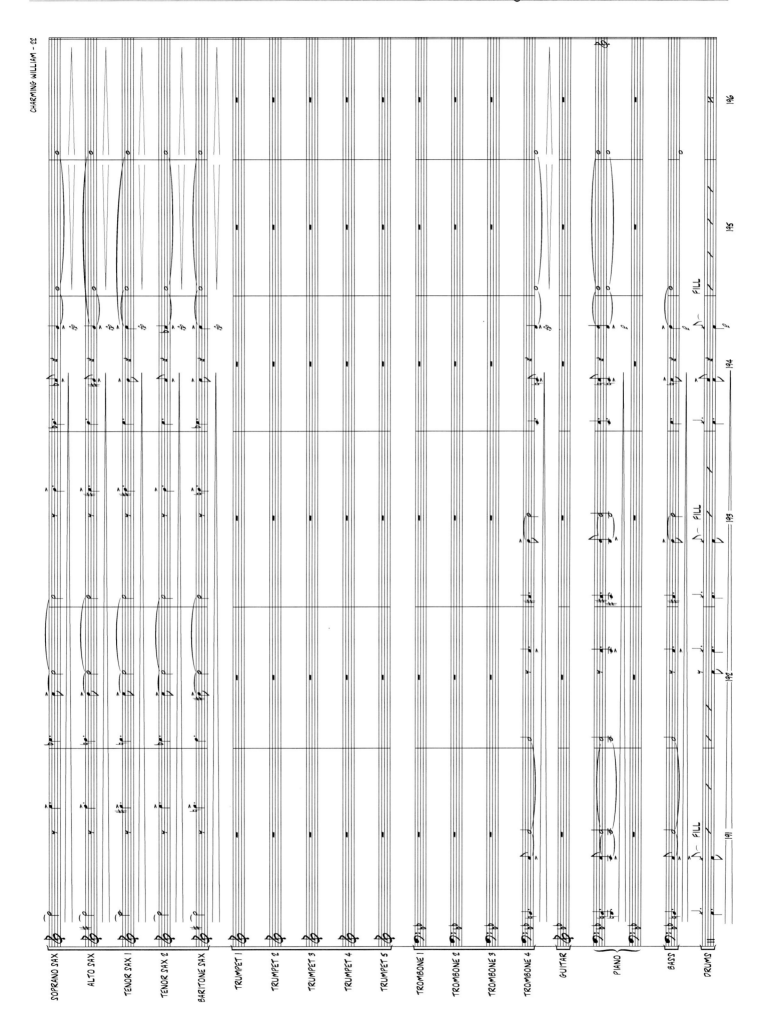

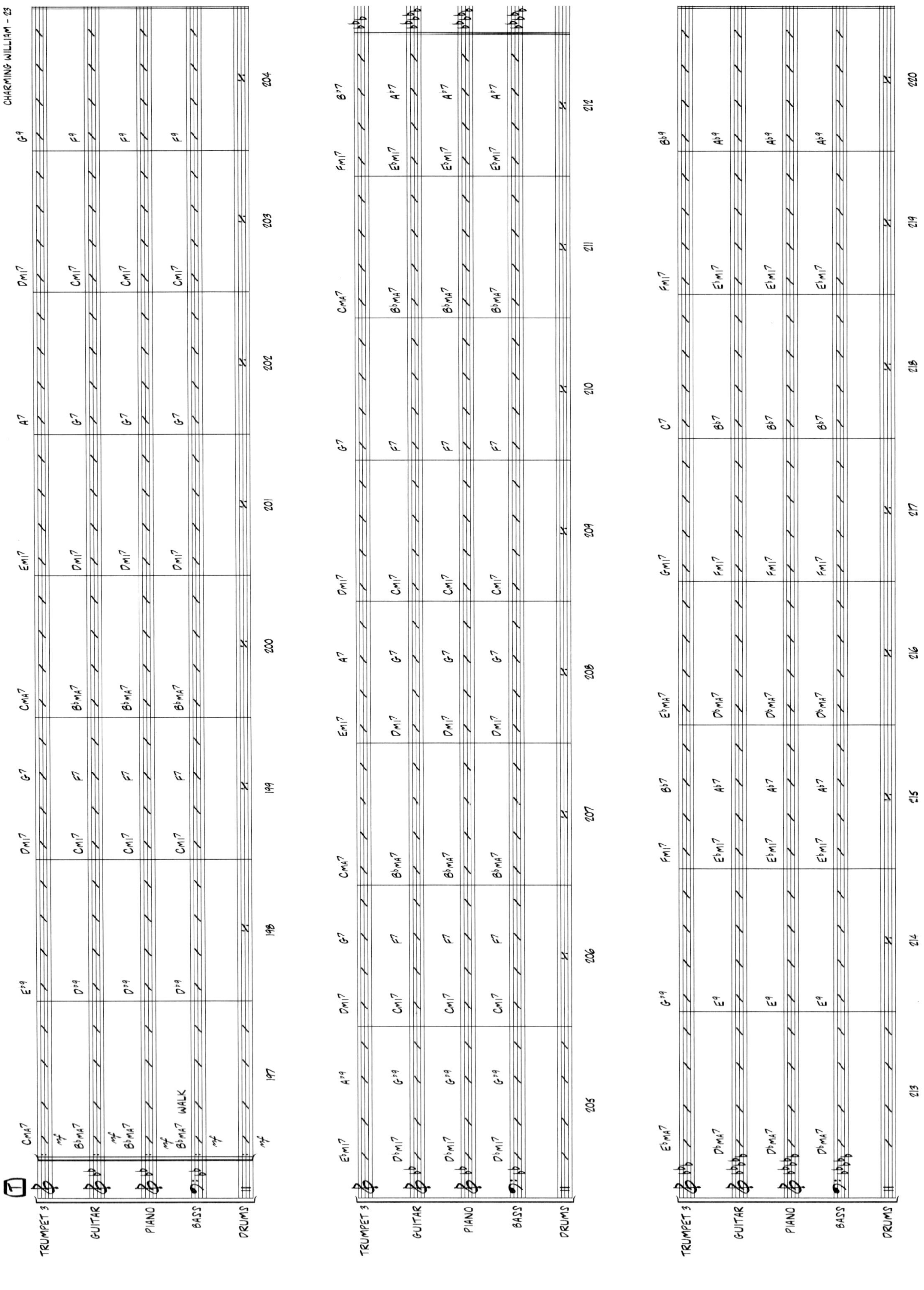
CHARMING WILLIAM - 23
TRUMPET 3
GUITAR
PIANO
BASS
DRUMS
WALK
mf
CMA7 E79 DMI7 G7 CMA7 EMI7 A7 DMI7 G9
B♭MA7 D79 CMI7 F7 B♭MA7 DMI7 G7 CMI7 F9
197 198 199 200 201 202 203 204
E♭MI7 A79 DMI7 G7 CMA7 EMI7 A7 DMI7 G7 CMA7 FMI7 B♭7
D♭MI7 G79 CMI7 F7 B♭MA7 DMI7 G7 CMI7 F7 B♭MA7 E♭MI7 A♭7
205 206 207 208 209 210 211 212
E♭MA7 G79 FMI7 B♭7 E♭MA7 GMI7 C7 FMI7 B♭9
D♭MA7 E9 E♭MI7 A♭7 D♭MA7 FMI7 B♭7 E♭MI7 A♭9
213 214 215 216 217 218 219 220

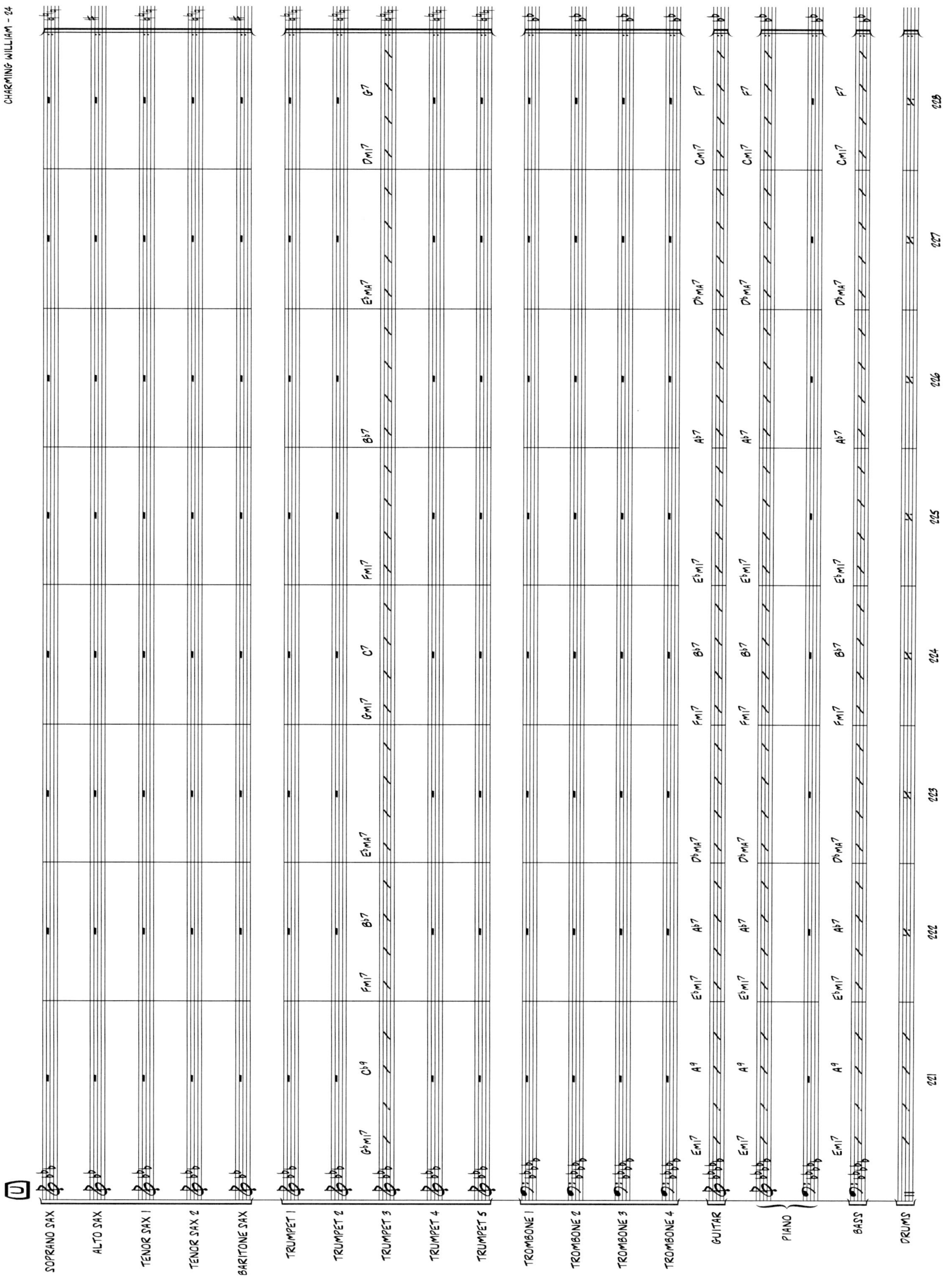
CHARMING WILLIAM - 24
U
SOPRANO SAX
ALTO SAX
TENOR SAX 1
TENOR SAX 2
BARITONE SAX
TRUMPET 1
TRUMPET 2
TRUMPET 3
TRUMPET 4
TRUMPET 5
TROMBONE 1
TROMBONE 2
TROMBONE 3
TROMBONE 4
GUITAR
PIANO
BASS
DRUMS
G♭mi7 C♭9 Fmi7 B♭7 E♭ma7 Gmi7 C7 Fmi7 B♭7 E♭ma7 Dmi7 G7
Emi7 A9 E♭mi7 A♭7 D♭ma7 Fmi7 B♭7 E♭mi7 A♭7 D♭ma7 Cmi7 F7
221
222
223
224
225
226
227
228

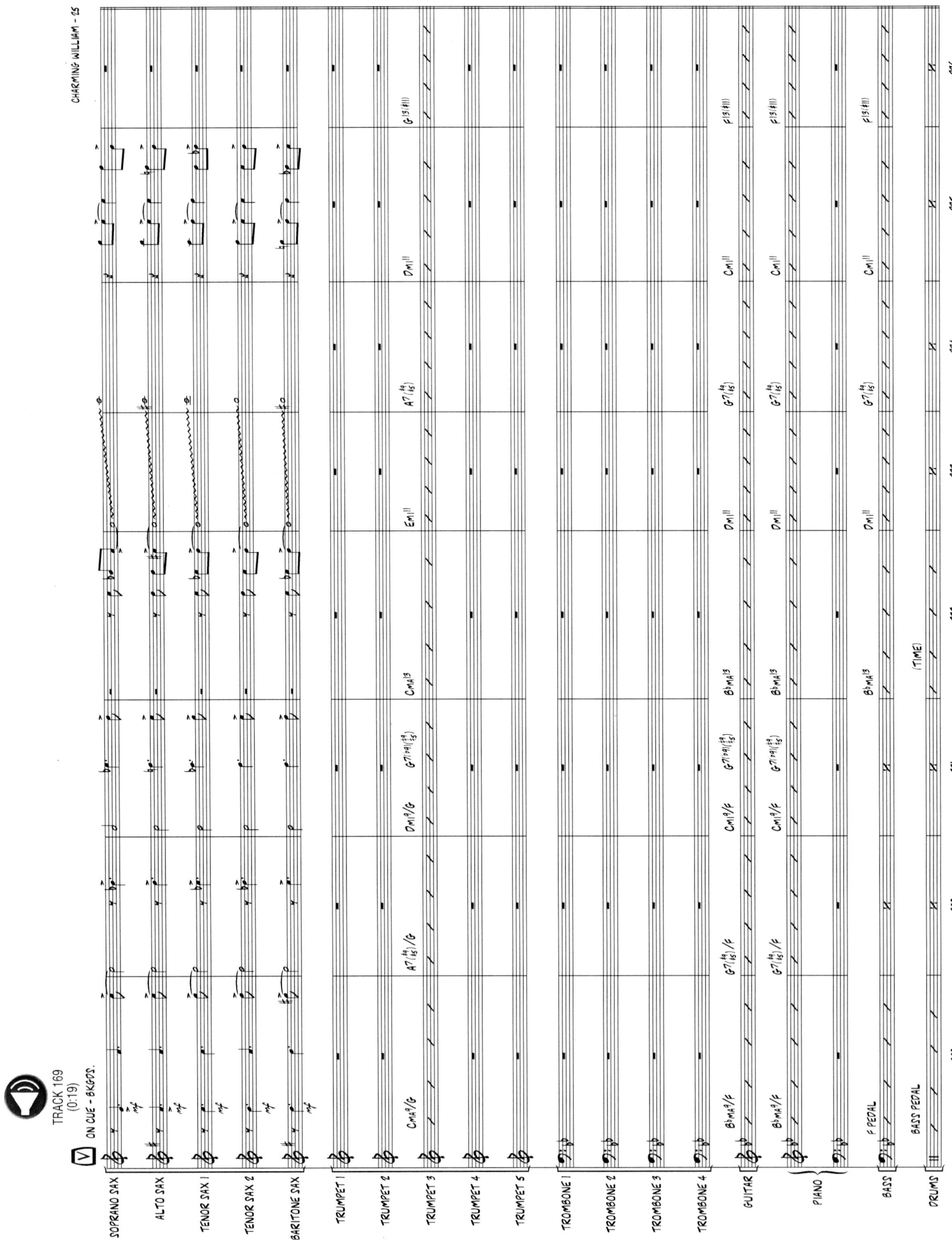

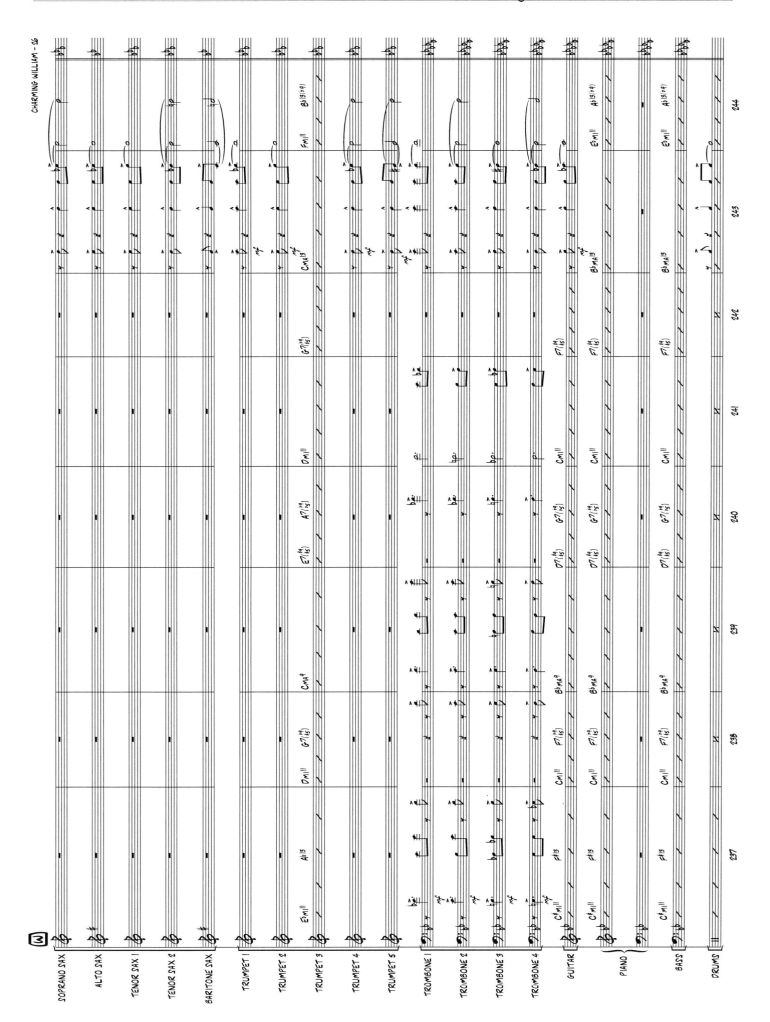

CHARMING WILLIAM - 27

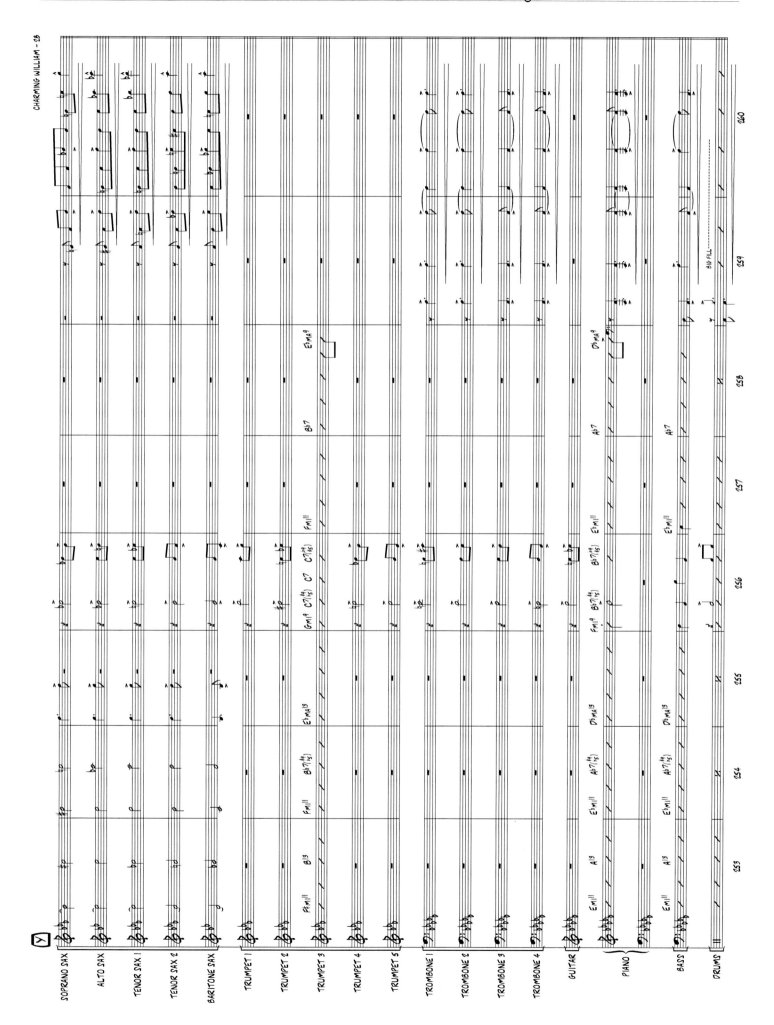

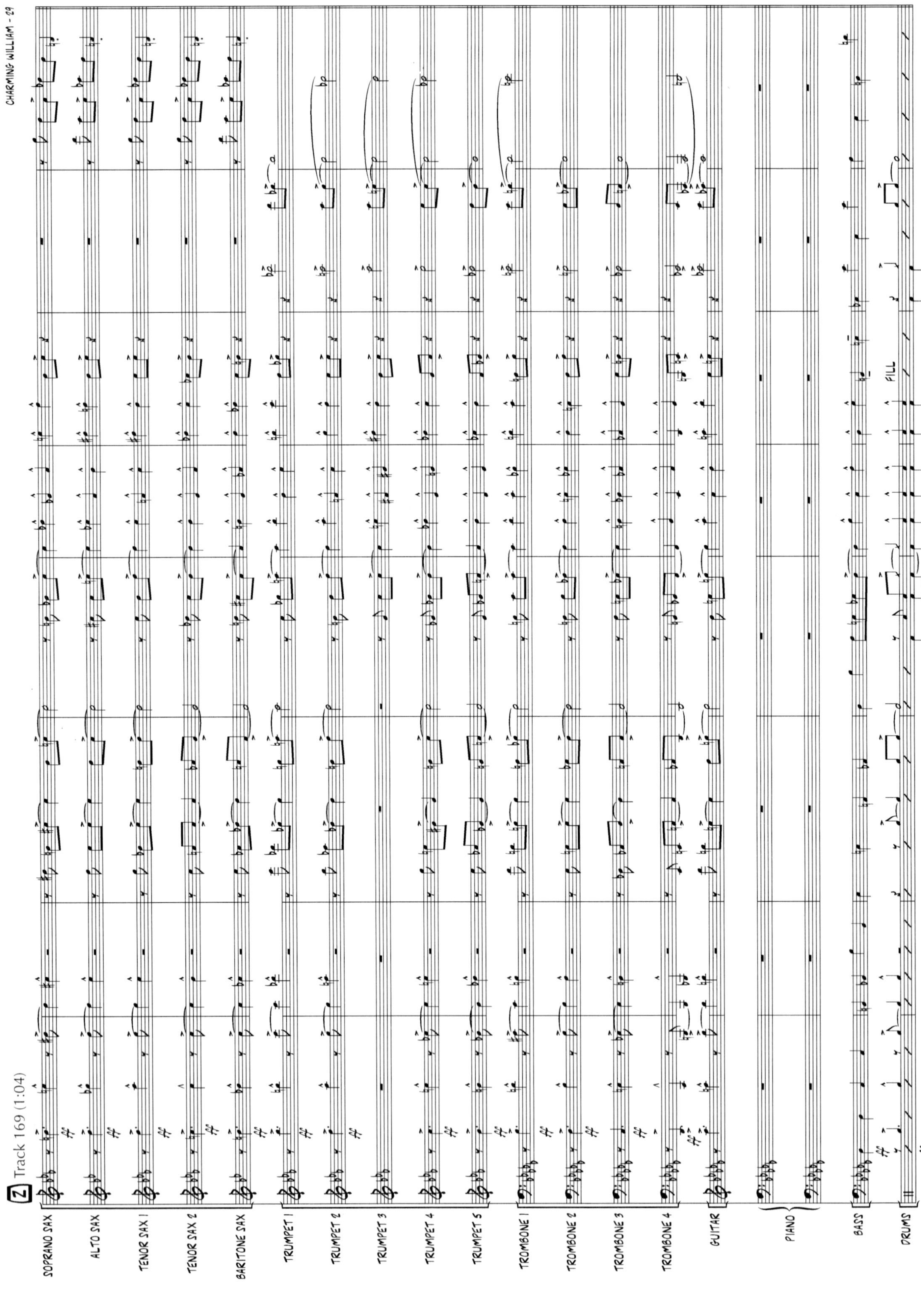

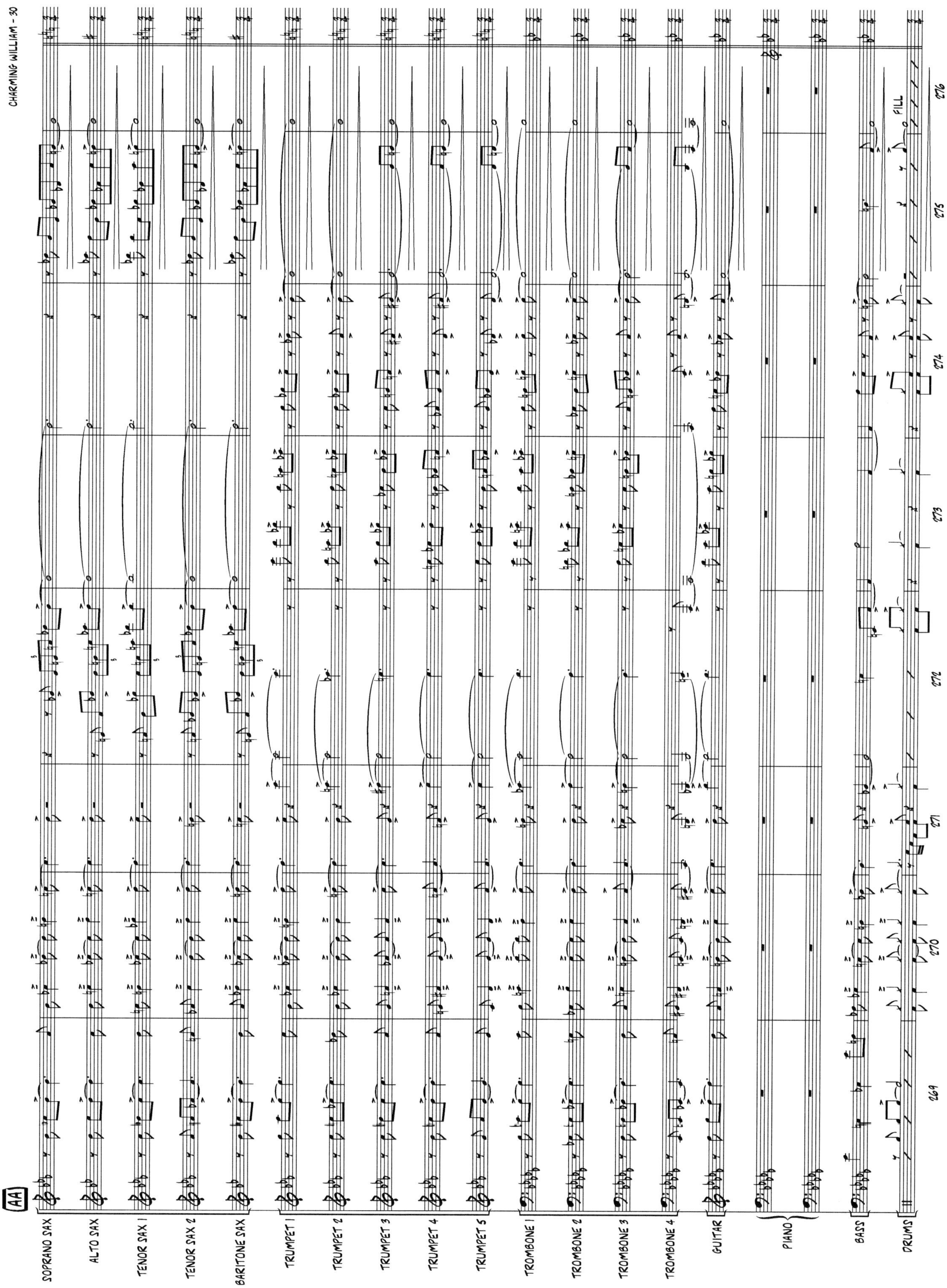
CHARMING WILLIAM - 30
AA
SOPRANO SAX
ALTO SAX
TENOR SAX 1
TENOR SAX 2
BARITONE SAX
TRUMPET 1
TRUMPET 2
TRUMPET 3
TRUMPET 4
TRUMPET 5
TROMBONE 1
TROMBONE 2
TROMBONE 3
TROMBONE 4
GUITAR
PIANO
BASS
DRUMS
FILL
269
270
271
272
273
274
275
276

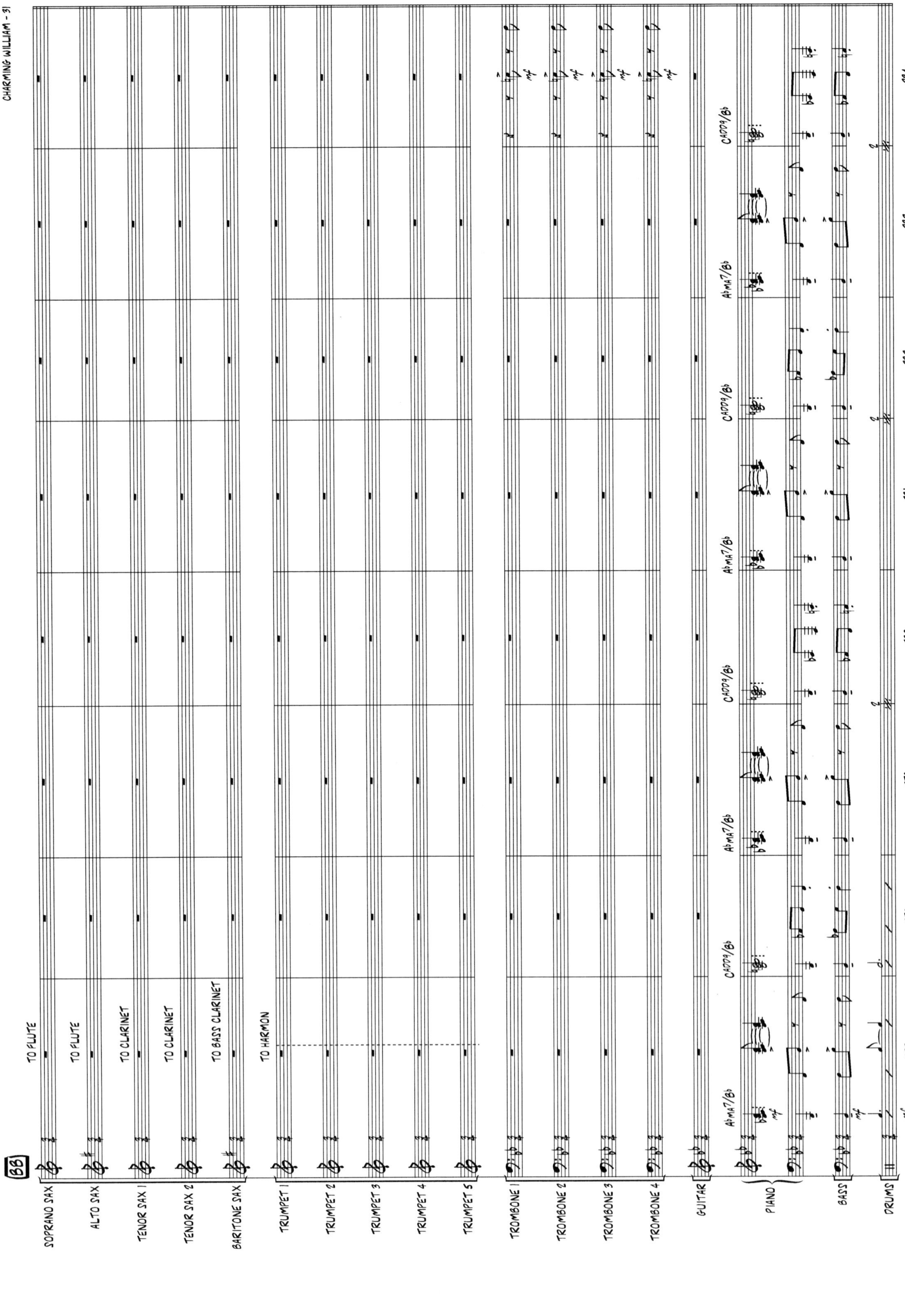
CHARMING WILLIAM - 31
BB
SOPRANO SAX
ALTO SAX
TENOR SAX 1
TENOR SAX 2
BARITONE SAX
TRUMPET 1
TRUMPET 2
TRUMPET 3
TRUMPET 4
TRUMPET 5
TROMBONE 1
TROMBONE 2
TROMBONE 3
TROMBONE 4
GUITAR
PIANO
BASS
DRUMS
TO FLUTE
TO FLUTE
TO CLARINET
TO CLARINET
TO BASS CLARINET
TO HARMON
AbMA7/Bb
CADD9/Bb
277
278
279
280
281
282
283
284

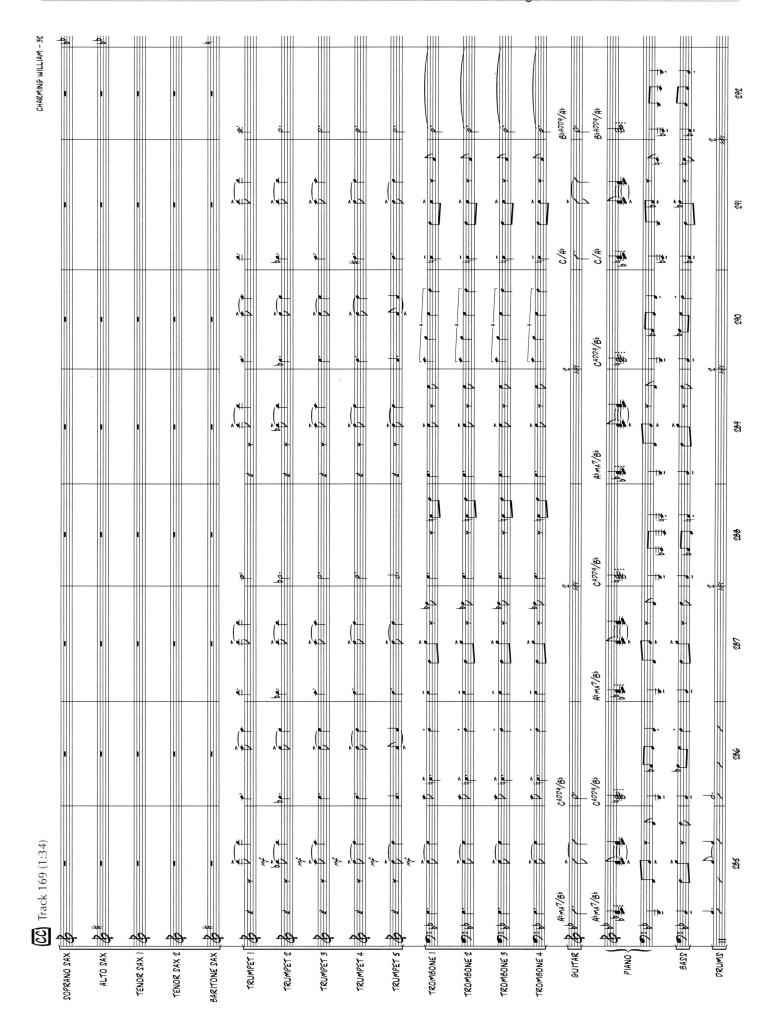

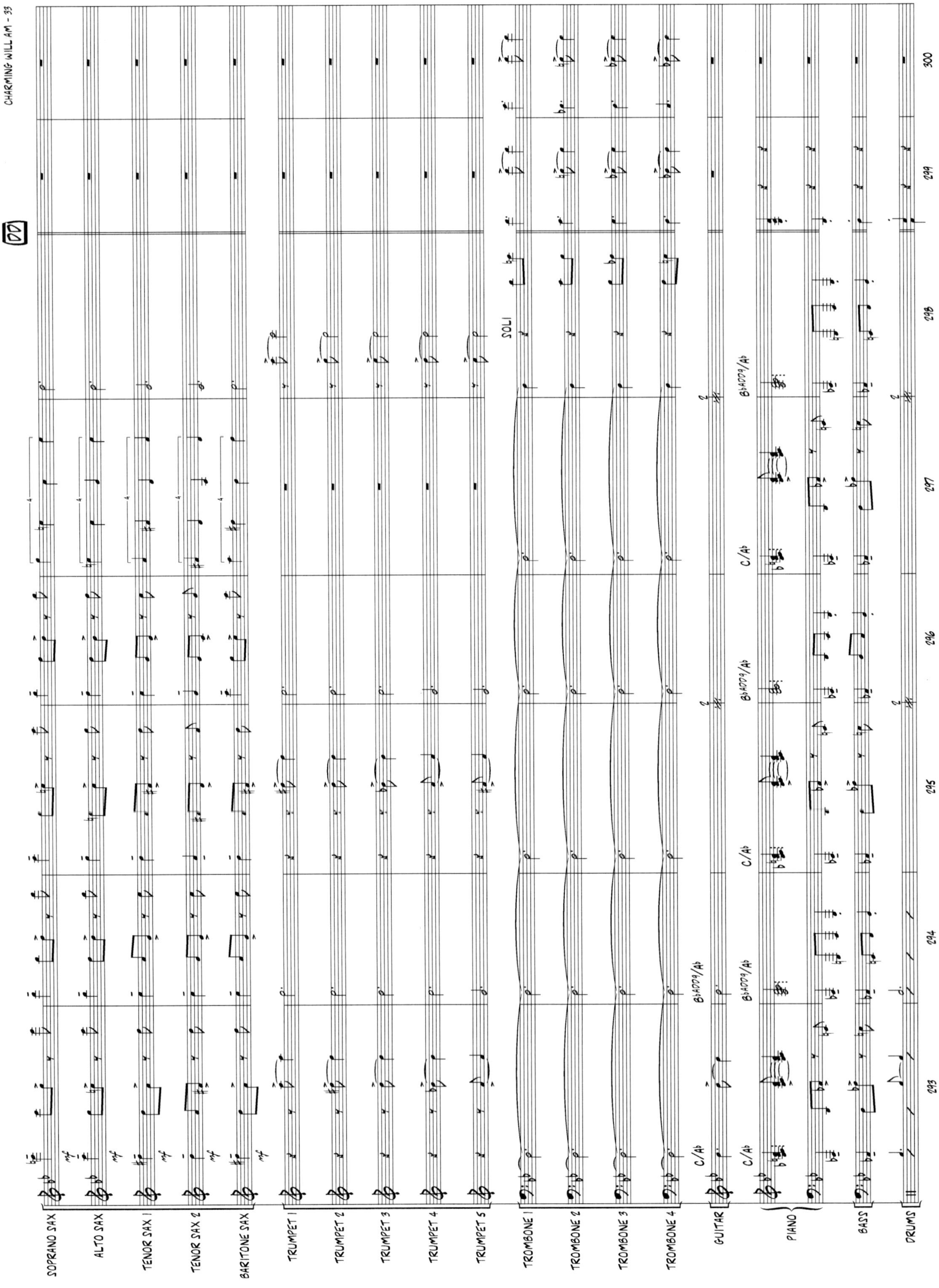

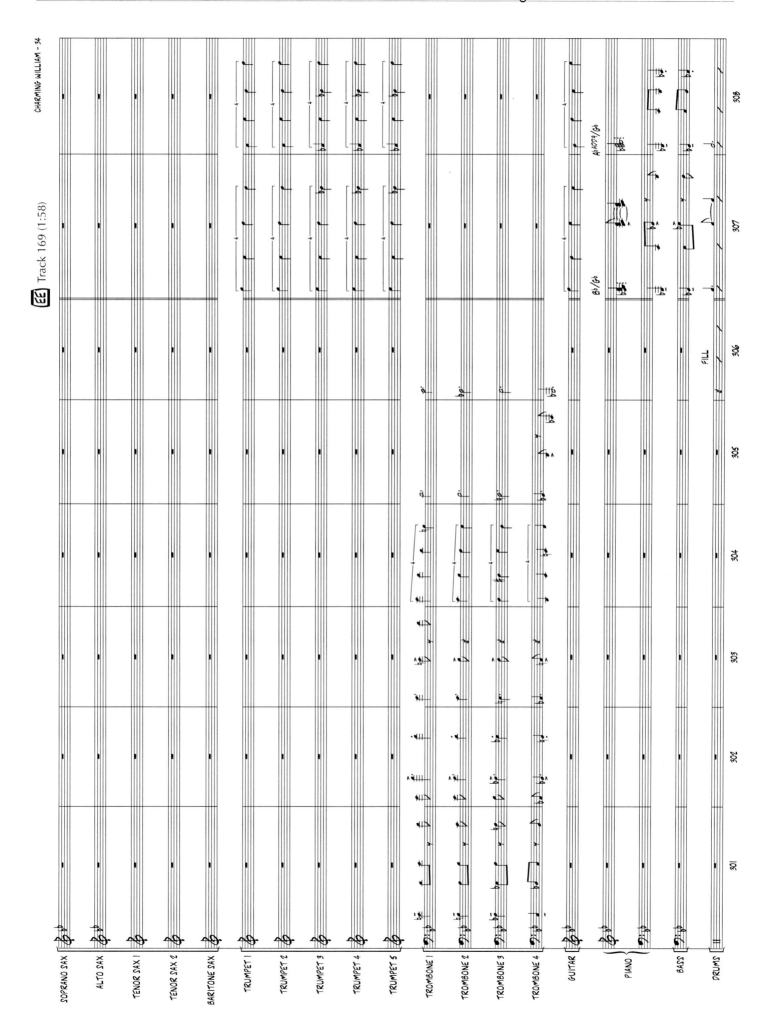

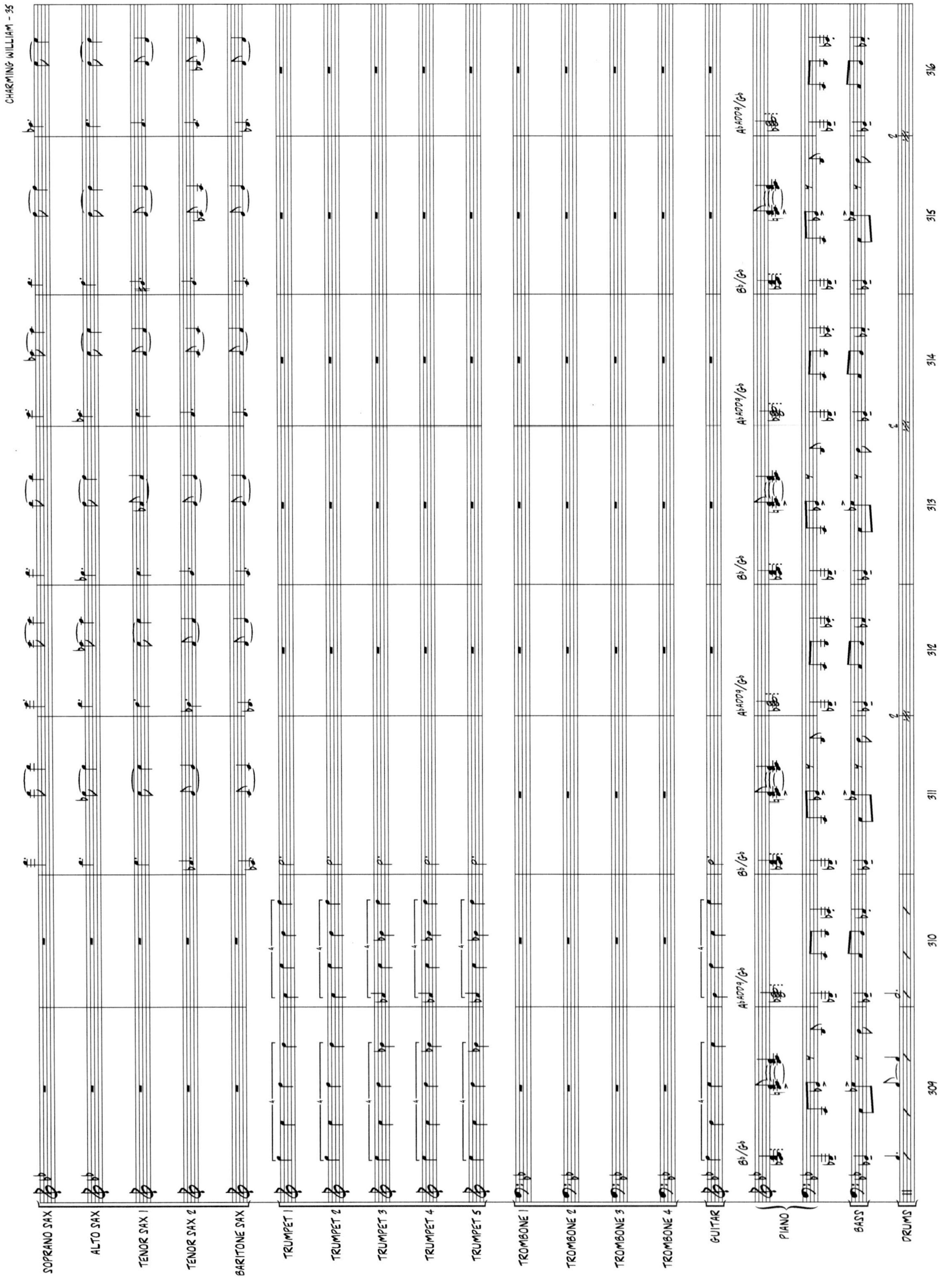

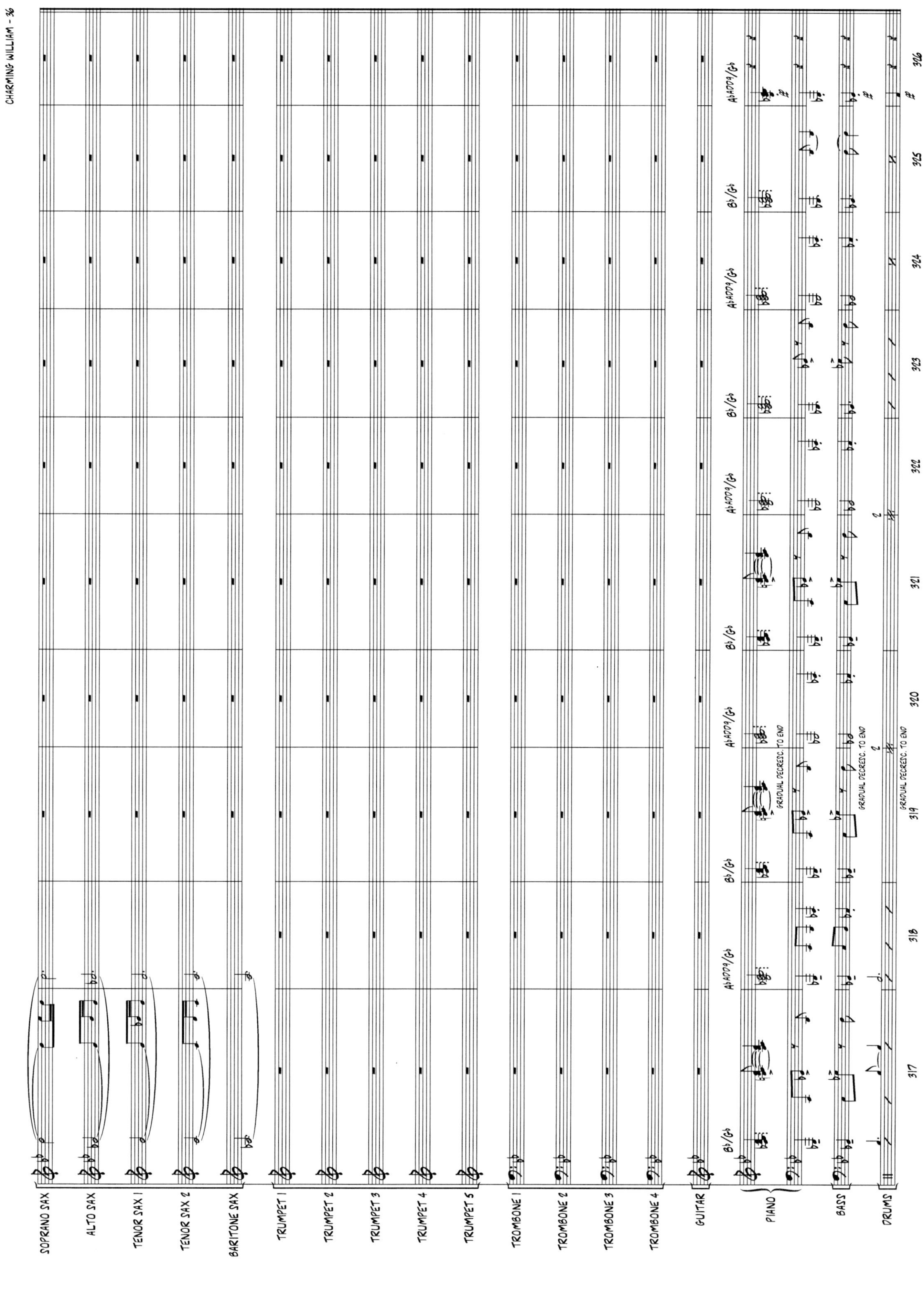

APPENDIX 8
Modulation and Melody Writing

Modulation

Modulation is one of the most important resources in tonal music. The origins of the practice can be traced back to the fifteenth century. By the eighteenth century, it was an integral part of the blueprint of every extended composition. It has long been the consensus of composers that to stay in one key for too long is aesthetically undesirable, and jazz arrangers have often been criticized for this. This criticism can be offset somewhat by the internal key movement (tonicization) that occurs in most jazz pieces.

Conversely, many arrangements dating back to the 1930s had frequent modulations and often ended in a different key than they began (for which the arrangers were also criticized). Jazz arrangements and marches are the only two genres in western music that can end in a different key than which they begin. There is no right or wrong solution to this dilemma. It is purely subjective, and each piece will hopefully offer its own solution.

The techniques of modulation are very similar to those of tonicization. The decision as to whether a tonicization or a modulation has occurred is also subjective and is generally dependent on three things:

- The degree of emphasis placed on the key change
- The length of time spent in the new key area
- Whether or not the new key has been confirmed by a cadence

Pieces like "Moten Swing" or "Polkadots and Moonbeams" in which the entire bridge is in a different key than the rest of the tune would most likely be considered a modulation. "Giant Steps" or the bridges to "Cherokee" and "Invitation," which move quickly through several keys, would be thought of as tonicizations.

The range of effect of a modulation is very large. The tonal shift can be so gentle that it is hardly noticeable or can be forceful and dynamic. It can happen suddenly and create surprise, even shock, or it can be lengthy and help to build suspense and momentum.

Modulations may be divided into three categories:

- Diatonic
- Chromatic
- Enharmonic

Diatonic Modulations

These are most often affected by means of a *pivot chord*, which is a chord common to both the initial key and the new key. The pivot chord should not be the dominant chord in the new key, but a dominant preparation—that is, either a II, IV, or VI. In jazz harmony, the II7 is the chord of choice, but IV7 and VI7 work well too, especially when modulating to a minor key. Modulation to several closely related keys can be accomplished with only four chords:

I	II	III	IV
Original Tonic	Pivot Chord	New Dominant Seventh	New Tonic

All of the diatonic chords of the major scale can function as pivot chords in at least one other key. The following example shows the chords of C major and their possible functions as dominant preparations in another key.

EXAMPLE A8-1.

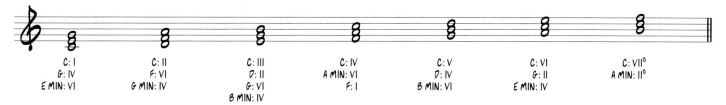

The following are examples of diatonic modulation to closely related keys through the use of a pivot chord that is common to both keys.

EXAMPLE A8-2.

One drawback to this type of modulation is that it is almost too easy. It can be accomplished so effortlessly that it becomes a nonevent.

Chromatic Modulations

In this type of modulation, the pivot chord is chromatic in one or both keys. This method can create striking shifts to more distant keys. One way to effectively modulate to keys on the flat side of the tonality is to use diatonic chords of the parallel minor as pivot chords. In the following example, modulations from C Major are accomplished by using diatonic chords of C minor.

EXAMPLE A8-3.

Enharmonic Modulation

Enharmonic modulation involves an enharmonic change of one or more notes in a chord. Perhaps the most common example is the diminished-seventh chord, which can, through enharmonic respelling, serve as a leading-tone chord (vii°7) in four different keys.

EXAMPLE A8-4.

It is common knowledge that the addition of a note a major third below the root creates an enlarged version of the chord, i.e., adding a major third below a VII°7 produces a V7(♭9) of II.

EXAMPLE A8-5.

The next example is more involved. This modulation from D♭ major to E major uses G♭mi7 as the pivot chord, but it must be respelled to F♯mi7 to show its function in the new key more clearly.

EXAMPLE A8-6.

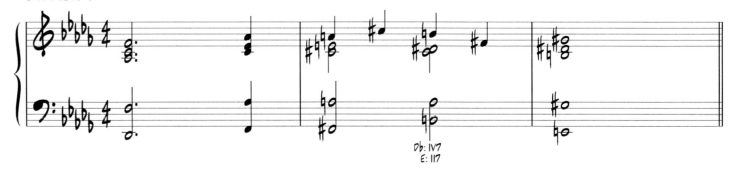

Other Modulations

Half-step root movement

Another effective device for modulating to remote keys is the use of half-step root movement. Here, the modulatory sketch would need to be expanded from four to five or six chords.

EXAMPLE A8-7.

Common-tone modulation

A completely different kind of modulation is referred to as *common-tone modulation*. In this type, a note common to two keys serves as a pivot between those keys. The common tone is usually a member of the tonic triad of one or both keys, but ninths, elevenths, thirteenths, and chromatically altered tones are possible. In this example, instead of harmonizing the note C as the root of a C major chord, it is harmonized as the third of an A♭ major chord. This effect is sudden and dramatic when done without preparation.

EXAMPLE A8-8.

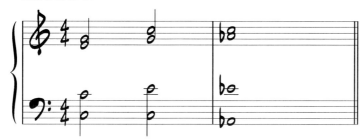

Bill Evans' recording of "The Days of Wine and Roses" uses this technique very effectively.

Modulation by sequence

A final method is *modulation by sequence*. Here a sequential pattern is established which can be manipulated to lead to any key.

EXAMPLE A8-9.

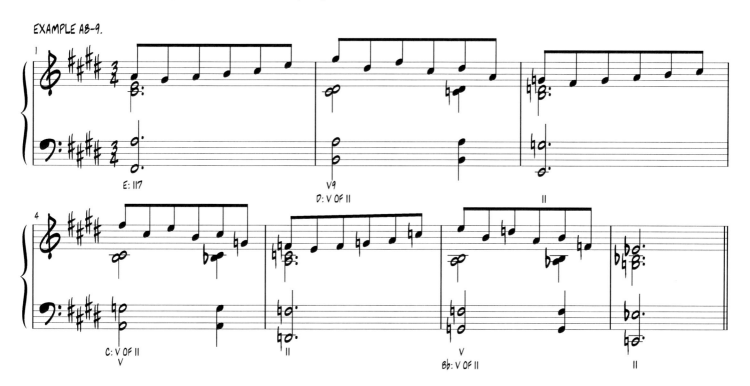

All of the above examples were presented in a very simple rhythmic format. When writing modulations, do not become so enamored with the harmonic aspects that the melodic, rhythmic, and metric details are neglected. Next is an example which is first worked out in sketch form, then fleshed out to include other necessary musical details.

EXAMPLE A8-10.

Melody Writing

While it is true that inspiration must be relied upon when creating a melody, knowledge and technique can be used to enhance and improve it. Below are a few suggestions that apply to all good melody writing:

- Each phrase should contain a characteristic feature in the form of an interval, motive, or rhythm.

- Repetition—either melodic, rhythmic, or both—is evident in most phrases. This, coupled with a characteristic feature, is a strong unifying device. Sequences are also possible, but they can quickly become monotonous.

- A limited number of rhythmic patterns used imaginatively is better than many diverse ideas.

- Stepwise motion is basic in melody writing. This should be balanced with leaps and repeated notes.

- Large leaps, except chord arpeggiation, are almost always followed by a change of direction, usually stepwise.

- In order to form a balanced musical period, the second phrase must contain some features which contrast with the first phrase. The most obvious would involve melodic contour and rhythmic activity.

APPENDIX 9
Suggested Assignments and Class Schedule

First Semester

Assignment 1: Melodic Paraphrase

Create a one-chorus melodic paraphrase of an American popular song in a swing-eighth style. Repeated sections of the form should be paraphrased differently (e.g., an AABA tune should present three different paraphrases of the A section). Avoid slow-tempo pieces for this as well as all assignments (unless otherwise indicated), as it is more difficult to create melodic paraphrase at slower tempos.

Assignment 2: Two-Part Harmonization

Create a one-chorus melodic paraphrase of an American popular song, then harmonize it using appropriate techniques discussed in class. Repeated sections of the form should be paraphrased and harmonized differently. Incorporate all types of movements, not just parallel.

Assignment 3: Countermelody

Create a one-chorus melodic paraphrase of an American popular song, then construct a countermelody using appropriate techniques discussed in class. Repeated sections should contain different paraphrasing and countermelody.

Assignment 4: Four-Note Close-Position Voicings

Select a tune from the list found in chapter 4. Paraphrase the melody where necessary, then harmonize every note using four-note close-position voicings. An attempt should be made to harmonize repeated sections differently (and not merely re-voice the same chords), focusing on the extension of all chord types and the alteration of dominant chords.

Assignment 5: Harmonization of Nonharmonic Tones and Tonicization

Select a tune that contains nonharmonic tones (look for scalar passages and conjunct motion). Paraphrase the melody where necessary, then harmonize every note using four-note close-position voicings, applying tonicization and parallelism whenever possible. An attempt should be made to harmonize repeated sections differently, focusing on the extension of all chord types and the alteration of dominant chords.

Assignment 6: Four-Note Open-Position Voicings

Select an eight-measure section of a tune containing some eighth-note lines. Paraphrase the melody where necessary, then harmonize every note using the indicated four-note open-position voicings. It is probable that the entire passage may need to be transposed upward to accommodate the open voicings. Continue to focus on the extension of all chord types and the alteration of dominant chords.

- First version: drop 2
- Second version: drop 2 & 4
- Third version: spread
- Fourth version: a logical combination of the above three techniques in the original key (not all the voicing types may be needed.)

Assignment 7: Three-Note Voicings – Close and Open Positions

Select an eight-measure section of a tune containing some eighth-note lines. Paraphrase the melody where necessary, then harmonize every note using the indicated three-note voicings. It is probable that the entire passage may need to be transposed upward to accommodate the open voicings. Continue to focus on the extension of all chord types and the alteration of dominant chords.

- First version: close
- Second version: drop 2
- Third version: a logical combination of the above techniques in the original key

Assignment 8: Five-Note Voicings – Close and Open Positions

Select an eight-measure section of a tune containing some eighth-note lines. Paraphrase the melody where necessary, then harmonize every note using the indicated five-note voicings. It is probable that the entire passage may need to be transposed upward to accommodate the open voicings. Continue to focus on the extension of all chord types and the alteration of dominant chords.

- First version: close
- Second version: drop 2
- Third version: drop 2 & 4
- Fourth version: spread
- Fifth version: a logical combination of the above four "drop" techniques in the original key (not all the voicing types may be needed).

Assignment 9: Accompaniment Devices: Pads, Punches, Melodic Fills, and Riffs

Select an eight-measure section of a tune that contains a sufficient amount of long note values and/or rests. Paraphrase the melody where necessary, then create three different accompaniments, each focusing on a specific technique. A fourth accompaniment should be created that consists of a logical combination of pads, punches, and melodic fills (riffs cannot be used in this situation). Continue to focus on the extension of all chord types and the alteration of dominant chords.

Assignment 10: Small Ensemble Arrangement (First Chorus – Introduction and Melody)

Choose a tune for this project. Arrange the first chorus for five horns (trumpet, alto sax, tenor sax, trombone, and baritone sax), guitar, piano (two staves, if necessary), bass, and drums. Paraphrase the melody where necessary. The horn parts should be comprised of at least two of the following: vertical sonorities (close, open, or spread voicings), melody and counter-melody, solo with accompaniment. All staves should contain appropriate notation styles for each instrument.

The composition of the introduction could take place at this time or occur later in the arranging process.

Assignment 11: Continuation of Small Ensemble Arrangement (Second Chorus – Improvised Solo with Backgrounds)

Using the score created for the previous assignment, arrange the second chorus, following these guidelines:

- Choose one horn soloist; this line will consist solely of chord changes.

- This section should consist of two choruses; the first containing changes for all instruments (with optional repeat), and the second, changes for the chosen soloist and rhythm section, and backgrounds for the remaining horns.
- Rhythm section parts should contain appropriate notation styles for kicks when necessary.

The composition of the introduction could take place at this time or occur later in the arranging process.

Assignment 12: Continuation of Small Ensemble Arrangement (Shout Chorus and Recapitulation)

Using the score created for the previous assignments, compose a shout chorus. Use the following guidelines:

- Half chorus in length
- Shout should logically link with the second half of the first chorus to create a recapitulation.
- Rhythm section parts should contain chord changes as well as appropriate notation styles for kicks when necessary.

At this time, the following should be placed where necessary:

- D.S. al Fine, D.S. al Coda, D.C. al Fine, or D.C. al Coda text
- D.S. symbol

The composition of the introduction could take place at this time or occur later in the arranging process.

Assignment 13: Continuation of Small Ensemble Arrangement (Ending)

Using the score created for the previous assignments, create and arrange an ending. This can be as compact or extended as musically appropriate. The ending should begin by producing a smooth transition from the end of the final chorus. At this time, the following text and symbols should be placed where necessary:

- *To Coda* text and *Coda* symbol at the appropriate place
- *Coda* text and *Coda* symbol at the first measure of the Coda

The composition of the introduction must be completed at this time.

Add the following items if they have not already been placed:

- Double bar lines at the end of each section
- Rehearsal letters or numbers at these double bar lines
- Final bar line at the end of the piece
- Style and tempo indication
- Title
- Composer/arranger credits
- Page header and any text that will aid the players during performance

Make one final check over the entire score for any last-minute fixes. Next, extract the parts and check each one for colliding text or notes and for overall appearance before printing. Print two copies of the score: one for grading and one for rehearsal. Be prepared to run the piece with the group.

Second Semester

Assignments 1a and 1b: Sax and Woodwind Section Solis

1a

Select an eight-measure section of a tune. Choose a key that places the lead alto in an appropriate register for harmonization. Paraphrase the melody where necessary, then harmonize it for sax section (AATTB) in the following ways:

- Four-note block voicing with doubled lead
- Four-note drop 2 voicing with doubled lead (Transpose upward if necessary to accommodate this harmonization.)
- Four-note drop 2 & 4 voicing with doubled lead (Transpose upward if necessary to accommodate this harmonization.)
- Five-note voicing (no doubled lead) using a logical combination of block, drop 2, and drop 2 & 4 voicings in the original key

1b

Select an eight-measure section of a tune with predominantly longer note values. Choose a key that places the flute in a strong register. Paraphrase the melody where necessary, then harmonize it for woodwind section (two flutes, two clarinets, and bass clarinet) in the following ways:

- Four-note voicing using a logical combination of drop 2 and drop 2 & 4 voicings with bass clarinet playing chord roots
- Five-note voicing using a logical combination of drop 2, drop 2 & 4, and spread voicings. (Avoid placing the bass clarinet exclusively on chord roots.)

Assignment 2a & 2b: Trumpet & Trombone Section Solis

2a

Select an eight-measure section of a tune. Choose a key that places the lead trumpet in an appropriate register for harmonization. Paraphrase the melody where necessary, then harmonize it for the trumpet section (four or five where specified) in the following ways:

- Four trumpets: four-note block voicing (four different pitches)
- Four trumpets: transpose upward so that the lead trumpet is centered on the second octave above middle C, then harmonize with four-note drop 2 voicings (four different pitches).
- Five trumpets: four-note block voicing with doubled lead in the original key
- Five trumpets: transpose upward so that the lead trumpet is centered on the second octave above middle C, then harmonize with four-note drop 2 voicings with doubled lead.
- Five trumpets: five-note voicing (no doubled lead) using a logical combination of block and drop 2 voicings in the original key

2b

Select an eight-measure section of a tune with predominantly longer note values. Choose a key that places the lead trombone mostly above the staff. Paraphrase the melody where necessary, then harmonize it for four trombones in the following ways:

- Block voicing (four different pitches)
- Drop 2 voicings (four different pitches). (If the lead line descends into the staff, some voicings may need to be converted to block.)
- Chorale voicing. (Construct a new lead line for the top voice using the existing progression.)

Assignment 3: Four- and Five-Note Chord Brass Section Writing

Select an eight-measure section of a tune with predominantly longer note values. Choose a key that places the lead trumpet no higher than concert Bb above the staff. Paraphrase the melody where necessary, then harmonize it for the brass section (four trumpets, four trombones) in the following ways:

- Double block voicing
- From the first configuration, retain the trumpet block voicing and lead trombone, then rearrange one or more of the three remaining trombone notes to create a combination of block and drop voicings.
- From the first configuration, retain the trumpet block voicing and lead trombone, then place the chord roots in the bass trombone. The interval between the first and fourth trombone should be wide enough to allow the placement of the remaining two parts between these notes (the interval must be at least a 7th and could be much greater). The selection of the remaining two trombone notes should result in a trombone voicing (block or drop) that contains all guide tones. If the root is in the melody, avoid a tripled root by placing the 5th in the bass trombone.

Assignment 4: Six- and Seven-Note Chord Brass Section Writing

Select an eight-measure section of a tune with predominantly longer note values. Choose a key that centers the lead trumpet on the second octave above middle C, extending as far as concert Eb above the staff. Paraphrase the melody where necessary, then harmonize it in six- or seven-note chords through the addition of color tones in all chord types and doubly altered 5ths and 9ths in dominant chords. Orchestrate this for the brass section (four or five trumpets, four trombones where specified) in the following ways:

- Four trumpets, four trombones: first and fourth trumpets doubled in octaves; open trombone voicings
- Four trumpets, four trombones: four different trumpet notes; open trombone voicings
- Four trumpets, four trombones: either of the above trumpet voicings; open trombone voicings with bass trombone playing chord roots
- Five trumpets, four trombones: first and fifth trumpets doubled in octaves or five different trumpet notes; open trombone voicings with or without bass trombone chord roots

Assignment 5: Integrating the Sax Section into Brass Section Voicings

- Using the double-block brass section voicing from assignment 3, write a four-note drop 2 voicing in the top four saxes, interlocking it with the brass section. The baritone sax should triple the melody, switching to chord roots at phrase endings when melodically feasible.
- Using the third voicing from assignment 4, write a five-note drop 2 voicing in the sax section, interlocking it with the brass section.
- Using either of the first two voicings from assignment 4, write a four-note drop 2 voicing in the top four saxes, interlocking it with the brass section, then write chord roots in the baritone sax part, keeping it below the fourth trombone notes.

Assignment 6: Sax Section Against the Brass Section

6a

Choose a familiar chord progression, then compose an eight-measure melody for lead trumpet that centers on the second octave above middle C, extending as far as concert E♭ above the staff. This line should be rhythmic, with syncopated figures taking precedence over long strings of eighth notes. The line should also contain some sustained notes as well as a few rests lasting two or three beats. Harmonize this line for eight brass instruments. Then, compose a countermelody for the sax section to be played in unison or two octaves. (Refer to chapter 3 for guidelines on writing countermelodies.)

6b

Choose a second familiar chord progression, then compose an eight-measure melody for lead alto or soprano that centers on the C one octave above middle C. This will place the majority of the melody within the treble staff. The line should be rhythmic, with syncopated figures taking precedence over long strings of eighth notes. It should also contain some sustained notes as well as a few rests lasting two or three beats. Harmonize this line for five saxophones. Then, compose a countermelody for the brass section to be played in octaves. (Refer to chapter 3 for guidelines on writing countermelodies.)

Assignment 7: Three Elements – Melody, Countermelody, Accompaniment

Select an eight-measure section of a tune to be played by the trumpet section in unison, paraphrasing the melody when necessary. Change the key if needed. Then, compose a countermelody below the melody to be played by the sax section in unison or octaves. Finally, compose a harmonized accompaniment to be played by the trombone section.

Select a second eight-measure section of a tune to be played by the top two trumpets and two altos in unison or octaves, paraphrasing the melody when necessary. Change the key if needed. Then, compose a countermelody to be played by the bottom two trumpets and two tenors in unison or octaves. It is possible that this line may cross the melody on occasion. Finally, compose a harmonized accompaniment in five parts to be played by the trombone section and baritone sax. The baritone can either play chord roots or be placed on a harmony note directly above the bass trombone.

Assignment 8: Large Ensemble Arrangement (First Chorus – Introduction and Melody)

Choose a tune or compose an original piece for this project. Arrange the first chorus for thirteen horns (five saxes, four trumpets, four trombones), guitar, piano (two staves), bass, and drums. Paraphrase the melody where necessary. The horn parts should be comprised of at least two of the following:

- Vertical sonorities
- Melody and countermelody
- Melody with accompaniment
- Melody, countermelody, and accompaniment

All staves should contain appropriate notation styles for each instrument.

The composition of the introduction could take place at this time or occur later in the arranging process.

Assignment 9: Continuation of Large Ensemble Arrangement (Second Chorus–Interlude and Solo Chorus with Backgrounds)

Using the score created for the previous assignment, arrange the second chorus. Use the following guidelines:

- Choose one horn soloist; this line will consist solely of chord changes.
- This section should consist of two choruses of the chord progression: the first for just the rhythm section and soloist (with optional repeat), and the second for backgrounds.
- Rhythm section parts should contain chord changes as well as appropriate notation styles for kicks when necessary.

The composition of the introduction could take place at this time or occur later in the arranging process.

Assignment 10: Continuation of Large Ensemble Arrangement (Third Chorus – Shout Chorus and Recapitulation)

Using the score created for the previous assignments, compose a shout chorus. Use the following guidelines:

- It may be a half or full chorus in length. Use a combination of the techniques discussed in chapter 14.
- The half chorus/shout chorus should logically link with the second half of the first chorus to create a recapitulation. A full-chorus shout should be followed by a full- or half-chorus recapitulation or link to a coda.
- Rhythm section parts should contain chord changes as well as appropriate notation styles for kicks when necessary.

At this time, the following should be placed where necessary:

- *D.S. al Fine, D.S. al Coda, D.C. al Fine,* or *D.C. al Coda* text
- *D.S.* symbol

The composition of the introduction could take place at this time or occur later in the arranging process.

Assignment 11: Continuation of Large Ensemble Arrangement – Ending

Using the score created for the previous assignments, create and arrange an ending for the arrangement. This can be as compact or extended as musically appropriate. The ending should begin by producing a smooth transition from the end of the final chorus. At this time, the following text and symbols should be placed where necessary:

- *To Coda* text and *Coda* symbol at the appropriate place
- *Coda* text and *Coda* symbol at the first measure of the *coda*

The composition of the introduction must be completed at this time.

Add the following items if they have not already been placed:

- Double bar lines at the end of each section
- Rehearsal letters or numbers at these double bar lines
- Final bar line at the end of the piece
- Style and tempo indication
- Title
- Composer/arranger credits
- Page header and any text that will aid the players during performance

Make one final check over the entire score for any last-minute fixes. Then, extract the parts and check each one for colliding text or notes and for overall appearance before printing. Print two copies of the score: one for grading and one for rehearsal. Be prepared to run the piece with the group.

Assignment 12: Arranging for Seven Horns

Choose either a binary or ternary tune and arrange the melody for two trumpets; two trombones; alto, tenor, and baritone saxes; guitar; piano; bass; and drums. If the form is binary, arrange a minimum of sixteen measures. If the form is ternary, arrange a minimum of twenty-four measures. Also, compose a shout chorus based on the first eight measures of the form using a homophonic texture.

Assignment 13: Contemporary Arranging Techniques

Experiment with any one of the techniques discussed in chapter 23 for any size ensemble.

CLASS SCHEDULE: FIRST SEMESTER

DATE	READINGS ASSIGNMENTS, DISSCUSSION TOPICS, WRITING ASSIGNMENTS, & REVISIONS
Week 1, Day 1	Discussion: Class Overview & Melodic Paraphrase; Reading Assignment – Chapter 1, Appendices 1, 10, and 11
Week 1, Day 2	Discussion: Melodic Paraphrase
Week 2, Day 1	Writing Assignment 1 due; Reading Assignment – Chapter 2
Week 2, Day 2	Discussion: Two-Part Harmonization
Week 3, Day 1	Writing Assignment 2 due; Reading Assignment – Chapter 3
Week 3, Day 2	Discussion: Countermelody; Assignment 1 Revision due
Week 4, Day 1	Writing Assignment 3 due; Reading Assignment – Chapter 4, Appendices 2, 3, and 4
Week 4, Day 2	Discussion: Four-Note Close-Position Voicings; Assignment 2 Revision due
Week 5, Day 1	Writing Assignment 4 due; Reading Assignment – Chapter 5
Week 5, Day 2	Discussion: NHT's and Tonicization; Assignment 3 Revision due
Week 6, Day 1	Writing Assignment 5 due; Reading Assignment – Chapter 6
Week 6, Day 2	Discussion: Four-Note Open-Position Voicings; Assignment 4 Revision due
Week 7, Day 1	Writing Assignment 6 due; Reading Assignment – Chapter 7, Appendix 5
Week 7, Day 2	Discussion: Three-Note Voicings In Close and Open Positions; Assignment 5 Revision due
Week 8, Day 1	Writing Assignment 7 due; Reading Assignment – Chapter 8, Appendix 6
Week 8, Day 2	Discussion: Five-Note Voicings In Close and Open Positions; Assignment 6 Revision due

Week 9, Day 1	Writing Assignment 8 due; Reading Assignment – Chapter 9
Week 9, Day 2	Discussion: Accompaniment Devices; Assignment 7 Revision due
Week 10, Day 1	Writing Assignment 9 due; Reading Assignment - Chapters 10 (Saxophone, Trumpet, and Trombone sections) and 12
Week 10, Day 2	Discussion: Saxophone, Trumpet, Trombone, and Rhythm Section; Assignment 8 Revision due
Week 11, Day 1	Writing Assignment – none; Reading Assignment – Chapters 13, 16, 17, and 18
Week 11, Day 2	Discussion: Small Ensemble Arranging, Planning An Arrangement, Introductions, and First Chorus; Assignment 9 Revision due
Week 12, Day 1	Writing Assignment 10 due; Reading Assignment – Chapters 19 and 20, Appendix 8
Week 12, Day 2	Discussion: Interludes, Improvised Solo with Backgrounds; No Revision due
Week 13, Day 1	Writing Assignment 11 due; Reading Assignment – Chapters 21 and 22
Week 13, Day 2	Discussion: Shout Chorus and Recapitulation, Endings; Assignment 10 Revision due
Week 14, Day 1	Writing Assignment 12 due; Assignment 11 Revision due
Week 14, Day 2	Writing Assignment 13 and Final preparation for live performance of small ensemble arrangement; Assignment 12 Revision due
	Live Performance of Small Ensemble Arrangement

CLASS SCHEDULE: SECOND SEMESTER

DATE	READINGS ASSIGNMENTS, DISSCUSSION TOPICS, WRITING ASSIGNMENTS, & REVISIONS
Week 1, Day 1	Discussion: Class Overview, Saxes and Woodwinds; Reading Assignment –Review Chapter 10 (Saxes and Woodwinds), Read Chapter 11 (Introduction & Sax Section)
Week 1, Day 2	Discussion: Sax and Woodwind Section Writing
Week 2, Day 1	Writing Assignment 1 due; Reading Assignment – Review Chapter 10 (Brass), Read Chapter 11 (Trumpet and Trombone Sections)
Week 2, Day 2	Discussion: Trumpet and Trombone Section Writing
Week 3, Day 1	Writing Assignment 2 due; Reading Assignment – Chapter 14 (to Example 14-2)
Week 3, Day 2	Discussion: Four- and Five-Note Homophonic Brass Section Writing; Assignment 1 Revision due
Week 4, Day 1	Writing Assignment 3 due; Reading Assignment – Chapter 14 (to Example 14-26)
Week 4, Day 2	Discussion: Six- and Seven-Note Homophonic Brass Section Writing; Assignment 2 Revision due
Week 5, Day 1	Writing Assignment 4 due; Reading Assignment – Chapter 14 (Exs. 14-3–14-6 and 14-27 to end of section)
Week 5, Day 2	Discussion: Integrating the Sax Section into Brass Section Voicings; Assignment 3 Revision due

Week 6, Day 1	Writing Assignment 5 due; Reading Assignment – Chapter 14 (Two Elements – Saxophone Section Against the Brass Section)
Week 6, Day 2	Discussion: Two Elements – Saxophone Section Against the Brass Section; Assignment 4 Revision due
Week 7, Day 1	Writing Assignment 6 due; Reading Assignment – Chapter 14 (Three Elements – Melody, Countermelody, Accompaniment)
Week 7, Day 2	Discussion: Three Elements – Melody, Countermelody, Accompaniment; Assignment 5 Revision due
Week 8, Day 1	Writing Assignment 7 due; Reading Assignment – Review Chapters 16, 17, and 18
Week 8, Day 2	Discussion: Planning An Arrangement, Introduction and First Chorus; Assignment 6 Revision due
Week 9, Day 1	Writing Assignment 8 due; Reading Assignment – Chapters 19 & 20
Week 9, Day 2	Discussion: Interludes, Improvised Solo with Backgrounds; Assignment 7 Revision due
Week 10, Day 1	Writing Assignment 9 due; Reading Assignment - Chapters 21 and 22
Week 10, Day 2	Discussion: Shout Chorus and Recapitulation & Endings; Assignment 8 Revision due
Week 11, Day 1	Writing Assignment 10 due
Week 11, Day 2	Discussion: Endings; Assignment 9 Revision due
Week 12, Day 1	Writing Assignment 11 due; Reading Assignment – Chapter 15; Final preparation for live performance of large ensemble arrangement
Week 12, Day 2	Discussion: Arranging for Six and Seven Horns; Assignment 10 Revision due
Week 13, Day 1	Writing Assignment 12 due; Reading Assignment – Chapter 23
Week 13, Day 2	Discussion: Where Do We Go from Here?; Assignment 11 Revision due
Week 14, Day 1	Writing Assignment 13 due
Week 14, Day 2	Assignment 12 Revision due
	Live Performance of Large Ensemble Arrangement

APPENDIX 10
Assignment Templates
and Assignment Comment Sheets

The templates that accompany this text have been constructed specifically for each assignment. They are designed to be projected onto a screen in scroll view, not printed (although this is certainly an option if so desired). Staves are provided for the subject of the assignment as well as one or two additional ones at the bottom of the score for chord roots and guide tones. The note values for both should mirror the harmonic rhythm of the song; consequently, most will be whole and half notes.

EXAMPLE A10-1. GUIDE TONE AND CHORD ROOT PLACEMENTS

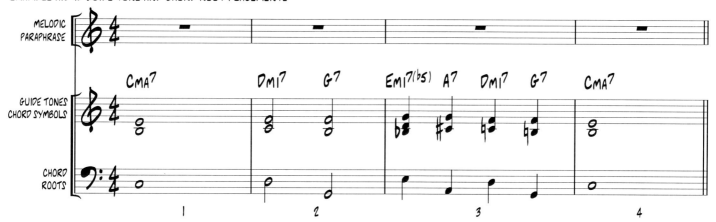

These staves will provide a skeletal outline of the song's chord structure and enable one to hear how the assigned task functions with it. Do not write a walking bass line as it will prove to be a distraction. Those assignments that are linear in nature (melodic paraphrase, countermelody, etc.) contain both additional staves, while those that are vertical (four-note voicings, tonicization, etc.) only contain the chord root staff.

Large measure numbers have also been provided at the bottom of each score to make it easier to locate specific places in the assignment.

The following is a detailed description of each assignment template:

First Semester

Assignment 1 – Melodic Paraphrase

- First staff: Paraphrased melody with appropriate dynamics and articulations
- Second staff: Guide tones with chord symbols above
- Third staff: Chord roots

Assignment 2 – Two-part Harmonization

- First staff: Paraphrased melody with appropriate dynamics and articulations
- Second staff: Harmonization with appropriate dynamics and articulations
- Third staff: Guide tones with chord symbols above
- Fourth staff: Chord roots

Assignment 3 - Countermelody

- First staff: Paraphrased melody with appropriate dynamics and articulations
- Second staff: Countermelody with appropriate dynamics and articulations
- Third staff: Guide tones with chord symbols above
- Fourth staff: Chord roots

Assignment 4 – Four-Note Close-Position Voicings

- First staff: Original input location of the four-note harmonization containing appropriate paraphrasing, dynamics, and articulations. After exploding the harmonization onto separate staves, it should contain the top line.
- Second–Fourth staves: Bottom three notes of the harmonization on separate staves so that the linear aspects of the harmonization can also be examined
- Fifth staff: Chord roots with chord symbols above

Assignment 5 – Harmonization of Nonharmonic Tones and Tonicization

- First staff: Original input location of the four-note harmonization containing appropriate paraphrasing, dynamics, and articulations. After exploding the harmonization onto separate staves, it should contain the top line.
- Second–Fourth staves: Bottom three notes of the harmonization on separate staves so that the linear aspects of the harmonization can also be examined
- Fifth staff: Chord roots with chord symbols above

Assignment 6 – Four-Note Open-Position Voicings

- First staff: Original input location of the four-note harmonization containing appropriate paraphrasing, dynamics, and articulations. After exploding the harmonization onto separate staves, it should contain the top line.
- Second–Fourth staves: Bottom three notes of the harmonization on separate staves so that the linear aspects of the harmonization can also be examined
- Fifth staff: Chord roots with chord symbols above

Assignment 7 – Three-Note Voicings – Close and Open Positions

- First staff: Original input location of the three-note harmonization containing appropriate paraphrasing, dynamics, and articulations. After exploding the harmonization onto separate staves, it should contain the top line.
- Second and Third staves: Bottom two notes of the harmonization on separate staves so that the linear aspects of the harmonization can also be examined
- Fifth staff: Chord roots with chord symbols above

Assignment 8 – Five-Note Voicings – Close and Open Positions

- First staff: Original input location of the four-note harmonization containing appropriate paraphrasing, dynamics, and articulations. After exploding the harmonization onto separate staves, it should contain the top line.
- Second–Fifth staves: Bottom four notes of the harmonization on separate staves so that the linear aspects of the harmonization can also be examined
- Sixth staff: Chord roots with chord symbols above

Assignment 9 – Accompaniment Devices

- First staff: Paraphrased melody with appropriate dynamics and articulations
- Second staff: Accompaniment devices using four-note voicings
- Third staff: Chord roots with chord symbols above

Assignments 10-13 – Small Ensemble Arrangement

- First staff: Trumpet
- Second staff: Alto sax
- Third staff: Tenor sax
- Fourth staff: Trombone
- Fifth staff: Baritone sax
- Sixth staff: Guitar
- Seventh and Eighth staves: Piano grand staff
- Ninth staff: Bass
- Tenth staff: Drums

Second Semester

Assignments 1a and 1b – Sax and Woodwind Section Solis

- First staff: Original input location of the five-note harmonization containing appropriate paraphrasing, dynamics, and articulations. After exploding the harmonization onto separate staves, it should contain the top line.
- Second–Fifth staves: Bottom four notes of the harmonization on separate staves
- Sixth staff: Chord roots with chord symbols above

Assignments 2a and 2b – Trumpet and Trombone Section Solis

- First staff: Original input location of the four- and five-note trumpet and four-note trombone harmonizations containing appropriate paraphrasing, dynamics, and articulations. After exploding the harmonization onto separate staves, it should contain the top line.
- Second–Fifth staves: Bottom notes of the harmonization on separate staves (the Fifth staff will not be used for either of the four-note solis)
- Sixth staff: Chord roots with chord symbols above

Assignment 3 – Four- and Five-Note Brass Section Writing

- First staff: Original input location of the four-note trumpet harmonization containing appropriate paraphrasing, dynamics, and articulations. After exploding the harmonization onto separate staves, it should contain the top line.
- Second–Fifth staves: Bottom three or four notes of the trumpet harmonization on separate staves
- Sixth staff: Original input location of the four-note trombone harmonization containing appropriate paraphrasing, dynamics, and articulations. After exploding the harmonization onto separate staves, it should contain the top line.
- Seventh–Ninth staves: Bottom three notes of the trombone harmonization on separate staves
- Tenth staff: Chord roots with chord symbols above

Assignment 4 – Six- and Seven-Note Brass Section Writing

- First staff: Original input location of the four- or five-note trumpet harmonization containing appropriate paraphrasing, dynamics, and articulations. After exploding the harmonization onto separate staves, it should contain the top line.
- Second-Fifth staves: Bottom three or four notes of the trumpet harmonization on separate staves

- Sixth staff: Original input location of the four-note trombone harmonization containing appropriate paraphrasing, dynamics, and articulations. After exploding the harmonization onto separate staves, it should contain the top line.

- Seventh–Ninth staves: Bottom three notes of the trombone harmonization on separate staves

- Tenth staff: Chord roots with chord symbols above

Assignment 5 – Integrating the Sax Section into Brass Section Voicings

- First staff: Original input location of the five-note saxophone harmonization containing appropriate paraphrasing, dynamics, and articulations. After exploding the harmonization onto separate staves, it should contain the top line.

- Second–Fifth staves: Bottom four notes of the saxophone harmonization on separate staves

- Sixth staff: Original input location of the four- or five-note trumpet harmonization containing appropriate paraphrasing, dynamics, and articulations. After exploding the harmonization onto separate staves, it should contain the top line.

- Seventh–Tenth staves: Bottom three or four notes of the trumpet harmonization on separate staves

- Eleventh staff: Original input location of the four-note trombone harmonization containing appropriate paraphrasing, dynamics, and articulations. After exploding the harmonization onto separate staves, it should contain the top line.

- Twelfth–Fourteenth staves: Bottom three notes of the trombone harmonization on separate staves

- Fifteenth staff: Chord roots with chord symbols above

Assignment 6 – Sax Section Against the Brass Section

- First staff: Original input location of the five-note saxophone harmonization containing appropriate paraphrasing, dynamics, and articulations. After exploding the harmonization onto separate staves, it should contain the top line.

- Second–Fifth staves: Bottom four notes of the saxophone harmonization on separate staves

- Sixth staff: Original input location of the four- or five-note trumpet harmonization containing appropriate paraphrasing, dynamics, and articulations. After exploding the harmonization onto separate staves, it should contain the top line.

- Seventh–Tenth staves: Bottom three or four notes of the trumpet harmonization on separate staves

- Eleventh staff: Original input location of the four-note trombone harmonization containing appropriate paraphrasing, dynamics, and articulations. After exploding the harmonization onto separate staves, it should contain the top line.

- Twelfth–Fourteenth staves: Bottom three notes of the trombone harmonization on separate staves

- Fifteenth staff: Chord roots with chord symbols above

Assignment 7 – Three Elements – Melody, Countermelody, Accompaniment

- First staff: Original input location of the five-note saxophone harmonization containing appropriate paraphrasing, dynamics, and articulations. After exploding the harmonization onto separate staves, it should contain the top line.

- Second–Fifth staves: Bottom four notes of the saxophone harmonization on separate staves
- Sixth staff: Original input location of the four- or five-note trumpet harmonization containing appropriate paraphrasing, dynamics, and articulations. After exploding the harmonization onto separate staves, it should contain the top line.
- Seventh-Tenth staves: Bottom three or four notes of the trumpet harmonization on separate staves
- Eleventh staff: Original input location of the four-note trombone harmonization containing appropriate paraphrasing, dynamics, and articulations. After exploding the harmonization onto separate staves, it should contain the top line.
- Twelfth–Fourteenth staves: Bottom three notes of the trombone harmonization on separate staves
- Fifteenth Staff: Chord roots with chord symbols above

Assignments 8-11 – Large Ensemble Arrangement

- First–Fifth staves: Saxophone section
- Sixth–Tenth staves: Trumpet section (if writing for four trumpets, tenth staff will not be used).
- Eleventh–Fourteenth staves: Trombone section
- Fifteenth staff: Guitar
- Sixteenth and Seventeenth staves: Piano grand staff
- Eighteenth staff: Bass
- Nineteenth staff: Drums

Assignment 12 – Arranging for Six and Seven Horns

- First staff: Alto sax
- Second staff: Tenor sax
- Third staff: Baritone sax
- Fourth staff: Trumpet 1
- Fifth staff: Trumpet 2
- Sixth staff: Trombone 1
- Seventh staff: Trombone 2
- Eighth staff: Guitar
- Ninth and Tenth staves: Piano grand staff
- Eleventh staff: Bass
- Twelfth staff: Drums

Assignment 13 – Contemporary Arranging Techniques

- First and Second staves: Saxes
- Third staff: Trumpets
- Fourth staff: Trombones
- Fifth staff: Guitar
- Sixth and Seventh staves: Piano grand staff
- Eighth staff: Bass
- Ninth staff: Drums

First Semester Jazz Arranging Grade and Comment Sheet
Assignment 1 – Melodic Paraphrase

STUDENT NAME _____ GRADE _____

Comment Key

1) Insufficient rhythmic alteration
2) Awkward rhythmic alteration
3) Excessive rhythmic alteration
4) Incorrect articulation
5) Excessive articulation
6) Non-defined quarter-note length
7) Awkward rhythmic notation
8) Incorrect bass note
9) Incorrect guide tones
10) Incorrect chord symbol
11) Musically awkward connecting tones, neighbor tones, or fills
12) Excessive use of dynamics
13) Lack of dynamics
14) Incorrect use of dynamics
15) Excessive use of ornamentation
16) Incorrect use of ornamentation
17) Wrong notes

MEASURE #	COMMENTS	MEASURE #	COMMENTS
1		21	
2		22	
3		23	
4		24	
5		25	
6		26	
7		27	
8		28	
9		29	
10		30	
11		31	
12		32	
13		33	
14		34	
15		35	
16		36	
17		37	
18		38	
19		39	
20		40	

General Comments:

First Semester Jazz Arranging Grade and Comment Sheet

Assignment 2 – Two-Part Harmonization

STUDENT NAME _____ GRADE _____

Comment Key

1) Insufficient rhythmic alteration
2) Awkward rhythmic alteration
3) Excessive rhythmic alteration
4) Incorrect articulation
5) Excessive articulation
6) Non-defined quarter-note length
7) Awkward rhythmic notation
8) Incorrect bass note
9) Incorrect guide tones
10) Incorrect chord symbol

11) Musically awkward connecting tones, neighbor tones, or fills
12) Incorrect or excessive use of dynamics
13) Incorrect or excessive use of ornamentation
14) Wrong notes
15) Ineffective harmonization of target note
16) Harmonization is too dissonant
17) Harmonization is uninteresting due to excessive use of consonance

MEASURE #	COMMENTS	MEASURE #	COMMENTS
1		21	
2		22	
3		23	
4		24	
5		25	
6		26	
7		27	
8		28	
9		29	
10		30	
11		31	
12		32	
13		33	
14		34	
15		35	
16		36	
17		37	
18		38	
19		39	
20		40	

General Comments:

First Semester Jazz Arranging Grade and Comment Sheet
Assignment 3 – Countermelody

STUDENT NAME _____ **GRADE** _____

Comment Key

1) Insufficient rhythmic alteration
2) Awkward rhythmic alteration
3) Excessive rhythmic alteration
4) Incorrect articulation
5) Excessive articulation
6) Non-defined quarter-note length
7) Awkward rhythmic notation
8) Incorrect bass note
9) Incorrect guide tones
10) Incorrect chord symbol

11) Musically awkward connecting tones, neighbor tones, or fills
12) Incorrect or excessive use of dynamics
13) Incorrect or excessive use of ornamentation
14) Wrong notes
15) Fragmented countermelody
16) Voices collide
17) Countermelody is too active
18) Incompatible rhythms

MEASURE #	COMMENTS
1	
2	
3	
4	
5	
6	
7	
8	
9	
10	
11	
12	
13	
14	
15	
16	
17	
18	
19	
20	

MEASURE #	COMMENTS
21	
22	
23	
24	
25	
26	
27	
28	
29	
30	
31	
32	
33	
34	
35	
36	
37	
38	
39	
40	

General Comments:

First Semester Jazz Arranging Grade and Comment Sheet

Assignment 4 – Four-Note Close-Position Voicings

STUDENT NAME _____ GRADE _____

Comment Key

1) Insufficient rhythmic alteration
2) Awkward rhythmic alteration
3) Excessive rhythmic alteration
4) Incorrect articulation
5) Excessive articulation
6) Non-defined quarter-note length
7) Awkward rhythmic notation
8) Incorrect bass note
9) Incorrect guide tones
10) Incorrect chord symbol
11) Musically awkward connecting tones, neighbor tones, or fills

12) Incorrect or excessive use of dynamics
13) Incorrect or excessive use of ornamentation
14) Wrong notes
15) Minor-second interval between top two voices
16) Omission of guide tones
17) Inconsistent tension and density level
18) Excessive dissonance
19) Coincidence of altered and unaltered fifth in the same voicing
20) Coincidence of altered and unaltered ninth in the same voicing

MEASURE #	COMMENTS	MEASURE #	COMMENTS
1		21	
2		22	
3		23	
4		24	
5		25	
6		26	
7		27	
8		28	
9		29	
10		30	
11		31	
12		32	
13		33	
14		34	
15		35	
16		36	
17		37	
18		38	
19		39	
20		40	

General Comments:

First Semester Jazz Arranging Grade and Comment Sheet
Assignment 5 – MHTs and Tonicization

STUDENT NAME _____ **GRADE** _____

Comment Key

1) Insufficient, awkward, or excessive rhythmic alteration
2) Incorrect or excessive articulation
3) Non-defined quarter-note length
4) Awkward rhythmic notation
5) Incorrect bass note, guide tones, or chord symbol
6) Musically awkward connecting tones, neighbor tones, or fills
7) Incorrect or excessive use of dynamics
8) Incorrect or excessive use of ornamentation
9) Wrong notes
10) Minor-second interval between top two voices

11) Omission of guide tones
12) Inconsistent tension and density level
13) Excessive dissonance
14) Ineffective tonicization
15) Ineffective use of diatonic parallelism
16) Ineffective use of chromatic parallelism
17) Absence of alteration in cycled dominant tonicizations
18) Inappropriate use of alterations in tonicizations
19) Coincidence of altered and unaltered fifth in the same voicing
20) Coincidence of altered and unaltered ninth in the same voicing

MEASURE #	COMMENTS	MEASURE #	COMMENTS
1		21	
2		22	
3		23	
4		24	
5		25	
6		26	
7		27	
8		28	
9		29	
10		30	
11		31	
12		32	
13		33	
14		34	
15		35	
16		36	
17		37	
18		38	
19		39	
20		40	

General Comments:

First Semester Jazz Arranging Grade and Comment Sheet
Assignment 6 – Four-Note Open-Position Voicings

STUDENT NAME _____ GRADE_____

Comment Key

1) Insufficient, awkward, or excessive rhythmic alteration
2) Incorrect or excessive articulation
3) Non-defined quarter-note length
4) Awkward rhythmic notation
5) Incorrect bass note, guide tones, or chord symbol
6) Musically awkward connecting tones, neighbor tones, or fills
7) Incorrect or excessive use of dynamics
8) Incorrect or excessive use of ornamentation
9) Wrong notes
10) Minor-second interval between top two voices
11) Omission of guide tones

12) Inconsistent tension and density level
13) Excessive dissonance
14) Ineffective tonicization
15) Ineffective use of diatonic or chromatic parallelism
16) Absence of alteration in cycled dominant tonicizations
17) Inappropriate use of alterations in tonicizations
18) Coincidence of altered and unaltered fifth in the same voicing
19) Coincidence of altered and unaltered ninth in the same voicing
20) Improper spacing
21) Voicing is unclear (too low)
22) Awkward voice leading

MEASURE #	COMMENTS	MEASURE #	COMMENTS
1		21	
2		22	
3		23	
4		24	
5		25	
6		26	
7		27	
8		28	
9		29	
10		30	
11		31	
12		32	
13		33	
14		34	
15		35	
16		36	
17		37	
18		38	
19		39	
20		40	

General Comments:

First Semester Jazz Arranging Grade and Comment Sheet

Assignment 7 – Three-Note Voicings

STUDENT NAME _____ **GRADE** _____

Comment Key

1) Insufficient, awkward, or excessive rhythmic alteration
2) Incorrect or excessive articulation
3) Non-defined quarter-note length
4) Awkward rhythmic notation
5) Incorrect bass note, guide tones, or chord symbol
6) Musically awkward connecting tones, neighbor tones, or fills
7) Incorrect or excessive use of dynamics
8) Incorrect or excessive use of ornamentation
9) Wrong notes
10) Minor-second interval between top two voices
11) Ineffective omission of guide tones
12) Inconsistent tension and density level
13) Excessive dissonance
14) Ineffective tonicization
15) Ineffective use of diatonic or chromatic parallelism
16) Absence of alteration in cycled dominant tonicizations
17) Inappropriate use of alterations in tonicizations
18) Coincidence of altered and unaltered fifth in the same voicing
19) Coincidence of altered and unaltered ninth in the same voicing
20) Improper spacing
21) Voicing is unclear (too low)
22) Awkward voice leading
23) Overuse of triadic voicings

MEASURE #	COMMENTS	MEASURE #	COMMENTS
1		21	
2		22	
3		23	
4		24	
5		25	
6		26	
7		27	
8		28	
9		29	
10		30	
11		31	
12		32	
13		33	
14		34	
15		35	
16		36	
17		37	
18		38	
19		39	
20		40	

General Comments:

First Semester Jazz Arranging Grade and Comment Sheet

Assignment 8 – Five-Note Voicings

STUDENT NAME _____ **GRADE** _____

Comment Key

1) Insufficient, awkward, or excessive rhythmic alteration
2) Incorrect or excessive articulation
3) Non-defined quarter-note length
4) Awkward rhythmic notation
5) Incorrect bass note, guide tones, or chord symbol
6) Musically awkward connecting tones, neighbor tones, or fills
7) Incorrect or excessive use of dynamics
8) Incorrect or excessive use of ornamentation
9) Wrong notes
10) Minor-second interval between top two voices
11) Omission of guide tones
12) Inconsistent tension and density level
13) Excessive dissonance
14) Ineffective tonicization
15) Ineffective use of diatonic or chromatic parallelism
16) Absence of alteration in cycled dominant tonicizations
17) Inappropriate use of alterations in tonicizations
18) Coincidence of altered and unaltered fifth in the same voicing
19) Coincidence of altered and unaltered ninth in the same voicing
20) Improper spacing
21) Voicing is unclear (too low)
22) Awkward voice leading
23) Excessive use of chord roots at the bottom of voicings
24) Improper guide tone placement in chorale voicing

MEASURE #	COMMENTS
1	
2	
3	
4	
5	
6	
7	
8	
9	
10	
11	
12	
13	
14	
15	
16	
17	
18	
19	
20	

MEASURE #	COMMENTS
21	
22	
23	
24	
25	
26	
27	
28	
29	
30	
31	
32	
33	
34	
35	
36	
37	
38	
39	
40	

General Comments:

First Semester Jazz Arranging Grade and Comment Sheet
Assignment 9 – Accompaniment Devices

STUDENT NAME _____ GRADE _____

Comment Key

1) Insufficient, awkward, or excessive rhythmic alteration
2) Incorrect or excessive articulation
3) Non-defined quarter-note length
4) Awkward rhythmic notation
5) Incorrect bass note, guide tones, or chord symbol
6) Musically awkward connecting tones, neighbor tones, or fills
7) Incorrect or excessive use of dynamics
8) Incorrect or excessive use of ornamentation
9) Wrong notes
10) Minor-second interval between top two voices
11) Omission of guide tones
12) Inconsistent tension and density level
13) Excessive dissonance
14) Ineffective tonicization
15) Ineffective use of diatonic or chromatic parallelism
16) Absence of alteration in cycled dominant tonicizations
17) Inappropriate use of alterations in tonicizations
18) Coincidence of altered and unaltered fifth in the same voicing
19) Coincidence of altered and unaltered ninth in the same voicing
20) Improper spacing
21) Voicing is unclear (too low)
22) Awkward voice leading
23) Melody and top voice of accompaniment collide
24) Accompaniment is too active
25) Incompatible rhythms between melody and accompaniment

MEASURE #	COMMENTS	MEASURE #	COMMENTS
1		21	
2		22	
3		23	
4		24	
5		25	
6		26	
7		27	
8		28	
9		29	
10		30	
11		31	
12		32	
13		33	
14		34	
15		35	
16		36	
17		37	
18		38	
19		39	
20		40	

General Comments:

First Semester Jazz Arranging Grade and Comment Sheet

Assignment 10 – Small Ensemble Arrangement – Melody Chorus

STUDENT NAME _____ GRADE _____

Comment Key

1) Insufficient, awkward, or excessive rhythmic alteration
2) Incorrect or excessive articulation
3) Non-defined quarter-note length
4) Awkward rhythmic notation
5) Incorrect bass note, guide tones, or chord symbol
6) Musically awkward connecting tones, neighbor tones, or fills
7) Incorrect or excessive use of dynamics
8) Incorrect or excessive use of ornamentation
9) Wrong notes
10) Minor-second interval between top two voices
11) Omission of guide tones
12) Inconsistent tension and density level
13) Excessive dissonance
14) Ineffective tonicization
15) Ineffective use of diatonic or chromatic parallelism
16) Absence of alteration in cycled dominant tonicizations
17) Inappropriate use of alterations in tonicizations
18) Coincidence of altered and unaltered fifth in the same voicing
19) Coincidence of altered and unaltered ninth in the same voicing
20) Improper spacing
21) Voicing is unclear (too low)
22) Awkward voice leading
23) Melody and top voice of accompaniment collide
24) Accompaniment is too active
25) Incompatible rhythms between melody and accompaniment
26) Absence of rhythm section involvement
27) Incorrect rhythm section notation
28) Notes are too close to the instrument's range extremities
29) Notes out of instrument's range

MEASURE #	COMMENTS	MEASURE #	COMMENTS
1		21	
2		22	
3		23	
4		24	
5		25	
6		26	
7		27	
8		28	
9		29	
10		30	
11		31	
12		32	
13		33	
14		34	
15		35	
16		36	
17		37	
18		38	
19		39	
20		40	

General Comments:

First Semester Jazz Arranging Grade and Comment Sheet

Assignment 11: Small Ensemble Arrangement – Improvised Solo w/Backgrounds

STUDENT NAME _____ GRADE _____

Comment Key

1) Insufficient, awkward, or excessive rhythmic alteration
2) Incorrect or excessive articulation
3) Non-defined quarter-note length
4) Awkward rhythmic notation
5) Incorrect bass note, guide tones, or chord symbol
6) Musically awkward connecting tones, neighbor tones, or fills
7) Incorrect or excessive use of dynamics
8) Incorrect or excessive use of ornamentation
9) Wrong notes
10) Minor-second interval between top two voices
11) Omission of guide tones
12) Inconsistent tension and density level
13) Excessive dissonance
14) Ineffective tonicization
15) Ineffective use of diatonic or chromatic parallelism
16) Absence of alteration in cycled dominant tonicizations
17) Inappropriate use of alterations in tonicizations.
18) Coincidence of altered and unaltered fifth in the same voicing
19) Coincidence of altered and unaltered ninth in the same voicing
20) Improper spacing
21) Voicing is unclear (too low)
22) Awkward voice leading
23) Background is too active
24) Absence of rhythm section involvement
25) Incorrect rhythm section notation
26) Incorrect use of endings and repeat
27) Notes are too close to the instrument's range extremities
28) Notes out of instrument's range

MEASURE #	COMMENTS	MEASURE #	COMMENTS
1		21	
2		22	
3		23	
4		24	
5		25	
6		26	
7		27	
8		28	
9		29	
10		30	
11		31	
12		32	
13		33	
14		34	
15		35	
16		36	
17		37	
18		38	
19		39	
20		40	

General Comments:

First Semester Jazz Arranging Grade and Comment Sheet

Assignment 12: Small Ensemble Arrangement – Shout Chorus and Recapitulation

STUDENT NAME _____ GRADE _____

Comment Key

1) Insufficient, awkward, or excessive rhythmic alteration
2) Incorrect or excessive articulation
3) Non-defined quarter-note length
4) Awkward rhythmic notation
5) Incorrect bass note, guide tones, or chord symbol
6) Musically awkward connecting tones, neighbor tones, or fills
7) Incorrect or excessive use of dynamics
8) Incorrect or excessive use of ornamentation
9) Wrong notes
10) Minor-second interval between top two voices
11) Omission of guide tones
12) Inconsistent tension and density level
13) Excessive dissonance
14) Ineffective tonicization
15) Ineffective use of diatonic or chromatic parallelism
16) Absence of alteration in cycled dominant tonicizations
17) Inappropriate use of alterations in tonicizations
18) Coincidence of altered and unaltered fifth in the same voicing
19) Coincidence of altered and unaltered ninth in the same voicing
20) Improper spacing
21) Voicing is unclear (too low)
22) Awkward voice leading
23) Accompaniment is too active
24) Absence of rhythm section involvement
25) Incorrect rhythm section notation
26) Lead trumpet register is too high
27) Voicings are too close or too spread
28) Improper guide tone placement in spread voicings
29) Improper use or placement of signs (e.g., D.S.)
30) Notes are too close to the instrument's range extremities
31) Notes out of instrument's range

MEASURE #	COMMENTS
1	
2	
3	
4	
5	
6	
7	
8	
9	
10	
11	
12	
13	
14	
15	
16	
17	
18	
19	
20	

MEASURE #	COMMENTS
21	
22	
23	
24	
25	
26	
27	
28	
29	
30	
31	
32	
33	
34	
35	
36	
37	
38	
39	
40	

General Comments:

First Semester Jazz Arranging Grade and Comment Sheet
Assignment 13: Small Ensemble Arrangement – Intro and Ending

STUDENT NAME _____   **GRADE** _____

Comment Key

1) Insufficient, awkward, or excessive rhythmic alteration
2) Incorrect or excessive articulation
3) Non-defined quarter-note length
4) Awkward rhythmic notation
5) Incorrect bass note, guide tones, or chord symbol
6) Musically awkward connecting tones, neighbor tones, or fills
7) Incorrect or excessive use of dynamics
8) Incorrect or excessive use of ornamentation
9) Wrong notes
10) Minor-second interval between top two voices
11) Omission of guide tones
12) Inconsistent tension and density level
13) Excessive dissonance
14) Ineffective tonicization
15) Ineffective use of diatonic or chromatic parallelism
16) Absence of alteration in cycled dominant tonicizations
17) Inappropriate use of alterations in tonicizations
18) Coincidence of altered and unaltered fifth in the same voicing
19) Coincidence of altered and unaltered ninth in the same voicing
20) Improper spacing
21) Voicing is unclear (too low)
22) Awkward voice leading
23) Accompaniment is too active
24) Absence of rhythm section involvement
25) Incorrect rhythm section notation
26) Ineffective link between intro and first chorus
27) Ineffective link between shout or recap and ending
28) Improper use or placement of signs (e.g., Coda)
29) Notes are too close to the instrument's range extremities
30) Notes out of instrument's range

MEASURE #	COMMENTS
1	
2	
3	
4	
5	
6	
7	
8	
9	
10	
11	
12	
13	
14	
15	
16	
17	
18	
19	
20	

MEASURE #	COMMENTS
21	
22	
23	
24	
25	
26	
27	
28	
29	
30	
31	
32	
33	
34	
35	
36	
37	
38	
39	
40	

General Comments:

Second Semester Jazz Arranging Grade and Comment Sheet
Assignment 1: Sax and Woodwind Section Solis

STUDENT NAME _____ GRADE_____

Comment Key

1) Insufficient, awkward, or excessive rhythmic alteration
2) Incorrect or excessive articulation
3) Non-defined quarter-note length
4) Awkward rhythmic notation
5) Incorrect bass note, guide tones, or chord symbol
6) Musically awkward connecting tones, neighbor tones, or fills
7) Incorrect or excessive use of dynamics
8) Incorrect or excessive use of ornamentation
9) Wrong notes
10) Minor-second interval between top two voices
11) Omission of guide tones
12) Inconsistent tension and density level
13) Excessive dissonance

14) Ineffective tonicization
15) Ineffective use of diatonic or chromatic parallelism
16) Absence of alteration in cycled dominant tonicizations
17) Inappropriate use of alterations in tonicizations
18) Coincidence of altered and unaltered fifth in the same voicing
19) Coincidence of altered and unaltered ninth in the same voicing
20) Improper spacing
21) Voicing is unclear (too low)
22) Notes are too close to the instrument's range extremities
23) Notes out of instrument's range

MEASURE #	COMMENTS	MEASURE #	COMMENTS
1		21	
2		22	
3		23	
4		24	
5		25	
6		26	
7		27	
8		28	
9		29	
10		30	
11		31	
12		32	
13		33	
14		34	
15		35	
16		36	
17		37	
18		38	
19		39	
20		40	

General Comments:

Second Semester Jazz Arranging Grade and Comment Sheet
Assignment 2: Trumpet and Trombone Section Solis

STUDENT NAME _____ GRADE_____

Comment Key

1) Insufficient, awkward, or excessive rhythmic alteration
2) Incorrect or excessive articulation
3) Non-defined quarter-note length
4) Awkward rhythmic notation
5) Incorrect bass note, guide tones, or chord symbol
6) Musically awkward connecting tones, neighbor tones, or fills
7) Incorrect or excessive use of dynamics
8) Incorrect or excessive use of ornamentation
9) Wrong notes
10) Minor-second interval between top two voices
11) Omission of guide tones
12) Inconsistent tension and density level
13) Excessive dissonance
14) Ineffective tonicization
15) Ineffective use of diatonic or chromatic parallelism
16) Absence of alteration in cycled dominant tonicizations
17) Inappropriate use of alterations in tonicizations
18) Coincidence of altered and unaltered fifth in the same voicing
19) Coincidence of altered and unaltered ninth in the same voicing
20) Improper spacing
21) Voicing is unclear (too low)
22) Notes are too close to the instrument's range extremities
23) Notes out of instrument's range

MEASURE #	COMMENTS	MEASURE #	COMMENTS
1		21	
2		22	
3		23	
4		24	
5		25	
6		26	
7		27	
8		28	
9		29	
10		30	
11		31	
12		32	
13		33	
14		34	
15		35	
16		36	
17		37	
18		38	
19		39	
20		40	

General Comments:

Second Semester Jazz Arranging Grade and Comment Sheet
Assignment 3: Four- and Five-Note Brass Section Writing

STUDENT NAME _____ GRADE_____

Comment Key

1) Insufficient, awkward, or excessive rhythmic alteration
2) Incorrect or excessive articulation
3) Non-defined quarter-note length
4) Awkward rhythmic notation
5) Incorrect bass note, guide tones, or chord symbol
6) Musically awkward connecting tones, neighbor tones, or fills
7) Incorrect or excessive use of dynamics
8) Incorrect or excessive use of ornamentation
9) Wrong notes
10) Minor-second interval between top two voices
11) Omission of guide tones
12) Inconsistent tension and density level
13) Excessive dissonance
14) Ineffective tonicization
15) Ineffective use of diatonic or chromatic parallelism
16) Absence of alteration in cycled dominant tonicizations
17) Inappropriate use of alterations in tonicizations
18) Coincidence of altered and unaltered fifth in the same voicing
19) Coincidence of altered and unaltered ninth in the same voicing
20) Improper spacing
21) Voicing is unclear (too low)
22) Notes are too close to the instrument's range extremities
23) Notes out of instrument's range

MEASURE #	COMMENTS	MEASURE #	COMMENTS
1		21	
2		22	
3		23	
4		24	
5		25	
6		26	
7		27	
8		28	
9		29	
10		30	
11		31	
12		32	
13		33	
14		34	
15		35	
16		36	
17		37	
18		38	
19		39	
20		40	

General Comments:

Second Semester Jazz Arranging Grade and Comment Sheet

Assignment 4: Six- and Seven-Note Brass Section Writing

STUDENT NAME _____ **GRADE** _____

Comment Key

1) Insufficient, awkward, or excessive rhythmic alteration
2) Incorrect or excessive articulation
3) Non-defined quarter-note length
4) Awkward rhythmic notation
5) Incorrect bass note, guide tones, or chord symbol
6) Musically awkward connecting tones, neighbor tones, or fills
7) Incorrect or excessive use of dynamics
8) Incorrect or excessive use of ornamentation
9) Wrong notes
10) Minor-second interval between top two voices
11) Omission of guide tones
12) Inconsistent tension and density level
13) Excessive dissonance
14) Ineffective tonicization
15) Ineffective use of diatonic or chromatic parallelism
16) Absence of alteration in cycled dominant tonicizations
17) Inappropriate use of alterations in tonicizations
18) Coincidence of altered and unaltered fifth in the same voicing
19) Coincidence of altered and unaltered ninth in the same voicing
20) Improper spacing
21) Voicing is unclear (too low)
22) Notes are too close to the instrument's range extremities
23) Notes out of instrument's range
24) Lead trombone is too high or too low for this voicing
25) Chord is unbalanced due to excessive or insufficient doubling of certain pitches

MEASURE #	COMMENTS	MEASURE #	COMMENTS
1		21	
2		22	
3		23	
4		24	
5		25	
6		26	
7		27	
8		28	
9		29	
10		30	
11		31	
12		32	
13		33	
14		34	
15		35	
16		36	
17		37	
18		38	
19		39	
20		40	

General Comments:

Second Semester Jazz Arranging Grade and Comment Sheet

Assignment 5: Integrating the Sax Section into Brass Section Voicings

STUDENT NAME _____ GRADE_____

Comment Key

1) Insufficient, awkward, or excessive rhythmic alteration
2) Incorrect or excessive articulation
3) Non-defined quarter-note length
4) Awkward rhythmic notation
5) Incorrect bass note, guide tones, or chord symbol
6) Musically awkward connecting tones, neighbor tones, or fills
7) Incorrect or excessive use of dynamics
8) Incorrect or excessive use of ornamentation
9) Wrong notes
10) Minor-second interval between top two voices
11) Omission of guide tones
12) Inconsistent tension and density level
13) Excessive dissonance
14) Ineffective tonicization
15) Ineffective use of diatonic or chromatic parallelism
16) Absence of alteration in cycled dominant tonicizations
17) Inappropriate use of alterations in tonicizations
18) Coincidence of altered and unaltered fifth in the same voicing
19) Coincidence of altered and unaltered ninth in the same voicing
20) Improper spacing
21) Voicing is unclear (too low)
22) Notes are too close to the instrument's range extremities
23) Notes out of instrument's range
24) Lead trombone is too high or too low for this voicing
25) Lead alto is too high or too low for this voicing
26) Chord is unbalanced due to excessive or insufficient doubling of certain pitches

MEASURE #	COMMENTS	MEASURE #	COMMENTS
1		21	
2		22	
3		23	
4		24	
5		25	
6		26	
7		27	
8		28	
9		29	
10		30	
11		31	
12		32	
13		33	
14		34	
15		35	
16		36	
17		37	
18		38	
19		39	
20		40	

General Comments:

Second Semester Jazz Arranging Grade and Comment Sheet
Assignment 6: Sax Section Against the Brass Section

STUDENT NAME _____ **GRADE** _____

Comment Key

1) Insufficient, awkward, or excessive rhythmic alteration
2) Incorrect or excessive articulation
3) Non-defined quarter-note length
4) Awkward rhythmic notation
5) Incorrect bass note, guide tones, or chord symbol
6) Musically awkward connecting tones, neighbor tones, or fills
7) Incorrect or excessive use of dynamics
8) Incorrect or excessive use of ornamentation
9) Wrong notes
10) Minor Second interval between top two voices
11) Omission of guide tones
12) Inconsistent tension and density level
13) Excessive dissonance

14) Ineffective tonicization
15) Ineffective use of diatonic or chromatic parallelism
16) Absence of alteration in cycled dominant tonicizations
17) Inappropriate use of alterations in tonicizations
18) Coincidence of altered and unaltered fifth in the same voicing
19) Coincidence of altered and unaltered ninth in the same voicing
20) Improper spacing
21) Voicing is unclear (too low)
22) Notes are too close to the instrument's range extremities
23) Notes out of instrument's range
24) Incompatible rhythms

MEASURE #	COMMENTS	MEASURE #	COMMENTS
1		21	
2		22	
3		23	
4		24	
5		25	
6		26	
7		27	
8		28	
9		29	
10		30	
11		31	
12		32	
13		33	
14		34	
15		35	
16		36	
17		37	
18		38	
19		39	
20		40	

General Comments:

Second Semester Jazz Arranging Grade and Comment Sheet

Assignment 7: Three Elements – Melody, Countermelody, and Accompaniment

STUDENT NAME _____ **GRADE** _____

Comment Key

1) Insufficient, awkward, or excessive rhythmic alteration
2) Incorrect or excessive articulation
3) Non-defined quarter-note length
4) Awkward rhythmic notation
5) Incorrect bass note, guide tones, or chord symbol
6) Musically awkward connecting tones, neighbor tones, or fills
7) Incorrect or excessive use of dynamics
8) Incorrect or excessive use of ornamentation
9) Wrong notes
10) Minor-second interval between top two voices
11) Omission of guide tones
12) Inconsistent tension and density level
13) Excessive dissonance
14) Ineffective tonicization
15) Ineffective use of diatonic or chromatic parallelism
16) Absence of alteration in cycled dominant tonicizations
17) Inappropriate use of alterations in tonicizations
18) Coincidence of altered and unaltered fifth in the same voicing
19) Coincidence of altered and unaltered ninth in the same voicing
20) Improper spacing
21) Voicing is unclear (too low)
22) Notes are too close to the instrument's range extremities
23) Notes out of instrument's range
24) Melody and top voice of accompaniment collide
25) Accompaniment is too active
26) Incompatible rhythms between melody and accompaniment
27) Fragmented countermelody
28) Voices collide
29) Countermelody is too active
30) Incompatible rhythm

MEASURE #	COMMENTS	MEASURE #	COMMENTS
1		21	
2		22	
3		23	
4		24	
5		25	
6		26	
7		27	
8		28	
9		29	
10		30	
11		31	
12		32	
13		33	
14		34	
15		35	
16		36	
17		37	
18		38	
19		39	
20		40	

General Comments:

Second Semester Jazz Arranging Grade and Comment Sheet
Assignment 8: Large Ensemble Arrangement – First Chorus – Melody

STUDENT NAME _____ GRADE_____

Comment Key

1) Insufficient, awkward, or excessive rhythmic alteration
2) Incorrect or excessive articulation
3) Non-defined quarter-note length
4) Awkward rhythmic notation
5) Incorrect bass note, guide tones, or chord symbol
6) Musically awkward connecting tones, neighbor tones, or fills
7) Incorrect or excessive use of dynamics
8) Incorrect or excessive use of ornamentation
9) Wrong notes
10) Minor-second interval between top two voices
11) Omission of guide tones
12) Inconsistent tension and density level
13) Excessive dissonance
14) Ineffective tonicization
15) Ineffective use of diatonic or chromatic parallelism
16) Absence of alteration in cycled dominant tonicizations
17) Inappropriate use of alterations in tonicizations
18) Coincidence of altered and unaltered fifth in the same voicing
19) Coincidence of altered and unaltered ninth in the same voicing
20) Improper spacing
21) Voicing is unclear (too low)
22) Notes are too close to the instrument's range extremities
23) Notes out of instrument's range
24) Melody and top voice of accompaniment collide
25) Accompaniment is too active
26) Incompatible rhythms between melody and accompaniment
27) Absence of rhythm section involvement
28) Incorrect rhythm section notation
29) Lead trombone is too high or too low for this voicing
30) Lead alto is too high or too low for this voicing
31) Chord is unbalanced due to excessive or insufficient doubling of certain pitches

MEASURE #	COMMENTS	MEASURE #	COMMENTS
1		21	
2		22	
3		23	
4		24	
5		25	
6		26	
7		27	
8		28	
9		29	
10		30	
11		31	
12		32	
13		33	
14		34	
15		35	
16		36	
17		37	
18		38	
19		39	
20		40	

General Comments:

Second Semester Jazz Arranging Grade and Comment Sheet

Assignment 9: Large Ensemble Arrangement – Solo Chorus w/Backgrounds

STUDENT NAME _____ GRADE _____

Comment Key

1) Insufficient, awkward, or excessive rhythmic alteration
2) Incorrect or excessive articulation
3) Non-defined quarter-note length
4) Awkward rhythmic notation
5) Incorrect bass note, guide tones, or chord symbol
6) Musically awkward connecting tones, neighbor tones, or fills
7) Incorrect or excessive use of dynamics
8) Incorrect or excessive use of ornamentation
9) Wrong notes
10) Minor-second interval between top two voices
11) Omission of guide tones
12) Inconsistent tension and density level
13) Excessive dissonance
14) Ineffective tonicization
15) Ineffective use of diatonic or chromatic parallelism
16) Absence of alteration in cycled dominant tonicizations
17) Inappropriate use of alterations in tonicizations
18) Coincidence of altered and unaltered fifth in the same voicing
19) Coincidence of altered and unaltered ninth in the same voicing
20) Improper spacing
21) Voicing is unclear (too low)
22) Notes are too close to the instrument's range extremities
23) Notes out of instrument's range
24) Lead trombone is too high or too low for this voicing
25) Lead alto is too high or too low for this voicing
26) Chord is unbalanced due to excessive or insufficient doubling of certain pitches
27) Background is too active
28) Absence of rhythm section involvement
29) Incorrect rhythm section notation
30) Incorrect use of endings and repeat

MEASURE #	COMMENTS	MEASURE #	COMMENTS
1		21	
2		22	
3		23	
4		24	
5		25	
6		26	
7		27	
8		28	
9		29	
10		30	
11		31	
12		32	
13		33	
14		34	
15		35	
16		36	
17		37	
18		38	
19		39	
20		40	

General Comments:

Second Semester Jazz Arranging Grade and Comment Sheet
Assignment 10: Large Ensemble Arrangement –
Shout Chorus and Recapitulation

STUDENT NAME _____ GRADE _____

Comment Key

1) Insufficient, awkward, or excessive rhythmic alteration
2) Incorrect or excessive articulation
3) Non-defined quarter-note length
4) Awkward rhythmic notation
5) Incorrect bass note, guide tones, or chord symbol
6) Musically awkward connecting tones, neighbor tones, or fills
7) Incorrect or excessive use of dynamics
8) Incorrect or excessive use of ornamentation
9) Wrong notes
10) Minor-second interval between top two voices
11) Omission of guide tones
12) Inconsistent tension and density level
13) Excessive dissonance

14) Ineffective tonicization
15) Ineffective use of diatonic or chromatic parallelism
16) Absence of alteration in cycled dominant tonicizations
17) Inappropriate use of alterations in tonicizations
18) Coincidence of altered and unaltered fifth in the same voicing
19) Coincidence of altered and unaltered ninth in the same voicing
20) Improper spacing
21) Voicing is unclear (too low)
22) Notes are too close to the instrument's range extremities
23) Notes out of instrument's range
24) Lead trumpet register is too high
25) Improper use or placement of signs (e.g., D.S.)

MEASURE #	COMMENTS
1	
2	
3	
4	
5	
6	
7	
8	
9	
10	
11	
12	
13	
14	
15	
16	
17	
18	
19	
20	

MEASURE #	COMMENTS
21	
22	
23	
24	
25	
26	
27	
28	
29	
30	
31	
32	
33	
34	
35	
36	
37	
38	
39	
40	

General Comments:

Second Semester Jazz Arranging Grade and Comment Sheet
Assignment 11: Large Ensemble Arrangement –
Introduction and Ending

STUDENT NAME _____ GRADE_____

Comment Key

1) Insufficient, awkward, or excessive rhythmic alteration
2) Incorrect or excessive articulation
3) Non-defined quarter-note length
4) Awkward rhythmic notation
5) Incorrect bass note, guide tones, or chord symbol
6) Musically awkward connecting tones, neighbor tones, or fills
7) Incorrect or excessive use of dynamics
8) Incorrect or excessive use of ornamentation
9) Wrong notes
10) Minor-second interval between top two voices
11) Omission of guide tones
12) Inconsistent tension and density level
13) Excessive dissonance
14) Ineffective tonicization

15) Ineffective use of diatonic or chromatic parallelism
16) Absence of alteration in cycled dominant tonicizations
17) Inappropriate use of alterations in tonicizations
18) Coincidence of altered and unaltered fifth in the same voicing
19) Coincidence of altered and unaltered ninth in the same voicing
20) Improper spacing
21) Voicing is unclear (too low)
22) Notes are too close to the instrument's range extremities
23) Notes out of instrument's range
24) Ineffective link between intro and first chorus
25) Ineffective link between shout or recap and ending
26) Improper use or placement of signs (e.g., D.S.)

MEASURE #	COMMENTS	MEASURE #	COMMENTS
1		21	
2		22	
3		23	
4		24	
5		25	
6		26	
7		27	
8		28	
9		29	
10		30	
11		31	
12		32	
13		33	
14		34	
15		35	
16		36	
17		37	
18		38	
19		39	
20		40	

General Comments:

Second Semester Jazz Arranging Grade and Comment Sheet
Assignment 12: Arranging for Seven Horns

STUDENT NAME _____ GRADE _____

Comment Key

1) Insufficient, awkward, or excessive rhythmic alteration
2) Incorrect or excessive articulation
3) Non-defined quarter-note length
4) Awkward rhythmic notation
5) Incorrect bass note, guide tones, or chord symbol
6) Musically awkward connecting tones, neighbor tones, or fills
7) Incorrect or excessive use of dynamics
8) Incorrect or excessive use of ornamentation
9) Wrong notes
10) Minor-second interval between top two voices
11) Omission of guide tones
12) Inconsistent tension and density level
13) Excessive dissonance
14) Ineffective tonicization
15) Ineffective use of diatonic or chromatic parallelism
16) Absence of alteration in cycled dominant tonicizations
17) Inappropriate use of alterations in tonicizations
18) Coincidence of altered and unaltered fifth in the same voicing
19) Coincidence of altered and unaltered ninth in the same voicing
20) Improper spacing
21) Voicing is unclear (too low)
22) Notes are too close to the instrument's range extremities
23) Notes out of instrument's range
24) Chord is unbalanced due to excessive or insufficient doubling of certain pitches

MEASURE #	COMMENTS	MEASURE #	COMMENTS
1		21	
2		22	
3		23	
4		24	
5		25	
6		26	
7		27	
8		28	
9		29	
10		30	
11		31	
12		32	
13		33	
14		34	
15		35	
16		36	
17		37	
18		38	
19		39	
20		40	

General Comments:

Second Semester Jazz Arranging Grade and Comment Sheet

Assignment 13: Contemporary Arranging Techniques

STUDENT NAME _____ **GRADE** _____

Comment Key

1) Insufficient, awkward, or excessive rhythmic alteration
2) Incorrect or excessive articulation
3) Non-defined quarter-note length
4) Awkward rhythmic notation
5) Incorrect bass note, guide tones, or chord symbol

6) Musically awkward connecting tones, neighbor tones, or fills
7) Incorrect or excessive use of dynamics
8) Incorrect or excessive use of ornamentation
9) Wrong notes

MEASURE #	COMMENTS	MEASURE #	COMMENTS
1		21	
2		22	
3		23	
4		24	
5		25	
6		26	
7		27	
8		28	
9		29	
10		30	
11		31	
12		32	
13		33	
14		34	
15		35	
16		36	
17		37	
18		38	
19		39	
20		40	

General Comments:

APPENDIX 11
Tips for Using the Assignment Templates

Note Input Method

By far, the most useful method of note input is via a midi keyboard using the *Speedy Entry* tool in Finale®. The *Hyperscribe* tool is useful only if you are an adept keyboardist. The least desirable method of input is with the *Simple Entry* tool as it is laborious and is more apt to lead to errors involving accidentals and unclear rhythmic notation. Another reason to avoid this tool is that vertical sonorities (two or more notes) cannot be entered at the same time. This inevitably leads to note errors.

The cost of a midi keyboard should not be an issue. Since the sounds are generated from within Finale®, any midi keyboard, no matter how cheap, can be used for input. There are many that have smaller keys that can be purchased for under $100. In fact, there is an advantage to using smaller-sized keys, as the range of notes played by one hand can exceed an octave, permitting easier input of open-position voicings, regardless of the instrumentation.

Metatools

Metatools are one of the most valuable features of Finale®. These hotkeys can cut input time considerably. There are essentially two different processes. For articulations and dynamics, hold down the number or letter corresponding to the desired figure, then click on the appropriate note. The articulation or dynamic should automatically be centered correctly, but some nudging may be necessary. For "mass edit" and "staff styles," select the measures or partial measures where the metatool is to be applied, then press the number or letter corresponding to the desired process or effect. In addition to the metatool lists below, Finale® contains several others, most of which are of little use to the jazz arranger.

User-Programmed Articulation Metatools (Articulation Tool)

These are programmed to be placed above the note (or between two notes in the case of the turn). The rationale is that the player does not have to continually look both above and below the staff searching for articulations. The first five of these will play back correctly.

1 – • 2 – ▬ 3 – ＞ 4 – ∧ 5 – ≳ 6 – ∿ 7 – ∼ 8 – ◠ 9 – + 0 – ○

User-Programmed Dynamic Metatools (Note and Measure Expression Tool)

The numbered metatools will play back correctly.

1 – *ppp*   2 – *pp*   3 – *p*   4 – *mp*   5 – *mf*   6 – *f*   7 – *ff*   8 – *fff*   9 – *fp*   0 – *sfz*

S – *sub. p*   C – *gradual cresc.* D – *gradual decresc.*

User-Programmed Staff Style Metatools (Staff Tool)

These are the most useful ones for the jazz arranger.

- S: Slash Notation
- R: Rhythmic Notation
- 1: One-Bar Repeat
- 2: Two-Bar Repeat

Pre-Programmed Mass Edit Metatools

These are the most useful ones for the jazz arranger.

1: Implode Music (useful when creating condensed scores)
2: Explode Music (essential for the distribution of individual notes when writing vertical sonorities)
4: Apply Note Spacing (essential to score and part writing; this takes place automatically when "Automatic Music Spacing" and "Automatic Update Layout" are selected under the Edit menu)
5: Check Elapsed Time (useful if writing within a particular time frame or for checking the length of a chorus)
6: User-Programmed Transposition–currently set to "Down One Octave"
7: User-Programmed Transposition–currently set to "Up One Octave"
8: User-Programmed Transposition–Unprogrammed
9: User-Programmed Transposition–Unprogrammed

View Percentage Metatools

Control 2: 200%
Control 1: 100%
Control 7: 75%
Control 5: 50%

Chord Suffixes

Select manual input under the chord menu to access the 125 available suffixes. They are grouped in the following manner:

1–7: Major chords with no altered pitches
8–11: Number suffixes with major quality
12–16: Unaltered dominant chords
17–31: Minor chords with no altered pitches
32–40: All suspended chords
41–45: All fully-diminished chords
46–52: All half-diminished chords
53–66: Major chords with altered pitches
67–80: All dominant chords with one altered pitch
81–90: Dominant 7th chords with two altered pitches
91–100: Dominant 7th chords with three or four altered pitches
101: Dominant 9th chord with two altered pitches
102–108: Dominant 13th chords with two or three altered pitches
109–122: Minor chords with altered pitches
123–125: Hybrids (pedal, 7alt, 7 over 4)

Writing Drum Parts

Time Slashes

Enter quarter rests in these measures before selecting slash notation. This will enable the placement of note expressions rather than measure expressions, which require an extra dialogue box.

Slashes with Rhythms Above or Below the Staff

Enter quarter rests in Layer 1, then select slash notation. For rhythms above the staff, change to Layer 2 and enter the desired rhythms using G two octaves above middle C. For notes below, change to Layer 3 and enter the desired rhythms using F above middle C. All stems, beams, and rests will automatically freeze in the correct positions (One exception is the half rest in Layer 2, which is a step too high. This can be left as is or manually moved downward in Speedy Entry).

Fully Notated Parts

Notes played by the foot should be entered in Layer 1, while those played by the hands in Layer 2. All stems, beams, and rests will automatically freeze in the correct positions. There is no real need for playback in the drum part. However, if this is desired, use the following pitches to attain the correct drum sounds. (When entering these notes, the sound will not be correct; however, they will play back properly.)

EXAMPLE AII-I.

Extended Measures of Time

As mentioned in chapter 12, there are two methods for indicating extended measures of time. If using one measure of slashes and several one-measure repeats, be sure to number at least the last repeat in the series so that the drummer knows how many measures to play. Don't forget to include the measure of slashes in the count.

The second method, which adheres more closely to tradition, involves a more complicated process:

- Using the *Mass Edit Tool*, clear all entries and smart shapes from the desired measures.
- Using the *Staff Tool*, clear all staff styles from the desired measures.
- Using the *Measure Tool*, go to "Multimeasure Rests" and click "Create."
- Using the *Measure Tool*, go to "Multimeasure Rests" and click "Edit."
- Input the number "0" in the *Shape Select* box and enter a number at least one higher than the number of measures selected in the "Start Numbering at _ Measures" box. This will produce an empty space where the multimeasure rest used to be.
- Using the *Expression Tool*, select the appropriate graphic rest (numbered 109–114) and center it in the empty space. If necessary, replace the dummy number with the correct one. Adjust its length by deleting bar segments and re-centering it in the space.
- Adjust the widths of the adjacent measures, if necessary.

Laisse Vibrer (let ring): Instead of notating a cymbal crash as a whole note, it is often more desirable to write it as a quarter or half that rings out. To obtain these alternate noteheads, first input the desired value (quarter or half) in Layer 2. Then, access the *Special Tools* menu and click on the "x" notehead button, then click on the measure where the L.V. tail is desired. Assuming that Layer 2 is selected, boxes will appear on all the noteheads in that measure that are present. Double-click on the specific notehead to be altered. This opens a symbol selection map for the jazz font. The quarter "x" notehead can be found at position 203, while the half is located at position 204. Double-click on the desired symbol and it will replace the existing one.

Note and Measure Expressions

Most of the typical text items necessary to an arrangement are contained within the *Expression Tool*. They are grouped as follows:

- 1–13: Dynamics and dynamic effects
- 14–20: Tempo and style indicators
- 21–29: D.S., Coda, and Fine indicators
- 30–40: Trumpet mutings and instrument changes (some of these are also applicable to the trombone)
- 41–52: Saxophone and woodwind instrument changes
- 53–55: Bass text
- 56–61: Drum text
- 62–66: Solo and soli indicators
- 67–75: Various repeat commands
- 76–77: Octave up and down
- 78: N.C. (no chord)
- 79–104: Alphabetical rehearsal markers
- 105: Double-letter alphabetical rehearsal-marker template
- 106–108: One-, two-, and three-digit numerical rehearsal-marker templates
- 109–114: Extended-time drum indicators
- 115: Number for one-measure repeats
- 116: Four-measure repeat sign
- 117: Filler for four-measure repeat sign

Exploding Parts

This has always been a major feature of Finale® and is essential to the jazz arranger as it creates individual parts on separate staves from vertical sonorities created on a single staff. Using the *Mass Edit* tool, select the appropriate measures. The *Explode Music Dialog Box* is located within the submenu *Utilities* found in the *Mass Edit* menu (as mentioned earlier, it is much quicker to select metatool 2, the shortcut for this command). Then, select how many staves the music will be exploded onto (Options: Split into ___ staves) and where to place the notes (Place Music Into: Existing staves starting with staff ___; use the pull-down menu to select the proper staff). In most circumstances, one note will be placed in each staff.

Swing Feel

This can be found under *Playback Settings*. The problem is that the provided settings are inaccurate. The percentage of swing is relative to tempo. For tempos below 100 bpm, use no more than the "Standard" setting (100 percent); this will produce a pronounced triplet effect. For tempos above 100 bpm, switch to the "Light" setting (75 percent). For those above 150 bpm, manually input 60 percent; above 200 bpm, switch to 50 percent and above 250 bpm, 40 percent.

"Select Partial Measures" and "Display in Concert Pitch"

These are two very important commands that are invaluable to any arranger. The problem is that they are located under the *Edit* and *Options* menus and are not easily accessible. The icons for both these commands can be placed onto the workspace by going to *Window Menu>Menu* toolbars and checking the *Edit Menu* and *Options Menu Toolbars*.

Measure Numbers for Printing

As mentioned in appendix 10, the assignment templates are not necessarily intended for printing as the measure numbers are much too large. If printed parts are desired, do one of two things: either delete the measure numbers or adjust them to the following specifications:

- Change the font size to 10 points
- For one-digit numbers, use the following settings–left alignment, H: -.03472, V: -.48611
- For two-digit numbers, use the following settings–left alignment, H: -.05208, V: -.48611
- For three-digit numbers, use the following settings–left alignment, H: -.06944, V: -.48611

Woodwind Transpositions

These are most easily accomplished through the use of the staff styles provided in the templates. Input the notes at concert pitch, then select the appropriate measures with the *Staff Tool*. Then select "Apply Staff Styles" under the *Staff* menu. Finally, choose the corresponding transposition from staff styles #14–21. This will affect the transposition and clef for the selected area. For patch changes, enter the corresponding instrument change from the list found in the *Expression Tool*.

Creating a Score with No Key Signature

For those compositions/arrangements where a key signature is unnecessary, it may be desirable to create a score without one. First, using the *Staff Tool*, access the *Staff Attributes* dialog box by double-clicking on the box at the beginning of each staff of those instruments not pitched in C. Then check the *Key Signature* box under the heading "Independent Elements." Next, select the *Key Signature Tool* and click on each staff again of those instruments that normally transpose. Select the key signature that is identical to the key in which the instrument is pitched (e.g., the alto sax is pitched in E♭, so the key signature of E♭ should be selected for that staff). The measure region should be selected as "measure 1 through end of piece" and the direction of transposition should be "up" for all instruments except piccolo. After following this same procedure for all the transposing instruments, the score will appear with no key signature when displayed in transposed pitch and will contain the key signature correspondent to each instruments' key when displayed in concert pitch.

Alternate Measure Numbers

If a pickup measure is selected, the measure numbering format for these templates will need to be adjusted. To fix this problem, select the *Measure Tool*, then access the *Edit Regions* dialog box via the *Measure* menu and *Measure Numbers* submenu. Then change the following numbers – Region 1: change "2 to 9" to "2 to 10"; Region 2: change "10 to 99" to "11 to 100"; Region 3: change "100 to 99" to "101 to 999."

Extracting Parts

Both the small and large-ensemble project templates are designed for live performance; that is, individual parts can be extracted and printed. However, before extracting any parts, be sure all the desired markings are on the score and most items are spaced correctly. This will save considerable time when proofing the individual parts. Check for the existence and proper placement of the following items:

- Double bar lines at the end of each section
- Rehearsal letters or numbers at all double bar lines
- Final bar line at the end of the piece
- Repeats and endings
- Atrticulations and dynamics
- Style and tempo indications
- Any text that will aid the players during performance
- D.S. or D.C. al Coda or Fine text, D.S. symbol, To Coda text and Coda symbol, Coda text and Coda symbol at the first measure of the Coda
- Title, composer/arranger credits, and page header–dummy versions of these are already in their proper place for extraction in the score. Simply replace these with the correct information. The title and composer/arranger credits are located on the first page; the header can be found in the top right corner of the second page of the score.

Next, extract the parts and check each one for colliding text or notes and for overall appearance before printing.

Printing the Score

Before formatting the score for printing, save it as a new file, renaming it so that it will not be confused with the original score (something like "print score" would be fine). This ensures that the score from which the parts were extracted also remains a separate file and can be revisited at any time to print a new set of parts if necessary.

Scores are typically grouped at eight measures per system. This can be accomplished by accessing the *Mass Edit Tool* and selecting the entire score by pressing "Control-A". Then press "Control-M" to bring up the *Fit Music* dialog box. Replace the default 4 in "Lock Layout with _ Measures per System" with an 8. There is no need to alter anything else in this box.

Select the *Staff Tool*, then access the *Staff Attributes* dialog box for the top staff by double-clicking on the box at the top of that staff. In the "Items to Display" box, unselect only "Measure Numbers." Access the remainder of the staves within this dialog box by clicking on the up and down arrows beside the staff name at the top of the box. For all the rest of the staves except the bottom one, unselect both "Measure Numbers" and "Endings and Text Repeats." For the bottom staff, unselect only "Endings and Text Repeats." This will display the endings and text repeats only on the top staff and the measure numbers only on the bottom staff.

Due to the reduced print size of the score, several items should be made larger so that the arranger or director can clearly see some of the more important information. These items are:

- Style and tempo indications
- Rehearsal letters or numbers

- Any text pertaining directly to the director (ritard, vamp, on cue, etc.)
- Measure numbers

The first three can easily be enlarged by right-clicking on each individual command and altering the font size. Measure numbers should be enlarged through a slightly more complex process:

- Access the *Edit Regions* dialog box via the *Measure* menu>*Measure Numbers* submenu.
- Delete all regions except for Region 1.
- Change the range of Region 1 from "1 to 10" to "1 to 999 (or the last measure of the arrangement)."
- Change the font size to 20.
- Change the position to center alignment, H: 0, V: -1

This will place all the measure numbers at a very readable point size.

Lastly, before printing the score, be sure to set the printer to landscape mode.

Jazz Instruction & Improvisation

BOOKS FOR ALL INSTRUMENTS FROM HAL LEONARD

AN APPROACH TO JAZZ IMPROVISATION
by Dave Pozzi
Musicians Institute Press
Explore the styles of Charlie Parker, Sonny Rollins, Bud Powell and others with this comprehensive guide to jazz improvisation. Covers: scale choices • chord analysis • phrasing • melodies • harmonic progressions • more.
00695135 Book/CD Pack......................................$17.95

THE ART OF MODULATING
FOR PIANISTS AND JAZZ MUSICIANS
by Carlos Salzedo &
Lucile Lawrence
Schirmer
The Art of Modulating is a treatise originally intended for the harp, but this edition has been edited for use by intermediate keyboardists and other musicians who have an understanding of basic music theory. In its pages you will find: table of intervals; modulation rules; modulation formulas; examples of modulation; extensions and cadences; ten fragments of dances; five characteristic pieces; and more.
50490581 ....$19.99

BUILDING A JAZZ VOCABULARY
By Mike Steinel
A valuable resource for learning the basics of jazz from Mike Steinel of the University of North Texas. It covers: the basics of jazz • how to build effective solos • a comprehensive practice routine • and a jazz vocabulary of the masters.
00849911 ....$19.99

THE CYCLE OF FIFTHS
by Emile and Laura De Cosmo
This essential instruction book provides more than 450 exercises, including hundreds of melodic and rhythmic ideas. The book is designed to help improvisors master the cycle of fifths, one of the primary progressions in music. Guaranteed to refine technique, enhance improvisational fluency, and improve sight-reading!
00311114 ....$16.99

THE DIATONIC CYCLE
by Emile and Laura De Cosmo
Renowned jazz educators Emile and Laura De Cosmo provide more than 300 exercises to help improvisors tackle one of music's most common progressions: the diatonic cycle. This book is guaranteed to refine technique, enhance improvisational fluency, and improve sight-reading!
00311115 ....$16.95

EAR TRAINING
by Keith Wyatt,
Carl Schroeder and Joe Elliott
Musicians Institute Press
Covers: basic pitch matching • singing major and minor scales • identifying intervals • transcribing melodies and rhythm • identifying chords and progressions • seventh chords and the blues • modal interchange, chromaticism, modulation • and more.
00695198 Book/Online Audio $24.99

EXERCISES AND ETUDES FOR THE JAZZ INSTRUMENTALIST
by J.J. Johnson
Designed as study material and playable by any instrument, these pieces run the gamut of the jazz experience, featuring common and uncommon time signatures and keys, and styles from ballads to funk. They are progressively graded so that both beginners and professionals will be challenged by the demands of this wonderful music.
00842018 Bass Clef Edition $17.99
00842042 Treble Clef Edition $16.95

JAZZOLOGY
THE ENCYCLOPEDIA OF JAZZ THEORY FOR ALL MUSICIANS
by Robert Rawlins and
Nor Eddine Bahha
This comprehensive resource covers a variety of jazz topics, for beginners and pros of any instrument. The book serves as an encyclopedia for reference, a thorough methodology for the student, and a workbook for the classroom.
00311167 ....$19.99

JAZZ THEORY RESOURCES
by Bert Ligon
Houston Publishing, Inc.
This is a jazz theory text in two volumes. **Volume 1 includes**: review of basic theory • rhythm in jazz performance • triadic generalization • diatonic harmonic progressions and analysis • substitutions and turnarounds • and more. **Volume 2 includes**: modes and modal frameworks • quartal harmony • extended tertian structures and triadic superimposition • pentatonic applications • coloring "outside" the lines and beyond • and more.
00030458 Volume 1 ....$39.95
00030459 Volume 2 ....$29.95

JOY OF IMPROV
by Dave Frank
and John Amaral
This book/audio course on improvisation for all instruments and all styles will help players develop monster musical skills! Book One imparts a solid basis in technique, rhythm, chord theory, ear training and improv concepts. **Book Two** explores more advanced chord voicings, chord arranging techniques and more challenging blues and melodic lines. The audio can be used as a listening and play-along tool.
00220005 Book 1 – Book/Online Audio................$27.99
00220006 Book 2 – Book/Online Audio...............$26.99

THE PATH TO JAZZ IMPROVISATION
by Emile and Laura De Cosmo
This fascinating jazz instruction book offers an innovative, scholarly approach to the art of improvisation. It includes in-depth analysis and lessons about: cycle of fifths • diatonic cycle • overtone series • pentatonic scale • harmonic and melodic minor scale • polytonal order of keys • blues and bebop scales • modes • and more.
00310904 ....$14.99

THE SOURCE
THE DICTIONARY OF CONTEMPORARY AND TRADITIONAL SCALES
by Steve Barta
This book serves as an informative guide for people who are looking for good, solid information regarding scales, chords, and how they work together. It provides right and left hand fingerings for scales, chords, and complete inversions. Includes over 20 different scales, each written in all 12 keys.
00240885 ....$19.99

21 BEBOP EXERCISES
by Steve Rawlins
This book/CD pack is both a warm-up collection and a manual for bebop phrasing. Its tasty and sophisticated exercises will help you develop your proficiency with jazz interpretation. It concentrates on practice in all twelve keys – moving higher by half-step – to help develop dexterity and range. The companion CD includes all of the exercises in 12 keys.
00315341 Book/CD Pack.....................................$17.95

HAL•LEONARD®
7777 W. BLUEMOUND RD. P.O. BOX 13819 MILWAUKEE, WI 53213

Visit Hal Leonard online at
www.halleonard.com

Prices, contents & availability
subject to change without notice.

0417

Presenting the Hal Leonard JAZZ PLAY-ALONG® SERIES

For use with all B-flat, E-flat, Bass Clef and C instruments, the Jazz Play-Along® Series is the ultimate learning tool for all jazz musicians. With musician-friendly lead sheets, melody cues, and other split-track audio choices included, these first-of-a-kind packages help you master improvisation while playing some of the greatest tunes of all time. FOR STUDY, each tune includes a split track with: melody cue with proper style and inflection • professional rhythm tracks • choruses for soloing • removable bass part • removable piano part. FOR PERFORMANCE, each tune also has: an additional full stereo accompaniment track (no melody) • additional choruses for soloing.

*These do not include split tracks.